BY ANY OTHER NAME

BY ANY OTHER NAME

A Novel

JODI PICOULT

THORNDIKE PRESS
A part of Gale, a Cengage Company

Thorndike Press, a part of Gale, a Cengage Company.

Thorndike Press® Large Print Top Shelf.

The text of this Large Print edition is unabridged.

Other aspects of the book may vary from the original edition.

Set in 16 pt. Plantin.

LIBRARY OF CONGRESS CIP DATA ON FILE.
CATALOGUING IN PUBLICATION FOR THIS BOOK
IS AVAILABLE FROM THE LIBRARY OF CONGRESS.

ISBN-13: 978-1-4205-1589-3 (hardcover alk. paper)

Published in 2024 by arrangement with Ballantine Books, an imprint of Random House, a division of Penguin Random House LLC.

Printed in the United States of America
1 2 3 4 5 6 7 28 27 26 25 24

For Elyssa Samsel and Kate Anderson:
adopted daughters, beloved collaborators,
gifted songwriters,
and most important,
fierce women

NOTE: The Emilia chapters are peppered with references to actual Shakespearean plays and poetry.

They are listed in the back of this novel, in case you would like to check to see how many you caught.

Come, you spirits
That tend on mortal thoughts,
unsex me here.
— Lady Macbeth, *Macbeth*

O God, that I were a man! I would eat his
heart in the marketplace.
— Beatrice, *Much Ado About Nothing*

To whom should I complain? Did I tell this,
Who would believe me?
— Isabella, *Measure for Measure*

My tongue will tell the anger of my heart
Or else my heart concealing it will break.
— Katherine, *The Taming of the Shrew*

Let husbands know
Their wives have sense like them.
— Emilia, *Othello*

MELINA

MAY 2013

Many years after Melina graduated from Bard College, the course she remembered the most was not a playwriting seminar or a theater intensive but an anthropology class. One day, the professor had flashed a slide of a bone with twenty-nine tiny incisions on one long side. "The Lebombo bone was found in a cave in Swaziland in the 1970s and is about forty-three thousand years old," she had said. "It's made of a baboon fibula. For years, it's been the first calendar attributed to man. But I ask you: what *man* uses a twenty-nine-day calendar?" The professor seemed to stare directly at Melina. "History," she said, "is written by those in power."

The spring of her senior year, Melina headed to her mentor's office hours, as she did every week. Professor Bufort had, in the eighties, written a play called *Wanderlust* that won a Drama Desk Award, transferred to Broadway, and was nominated for a Tony. He claimed that he'd always wanted to teach, and that when Bard College made him head of the theater program it was a dream come true, but Melina thought it hadn't hurt that none of his other plays had had the same critical success.

He was standing with his back to her when she knocked and entered. His silver hair fell over his eyes, boyish. "My favorite thesis student," he greeted.

"I'm your *only* thesis student." Melina pulled an elastic from her wrist and balled her black hair on top of her head in a loose knot before rummaging in her backpack for two small glass bottles of chocolate milk from a local dairy. They cost a fortune, but she brought Professor Bufort one each week. High blood pressure medication had robbed him of his previous vices — alcohol and cigarettes — and he joked that this was the only fun he got to have anymore. Melina handed him a bottle and clinked hers against it.

"My savior," he said, taking a long drink.

Like most high school kids who had notched productions of *The Crucible* and *A Midsummer Night's Dream* on their belts, Melina had come to Bard assuming that she would study acting. It wasn't until she took a playwriting course that she realized the only thing mightier than giving a stellar performance was being the person who crafted the words an actor spoke. She started writing one-acts that were performed by student groups. She studied Molière and Mamet, Marlowe and Miller. She took apart the language and the structure of their plays with the intensity of a grandmaster chess champion whose understanding of the game determined success.

She wrote a modern *Pygmalion,* where the sculptor was a pageant mom and the statue was JonBenét Ramsey, but it was her version of *Waiting for Godot,* set at a political convention where all the characters were awaiting a savior-like presidential candidate who never arrived, that caught the attention of Professor Bufort. He encouraged her to send her play to various open-submission festivals, and although she never was selected, it was clear to Melina and everyone else in the department that *she* was going to be one of the few to *make it* as a produced playwright.

"Melina," Bufort asked, "what are you going to do after graduation?"

"I'm open to suggestions," she replied, hoping that this was where her mentor told her about some fabulous job opportunity. She wasn't naïve enough to believe that she could survive in New York City without some sort of day job, and Bufort had hooked her up before. She'd interned one summer for a famous director in the city — a man who once threw an iced latte at a costume designer who hadn't adjusted a hem, and who took her to bars even though she was underage because

13

he preferred to drink his lunch. Another summer, she'd been behind the cash register at a café at Signature Theatre and behind a merch booth at Second Stage. Professor Bufort had connections.

This whole business ran on connections.

"This is not a suggestion," Bufort said, handing her a flyer. "This is more of a command."

Bard College would be hosting a collegiate playwriting competition. The prize was a guaranteed slot at the Samuel French Off-Off-Broadway Short Play Festival.

The professor leaned against the desk, his legs inches away from Melina's. He set down his chocolate milk, crossed his arms, and smiled down at her. "I think you could win," he said.

She met his gaze. "But . . . ?"

"But." He raised a brow. "Do I have to say it? *Again?*"

Melina shook her head. The only negative comment she ever received from him was that although her writing was clean and compelling, it was emotionally sterile. As if she had put up a wall between the playwright and the play.

"You are good," Bufort said, "but you could be *great.* It's not enough to manipulate your audience's feelings. You must make them believe that there's a reason *you* are the one telling this story. You have to let a bit of yourself bleed into your work."

And therein lay the problem: you couldn't bleed without feeling the sting of the cut.

Melina began to pleat the edge of her T-shirt, just to avoid his gaze. Bufort pushed off the desk and circled behind her. "I've been acquainted with Melina Green for three years," he said, drawing close. "But I don't really *know* her at all."

What she loved about playwriting was that she could be anyone but herself, a technically Jewish girl from Connecticut who had grown up as the least important person in her household. When she was an adolescent, her mother had had a terminal illness, and her father was struck down by anticipatory grief. She learned to be quiet, and she learned to be self-sufficient.

No one wanted to know Melina Green, least of all Melina herself.

"Good writing cuts deep — for both the playwright and the audience. You have talent, Melina. I want you to write something for this competition that makes you feel . . . vulnerable."

"I'll try," Melina said.

Bufort's hands came down on her shoulders, squeezing. She told herself, as she did whenever it happened, that he meant nothing by it; it was just his way of showing support, like the way he had pulled strings to get her jobs in the city. He was her father's age; he didn't think about boundaries the way that younger people did. She shouldn't read into it.

As if to underline this, suddenly, he was no longer touching her. Professor Bufort raised the chocolate milk again. "Show me what scares you," he said.

That year Melina lived in an apartment above a Thai restaurant with her best friend, Andre. They had met in a sophomore playwriting class and bonded over the fact that *Our Town* was overrated, that the musical *Carrie* was underrated, and that you could both love *Phantom of the Opera* and find it uncomfortably rapey.

As soon as she walked through the door, Andre looked up from where he was watching the Real Housewives. "Mel! Vote on dinner," he said.

Andre was the only person who called Melina by a nickname. Her name, in Greek, meant *sweet,* and he said he knew her too well to lie to her face every time he addressed her.

"What are my options?" Melina asked.

"Mayonnaise, Vienna fingers, or take-out Thai."

"Again?"

"You're the one who wanted to live over Golden Orchid because it smelled so good."

They looked at each other. "Thai," they said in unison.

Andre turned off the television and followed Melina to her bedroom. Although they'd been living in the apartment for two years, there were still boxes on the floor and she'd never hung up any art or strung fairy lights around the headboard the way Andre had. "No wonder you get shit done," he murmured. "You live in a cell."

Like her, Andre was a playwriting major. Unlike her, Andre had never actually finished a play. He would make it to the end of the second act and decide he needed to revise the first before he could finish, and then get stuck endlessly rewriting. For the past semester he'd been working on a retelling of *King Lear* with a Black matriarch who was trying to decide which of three daughters deserved her secret recipe for gumbo. He'd based the main character on his grandmother.

He handed her the mail, which today consisted of a manila envelope addressed to her in her father's messy handwriting. The relationship between Melina and her father had decayed during her mom's illness to the point where putting any weight on it was too tender, but in his own sweet and distant way, he tried. Lately, he had gotten interested in genealogy, and he told Melina he'd discovered she was related to a Union general, Queen Isabella of Spain, and Adam Sandler.

She tore open the packet. *Just found this ancestor on Mom's side of the family. First*

17

published female poet in England — 1611.
Maybe this writing thing is in your blood!

The note was clipped to a small sheaf of papers. She glanced at a photocopied picture of a severe-looking Elizabethan lady with a stiff white ruff around her neck, and then tossed the packet onto the mess of her desk. "My ancestor was a poet," she said dismissively.

"Well, my ancestor was Thomas Jefferson, and you see where *that* got me." Andre propped himself up on an elbow. "How was Bufort?"

She shrugged.

"What are you submitting for the competition?"

Melina rubbed her forehead, where a dull ache had started. "What makes you think I'm going to submit anything?"

Andre rolled his eyes. "A Bard playwriting competition without an entry from you would be like Scotland going into battle without Mel Gibson."

"I don't even know what that *means.*"

"To be fair, he's better at makeup than you are, which is criminal because I've never met anyone else with those weird-ass silver eyes of yours, and if you *knew* what mascara was, they'd pop even more," Andre said, looking her over from her messy braid to her torn cargo pants to her ratty sneakers. "Do people who see you ever, like, offer you handouts?"

Andre was always harping on how she put

18

no effort into her appearance. It was true that sometimes she was writing so fiercely she forgot to shower or brush her teeth. And that she liked to wear leggings and fuzzy sweatshirts when she knew she had a long night at the laptop ahead of her. "What are *you* entering in the competition?" she asked, changing the subject.

"I don't think I'll have anything ready," Andre hedged.

"You could," Melina said, looking him directly in the eye.

"But you're going to win," he said, without even an ounce of rancor. It was one of the reasons she loved him. They were in the same program, and instead of their relationship being competitive, it was supportive. Andre, she knew, would have and had clapped back at other students who were convinced her success at Bard wasn't deserved, but rather the rumored result of an affair with Bufort. It would have been funny, if it hadn't hurt so much — she hadn't even kissed a guy in the four years she'd been at college, much less embarked on a torrid May-December romance.

She sighed. "I . . . don't know what to write about."

"Mm. You could try that idea about the thing that happened in Vegas that didn't stay in Vegas."

"I feel like comedy wouldn't be taken seriously," Melina said.

"Isn't that the point?"

"Bufort wants me to do something *personal*," she said, pronouncing the word like a curse. "Something painful."

"Okay then," Andre said, "write about something that hurts you."

She wrote a play called *Reputation,* where none of the characters had names. They were The Girl. The Boy. The Best Friend. The Nemesis. The Father.

The Girl was fourteen, and invisible. For years she had been fading, in direct proportion to The Mother's illness. After the funeral, she disappeared entirely, edged out of sight by The Father's grief. Until one day, The Boy — eighteen — said hello.

She was certain that it must be a mistake, but no. He saw her. He spoke to her. And when he touched her, she could see herself again — hazy, but coming back into focus.

The Boy was everything she was not: he took up space, he knew everyone, he was impossible to miss. In his presence, she felt bigger and solid and seen.

It started with kisses. Each time his mouth touched hers, she felt a little more substantial. Wherever he put his hands on her, she could see the outline of her body. But when he rucked up her skirt and started to unbutton his pants, she shoved him away and said no.

The next day at school, the Boy's Best

Friend was talking about her to people she did not know. *The Boy said she climbed him like a tree,* he said. *She was tight as a fist.*

Her Nemesis walked by with a friend. *I knew she had to be a slut if he was interested in her.*

The Girl's face burned so hot she was certain people could feel her embarrassment, even if they could not see it. She found The Boy and demanded to know why he'd lied.

Don't you want to be with me? he asked.

Yes but.

I have a reputation to uphold, The Boy said. *Does it really matter what they think, as long as you and I know what's true?*

She wanted to walk away, but he caught her hand, and like magic, she flickered into view.

The Girl had a reputation now, too. When she stood in the line at the cafeteria, unseen, she heard herself described as easy. Changing in the locker room for gym class, she heard herself described as desperate.

The Girl spent more and more time with The Boy, because he was the only person who seemed to know who she really was. In private, he was mostly kind and sweet. She thought maybe she saw a version of The Boy that was invisible to everyone else, too.

One night, he pushed up her skirt again and began to unbutton his pants. *Everyone thinks you're doing it,* he said. *So you might as well.*

This time, The Girl didn't say no.

21

Did she choose? Or did she give in under pressure?

Did it matter?

Because at the moment The Boy pushed into her, she manifested fully and permanently into view — albeit a messy, aching footnote in someone else's story.

Professor Bufort loved the play. He called it raw and thoughtful and provocative. Melina's play was chosen as one of the three finalists in the competition, along with one from a Middlebury student and another from Wesleyan. On the day of the judging, where there would be a reading of each play performed by Bard theater students, Melina spent the morning riddled with nerves and throwing up. This was the first play she had crafted where she was the main character, albeit buried under layers of language.

If people found the play lacking, was *she*? She couldn't separate herself from the script, she couldn't look at the actors playing The Boy and The Girl without seeing herself at fourteen, untethered after her mother's death, latching on to the only person who seemed to want her company. She couldn't hear the words she had written without remembering that lost autumn, when she had no voice, and others filled in the silence with lies about her that became truths.

If that wasn't stressful enough, she had

altered the play the tiniest bit, adding a scene for the final reading that Professor Bufort did not know about. For all she knew, it could get her disqualified. But the play wasn't finished, not without the epilogue, which made it relevant in the present day.

The auditorium was packed. Andre had saved her a seat in a spot that was all too exposed for her tastes, only a few rows back from the stage. She mumbled apologies as she clambered over people who were already seated.

"I had to tell people I had mono to keep them from sitting here," Andre said.

She rolled her eyes. "I'm fashionably late."

He glanced from her messy bun to her Crocs. "No. You're just late."

Professor Bufort stepped onto the stage. "Thank you all for attending the readings that constitute the final round of the inaugural Bard College Playwriting Competition. It has been a struggle keeping our judge this year a secret," Bufort said. "You know him for his incisive reviews, and his coverage of the theater industry as a whole. Please welcome, from *The New York Times,* theater critic Jasper Tolle."

Andre and Melina looked at each other. "What life is this?" Melina whispered. "*Jasper Tolle* is going to judge *my* play?"

Everyone knew him — even people outside the business. Hailed as a wunderkind who had been hired by the *Times* at twenty-six, and then — with his sharp and cutting commentary — he'd attracted a following that either despised or adored him. Within three years he'd moved from covering black box productions in northern New Jersey to Off-Off-Broadway to select shows geared toward Millennials, like *The Agony and the Ecstasy of Steve Jobs* and *Murder Ballad.* Jasper Tolle was half the age of the senior critic at the paper. He had fan accounts on Instagram and Facebook. He made theater — an art form usually embraced by audiences with gray hair — cool again.

"Holy shit," Andre breathed. "He's *hot.*"

He was, Melina supposed, for someone in his early thirties. He had white-blond hair with a cowlick in the back, and behind his tortoiseshell glasses, his vivid blue eyes glittered like cut glass. He was tall, lanky, and looked aggrieved, as if this was something he'd put on his calendar months ago and now regretted.

"He is giving sexy Voldemort vibes," Andre murmured.

"*Never* say that again."

Bufort pushed the handheld mic toward the critic, who cleared his throat, cheeks reddening.

Interesting, Melina thought. He was a critic who liked to hide behind his words.

Not much different than a playwright.

Melina's reading would be the third of the three. After each, Tolle would take the stage and give his reaction, choosing a winner after the final performance. The first play, written and acted by the Wesleyan student, was a one-man show about the multiverse. The second, written by the Middlebury student, put the Marvel Avengers into group therapy.

When the student actors filed in to perform *Reputation,* each carrying a chair and a music stand on which to place their script, Melina felt her heart careen in the cage of her ribs. If she passed out, Andre would have to wake her so that she could hear Jasper Tolle's comments on her work. She was about to tell him this when she saw Professor Bufort lean toward the critic and murmur something.

She imagined he was telling Tolle that Melina was his student, maybe even his protégée.

She swallowed hard and threaded her fingers through Andre's.

In rehearsals, her play had run twenty-eight minutes — which was two minutes under the allotted time for each reading. But that was before she had given a two-page epilogue to the actors at last night's final rehearsal.

As Melina watched the reading now, the dialogue felt as if it were being pulled out of her own throat: painful, familiar, jagged. The audience laughed where they were supposed to.

They fell silent when the narrator described how The Boy tugged at The Girl's clothes. At the last line of the version she had submitted to the festival, she heard a single, thunderous clap from the front row and realized it was Professor Bufort, trying to drive applause.

He didn't know it, but the play was not over.

Eight years later, the narrator said.

All the actors sat, except for The Girl and the narrator.

The narrator walked behind The Girl's chair. *It's different from your other work,* he said, his voice playful, a character who was no longer an observer but a participant.

Yes, The Girl agreed.

I've been acquainted with you for three years, but I don't know you at all.

The narrator put his hands on The Girl's shoulders and kneaded them.

The actress froze. *Professor?* she whispered.

The narrator leaned close to her ear. *Show me what scares you.*

The play ended there. *"Damn,"* Andre murmured.

There was a scattering of awkward claps — how do you applaud harassment? — but Melina barely noticed. She was focused on the profile of Professor Bufort, on the tight set of his jaw.

I'm sorry, she wanted to say.

It had been Bufort who wanted her to bleed on the page. And when she dug up the high school memory of being gaslit by a villain who had convinced her he was a hero, Melina had realized that history was repeating itself.

Jasper Tolle took the stage, bouncing on the balls of his feet, completely unaware that the last playwright had blown up her academic career. "Okay," he said, looking at his little black notebook. "Melina Green? Where are you?"

When she didn't move, Andre grabbed her wrist and yanked her hand in the air.

"Ah," Tolle said. "Well. That was . . . a lot. I suppose we should just discuss the biggest hurdle here . . ."

Melina saw black spots in front of her eyes.

". . . namely, that this is a coming-of-age story, which lands it squarely in the TYA camp."

Theater for Young Artists — in other words, kiddie theater. Melina's face burned. In what world was losing your virginity under morally gray circumstances considered children's fare?

"That's not true," she blurted out.

Jasper Tolle literally took a step backward, as if she had punched him. "I beg your pardon?"

"*B-brighton Beach Memoirs,*" she stuttered. "*Billy Elliot. Equus. Spring Awakening.* Those are all coming-of-age stories."

"Yes, but those works have critical merit," he countered, and her jaw dropped at the jab. "Those don't read as . . . small."

"Because they're about male characters?" Melina asked. She realized, for the first time, that she was the only female finalist. It hadn't occurred to her that would be like running a race with extra hurdles.

"Because their main characters aren't unlikable. Don't get me wrong, there is some truly impressive writing in here, but is this really a story an audience can relate to in a more universal way?"

She ground her teeth together. For God's sake, one of the other plays was about superheroes in a mental hospital.

"The play is supposed to make you uncomfortable," Melina said.

"Well, it did, but not for the reasons you think. It was overly sentimental. To fashion it all as a prelude to the last scene — which felt tacked on, incidentally — makes you wonder if The Girl even learned anything."

Melina was so angry she was shaking. She felt Andre's hand creep protectively around her knee. "That," she ground out, "is the point."

Tolle paused, assessing her. "May I ask if this play was inspired by an incident that happened to you?"

She didn't want to answer, but she nodded.

"In the future," Jasper Tolle said, "steer clear of those subjects. If you're too emotional to handle criticism because a play is so personal, you won't make it as a playwright."

She opened her mouth, but he held up a hand.

Literally, *held up a hand,* as if he could block whatever was about to come out of her mouth.

"You're — what? Twenty-one?" Tolle asked. "You have a lot to learn. Arguing doesn't make you look provocative. Just . . . difficult."

Melina grabbed her messenger bag and vaulted over the row's thicket of knees and legs and backpacks to get to the aisle. She burst through the auditorium door into the hallway just as Jasper Tolle announced that the winner of the Bard Playwriting Competition was the Middlebury student, for his fresh exploration of Iron Man with attachment disorder.

Melina didn't care if she looked like a sore loser. She didn't care if Jasper Tolle thought she was a bitch. She had tried to put herself into one of her plays, but she clearly hadn't fictionalized the experience enough. Lesson learned.

A few moments later, people began to trickle out of the auditorium, webbed in conversations. She turned away when Jasper Tolle and Professor Bufort walked by, paying no attention to the girl who had just lit the fuse to blow up her future.

An arm curled over her shoulders. Melina fell against Andre, finally letting herself cry. "Not sexy," he said, patting her on the back. "Just Voldemort."

Melina felt a laugh bubble up her throat.

29

"I thought it was amazing, Mel," Andre said, holding her at arm's length so that he could meet her gaze. "And I'm sorry if even a splinter of that happened to you in real life."

That was why she had written it. Maybe there was another girl in that auditorium today who would be bolstered to say no when she was pressured to say yes. Maybe there was someone *in* power who would pause before they crossed a line.

Maybe there needed to be more stories like this, not fewer.

"Fuck Jasper Tolle," Melina said.

Andre steered them out of the auditorium. "You took the words right out of my mouth," he replied.

The following week she wrote to Professor Bufort, asking for a meeting. He didn't respond, and so she went to his office hours. His door was locked, and there was an envelope taped to the door with her name on it.

Inside was the grade for her thesis. She had submitted five plays, including *Reputation.* In her major, she had never gotten less than an A on any assignment.

C+. Requires too much suspension of disbelief.

She went home to an empty apartment. Andre was in class, probably, and Melina was grateful for that. She walked into her spartan bedroom and fell facedown on the bed.

She would graduate without a recommendation from her thesis adviser. Other teachers in the theater department would brand her a troublemaker. Students she had considered friends would avoid her in case rejection was contagious. She had become persona non grata.

Andre was the only person on the campus who defended her. He insisted that nothing had changed; they would move to New York City as planned after graduation to try to make it as playwrights. But Melina didn't know if she had the courage for public excoriation again. If you didn't want to face a guillotine, you stayed far away from the chopping block.

And yet. Bufort had told her once: *Real writers can't not write.*

She looked at the piles of paper on her desk. She took the title page of her doomed play and crumpled it in her fist. Her rage became an engine. She grabbed more pages, tearing and tossing them like confetti, until the floor was a sea of print.

Then Melina's gaze snagged on a black-and-white printed image of a woman. The lady's eyes seemed to follow her. Her father's note was still clipped to one corner.

Emilia Bassano. Her ancestor. The poet.

The historian A. L. Rowse, in 1973, called Emilia Bassano the "dark lady" of Shakespeare's sonnets — a black-haired, Jewish woman of

31

dubious virtue. Although this was disproved, she deserves recognition on her own merits as the first published female poet in England, at a time when women were forbidden to write for a public audience.

Melina's chest loosened as she realized she was not the first in her family to struggle to find her place as a writer.

She flipped through her father's genealogy packet, tracing the generations from Emilia Bassano to herself.

> EMILIA sits on a carved
> bench beneath the embrace
> of a lush emerald willow.
> At her feet a faerie house.
> THE WOMAN enters.

THE WOMAN

A theater.

EMILIA

An audience.

THE WOMAN

A comedy.

EMILIA

A tragedy.

THE WOMAN

There once was a girl who became
invisible so that her words might
not be.

EMILIA

There once was a girl. A
beginning and an end.

> EMILIA becomes her younger self.

THE WOMAN

There was a story, whether or not others ever chose to listen.

EMILIA
(places a chess king in the faerie house)

Greetings Oberon, King of the Elves.

THE WOMAN

Emilia named him after the elf king from a French poem she had translated.

EMILIA
(places a chess queen in the faerie house)

And you shall be his Queen.

THE WOMAN

The poem made no mention of a Queen. She wasn't important enough to be recorded.

EMILIA

What to call a larger-than-life faerie queen?

EMILIA, THE WOMAN

Titania.

EMILIA
1581

Emilia is 12

By the age of twelve, Emilia Bassano knew that most people saw only what they expected to see. She thought about this as she lay on her belly, her skirts bunched up beneath her, her chin on one fist. With her free hand, she was building a faerie house. The whitest pebbles from the front drive of Willoughby House ringed a carpet of moss. On it, she had crafted a tiny home of twigs, laced together with long shoots of grass and capped with a roof made of birchbark. Dog-rose blossoms served as windows; twined columbine and kingcup lined the entrance. She added a spotted red toadstool she'd found in the woods, a perfect throne.

She'd filched a polished obsidian king from Peregrine Bertie's chess set. Also known as the Baron Willoughby, he was the brother of Emilia's guardian — Susan Bertie, the Countess of Kent. It was their quarrel that

35

had made Emilia flee outside to escape. She placed the chess piece close to the toadstool. *I'll call him Oberon,* Emilia thought, naming him after the king of the elves in the French poem *Huon de Bordeaux,* which she'd studied last week with the Countess. "Your Majesty," Emilia said, "here's your lady wife." She reached for a second piece she'd taken from the chess set, a smooth ivory queen.

If Oberon had a wife in the poem, she wasn't important enough to mention.

Emilia needed a name that made her unforgettable. *A faerie queen who's larger than life,* she mused. "Titania," she pronounced.

Finally, she set down the third chess piece between the king and queen. A small, dark pawn.

She could still hear the argument between the Baron and the Countess, as clear as day.

I can't bring Emilia with me, the Countess had said, when Emilia hadn't even known she was going somewhere.

Nor I, Susan, her brother argued. *I must leave for Denmark soon.*

Take her, the Countess replied. *She's a girl, not gunpowder.*

Now Emilia stroked the pawn with a fingertip and reimagined the story. The pawn was a child. An orphan. *The king and queen both want you,* she mused. *They cannot stop fighting over who gets to keep you. They love you so much that it will tear the whole world apart.*

"There you are!" With a rustle of skirts, the Countess sank down beside her. She didn't scold Emilia for disappearing or tell her that there would be grass stains on the silk of her dress, and for this, if for nothing else, Emilia adored her. The Countess was only in her twenties, and had already been widowed. For most women that would spell freedom — no longer owned by their fathers or husbands — but she'd been summoned back to court by Queen Elizabeth. Sometimes the Countess made Emilia think of a wolf willing to chew off a limb to escape a golden trap.

It was not extraordinary for a girl of limited means to be trained up into service in an aristocratic household. Emilia's family were court musicians and had emigrated from Italy at the request of King Henry VIII, after he heard them play their recorders. Emilia's own father had taught Queen Elizabeth, then a princess, how to play the lute and speak Italian. However, although Emilia's family now played for the entertainment of the Queen, they never would be nobility.

Emilia had been sent to the Countess at age seven, when her father had died and her mother had left London in service to another aristocratic family. Her parents had not been married, but they lived together while her father was alive. Emilia did not remember her mother very well, except for the fact that she was young, much younger than her father, and so lost in her own daydreams that, even as a child, Emilia knew not to rely on her. Baptista Bassano, her father, had the same olive skin as Emilia, and called her *passerotta* — little sparrow. She remembered the melodies he played on his recorder, some haunting, some jaunty; how the notes curled through her. She remembered her mother saying, almost regretfully, that her father's music could coax the stars from the sky. Those were the only bits she had left of her parents now. Emilia took the memories out regularly, like silver that had to be polished, lest you become unable to see the intricacies of its pattern.

"What have we here?" the Countess asked, as if it were perfectly normal to play in the dirt under the shrubbery. "A faerie house?"

"Another world," Emilia confirmed. She considered asking the Countess where she was going and begging to come along.

The Countess's mouth tipped at one corner. "What a pity we live in *this* world, where it's time for lessons." She extricated herself from the hedge more gracefully than Emilia did, but not before she gathered up the chess pieces. "If the Baron finds these missing, he'll become a bear."

Emilia pictured a wild beast dressed in the Baron's doublet and breeches, a stiff lace ruff beneath its bristled snout.

"Cheer your heart, child," the Countess said, chucking Emilia under the chin. "Once we're gone, perhaps the *real* faeries will come live in the house you've built them."

Emilia fell into step behind the Countess. She wondered if it were that simple; if anything became possible when no one was watching.

Emilia sat in the great hall, which was the room in the Baron's home where the family gathered. In their Lincolnshire country home, Grimsthorpe, there was a separate room for tutoring, but in London the library was used by the Baron. Emilia studied languages, reading, writing, and dancing (music had been dropped after it became clear that Emilia could have taught her tutor more than he could teach her). Because the Countess herself had been educated — which was far from the norm for a woman — she oversaw Emilia's reading. The Bible, of course, but also tracts on decorum and Christine de Pizan's *City of Ladies.* Today, the Countess had Emilia translating Marie de France's lai "Bisclavret." It was about a baron whose wife worried about his repeated disappearances. To Emilia's delight, the husband confessed: at times he transformed into a werewolf, and only donning his human clothes allowed him to turn back into a man. The wife, disgusted, promised to give her love and her body to a knight who'd been flirting with her if he stole Bisclavret's clothes — ensuring that the baron would not return. But when the werewolf pledged his fealty to the king, the wife's plan was thwarted.

"This cannot be right," Emilia said, doubting her own translation. *"More than one woman of that family / Was born without a nose to blow, and lived denosed."*

The Countess laughed. *"Oui, parfait,"* she said. "And what is the message of this poem?"

"Men are beasts," Emilia said flatly. She imagined, again, the Baron with the face of a bear.

"No, my dear. This is a poem about loyalty," the Countess said. "The wife turns on Bisclavret, and is punished for it. Bisclavret is loyal to his king, and is rewarded for it."

"So they're both beasts," Emilia answered.

"Should the wife be forced to stay married to a werewolf? And if not, what tools does she have to extract herself from that bond? Teeth and claws are weapons . . . but so are a woman's body and her love." She shrugged. "You can't blame Bisclavret for being cursed as a werewolf. Yet nor can you blame a woman cursed by her sex."

"But she loses her nose," Emilia pointed out.

"Life as a woman is not without risks," the Countess said. She covered Emilia's hand with her own. "Which is why," she added softly, "I am to wed Sir John."

Emilia had met the man when he visited.

The Countess cupped her cheek. "Afterward, he will take me to Holland. I shall write," she promised.

Emilia felt her eyes burn. She thought of the little dark pawn on the chessboard, being moved around at the whims of whoever was playing the game. Yet she had learned to show people what they wanted to see, so she smiled until a dimple appeared in her cheek. "I wish you all joy," she said.

The first thing you noticed about London was the stench — body odor, feces, and vomit, mingling with the smells of woodsmoke and cooked meat. The streets knotted and tangled as if they had been mapped by a child. Sellers hawked their wares, from feathers to jugs of milk to rush lights, their voices competing with the clatter of hooves and the rattle of carriage wheels. Emilia darted out of the way of conveyances and the occasional diving bird, the kites scavenging a moldy crust or a scrap of thread for their nests. Her leather boots slid on cobblestones that were slick with mud and refuse. Beggars with rags wrapped around their oozing limbs sat on the thresholds of doorways, hands plucking at Emilia's skirts. She passed a cockfight ringed with men shouting out their bets; and when a brawl between two skinny boys spilled into the street, she ducked into an alley. There, a light-skirt was making a quick coin, her skirts

41

pulled up to her waist. She stared blankly over the shoulder of the man rutting into her, as Emilia hurried by.

When in London, Emilia visited her cousin Jeronimo's family for Friday supper. Although she'd grown up outside the city gates, in Spitalfields, with her mother and father, the rest of her cousins now lived on Mark Lane, in the Italian community.

Mark Lane was jammed with two-story wooden homes that listed drunkenly, like a smile made of uneven teeth. Before Emilia had even turned the corner, she could hear music spilling from various houses. She could play almost any instrument, but she would never be as fluent as her cousins. They effortlessly strung together notes the way she entwined words — spinning a melody so perfect you couldn't imagine that a moment before it had not existed in the world.

The red belly of the sun was scraping the roof of her cousin's home when Emilia finally stepped inside. Jeronimo's sons, Edward and Scipio, barreled into her legs in greeting. Their mother, Alma, laughed. *"Piccolini,* let her breathe."

From the corner of the room closer to the hearth, her cousin looked up from the lute he was stringing and smiled. "How is the world of the nobility?" he teased.

"The same as it was yesterday when you were at court," Emilia said.

Jeronimo made a noncommittal sound. She knew, as did he, that the Bassanos' reign as Queen Elizabeth's musicians would last only as long as her favor — and that it could be revoked at any time. Then what would become of them?

Emilia swung one of her small second cousins onto her hip and glanced around the little home. Her relatives were not as wealthy as the Countess and the Baron, of course, but thanks to their roles at court, they were still gentry. They had carved wooden chests brought from Italy and curtains instead of plain wooden shutters. But they also had only a single loft bed, in which they slept with the children. Even if she asked her cousin to take her in after the Countess wed, there was not space for her. She was a shadow caught between two worlds, like the faeries.

"Tell us a story, Emilia," the smaller boy said, reaching for the braided rope of Emilia's hair. When she came to Mark Lane she dressed as a commoner, with her hair down and a plain kirtle over her chemise.

Emilia sat on the hearth with the boy in her lap, letting his brother settle beside her. "Do you know who I met today?" she said. "A faerie queen."

"Was she beautiful?" one boy asked. "Like you?"

Beauty, Emilia knew, was relative. Her olive coloring was far from the fashionable pale skin on display at court; her hair was darker than night; her eyes a ghostly silver. Taken separately, her features were arresting, odd. But combined, they drew attention — men's glances, their wives' narrowed eyes.

"Prettier even than Queen Elizabeth," Emilia said, and she heard her cousin muffle a snort.

Alma winked at her, opening a cupboard to retrieve a folded square of linen embroidered at the edges. It was probably the finest item in the household.

"The faerie queen had promised to care for a friend's orphaned babe, but her husband, the faerie king, wanted to take it away from her."

"Why?" one of the boys asked.

Emilia considered this. She could not remember being as young as her little second cousins, and certain that nothing on God's earth could separate a child from their parent.

"Because the faerie king feared that the queen would love the babe so much, she would forget him."

The boys leaned toward her, rapt. "What happened?"

"The king . . . wanted to teach the queen a lesson. So he told his faerie servant to find a purple flower that would make someone fall in love with the very first thing they saw. And he brushed that flower over the queen's brow as she slept."

Alma smoothed the embroidered linen over the scarred wooden table in the center of the room. "Emilia, *cara*," she said, "the shutters?"

Emilia slid away from the children and stood, dusting off her skirts as she crossed to the open window that lacked the leaded glass panes the Baron had. "But who did she fall in love with?" asked one boy.

A donkey cart rattled past outside. "Why . . . an ass!" Emilia said, and the children fizzed with giggles.

"That's enough," Alma chided. "Jeronimo?"

The sun had slipped below the horizon. Emilia's cousin made sure the shutters were closed and then wriggled a loose stone from the fireplace. Behind it was a small safehole, from which he drew a parcel wrapped in muslin, and another piece of folded linen. He unwound the muslin like he was peeling an apple, revealing two brass candlesticks that he set on the table. Alma added tallow candles and then reached for the linen to drape over her head. Emilia took her little cousins' hands and led them to the table, bowing her head. "*Baruch atah Adonai,*" Alma sang, lighting the candles with tinder from the hearth. "*Eloheinu melech ha-olam asher kid'shanu b'mitzvotav v'tzivanu l'hadlik neir shel Shabbat.*"

Amen, the rest replied, in perfect harmony.

A secret prayer, for a forbidden religion. Like the other converso Jews who had come from Spain and Italy, the Bassanos were

Christians now in the eyes of the world, attending church and praying to the Virgin and her Blessed Son.

People saw what they wanted to see.

Going to court had always felt to Emilia like a performance. Although she did not play recorder or lute beside her male relatives in the great hall, she had been carted along as an apprentice of sorts even when she was very young. She knew the frenetic scramble to present competent nonchalance as the Queen arrived in the room; she understood how music was meant to regale at times and fade into the background at others. Being a courtier was not that much different.

The Queen and her entourage had only recently returned to the palace at Whitehall from St. James's, moving between those properties and Hampton Court, Greenwich, Richmond, and Windsor Castle. There were so many confidants and advisers to Her Majesty, in addition to ladies-in-waiting and visitors from other royal houses, that a palace would periodically become overrun and foul with debris and waste. Then the entire troupe would relocate while it was cleaned and aired.

Dressing for court was the opposite of dressing for her forays to the Italian community in London. Emilia would be rubbed down by a maidservant with clean cloths, and then with perfume. Over a long linen smock she wore a pair of *bodies* — an outer layer made of brocade with whalebone stitched in vertically, a busk jammed between her budding breasts all the way to her belly. The *bodies* were ratcheted tight down the back through eyelet holes and finished with false sleeves crusted with lace and pearls. Tiers of skirts in black and white — the Queen's colors — completed the outfit, until Emilia could not even breathe without rustling. Her hair was dressed and a headpiece fitted to her scalp, ensuring a megrim at her temples before the end of the night. She looked like a miniature version of the Countess, without the swells of cleavage.

The Baron was in attendance, too, although he wasn't happy about it. "If Oxford is here," he muttered, as they waited to enter the crush of the great hall, "I shall not be held responsible for my actions."

"If Oxford is here," the Countess said with a laugh, "I shall eat my fan."

The pumping lifeblood of court was gossip, and the Earl of Oxford, Edward de Vere, had provided plenty this spring. Back in April, one of the Queen's ladies-in-waiting — Anna Vavasour — had given birth to Oxford's son. The scandal wasn't that Oxford was already married, but that this love affair had happened without the Queen's consent. She had thrown both of them into the Tower, and rumor was that Oxford had been released this week.

There was no love lost between the Baron and Oxford, who was the brother of the Baron's wife, Mary. The Baron's marriage nearly hadn't been allowed because the Queen didn't like how Oxford treated his own wife, accusing her of adultery and declaring their child a bastard. He was, simply, a wild card.

They were swept forward into a glittering sea of people. Entertainment varied from masques to bearbaiting to jousting in the tiltyard to Emilia's favorite: plays performed by troupes that had the patronage of a noble. She had grown up with music filling all the spaces of her childhood and knew that the right notes in the right order could make one weep or make one feel lighter than air. The same could happen with the right words, spoken in the right order, by the right actor.

Tonight, though, the entertainment was to be dancing. Emilia could hear the lively strains of her cousins' instruments, but the gallery for the musicians was on the far side of the hall, and she had about as much chance of reaching them in this crush as she did of getting to the Far East. Long, narrow windows let a spill of moonlight wash over those partnered in the vigorous dance. An enormous fireplace held banked flames even though it was warm outside, so the room reeked of sweat and soot. Tonight's music was a galliard — a pantomime of courtship, where the men chased the women. Sometimes the man would reach under a lady's busk to lift her in the air, or raise his thigh and balance his partner upon it. It was shocking to watch, and even more shocking to perform — which was exactly why the Queen used to dance it with her favorite — Robert Dudley, the Earl of Leicester — before he'd lost her regard. Now she was in the middle of the floor, partnered with Sir Christopher Hatton.

It was easy for Emilia to slip away, though she knew it would be frowned upon, or worse. She ducked past the guards at the edge of the room, trying to find a space less crowded and cooler, only to be cornered by Lord Archley. Although she did not know all the nobles at court, she'd had the bad fortune to meet this one before. He was nearly as wide around as he was tall, with a nose like a pomegranate and a ruff so stiff that it tilted back his head. When he saw Emilia, his eyes gleamed. "Ah," he said, his breath stale and gusty. "The lioness has let the young cub from her sight."

It was true that the Countess discouraged male courtiers from getting too close to Emilia. Archley dropped a kerchief and bent, his hand sliding under her skirts to graze her ankle. Emilia's jaw tightened and she stepped back. "My Lord Archley," she said, and curtsied. *Lord Arsely,* she thought.

"Such pretty manners," he said. "In one as fair as the sun."

Emilia refrained from rolling her eyes. Like

every other woman at court, she had powdered her face white as an homage to the Queen. Against her olive skin, however, the powder looked like a mask and only drew attention to how different she was from the rest. "Merely a daughter; no sun am I," she quipped.

Archley leaned close enough for her to see the food stuck in his teeth. "And yet, you make me rise."

Well, he wasn't the only one experiencing an anatomical upsurge, Emilia thought, suddenly queasy. "My mistress calls," she lied, and she tried to edge past him, but Archley's arm snatched her around the waist. She thought of the places the Countess had told her about, soft tissues where one could unman a man with a knee. Archley wore a codpiece, so instead Emilia lifted her foot and ground her heel into his instep. A moment later she was running away blindly. She flew around a corner and smacked hard into another gentleman.

"Please, my lord, excuse me," Emilia gasped.

The man grasped her shoulders to steady her. "I cannot," he said, "as I am the one who stepped in your path."

He was lean and old, with silver hair and kind eyes. There was gold thread in the brocade of his doublet, which marked him as the highest of nobility, a privy counselor.

"You are Countess Bertie's ward," he said. She sensed that he knew more about Emilia than she maybe knew of herself.

Straightening her spine, she met the stranger's gaze. "If you tell Her Majesty I stepped out of the room," Emilia said, "I shall tell her you were already outside it."

The man smiled, delighted. "You know . . . I believe you would."

Flustered, Emilia dropped another curtsy and spun, edging back into the great hall, where the dancing had reached fever pitch. The crowd swelled and receded like a great beast. Emilia picked the Countess out of a knot of women and fought her way to her side.

The Countess glanced down, smiling faintly. "And where were you?" she asked.

"Visiting my cousins," she lied, glancing toward the musicians' gallery, her eyes snagging instead on the gaze of the gentleman with the gold-threaded doublet. He stood talking to the Baron now, watching Emilia over the rim of his goblet.

After the Countess was remarried and living in the Netherlands, Emilia was shuttled between London and Grimsthorpe with the Baron and his wife. Emilia knew that the Baroness did not particularly like her, and when the Baroness fell pregnant, she became even less willing to look after Emilia.

Which is how Emilia found herself on a rain-lashed, three-decked merchant galleon headed to Denmark, certain that she was going to die.

The Baron had been sent on a diplomatic mission and had no alternative but to drag Emilia along. Unlike him, she had never been on a ship, much less one in a storm. Emilia spent the first half of the voyage battling seasickness. After a week, she had become accustomed to the rolling of the world beneath her feet, but she still spent most of the time in her tiny cabin. Sometimes she wrote to the Countess, using a writing box that she'd been given as a goodbye present *(Put your stories to paper, Emilia, and send them to me).* Other times she read books on decorum in the hope that she could make herself as unobtrusive as possible in the Danish court. On the Sabbath, she lit the candle on her bedside table and silently recited a Hebrew prayer, worshipping in the secret temple of her own mind.

That was, in fact, what she was doing when the ship listed so sharply that the candle tumbled, rolling across the cabin's wooden floor. Emilia dove for it, imagining there could be nothing worse than a fire on a galleon. As the flame fizzled in a growing puddle, she realized how wrong she was.

Emilia was certain a leak was something the captain ought to know about. She pulled a wrapper over her night rail and opened the cabin door.

It was like stepping through the doorway of Hell.

A spray of salt water lashed her face, making

her eyes burn. The water was ankle deep here, and more was streaming through the scuttle, the hatchway that led to the galleon's third deck. Wood creaked, stretched to its seams. A rending like a splintering tree roared in Emilia's ears, and then a crash shook the entire ship.

Emilia hovered, her slippers soaked, until the galleon tilted again and smacked her hard against the wall. She rubbed her head where it had struck the wood as one of the young sailors streaked past her, holding coils of rope. "Get back below, milady," he yelled out.

She pictured herself trapped in the little room as the ship drifted in a slow ballet to the bottom of the ocean. Then she turned to the ladder the boy had shimmied, tucked her skirts between her legs, and started to climb.

The hub of the ship was the third deck, the one exposed to the elements. Emilia had taken a turn there on calmer days, but this was a different world. Each strike of lightning illuminated chaos: One of the three masts broken in pieces, having crushed a railing on the side of the ship. Great billows of canvas sails whipping free in the wind, the crew in a losing battle to pull them in. Orders being piped through the boatswain's whistle, drowned out by the gales. A sailor, drenched and wild-eyed, tied to a mast that still stood, squinting into the darkness with a spyglass.

Emilia screamed when a wave rose, knocking

53

her off her feet and sending her skidding across the deck. She scrabbled with her fingernails and managed to grab on to an iron cleat. She heard her name, torn like parchment, and looked up to see the Baron struggling with the steersman to hold the whipstaff, the pole that attached to the rudder. The Baron wore only his linen underclothes and trousers, molded to his body by the pounding rain. "Emilia," he cried, hoarse. "Go below!"

The driving rain and seawater seemed to seal her to the pitched deck until she felt an arm jerk her upright. The boatswain, a beefy man who had let her play his carved bone flute once, yanked Emilia to his side. He half-dragged her, half-threw her down the scuttle, where she landed in a heap at the bottom of the ladder in six inches of standing water.

Shivering, aching, Emilia crawled back to her tiny cabin. The silence, after the scream of the wind, hurt her ears. She hauled herself onto the canvas that served as a bed, folding her legs beneath her.

As her eyes adjusted to the black of the cabin, she saw her nails were ragged and there were splinters in her palms from the wood on the deck. But what drew her attention was the spreading dark stain on her wet night rail. Emilia twisted, scanning her body to find the source of the wound. She was tender in places that would be bruises, but she could not find a cut or a scrape. It wasn't until she held her hand between her legs and her fingers came back streaked with blood that she realized she must have grievously injured something inside her.

Emilia lay back on the cot, crossing her arms over her chest, tears leaking from the corners of her eyes. Her lips moved silently, praying for the second time that night to her god.

She would die here, either drowning in the storm or bleeding until her breath stopped. Her body would be wrapped in a canvas and tossed overboard, among the mermaids and sea dragons. Finally, she would no longer be anyone's problem to solve.

The galleon didn't sink, and Emilia did not die. But she did not recover, either. She continued to bleed slowly but surely, like air being let out of a bladder.

Days later, when the galleon limped into the port of Helsingør, Emilia joined the Baron and his small entourage to seek an audience with King Frederick and Queen Sophie of Denmark on behalf of Queen Elizabeth.

Emilia blinked up at Kronborg Castle, still under construction. It rose impressively tall, shining pale walls capped with a glittering copper roof. It was, in her opinion, much lovelier than Her Majesty's Whitehall, which wasn't white at all but tarnished with soot and grime.

They had been given chambers to refresh

themselves, which was critical because their clothing was all but destroyed by the storm. Emilia sat while a maid who did not speak English brushed her hair until it shone like a raven's wing and braided it into an intricate puzzle. She was given a robe while her court clothes were dried and pressed. But when the little maid tried to help Emilia into her velvet *bodies,* she panicked. Wadded in her drawers was a strip torn from a shift, which she had been using as a bandage. Emilia grabbed the edges of the robe and held it tight, but the maid said something she did not understand and yanked, revealing Emilia in her linen underthings, speckled with dried blood.

Emilia's cheeks burned. She kept her eyes averted as her laces were done up, and then she went to meet the Baron, taking quick, tiny steps so as not to dislodge the wad of linen between her thighs. Her *bodies* was black and her skirts were white, and she feared the blood would stain.

The Baron was pacing in the hallway before the throne room. He gave her an appraising look. "We represent the Queen today," he said, his pale eyes meeting hers. "Consider this a test."

Emilia's mouth dropped open. What was she being tested for? Her usefulness at court upon her return? Was she to charm the Danish monarchs enough to be left behind as *their* new responsibility?

With that, the heavy paneled doors opened, and they were ushered inside. Courtiers flanked the hall, dressed in a flamboyance of velvet and brocade. There were other diplomatic envoys presenting flowery speeches to the monarchs. Emilia shifted from foot to foot as she and the Baron waited their turn. The maid had tied her laces so tight she could barely draw a breath, and her belly felt as if someone was making a fist inside of it. As stars danced at the edges of her vision, she tried to remember when she had last eaten.

Instead, she forced herself to focus as bags of pungent spices were lifted from a chest inlaid with cabochon gems, as a ceremonial sword from a Spanish explorer was offered up to the Danish king. When it was the Baron's turn, they proceeded toward the thrones with guards who bore the ceremonial jewelry of the Order of the Garter, an honorary knighthood for King Frederick from the Queen. They hoped, in return, to receive assurance for Her Majesty that English ships would not come to any harm in Danish waters.

The Baron bowed, and Emilia sank into a deep curtsy. From beneath her lowered lashes, she looked up at the royals. Queen Sophie was delicate, like a wren that had once made a nest outside Emilia's bedroom window at Grimsthorpe. King Frederick was much older, which was the way of things. But his hand rested on the arm of the Queen's throne, their fingers laced together. There was something unexpected about that that made Emilia's heart thump.

The King spoke, and the Baron straightened. Emilia did the same, but the room swam a little, and she stumbled. From the edge of her vision, she saw the Baron's jaw twitch at her mistake.

Then she felt the drip of blood down her leg.

Sucking in a breath, she shifted her foot to cover the red spot she'd left on the flagstone, trying to rub it away with her slipper. She clenched her legs together. A bead of sweat ran down the busk between her breasts.

Minutes, Emilia told herself. *You have only to last minutes, and then you may retreat to your chamber and expire.*

The Baron droned on in French, and Emilia followed the puffery of compliments being winged to the dais on behalf of the Queen of England. Finally, he gestured for the king to be given the carved wooden box that held the Garter Star. A member of the Danish privy council ferried the box the last few feet to the king. *"Vi acceptere denne ære fra den engelske domstol. Må Guds velsignelse overøse Elizabeth Regina,"* King Frederick intoned, pointing to the spot on his velvet cape where he wanted the jewels pinned.

Emilia hoped it would be done quickly. There was a buzzing in her ears.

Then King Frederick gestured at the star

58

and switched back to French. *"Et maintenant, nous célébrons."*

A celebration? *Now?*

The Baron began to back away from the thrones, expecting Emilia to do the same, but she was terrified to move and reveal the smear of blood under the cover of her belled skirts.

"Attends," Queen Sophie said, rising. *Wait.* In French, she asked Emilia her name.

Emilia opened her mouth to answer, and promptly fainted.

When Emilia woke, she was in an unfamiliar bed, a heavy counterpane pulled up to her chin. The maid who had dressed her was sitting in the corner on a stool and popped to her feet as soon as Emilia tried to sit up. Immediately, her debacle in the throne room rushed back. She vaguely remembered a guard hoisting her into his arms and carrying her up the stairs as whispers followed her like the train of a coronation gown. She groaned just as the door opened and Queen Sophie entered, trailed by her ladies-in-waiting.

Emilia tried to scramble to her feet to curtsy, but the Queen waved her off. *"Êtes-vous bien?"* she asked. *Are you well?*

She bit her lower lip, trying to keep herself from crying. *This is a test,* she reminded herself. But surely it was wrong to lie to royalty?

Emilia shook her head, staring down at the bed linens. *"Je pense que . . ."* she began, and

59

then swallowed hard. *"J'ai peur de mourir."* I fear I am dying.

At that the ladies-in-waiting all tittered, hiding their smiles behind feathered fans. Emilia thought how unfair it would be to die far from home, in the company of such cruelty.

To her shock, Queen Sophie climbed the small stool beside the bed and sat on its edge. *"Le Baron a dit que vous n'avez pas de mère."* The Baron said you do not have a mother.

She beckoned to one of the ladies behind her, who produced what seemed to be a miniature pillow, like one a mouse might dream upon. The Queen handed it to Emilia. It was in fact a small pouch, stuffed with what seemed to be dried moss.

"You are not dying," the Queen said, explaining what was happening to her — that her butterfly body was rising from a cocoon of childhood, that she could count the weeks between the flow, that certain herbs would help with the dull ache inside her.

Emilia grimaced. "What a nuisance," she muttered.

She had spoken in English, and Queen Sophie turned to one of her ladies to translate. Then the Queen shook her head. *"Mais non,"* she corrected. *"C'est un cadeau."*

"A gift?" Emilia scoffed. Of what?

The Queen's lips curved, the same smile that Eve had tossed over her shoulder at Adam, that had been used by the Sirens in

Ancient Greece, that Medusa gave a moment before turning a man to stone. *"La puissance,"* she said. *Power.*

Weeks passed as the galleon's mast was repaired for their return voyage, and the Baron used the time to curry the King's favor. As Queen Sophie had promised, Emilia soon felt well enough to join the festivities King Frederick organized to showcase Denmark's wealth and command — twenty-four-course meals, commissioned plays, raucous music and dancing, and endless vats of wine.

There were other guests in attendance — artists and scientists summoned to feed the King's thirst for knowledge and beauty. One evening, in the massive hall, Emilia watched players enact the story of a mythical prince, Amleth, who at the moment seemed to be feigning madness. Emilia was trying very hard to follow along, but the performance was in Danish and it was nearly midnight. She surreptitiously covered a yawn.

A voice spoke behind her in heavily accented English. "The name Amleth, you know, means *stupid.*"

Without turning, she hid a smile. "Fitting, perhaps, as his plan does not seem particularly sound," Emilia whispered.

The play, adapted from Saxo's tale, was about two brothers who ruled Jutland. One brother married the king's daughter Gerutha and had a son named Amleth. Jealous, the other brother murdered his sibling, married his brother's widow, and ascended to the throne. Amleth, certain he was going to be the next casualty, faked insanity while plotting his revenge.

Emilia leaned forward as a beautiful woman — or in this case, a young male actor who was bewigged and skirted — was sent to seduce Amleth into betraying his true motives. When the woman sided with Amleth, the crowd cheered.

Next the king sent a spy to listen in Queen Gerutha's chambers when Amleth chastised his mother for her hasty remarriage. Amleth killed the spy, hacked up the body, and left it to be devoured by a feral boar.

"Temper tantrum," the man behind her murmured.

Emilia giggled. "Sir," she murmured, "you shall ruin the story for me."

"Can one ruin a tale that relies on wild pigs for plot?"

The rest passed by quickly: the king sending Amleth to England with a note directing the recipient to execute him; Amleth swapping out the letter for one saying his escorts should be killed instead. Arriving back in Denmark during his own funeral, Amleth finally murdered his uncle and became monarch.

A rousing wave of applause swallowed the actors as they finished the play, bowing to the

King and Queen. A lavish meal would now be served for hours, until the sky turned a bashful pink.

"I insist upon your delightful company during supper," the man behind her said. Smiling, Emilia turned toward him for the first time.

He was missing a nose.

Instead, a polished gold triangle was affixed to his skin where the feature would be.

Bisclavret, Emilia thought with a pang, remembering the French medieval poem she had translated with the Countess.

He bowed. "Tycho Brahe, at your service."

Emilia knew that this was all wrong; that he was a favorite of the Danish King and she was a nobody, and because of that, *she* should be the one being introduced to *him,* so that he could refuse the conversation if he didn't want to speak with her. And yet, he didn't seem to stand on ceremony. "Emilia Bassano," she said, dropping a quick curtsy.

He was elaborately dressed and had ginger hair, in addition to a mustache with two long tails like an inverted V beneath the prosthetic. He offered his arm to escort her into the dining hall. "A sword fight," he said.

"I beg your pardon?"

"You are wondering how I lost it." He lifted his free hand, circling his face. "At the university in Rostock. My cousin and I were arguing over which of us was the better mathematician." He slid his glance toward Emilia, grinning. "He won . . . by a nose."

"So you are a mathematician?" she asked.

"An astronomer," he corrected. "And you, I assume, are a lover of theater?"

"I love stories of all sorts," Emilia said.

"Then I must know what you thought of our production."

She considered her answer. "I find it truthful," she offered, "as a fool is rarely thought to be a threat. And yet the play has flaws."

The astronomer paused, his brows raised. "Flaws?"

"The young woman sent to seduce Amleth instead saves his life without wielding so much as a knife. Is that not an intriguing character? And yet, she is never named — nor fully developed. And Gerutha — daughter of the Danish king — must outrank both her husbands. But she is an object in the play, not a subject. Had she been allowed to speak, why" — Emilia smiled cheekily — "we might have had a first course before daybreak."

Brahe threw back his head and laughed. "One day I shall read your version of the tale, which no doubt shall surpass this one."

They entered the feast hall, down the center of which ran a long wooden table. A tongue of red brocade licked from one end to the other, dotted with venison cooked in ale and platters of mackerel, roasted capon and shellfish pies,

64

honey tarts and bread pudding. A wooden trencher sat at each place setting, and Emilia let Tycho Brahe steer her toward one. He waved his arm in the direction of two gentlemen sitting across the table. "Cousins, may I introduce Mistress Bassano, whose wit and charm has been the finest entertainment of this evening."

She was not a mistress, technically, because she was not a gentlewoman. But she was having too much fun to reveal the hand that would end the game.

"I am Rosenkrans, mistress." A fair-haired man offered a quick bow.

The second fellow, taller and balding, followed suit. "Guldensteren."

As they dined, Emilia turned to the astronomer. "What is the most glorious thing," she asked, "that you have ever seen in the sky?"

He thought for a moment. "Almost ten years past now, I marked a new star. It was brighter than Venus, and had appeared in a spot beyond the moon, where there never had been a star like that before. A supernova, I called it, because it was new, and brilliant."

"Can one still see it?" Emilia asked eagerly.

"Not anymore, mistress. But it can still be felt. You see, all the scholars and scientists believed until then that the harmony of the world was ensured by the stars, which were fixed and ageless. But my star, my supernova? It proved otherwise. It meant that the Heavens can shift and alter. And if that is true . . . then the world itself can change."

Emilia thought, inexplicably, of the unnamed woman in the play and wondered what became of her. If she, too, might be driven mad by being a pawn in someone else's game. "Do you believe such a thing?" Her words were so soft, they might have been missed. But Tycho Brahe was good at seeing things that were not visible to others.

He nodded gravely. "Indeed, my lady."

She met the gaze of this man who'd rewritten the stars. "So do I," she breathed.

The voyage back to England was uneventful. There, the oppressive summer was cooling to autumn, and a letter from the Countess was waiting for her. She wrote of a stray cat that had claimed their Amsterdam home as its own. When Emilia read it, she could hear the Countess's voice telling the story, and she scanned it over and over until she had the words memorized.

Two days after their arrival, the Baron went to see the Queen. When he returned, he summoned Emilia, telling her to dress for travel and to report to his study. She hesitated at the threshold of the room, her gaze falling on the chessboard in the middle of an unfinished game. Oberon, the former faerie king, was two moves from checkmate.

The Baron stood with his back to her, hands

clasped behind his doublet. "There is a matter to discuss, Emilia," he said. "It would not be right, you understand, for you to stay here."

"Yes, my lord," she agreed. She knew that the Baron's wife would be having their baby soon. They would leave soon for Grimsthorpe, naturally.

"It would not be right for you to stay *with me*," he clarified. "You are no longer a child. My sister was married at your age, after all. You were a credit to Her Majesty in Denmark. The Countess versed you well in conversational skills and languages." His gaze slid away.

Emilia stilled. Was she to be wed, then?

Her head swam. Who was her suitor to be? Would he be handsome? Kind? Wealthy? Had they crossed paths during a masque at court, or in this very house?

The Baron cleared his throat, his face fiery. "You have but one talent left to master," he said. "And then I have no doubt that you will bring great happiness to a man."

Emilia's stomach churned as he led her to the waiting coach. She was too afraid to ask the Baron anything about her intended, lest he find her ungrateful. She had no dowry, which meant that maybe the Countess or the Baron himself had settled a small portion upon her.

The coach rattled over the cobblestones for some distance before she rallied the courage to speak. "My lord," she said softly. "In case I forget to say it later . . . many thanks."

Before he could respond, the coach swayed to a stop. The Baron stepped out and handed down Emilia, who stood on the muddy road, puzzled. They were in St. Helen's Bishopsgate, a part of London filled with affluent foreigners.

Emilia followed the Baron toward one narrow building. He rapped three times, and a servant opened the door. *Gentry then, at least,* thought Emilia. "My lord," the maid said as she bobbed, stepping aside to let them enter.

"Ah, *tesoro,* perhaps I should not let you in, and torture you with my absence as you've tortured me." The voice, flecked with an Italian accent, belonged to the woman who was gliding down the stairs toward them. She must have been sleeping, although it was midday. She was wrapped in a silk robe without even a shift below it. She wore a triple strand of pearls with a ruby clasp in the shape of a flower. She had the largest breasts Emilia had ever seen, and fingernails like talons.

If that wasn't shocking enough, the Baron let her mold herself against him and press her mouth to his.

A small huff of breath escaped Emilia. It was not a surprise that he had a mistress; most men at court did. But she had never really thought about *who* those mistresses were, where they lived, what they did when they were not entertaining the gentlemen who supported them.

The woman unraveled herself from the Baron and stood in front of Emilia. Her lips were rouged; kohl angled from the corners of her eyes. She was monstrous and fearsome and so beautiful that Emilia could not turn away. "So," she said. "This is the one?"

"Emilia," the Baron said. "This is Isabella. You will stay with her while she tutors you for the next few months. I trust you'll listen well to her instruction."

With a curt nod, he left. Emilia could hear the coach pulling away, a thunderstorm of hooves.

"Hmm," Isabella said, walking in a slow circle around Emilia. She felt like a fly being wound in the silk of a spider. "What am I to do with you."

It wasn't a question, not really, but Emilia pretended it was. "I am to be married," she said, hoping that if she spoke it, it would be true.

Isabella's wide red mouth opened like a wound, and a laugh spilled out of her. "Married," she repeated. "To whom?"

Emilia's imagination had always been both a blessing and a curse, and she suddenly could see herself in a robe like the one Isabella wore, her feet bare, her mouth painted. Never married, no.

Suddenly she thought she might be sick on

the thick carpet that the Baron had surely bought. Murmuring excuses that made no sense, Emilia turned and raced out of the house, mud splattering on her hem as she ran through the streets. She made her way to Mark Lane, tears streaking her face. By the time she banged on the door of her cousin's home, it was so dark that vagrants were becoming shadows, and shadows were becoming nightmares.

The door opened only a slice, and then it was wrenched wide. "Emilia!" Alma cried, alarmed at her ravaged face.

"He is selling me," Emilia burst out.

"Now," Alma said evenly. "What is all this?"

"The Baron," Emilia said, sobbing. "He expects me to be someone's whore." On the table were the Sabbath candles, already lit, but all she could see was herself diligently studying with her Latin tutor to master Ovid, and the Countess carefully teaching her to navigate the maze of social politics at court. What was the point, if she were always going to wind up on her back with her knees spread?

When she lifted her gaze, Jeronimo was standing in front of her, but he would not meet her eye. Two spots of color burned on his cheeks. "He will treat you well, *piccolina,*" her cousin said, and at that moment Emilia realized that it had not been the Baron who had brokered her future.

It had been her own cousin.

"You," she seethed. "You chose this for me?"

"Chose?" Jeronimo scoffed. "As if there are options! You are not one of us any longer, Emilia. Look at you, in your finery. It's a wonder you weren't robbed blind on your way here. But you are also not one of *them,* and you never will be." He sighed.

Emilia's cousin was more than a head taller than she was, but she lifted her chin and stared at him. "What did you get in return?" she demanded.

"Emilia —"

"What," she repeated, "did you get?"

He rubbed the back of his neck. "The Bassanos will remain the court musicians. And Hunsdon will allow us to bring over a dozen more relatives from Italy to join us."

Hunsdon. A name. Emilia filed this away.

She had been sold *by* her family, *for* her family.

She felt brittle and empty, as if a gust of wind might scatter her. With a nod, she turned and wrenched open the door of her cousin's home.

She stepped into the night, drew the stars around her like a cloak, and grew up in the space of a heartbeat.

It was hours before Emilia made her way back to the house of the Baron's courtesan. It was a marvel she wasn't assaulted or knifed or robbed, although in her state of mind she would have welcomed it. But that was not her

71

fate this night, and Isabella herself greeted her at the door, holding a goblet of wine.

Without saying a word, Isabella fell back, inviting Emilia to enter. Emilia stepped onto the thick carpeting in the hallway, giving no consideration to the mud on her slippers. Her head throbbed; she felt raw and flayed.

Isabella took her hand and led her up the staircase, Emilia following like a lamb on a lead. She sank onto a peach velvet settee indicated by Isabella. The woman crossed to a table near the tremendous bed and poured a second glass of wine from a decanter. "Drink," she ordered.

She sank to the floor in front of Emilia in a rustle of silk and took a long sip from her own goblet. "French," she said, lifting it in a toast. "And very expensive. You see, it is not *all* bad."

"Do you love him?" Emilia blurted out.

The question surprised Isabella. "Does it matter?" she asked. "Anything that signifies in this world is a business transaction. Including my relationship with the Baron. And, for the record, his marriage to his wife." She leaned forward, conspiratorial. "There is a difference, Emilia, between being kept — like me — and being owned — like a wife. That difference is *freedom*. I do what I want and I go where I want, as long as I make myself available otherwise."

The world began to spin. Emilia hadn't

eaten today, she had gulped this wine, and none of the words Isabella was saying were right . . . yet they made sense.

Isabella stood and plucked the goblet from Emilia's hand. "Come," she said. Then she gently tugged Emilia's wrist until she, too, was upright. They walked toward a mirror, a large rectangle of polished glass that was set by the bed. Emilia watched her reflection as Isabella stepped behind her, putting her hands on Emilia's shoulders. "You've been to a masque, yes?" Emilia nodded. "Then you know what it is to play at being someone you are not. We are all actors, *cara*. There is only one caveat to accepting this role," Isabella said. "Be sure you make yourself worth keeping. And for that, you must learn how to use your body as a tool. A weapon."

Emilia stood motionless as Isabella pulled off her sleeves, untied the laces of her *bodies,* tugged it over her head, slid her skirts to a froth on the floor. She stood in her shift, Isabella's hand on the small of her back.

"What do you see?" Isabella asked.

Emilia cataloged what was before her. A question mark of posture. Legs knobby as a colt's.

But, too, there were now curves at her waist, her hips. Small, high blooms of breasts, her nipples beading under the linen as she stared.

Thick black hair, and skin that wasn't unfashionably dark, but only brushed in shadow.

73

A head that held a library's worth of knowledge.

A mouth made to keep secrets.

Like Queen Sophie had said: Emilia saw power.

Isabella's hands began to knead Emilia's shoulders, relaxing the knots, accustoming her to the touch of another's hand. "I will teach you how to give a man pleasure," she said.

In the mirror, Emilia watched a flush climb from her chest to her neck to her face. "Are women not given pleasure, too?"

Isabella's eyes sparked. "Women are given nothing," she said flatly. "You must learn how to take what you want."

She stepped to the side so that Emilia could see Isabella's image in the mirror, too. Reaching between the shadows of her robe, Isabella slipped her fingers between her own thighs. She met Emilia's gaze. "We know what we are," Isabella said. "But we know not what we may be."

Emilia had always been an excellent student. She lowered her hand to her own dark triangle, visible through her thin shift. She pressed down, and gasped.

Isabella smiled in the reflection of the mirror. *Allora,* she said. "Let's begin."

MELINA
JULY 2023

In addition to still being Melina's best friend and roommate in Washington Heights, Andre remained her critique partner. For two years after the Jasper Tolle fiasco, she had not written anything but a grocery list. For another year after that, she had tried her hand (unsuccessfully) at poetry and had attempted a TV pilot. When she finally allowed herself to start a new play, it felt like a dam had burst. Nature, always, would win out.

She had written a handful of mediocre plays since then, and had shown them to Andre, who was working at a casting agency doing zero playwriting of his own. After college, he'd been too cowed by the lack of opportunities for Black playwrights in the "real world" — so he'd convinced himself the best way into the business was by making connections through his current job. When Andre gave feedback to her, he was gentle in his comments, but he said that her writing felt both beautiful and too careful. "It's like really good

AI," he said. "Super polished, but without a beating heart." He wasn't wrong — but that was by intent. The only personal thing she wrote, rewrote, and finessed — for years now — she had never showed to anyone.

Until Andre discovered her secret. He had burst into her bedroom one morning a few years ago, cradling her laptop, and had plopped down on the mattress. "Um, hello?" he said. *"By Any Other Name?"*

The title of her play was a nod to *Romeo and Juliet,* to Juliet's assertion that a label mattered less than the content. Even in her sleep-haze, Melina had snatched the laptop away from him. "What are you doing with my computer?"

"Making an appointment to get a pedicure, because my phone's dead," Andre said. "Number one, your passcode should never be your birthday. Number two, what are you doing writing a play this good and not letting me read it?"

"I'm not done yet," Melina said, and then in a smaller voice: "You like it?"

The play was about her ancestor Emilia Bassano. In the years since her father had made her aware of the poet, she had become an armchair expert on Emilia, and the more she had learned, the more Melina became determined to give her a voice.

She couldn't quite bring herself to complete it, though.

Because *this* story, *Emilia's* story, was the

story of Melina's heart — the one she kept coming back to, the one she felt maybe she was destined to tell. Completing it meant a reckoning of sorts: what if, after all this time and passion, it wasn't any good?

On the other hand, if Melina didn't finish it, she'd never have to face that possibility.

Andre had shaken his head. "This is the *one,*" he predicted.

Melina had rolled her eyes. "Let me just text my agent," she joked. "Oh right. I don't have one."

Thus began Andre's campaign to get Melina to stop hiding her light, or play, under a bushel. He pestered her about submitting samples to emerging writers' groups. He left flyers for play competitions and fringe festival submissions taped to the bathroom mirror. Sometimes, just to get him off her back, she would send off one of her plays — one whose success carried lower stakes.

Because the deeper Melina had dug while researching her ancestor, the more certain she had become that Emilia Bassano was not only the first published female poet in England and might very well have been a playwright, too.

The playwright, actually. The most famous one in history.

During a Shakespeare course in college, Melina's professor had spent fifteen minutes glossing over the fact that some scholars felt the man from Stratford might not have written his plays. He'd then sniffed and said it was elitist to think that just because Shakespeare wasn't formally educated or rich he couldn't be brilliant.

Melina's first instinct was a knee-jerk response: *of course* Shakespeare had written his own plays. He was the Bard, the greatest playwright of all time.

She got an A in the course and promptly forgot about this controversy.

After Melina graduated, when she found herself too paralyzed to write, she took temp jobs to survive. In between gigs, she would go to the New York Public Library's Manuscripts and Archives room, which was free and air-conditioned in the summer and heated in the winter. It was there she started diving into the life of her ancestor — quickly coming to realize that Emilia Bassano deserved to be more than a footnote in someone else's history.

Very few people had ever heard of Emilia, but if they had, it was because she was a potential answer to the mystery of the identity of the Dark Lady of Shakespeare's sonnets: the lover to whom some of the poems were addressed. Then one day Melina read a chapter in an academic tome that suggested Emilia might not be just the subject of the sonnets — but potentially the author.

Suddenly, Melina remembered her Shakespeare professor talking about people who questioned the authorship of the plays. She discovered that the first of the anti-Stratfordians (as this group was sometimes called) was a woman — Delia Bacon — and she was joined over time by esteemed authors, Supreme Court justices, and acclaimed actors, among others. Mostly, the alternative candidates they suggested were men who were Shakespeare's contemporaries.

Mostly. Occasionally a woman's name was mentioned as a candidate for the "real" author. Mary Sidney, Countess of Pembroke, was cited. Queen Elizabeth herself. And Emilia Bassano.

Melina struck up a friendship with a reference librarian who forwarded her links to scholarly articles and found her books about the Bassano family. Melina learned that her ancestor came from a family of musicians who performed for the Queen. She was educated by a countess, receiving instruction that was extremely rare for a young girl — especially one who was not noble. At age thirteen, Emilia became mistress to the Lord Chamberlain, the man who controlled all theater in London. Later in her life, she was the first woman in England to publish a book of poetry.

So, yes. She had a more classical education than Shakespeare did — it wasn't even known if he'd attended grammar school. Emilia had been born into a creative, musical family. She had access to and awareness of any dramatic productions that were launched through Lord Hunsdon, the Lord Chamberlain, who was responsible for vetting all theater performed in Elizabethan England. She was an established poet at a time when no women were being published. But none of that yet proved anything.

Three years after arriving in New York City, Melina got a job as an usher at an Off-Broadway house where *Hamlet* was running. As she watched the show night after night, she wondered how Shakespeare had known so much about Denmark. She asked her reference librarian friend and a few days later got her answer: unclear, because there was no record that Shakespeare had left England, much less visited the Danish court.

Melina became an amateur sleuth. She learned that when Emilia was twelve, the countess who'd been educating her got married. There was a short gap of time unaccounted for, before Emilia became the Lord Chamberlain's mistress, when she was in limbo, living at the home of the Countess's brother, a baron named Peregrine Bertie.

That baron was the ambassador to Denmark.

During a diplomatic mission he'd taken during that gap of time when Emilia was in his care, he'd met the monarchs of Denmark;

he'd stayed at the castle that was the model for the one in *Hamlet,* and he had dined with two men named Rosencrantz and Guildenstern — characters in that play.

Shakespeare did not move in the same social circle as the Baron; it would have been highly unlikely they knew each other. On the other hand, Emilia had lived with him. She would have heard his stories of the Danish court, or — since she was a child under his protection at the time — she might have traveled to Denmark with him.

That night when Melina watched Hamlet rage and Ophelia go mad, she saw the play in a new light.

What she knew: Shakespeare was an actor, a theater shareholder, and a businessman. There were plenty of documents to prove it. But there weren't any documents that proved he was the writer of the plays.

What she knew: Women were not allowed to write for the stage. At the very least, playwriting could lead to scandal and ostracism for a woman's entire family. At the worst, it could land her in jail.

What she also knew: When it came to history, absence of evidence was not evidence of absence. Just the fact that Emilia Bassano hadn't been published under her own name until 1611 did not mean she wasn't writing before that . . . as someone else.

It had been almost three years since Jasper

Tolle had destroyed Melina's self-esteem, three years since she had written a play . . . but that night, after she finished her ushering job, she took the subway home, opened her laptop, and typed: *Act I Scene I: A manicured garden in Westminster.*

She wrote: *Emilia sits on a carved bench beneath the embrace of a lush emerald willow.*

Living in New York City as a writer meant either having a day job or selling a kidney. At the moment, Melina was nannying to pay for her expensive playwriting habit. She had just dropped off her current charge, four-year-old Kingsley, and faced his mother's icy fury for being late. He'd had a casting call that ended at four-fifteen and an interview uptown for the Episcopal School at four-thirty, which was physically impossible to navigate. As Melina left, she heard Kingsley's mother tell his father that good help was hard to find.

By the time Melina got to the apartment she shared with Andre, she was fantasizing about a big glass of rosé and her pajamas. But when she opened the door, Andre was waiting, dressed far too well for a Friday night in. "Mel! Where have you *been?* We were supposed to be at my mother's birthday dinner a half hour ago."

"Oh, God, Andre. I totally forgot. Okay, let's go."

"Is that what you're wearing?"

She glanced down. "What's wrong with it?"

"What's *right* with it?" He grabbed her arm, yanking her into the apartment.

Melina sat on her bed while Andre detonated a small explosion in her closet. He emerged with a men's shirt she had bought at a consignment shop and a colorful scarf. "Strip."

Melina shucked off her cargo pants and tank top, shimmied into the shirt, and let Andre wrap the scarf around her waist, creating a minidress. "Why are you so good at this?" she muttered.

"If I'm in the closet," he said, "I might as well *do* something there."

In the years they had been living together, Melina had watched Andre love — and lose — numerous men: the semiprofessional tennis player, the bassist for a grunge band, the hedge fund wiz. If he had a type, it was that no two of his crushes were similar with the exception of the fact that they, too, kept their sexual orientation hidden from their colleagues or their fans or — in Andre's case — his parents.

She grabbed his hand. "Andre," Melina said. "Why don't you just *tell* them?"

He looked her dead in the eye. "Why don't you submit your Emilia play for the O'Neill summer conference?"

She huffed out a sigh, annoyed, unwilling

83

to engage. "I'm wearing sneakers," she muttered.

"You do you," Andre answered.

Melina had met Andre's parents twice. They thought she was his girlfriend, a lie that Andre had cultivated on purpose. "They're so upset I'm dating a white Jewish girl," he'd said, "that when I finally say I'm gay, it's going to be a relief."

Letitia, Andre's mother, was employed by a national insurance agency and had worked her way up through the ranks to become an executive in charge of fifty employees. "And then," she said, as they lingered over dessert, "HR told me that the feedback from my colleagues was that I hogged the conversation during meetings. *Hogged.* Can you believe that?"

Letitia looked at her husband, Darnell, who held up his hands. "I wisely learned to stay quiet years ago," he said.

She narrowed her eyes at him. "Anyway. I started to count the minutes I actually spoke at these meetings, and it was far less than any man did. In fact, it was a quarter of the time."

"I once read an article about that," Melina said. "When women talk twenty-five percent of the time in a room, people think it feels balanced. If they talk twenty-five to fifty percent of the time, it's seen as monopolizing the discussion."

"Maybe if men were smarter, we wouldn't have to keep explaining for that other twenty-five percent," Letitia huffed.

"Like I said . . . learn to stay quiet." Darnell nodded at Andre. "Let that be a lesson, son, for when you two get married."

"Which, honestly, should have happened by now," Letitia added. "You've been together for a *decade.* If I'm going to have grandbabies before I die —"

"Mom, you're hogging the conversation," Andre announced, and then he blurted out the first thing he could think of to change the subject. "Pop, Mel's writing a play about Shakespeare!"

Melina glared at Andre, who shrugged apologetically. "Shakespeare!" Darnell exclaimed, delighted. He was an English teacher at a high school in Brooklyn. He taught an entire class on Shakespeare and race, citing examples from *Othello, The Merchant of Venice, Titus Andronicus, As You Like It.* It was from Darnell that Melina had first heard the quote from Maya Angelou: *Shakespeare must be a Black girl.* The bleak desperation of Sonnet 29 seemed odd coming from a poet at the peak of his fame . . . but it made a lot of sense if you imagined the writer as someone who'd experienced racism or poverty or sexual abuse.

"My play isn't actually about Shakespeare," Melina explained. "And I've only just started it, really."

"She started it seven years ago," Andre said, and Melina kicked him beneath the table. "You've been working on it for years, *babe,*" he said pointedly. "Maybe if you start telling people the idea, it will stop being an idea and become a *finished play.*"

Melina looked at the expectant, polite faces of Darnell and Letitia and gave up the fight. "You know that there are people who think Shakespeare might not have been the author of the plays," she began.

"Oh, you mean the hogwash about him not going to Oxbridge?" Darnell said, waving dismissively. "He wasn't the only poet to come from the working class. Christopher Marlowe's father made shoes."

"But Christopher Marlowe got a scholarship to Cambridge," Melina said. "Shakespeare would have needed to *know* things to write all those plays. Philosophy, history, classics, astronomy, military strategy, a whole bunch of languages — French, Italian, Spanish, Latin, Hebrew . . ." She shook her head. "Even if he somehow managed to educate himself, there are subjects in the plays that he couldn't have written about without experiencing them firsthand."

Darnell looked dubious. "Like?"

"Legal knowledge, for one. Since there weren't legal libraries, you had to be invited to study the law. Or the geography of Italy — there weren't any guidebooks that explained the canal system in the interior of the country, but it's in *The Two Gentlemen of Verona.* The town of Bassano in Italy has a fresco in it that Iago describes in *Othello,* but there's no proof that Shakespeare ever went there."

"But it's not like there were travel records back then —"

"Actually, there were. There's all kind of records of the trips of people who were as famous as Shakespeare."

"So you think because he didn't leave behind documentation of his travel, he's a fake?" Darnell scoffed.

"No," Melina admitted. "I think William Shakespeare was a guy who lived in Stratford and London, acted sometimes, and invested in theater companies. But I think Shakespeare's reputation as a playwright is unfounded."

Melina wasn't ready to say Emilia Bassano's name out loud. Instead, she said, "Did you know that in 1687 a playwright named Edward Ravenscroft said that Shakespeare brought the manuscript of *Titus Andronicus* to a theater troupe, but that it had been written by someone else?"

"If the greatest playwright of all time was a hoax, wouldn't that have been exposed in the last, oh, four hundred years?" Darnell said.

"I think a hoax can look like history," Melina replied, "if you mistake mythology for truth."

Darnell turned to Andre. "You better put a ring on that one, boy. She's a smart cookie."

"At the risk of *hogging the conversation*," Letitia chimed in, "that is what I was saying."

Melina smiled sweetly at Andre. "Yeah," she said. *"Babe."*

Melina woke with a start and looked out her bedroom window. Her eyes were drawn to a star that burned even in the ambient lights of the city, one she could not remember seeing before, and the most extraordinary thought tumbled into her head:

> *The Heavens can shift and alter.*
> *The world itself can change.*

Melina pushed the tangle of sheets from her legs and grabbed her laptop. She opened it, the glow of her unfinished play illuminating her features. Her thoughts came faster than her fingers could fly, and she was still typing when dawn set the skyline on fire.

Andre entered her room without knocking. "I didn't sleep at all," he moaned. "I either had too much wine or too much of my parents, not sure which." He tossed himself dramatically onto the bed next to Melina, who remained frozen, reading, her eyes on the screen.

When she still didn't respond, Andre glanced at her. "Hello?"

"I finished. I finished my play." A little laugh bubbled up her throat; she caught her hand over her mouth, as if to stifle it.

"And?"

Melina looked at him. "Andre," she whispered. "I love it."

While Andre read her play, Melina paced. She tried to make (and burned) toast. She hummed until he told her to shut up. Finally, he said, "Did I ever tell you I failed high school American history?"

"Really?"

"I hated it. The Trail of Tears, the Civil War, JFK's assassination, Dr. King's assassination — each thing we learned was more fucked-up than the last. I didn't understand why we had to study this terrible stuff that couldn't be fixed." He looked up at Melina. "Now I get it."

"What do you mean?"

"Your play isn't about history. What happened to Emilia is still happening, every day."

"Yeah," Melina said, feeling that little twist of her heart that let her know her words had communicated exactly what she wanted. "Do you know I've been rejected by twenty-two emerging writers' groups since I moved to New York? I'd say I'm not good enough, but they're all run by male artistic directors, who *always* pick more men than women. They say it's because the stories they tell are ones they can relate to. But when they keep prioritizing those kinds of stories, the result is there are so many others that don't ever get told."

"Girl," Andre said, nodding.

She smiled. If anyone understood what it was like to feel sidelined, it was Andre, who existed at the nexus of not one but *two* marginalized groups. "I know you get it. When I get rejected for the zillionth time by a man who has more power than I ever will, I'm supposed to say, *It's fine.* Because a man who argues is ambitious, but a woman who argues is just a bitch."

Her computer dinged with a message. They both leaned forward to read the note from the nanny agency: *Kingsley's parents requested different nanny — said you were reliably unreliable. Will be in touch if other opptys arise.*

"Great," Melina moaned. "I'm going back to bed. Wake me in 2040." She pulled a blanket over her head.

"This is a sign." Andre yanked the throw from her. "You're not supposed to be a nanny."

"That was evident already to everyone, including me."

"You're supposed to be a playwright, Mel. If they're going to call you a bitch no matter what," he said, "you might as well earn the title."

"What's that supposed to mean?"

"There's a fringe festival I heard about at

the office. I think you should submit your play."

"Andre —"

"What's the worst that could happen?"

She raised her brows. "Were you not just listening?"

"What's the *best* that could happen?" Andre countered.

Melina picked at the weave of the blanket. "It speaks to someone. My play."

Andre tilted his head. "You can't complain about the lack of stories like yours in the world if you don't even bother to submit them."

She could have said the same to Andre . . . but he *wasn't* complaining. By working with casting agents and networking daily, he was trying to find another way into a system that didn't inherently value the stories he wanted to tell. On the other hand, Melina *was* complaining . . . and she hadn't done any work to try to change things.

Melina considered a future working terrible jobs to pay the rent. All the anger she felt toward her chosen profession was just fear, distilled to its purest form. "Okay," she conceded.

Andre leaped to his feet, ready to argue, and then stilled. "Wait, what?"

"Yes." Melina smirked. "We can work on the application today."

Andre's face split with a smile. "But first," he said, "champagne."

■ ■ ■ ■

Submitting a play to a fringe festival was never as simple as sending an email with a copy of your script attached. The festival organizers required everything from your résumé to recommendations to a précis of what the play was about. Andre and Melina sat shoulder to shoulder at her laptop, attempting to write summaries for her play that got sillier and sillier as they finished one, then two, then three bottles of prosecco. By then, the letters were dancing on the screen and Andre had crafted a fake letter of recommendation from Horace J. Sneed, the fictional artistic director of a mythical theater.

After several hours, the application was finished, and so were Melina and Andre, who couldn't sit up without leaning on each other. Andre looked at Melina, his hand hovering over the mousepad. "Ready?"

"Waitwaitwait," she slurred. "Lemme check it again for typos."

"You've read it thirty-teen times," Andre said. "Stop procrash . . . percast . . . procass . . . just send it already."

Melina wrenched the laptop into her arms and fell backward on the bed. She tucked the keyboard under her chin, squinting as she scrolled down the application page. Village Fringe was being presented by The Place, an Off-Off-Broadway theater space with a reputation for edgy and innovative work, and its artistic director, Felix Dubonnet.

Felix Fucking Dubonnet.

"No," Melina gasped, jackknifing so fast that the laptop tumbled onto Andre's belly. *"No no no no no."*

"Ow," Andre said, wincing. "Did your computer crash again? Did we run out of prosecco?"

"Do you know Felix Dubonnet?" Melina asked.

"Isn't that a drink?"

"He's an artistic director who's notorious for only producing plays written by men. Remember when Theresa Rebeck wrote about gender discrimination in theater in the *Times*? He wrote a counter opinion, saying that there were plenty of women in theater — *onstage.*" Melina shook her head. "If he's in charge of submissions for this contest, I'm out, Andre. I'm not doing this."

"Calm your tits, Mel," Andre said, sitting up with the laptop on his knees.

She looked at him, sobering. "Do you have any clue what it's like to be a woman?"

"Is that a trick question?"

"It's being judged constantly. For your clothes. For your curves. It's being told every time you turn on the TV that you have to be thinner or more beautiful. It means doing the same job as a man and getting paid less for it. It means if you age naturally you're letting yourself go, and if you get work done, you're trying too hard." She drew in a shaky breath. "Being a woman means being told to speak up for yourself in one breath, and to shut up in the next. It means fighting *all the fucking time.*"

Andre stared at her with empathy. "Different origin story," he murmured, "but I might know a little something about that."

Melina sighed, setting aside her laptop. She was beginning to understand why Andre didn't write anymore — if you didn't put yourself out there to be rejected, you couldn't get hurt. "Forget the fringe festival. I'm not a glutton for punishment, even if I am female."

Andre blinked. "What if you weren't?"

"Brilliant. I'll get right on that," Melina said, stumbling off the couch. "But first I've gotta pee. *Sitting down.*"

With the room still whirling, she staggered into the bathroom.

Andre looked at the screen and Melina's application to the Village Fringe. With one finger, he deleted three letters of her name, until only his nickname for her remained. *Mel.* He did the same on the script, then pressed send. *She'll thank me,* he thought drunkenly; then lay back against the pillows and passed out.

Melina returned to find her best friend snoring. Her laptop was shut on the coffee table, the last prosecco bottle empty. Yawning, she sank onto the couch and fell into a deep sleep, blissfully unaware that Andre had submitted her play under the alias of a man.

BY ANY OTHER NAME
Rehearsal Script

Lights up on HUNSDON
and EMILIA in box seats
watching a play.

EMILIA

My lord, did we not meet at the
Queen's masque?

HUNSDON

Yes, a fond memory.

EMILIA

Why is it that a woman might
perform *with* the Queen, but not
onstage at the Rose?

HUNSDON

The Puritans believe theater
attracts heathens. A woman acting
for profit would be indecent.

THE WOMAN

Emilia was a woman acting for
profit, too.

EMILIA

If they cannot act . . . do
women ever *write* plays?

HUNSDON

Emilia, you never fail to entertain.

THE WOMAN

Entertainment *was* on the menu that night.

> The theater box becomes a bed. EMILIA straddles HUNSDON.

> He climaxes, falls asleep.

THE WOMAN

Perhaps, with some reading, she would be drowsy enough to forget who she'd become.

> The stage continues to revolve, revealing HUNSDON'S study.

EMILIA
(reading the title of a play)

"The Reign of a Great King."

(yawning)

The dialogue's stilted. The characters are boring. The plot's dull.

THE WOMAN

Hunsdon said women couldn't write
plays. But that didn't mean they
shouldn't.

EMILIA

Who wrote this trash?

(flips to the front)

William . . . Shakespeare.

(She tosses it into the fire.)

EMILIA

1582

Emilia is 13

The first thing Emilia saw were the feet. Boots peeped out from the heavy brocade curtains in the library, where she had ostensibly come to practice her recorder part before the masque. She tucked her instrument under her arm, tiptoed to the lead-paned window, and tried to yank back the fabric — but instead wound up tangling herself in the long silk butterfly wings that trailed behind her as part of her costume, and dropped the recorder.

On one of the feet.

"Ow," a voice said.

Emilia tugged back the curtain to find a boy sitting with his back to the wall. He was younger than she was, with a shock of auburn hair. He was holding her recorder and he had tears in his bright blue eyes. "If that hurt," she said, "then you are weak indeed."

"I'm not weak," the boy said. "I'm hiding."

99

She settled down beside him in a balloon of painted silk. "Have you room for company?"

He wiped his eyes with the back of his hand. "Who are *you* hiding from?"

"Not who . . . *what,*" Emilia said. "I do not like playing for an audience." Unlike the rest of her family, she was not a performer. But Queen Elizabeth had commissioned this masque about famous warrior queens, and she was to play at the finale, when they all danced. Why she was dressed as a butterfly was baffling.

"You don't wish to be a butterfly," the boy said. "I don't wish to be an earl."

Emilia folded her legs beneath her skirts. "Perhaps we could trade roles."

He looked up, hopeful.

She had heard the gossip at court; this must be young Henry Wriothesley, the newly minted Earl of Southampton. He was only eight years old, so he had been given into the care of Lord Burghley, who would manage his upbringing and arrange his marriage.

Like Emilia's, the track of his life was being decided for him. The difference was that at some point, he would be able to take hold of the reins.

But right now, he was just a sad child.

"If I'm to be the earl and you're to be the butterfly, you must learn to play the recorder," Emilia said. "Take a deep breath and blow it out like so." She demonstrated, a long, steady stream of air.

The boy followed suit, and then she raised the recorder. "Now close your lips around the mouthpiece and do the same."

A long, high note curled into the space between them. The Earl broke into a smile. "Brilliant!" he said.

Emilia positioned his thumb and finger, and he blew again. "That note is a B," she told him. "And that's G."

His expression brightened. "Do they spell a secret message?"

She took the recorder and held it to her mouth, pushing her tongue against the mouthpiece to shape the notes as she blew, while her fingers danced over the wood. The music was impish, a cascade of notes that made her think of raindrops chasing one another down a pane of glass. Emilia had been playing since she was three, so it was effortless. Now, as her hands held the recorder, she thought of her lessons with Isabella. She imagined a staff of a different kind, her fingers playing a man's cock like an instrument, her breath hot around him. Although it had all been mere practice so far, one day soon it would be real, and that was enough to make her drop the recorder as if it had burned her.

The young earl, however, didn't see her existential crisis . . . he saw only her musical skill. *"Zounds,"* he swore, awed. "You're a bloody nightingale."

Emilia smiled faintly. "Butterfly, more like."

There was a rush of activity as the door to the library opened and one of the Queen's ladies-in-waiting entered. Lady Leighton gave Emilia a long-suffering glance and stopped directly in front of her. "Emilia Bassano. Where have you *been*?"

Emilia scrambled to her feet. "Right here," she said.

Southampton stood, her unlikely savior. "Apologies, my lady. She was giving me a music lesson, you see."

Lady Leighton frowned, suspicious, but even she could not ignore an earl, no matter his age. She dropped a curtsy to the boy and then slipped her arm through Emilia's, tugging her forward.

"Practice makes perfect, my lord," Emilia said, her lips twitching.

Southampton's unholy eyes lit up, and he winked. When he was grown, he would be beautiful . . . and dangerous. "Perhaps one day I shall return the favor and teach *you* something."

"I look forward to it," Emilia said, and she let herself be dragged from the library.

She did not really blame Lady Leighton for panicking at her absence. She was a lady of the privy chamber for the Queen, as her older sister Lettice had been. But Lettice had secretly married Her Majesty's favorite object of flirtation, the Earl of Leicester, and Lady Leighton likely assumed she was one misstep away from being banished from court, too.

More important, though — Lady Leighton's uncle was Lord Hunsdon, the man to whom Emilia had been bartered.

She had tried to learn as much as she could about the man who would become her protector. Henry Carey — Lord Hunsdon — was the Queen's cousin, the son of Mary Boleyn and William Carey, although that had been the subject of much speculation, since at the time his mother had also been the mistress of King Henry VIII. He had been knighted by the Queen and served as Lord Chamberlain, in charge of all entertainment — from the plays that were performed in town at the Theatre and the Curtain and the Rose, to the masque that would be presented that night, to retaining her relatives as court musicians. He was forty-three years older than Emilia.

He was also estranged from his wife, who lived in the country.

Which was where Emilia entered the story.

"Your uncle?" Emilia asked. "Will he be here tonight?"

"Of course," Lady Leighton said. "It is his duty."

Emilia had tried to learn from the Baron when she was to be conveyed to Lord Hunsdon's residence, Somerset House, but he

103

had been in the country for the birth of his child and had only just returned for to-night's festivities. The Queen had requested Emilia's participation because the masque was about virtuous warrior women, and it wouldn't do to have a man playing the musical accompaniment.

It seemed to Emilia that Her Majesty spent a good deal of time trying to convince everyone that a woman could be as skilled at running a country as a man. Once, the Countess had shown her a poem written by the Queen when she was under house arrest during the reign of her half sister, Mary. It had been scratched into the window with a diamond:

Much suspected by me,
Nothing proved can be.
Quoth Elizabeth prisoner.

Emilia wondered if the best revenge against those trying to erase you was, simply, existing. No matter what, Queen Elizabeth was still the monarch, and performances like this one were meant to remind everyone of that fact.

Two guards opened a doorway, admitting them into an antechamber where other ladies-in-waiting were lining up. The anticipation of the performance was like a charge in the air that lets you know lightning was coming.

An abundance of candles cast shadows over the painted faces of the women, including

Queen Elizabeth, who would, of course, play herself.

"Ah," the Queen said, her lips curving faintly as she regarded Emilia. "Our little butterfly, emerging from her cocoon."

The Queen sat on a heavy carved chair. She was dressed in golden armor, with jewels studding the fine metalwork. Her face was as pale as snow, as different from Emilia's complexion as possible. Her hair wound around a helm with a spiked crown welded to its top. She looked like an avenging angel — fierce, imposing, unassailable. Emilia immediately sank into her deepest curtsy, eyes lowered. "I am a butterfly, Your Majesty, yet I shall never be a Monarch," she quipped.

Her pun delighted the Queen, who replied, "No, just a well-made maid who shall soon be made." The two ladies attending her laughed behind their hands.

Emilia's face burned. It seemed even the Queen knew of her imminent change in position.

The Queen stood, and the room fell silent. "Come," she said. "We wait no longer."

Emilia did not know which playwright had written the masque, but it began in an unorthodox way — a troupe of male actors dressed as witches snaked through the crowd, bumping up against lords and making ladies shriek. One actor dropped a flash pot and red smoke rose in the center of the great hall.

The witches curved their hands to the ceiling, calling forth a firedrake with wings as wide as the horizon, come to incinerate the impious for their sins. *"Awake, thou spirits foul, come manifest . . . No man shall have the power to you repress . . ."*

At that, a flare of trumpets sounded, and the costumed ladies-in-waiting glided one by one into the room. Here was Boudicca, leading the uprising against the Romans. Judith, carrying the severed head of Holofernes. Zenobia, conquering the Egyptians. The women warriors turned in unison to the firedrake, whose fiery breath plumed from some theatrical device that had been rigged above the great hall.

That was Emilia's cue. She entered, playing her recorder, preceding the Queen — whose arrival was greeted with a thunderous cheer. Her Majesty brandished a sword to slay the monster and save the country.

No man shall have the power to you repress . . . but a woman would.

Emilia began to play a pavane, and her notes fell like snowflakes, spiraling, thickening, blanketing the room. The ladies-in-waiting and the Queen performed a stately dance, vanquishing the firedrake at last.

At the end of the performance, Emilia's composition morphed into a fast galliard. The other musicians — her cousins — joined in, and the crowd swelled toward the performers, becoming part of the act. They began to dance *la volta,* the Queen standing to the side and accepting the praise of her courtiers.

Emilia lowered the recorder. The court musicians would continue late into the night, but her own role in the entertainment was officially at an end. When she lifted her gaze, someone familiar was staring at her: the older gentleman who had saved her from Lord Archley last time she had been at court. She remembered him standing beside the Baron, across the room, watching her.

And suddenly she knew.

As he approached, Emilia's heart pounded so hard she was certain everyone could hear it. She tried to imagine the risqué illustrations that Isabella had shown her, but superimposed with his face. She wondered what his body looked like beneath that doublet, and if his legs were pale and skinny under his hose.

"Emilia," a voice said sharply, and she blinked to find the Baron standing beside her. He grabbed her elbow to keep her upright, not looking directly at her but instead gesturing in the general direction of the Lord Chamberlain. "Lord Hunsdon," he said, "might I present Emilia Bassano."

Hunsdon took her hand and brought her knuckles to his lips. "My dear," he said. "Would you honor me with a dance?"

He took the recorder from her hands, passing it to a footman. She stood frozen until the Baron put his hand between her shoulder blades and shoved her toward this stranger with whom she would share a bed. *He is old,* she thought.

She stumbled forward, and Hunsdon caught her. "The flagstones can be slippery," he said.

He is kind.

He led her to the throng of dancers, and they joined in *la volta.* These steps, too, had been part of Isabella's lessons. Emilia's work as a courtesan would occur not just in the bedroom but over the breakfast table or at court or wherever her keeper chose to bring her. Her conversation would ring like crystal. She would be fluent in every social grace and would know the steps to every new dance. She was polish, meant to make him shine.

"Do you enjoy performing?" Hunsdon asked her.

What a question. The answer was no, and yet wasn't her life, now, to be a performance? "I prefer to be the one dreaming up the stories," Emilia said.

"And what else do you enjoy?"

She did not meet his eye. Contracts had been signed; arrangements had been made. This was not a wooing; it was a fait accompli. "What does that matter?"

"It matters," he said. "And it is not so difficult a question. Let me go first: I find pleasure in gardening. And music."

And you will find pleasure in me.

"What of your desires?" he tried again.

"I desire we be better strangers," she blurted out, and immediately clapped her hand over her mouth.

But instead of getting angry, Hunsdon grinned. He plucked at the silk wing of her costume. "Perhaps you are no butterfly, but a wasp."

Despite herself, Emilia felt a smile tug at her lips. "Best beware my sting."

"My remedy would be to pluck it out."

She thought of Isabella, who had trained her in the art of bedroom talk.

Emilia lowered her lashes, slipping seamlessly into her role. "If love be rough with you, be rough with love. Prick love for pricking."

"You" — Hunsdon laughed — "are a delightful surprise."

"You do not know me."

"But I shall." He squeezed her hand, pulling her away from the other dancers. As crowded as the room was, Emilia felt the space contract around the two of them. Isabella called this freedom, yet to Emilia, it felt like being locked away.

She felt his finger under her chin, urging her to meet his gaze. "Speak your mind, Emilia."

It surprised her, for it was her body he wanted, presumably. "Why me?" she asked.

His eyes softened. "I am not unaware that you must be apprehensive. I know that even as I count the days we are apart, you cherish them." He reached for a curl that rested over her shoulder, wrapping it around his finger. "Yet I would that one day you come to enjoy my presence, instead of resenting it."

Emilia swallowed. He had given her truth; he deserved the same. "The course of true love ne'er did run smooth," she admitted.

Lord Hunsdon smiled. "Why you?" he said, finally answering her earlier question. "Because you shall keep me young."

The two ghostly globes of the man's arse pistoned up and down, making the bed knock against the wall. His hands were full of the breasts of the whore servicing him, her legs wrapped around his back. She hadn't even taken off her shoes.

Emilia pressed her face to the peephole in the wall. Isabella was crammed into the little antechamber, too. She wasn't watching, but then, she'd seen it all before.

She'd *done* it.

Emilia understood the logistics — what went where — and at this point even could have suggested some tricks to the woman on her back in the adjoining room, should she have wanted her partner to last longer. But from what Emilia could see, the prostitute only wanted this to be over as quickly as possible.

Isabella had arranged for this . . . *tutorial* with the madam of a brothel who was an acquaintance. It was the closest Emilia could get to sex without being spoiled goods for Lord Hunsdon. Innocence was a commodity, Isabella had explained. Emilia could relinquish it only once. "Isn't it wrong," Emilia whispered to Isabella, "that we're watching him, when he wasn't told?"

"Darling, there are men who'd pay *extra* for this."

Emilia blinked. Just when she thought she was learning, she realized she knew absolutely *nothing*.

With an arpeggio of exultation, the man finished, climbing off the woman and pulling up his slops. He yanked down the tails of his leather jerkin and withdrew a small pouch, tossing a coin onto the straw ticking beside the woman. "Ta, luv," she said, and she yawned.

Isabella slid home the slat that would close the peephole. She crawled out of their cramped quarters, and Emilia followed. "Well?" Isabella said, as another light-skirt passed, pulling a man up the stairs.

"It's . . . messy. And undignified."

"It's about keeping your head," Isabella said. "You retain yours, and the lord loses his."

Emilia frowned. "Well, they looked like a beast with two backs," she said after a moment.

Isabella considered this and shrugged. "You're not wrong."

On the way out of the brothel, Isabella thanked the madam and then led Emilia into the brightness of a rare bluebird day in London. That was another surprise — the fact that coupling happened at all times of the day and night, not just before sleep. As she walked beside Isabella, she saw a bricklayer turn his head, and then a drayman. Two well-dressed women in this part of town were an anomaly, but that wasn't why the men were staring. It was Isabella's lush figure and low-cut dress, Emilia's striking eyes and dark hair. To these men, they were sweets on a shelf just out of reach.

These days as Emilia passed strangers in the street, she found herself wondering if they had sex, and how often, and with whom. She felt as if she had been given a password to a secret society but had not yet used it. She stared at the bricklayer, who was sweaty and broad and not much older than Emilia herself. He pulled off his cap and held it to his chest.

Cheeks heating, Emilia hurried to catch up to Isabella, who held a kerchief to her mouth. "This dust," she muttered. "I don't know what's worse, this or the mud."

"Where are we going?"

"To the herbwoman," Isabella said. "So you can bring down the flowers."

Emilia's brow furrowed. "What flowers?"

Isabella paused in front of a small shopfront. Inside, Emilia could see broad beams strung with clusters of chamomile, Saint-John's-wort, and lavender. Ropes of garlic were braided and draped on the walls. At a scarred wooden table, a woman in a stained apron was grinding diligently with a brass mortar and pestle.

"You do recall," Isabella said, "how babes are created."

Emilia rolled her eyes.

"There is duty, and then there is pleasure. Creating an heir is a duty. Intimacy without issue is pleasure."

Isabella entered the shop, a bell jangling overhead. The woman smiled, toothless. "Dearie," she said, setting down her pestle. "I wondered when ye'd come. You're late, this month."

"Only in my visit," Isabella replied, dimpling. "Yet not where it would count." She lifted her kirtle to reveal her red petticoat, worn during the week she bled, to hide any stains.

The herbwoman wiped her hands on her apron. "I've saved ye what ye need," she said and bustled to the rear of the shop, behind a curtain.

Emilia wandered, her fingers brushing the brittle leaves of drying herbs and flowers. "Rosemary, pansies, fennel . . . columbine," she murmured, and she turned to Isabella. "You are a regular customer here. . . . Do people not accuse you of being a witch?"

Isabella laughed. "Are not all women? The mistake lies with the men who think we cast spells with eye of newt and skin of toad, when all we need is our bodies and our wit."

The herbwoman reappeared, holding two small bunches tied with string and crowned with delicate yellow flowers. "Herb o' grace," she said. "For divine intervention."

Isabella took them from her, trading a coin. She handed one bunch to Emilia. "There's rue for you, and some for me."

"It's pretty," Emilia said.

Isabella playfully tugged one stalk from the batch and tucked it behind Emilia's ear. "You may wear yours with a difference," she said. "But I'll mix mine with myrtle and laurel and wine."

As they left the shop, Isabella threaded her arm through Emilia's. They skirted a fishmonger arguing with a servant over the price of carp, and sidestepped the debris tossed down from a roof by a tiler. "I fail to see why it is the work of the woman to provide the pleasure *and* prevent the consequence," Emilia said. "What do we get out of it?"

Isabella stopped in the middle of the road, letting foot traffic eddy around them. "Security," she said, her face suddenly serious. "Companionship. Protection." She leaned closer, her words low and harsh. "And you may voice such thoughts to me, but mind you silence them starting tomorrow. This is not a banquet where you get to choose your courses. You get what you've been served, or you go hungry. Best relish your good fortune, lest you find yourself on your back like the whore we just watched."

A shiver ran down Emilia's spine. "Tomorrow?" she whispered, the only word she'd heard.

Isabella's gaze softened. With a gloved hand, she cupped Emilia's cheek. "Tomorrow," she confirmed.

Emilia's first impression of her new home was that it was a bloody *castle*. No doubt she would get lost in its halls, and someone would find her desiccated skeleton years later in a privy closet or a wine cellar. Somerset House sported a two-story stone façade on the Strand, and a walled courtyard behind backed up to the river. It looked like a palace because it had been one: the home of Queen Elizabeth, until she gifted it to Lord Hunsdon a few years earlier.

The coach that had come to collect her was the fanciest transport she had ever been in, so well sprung that she barely felt the jarring of the cobblestones beneath the wooden wheels. Painted on the door was Hunsdon's coat of arms — a silver shield with a black bar, three roses slicing through it.

When the conveyance stopped, she smoothed her skirts with her gloved hands and waited for the door to be opened and a servant to hand her down. She lifted her chin, thinking of Isabella, who had hugged her tight before she left and whispered: *Carry yourself as if you own the place.*

She was dressed in her finest court clothing, but her hair had not been pulled back as she had worn it at Whitehall. It fell loose down her back like the river Styx, curling to her bottom. Long flowing hair was the sign of an untried maiden.

And, Emilia mused, madwomen.

At the massive door of the house, she glanced up. Again the coat of arms was displayed, but the Hunsdon crest was here, too — a swan — as well as his motto: *Comme je trouve.*

As I find it.

Emilia considered that. Hunsdon had found her, and now he would take her.

The heavy door swung open, revealing a servant in livery. He did not make eye contact with Emilia as she entered a cavernous room with a stone staircase and more servants, some cleaning, some setting out vases of flowers, some replacing candles in sconces. It reminded her of the beehives at Grimsthorpe, all the inhabitants far too industrious to bother with the likes of her.

She had been schooled in the best way to remove her clothing to entice a man; she could recite erotic poetry in Italian; she could compose a soothing melody on a lute to wash away the residue of a trying day. But she did not know what to do next.

Emilia watched the afternoon light slide through the arched windows. Perhaps if she stayed still enough, she could be mistaken for a statue.

"Ah! Mistress!" A woman as round as she was tall hurried toward Emilia. She wore a heavy ring of keys at her waist, marking her as the head housemaid. "You must wish to freshen up after your journey," she said, although the distance from Isabella's home to Somerset House was negligible. Maybe this was the way of telling Emilia she should stay in her room until told otherwise.

The head housemaid began to waddle up the wide staircase, looking over her shoulder to ensure that Emilia was following. "You're a wee thing, ain't ye," she murmured. Emilia barely heard her. She was too busy looking at the paintings that lined the walls — men and women who all had Hunsdon's long, narrow face and high forehead. Their eyes seemed to follow her.

"His Lordship had this chamber readied," the housemaid said, unlocking a door. "The footmen will bring up your trunks, and Bess — she'll be your lady's maid. I can send her up if you please."

Emilia's eyes moved from the vaulted ceiling to the pale raw silk wallpaper to the bed — a massive canopied square with a velvet counterpane the color of fresh cream. There was a silver-handled brush on a dressing table and bottles of perfume and a filigreed hand mirror. There was so much air and light in the room that Emilia felt as if she were flying.

If this was a cage, it was a beautiful one.

She realized that the housemaid was waiting for her response, so she smiled and shook her head. "Thank you, but I'd like a moment to myself."

Bobbing, the woman started from the room.

"Wait — what are you called?"

The woman's jaw dropped, revealing a wide gap between her two front teeth. "Mary, mistress."

"Mary, I'm Emilia," she said. She might be the one sleeping in this stunning room, but like Mary, she was here to serve Hunsdon. The distinction between them was a fine one.

As soon as the door closed behind Mary, Emilia stripped off her gloves and looked out the window. Her view was of a prayer labyrinth and other gardens, which were being clipped and shaped into submission by servants. Beyond them was the Thames, dark and sluggish. She turned, eyes gleaming, and ran toward the bed, taking a flying leap to land sprawled on the mattress. It was stuffed with something soft and sweet smelling, and she flipped from her belly to her back to stare up at the pleated silk canopy.

She was in a chamber literally fit for a queen. Suddenly, Emilia understood what Isabella had tried to explain: that what she got from this bargain was equal to what Hunsdon would get. She would be another pretty object in his home; he would give her a home without objection.

There was a soft knock, and a moment later the door opened. Hunsdon stood with his hand curved around the wood. "May I come in?" he asked.

She sat up, flustered, and slid from the mattress to her feet — a moment of grace marred by the fact that she'd kicked off her slippers and now stood in her stocking feet on the thick carpet. She curled her toes, leaning forward a little so her skirts belled over them. "My lord," she said, curtsying. "It's your home. I should think you may go anywhere."

He took three steps, which still put him a body's distance from Emilia. She bit her lip. Would it happen *now*? *Right* now?

She knew what to expect, but that didn't mean she wasn't afraid.

"You are pleased with the chamber?" he asked.

"Very, my lord."

"If there is anything you need, you have but to ask for it."

Emilia nodded.

She could hear Isabella's voice ringing in her mind. *These men do not want you to be passive, to make them do all the work. That's how it is with a wife.*

Steeling herself, she raised her chin and

looked directly at him. He was wearing a doublet of blue damask, with silver buttons and pickadils at the waist. A stiff linen ruff covered his neck and wrists. His trunk hose were gray, and he held leather gloves in one hand, as if he'd just come inside. On his left hand was a large ruby ring.

His hair was silver, but she could tell that it used to be red. His beard was gray and cropped close. His eyes, she decided, were the best part of him. They were the soft blue of your most comfortable dress — faded, but full of your best memories.

Emilia reached to the laces that crisscrossed her *bodies.* She took a deep breath and pulled, unraveling the knot.

Hunsdon stepped toward her so quickly that her breath snagged in her throat. He covered her hands with his own. Then with slow, careful movements, he retied the knot. The corner of his mouth lifted. "We have time, do we not?"

Emilia swallowed.

"I wonder," he said, the tips of his ears going red, "if you might like to see my orangery."

"Your . . . orangery?"

"Yes." He smiled. "For my plants."

"I would like that very much, my lord," Emilia said.

Hunsdon waited for her to toe on her slippers and then reached for her hand. She went still for a beat of her heart, and then, deliberately, laced her fingers with his. He looked down at the spot where her palm was pressed to his, and he squeezed gently.

He led her down the stairs and past the great hall to the rear of the house, into the gardens. There were cabbage roses and crowflowers, pansies and long purples, manicured hedges of hawthorn and juniper. A structure of wood and windows had been erected in such a way that sunlight — when it was available in rainy London — would strike it from every side. When Hunsdon opened the door and ushered her through, a blast of heat struck her face, like the breath of a dragon.

Inside were the orange trees and lemon trees with bright pops of ripe fruit dangling from leafy branches. The smell was fresh and sweet. Emilia tugged at her clothing, which clung against her skin in the damp heat, as Hunsdon picked up a watering pot and tipped it into the earthenware base of a lime tree. "I spend much time in here," he admitted. "I find myself most at peace when my hands are buried in the dirt."

"And I warrant that the plants don't require witty conversation," Emilia added. Being at court all the time had to be exhausting.

His lips twitched. "Indeed, many of the seedlings are very good listeners."

She walked through the neat aisle, past the workbench with its sack of potting soil and spades. Hunsdon came up behind her as she

paused before a row of medicinal plants —
rosemary, parsley, sage, mint. "I grow those
for the maids, for healing," he explained.

Emilia nodded. "Comfrey," she said, touching her hands to leaf. "And foxglove . . . and
henbane." She turned to him. "Are these not
poisons?"

He smiled faintly. "Plotting my demise already, are you?"

She caught sight of what seemed to be a sun
floating on a tall stalk and hurried down the
aisle to take a closer look. "I've never seen the
like!"

Hunsdon clasped his hands behind his back.
"It comes from the New World."

"How fitting," Emilia said, as the thick,
damp heat of the glasshouse beaded on her
skin. "As I feel I have washed up on the shore
of a tropical island." She stepped up to a lat-
tice of wood with a vine woven through it.
Small red globes beat from the vine, their skin
shiny and warm to the touch. "And do you
also grow hearts, my lord?"

"Needs must," he said. "As the very instant that I saw you did my own heart fly to
your service." He cupped the weight of one
sphere in his palm. "This is called a tomato. I
brought it back from a journey to Italy. Quite
pretty, but poisonous." As if a thought had
just occurred to him, he walked back to the
worktable and picked up a dagger, then used
it to saw through the strangest flower Emilia

122

had ever seen. Nestled at the center of a bed of spiked leaves was a yellowish shape, scaled like a basilisk, and topped with a small crown of spikes. The spines and the sharp points of the entire plant seemed to warn off anyone who might try to get close.

But Hunsdon sliced the oval off at its base, carrying it back to the table. He deftly cut the spikes and scales away, speaking as he worked. "This pineapple is far from inviting," he said, splitting the fruit in half. "But what does the outside signify, when it is the inside that matters?"

The flesh of the fruit was vivid and juicy. Hunsdon cut it into smaller pieces. "A good leg will fall. A straight back will stoop. A black beard will turn white. A curled pate will grow bald." He held out a small triangle of fruit toward Emilia. "But a good heart, my dear . . . well, a good heart is the sun and the moon."

Hunsdon placed the wedge on her tongue. It burst with sweetness — wine, sugar, and flowers mixed together — almost too much to bear.

That night, Emilia washed and braided her hair and dabbed perfume at all the spots Isabella had instructed her. She dismissed the maid and regarded the massive bed, plagued by questions: Should she be on top of the counterpane? Beneath it? Would he want her nude, or would he prefer to unwrap her like a gift? Should she leave a candle burning, or snuff it?

She decided to sit at the head of the bed in her night rail, and draped herself with the covers. She left the light to spill from the bedside table into her lap, where her tightly clutched hands left fingernail marks on her skin.

Emilia knew what to expect of the mechanics. Isabella had pinched her thigh, hard. "Like that," she had said, "and then no more pain." She only wondered if, after, she would feel different. Older.

She thought, too, of what might happen when Hunsdon appeared before her unclothed. This must be the performance of her life, Isabella had said. He must be made to feel like the most virile male the world had ever known. Flattery, Isabella told her, would get her everywhere.

She lay down, and then sat back up and pulled the ribbon binding her braid, loosening her hair.

He didn't knock this time before opening the door. He was dressed in a brocade robe, with a cap on his head and slippers on his feet. His calves were bare and the skin was translucent, stretched over blue-veined tributaries like a faded map. He was carrying a candle that exaggerated the hollows and shadows of his face, turning it gruesome.

Emilia tried to relax, she really did, but her

124

hands clung tight to the counterpane. "My lord," she murmured.

Hunsdon looked around the room. "You are well? You have all you need?"

She nodded, one quick jerk of her chin. He approached the bed, set his candle down on the nightstand, and leaned toward her.

She closed her eyes, heart cartwheeling, and felt his hands on her face. Dry, cool, like leaves in autumn.

He kissed her forehead and drew back, picking up his candlestick. The flame swayed, dizzy.

Emilia bit her lip. "Do you not wish to . . . ?"

Hunsdon smiled down at her. "It is but your first night here," he said, as if that mattered.

As if *she* mattered.

"What shall you do today?" Hunsdon asked Emilia on the morrow, when they were seated in his dining room eating the midday meal. The first course of marchpanes and dried suckets and baked apples had been cleared, and the serving maids brought out a grand salad, a shield of brawn with mustard, a roasted goose, and an olive pie. She had eaten well with the Countess and the Baron, but not like this. Every meal was a feast.

Emilia looked up at him over her trencher. She had not thought of her own agency in the household; of what she would do when she

125

was not summoned to entertain Hunsdon. "I . . . don't know."

He frowned. "How did you pass the time at Grimsthorpe?"

"In lessons," Emilia said. "Reading. Dancing. Playing the recorder or the lute."

Making up stories, she thought, but surely that would be regarded as the pastime of a child.

"All those things, you may do here," Hunsdon said. "I would also ask that you choose fabrics for new clothing."

"I have gowns, my lord."

He smiled. "Indeed. And now you will have more."

Emilia wouldn't risk his displeasure by turning aside his gift, but she was uneasy. It felt . . . imbalanced. He hadn't touched her, hadn't taken her, hadn't even shown interest in it. Was it because he found her lacking? Was she doing something wrong, despite Isabella's lessons?

Still, a reprieve.

She watched him set aside his knife and take a sip of beer. Perhaps he genuinely wanted a companion. That, she did not mind. "And you, sir? How shall you spend your day?"

He looked surprised, as if he were not used to being accountable — or interesting — to anyone. "I shall peruse the plays that have been sent to me," Hunsdon said, "and decide which is to be performed for the Queen."

"It must be challenging to find entertainment for Her Majesty, when everyone is already acting a part at court." She stood, puffing out her chest. "'Tis I, your sweet Robin, your favorite," Emilia murmured, pitching her voice low like the Earl of Leicester. "We shall ride to the ends of the earth together on our swift-footed mounts. . . ." Then she smirked. "Until I secretly marry your cousin and you banish me."

For a moment, Hunsdon froze — and Emilia thought she may have gone too far. It was one thing to jest privately with Isabella about court politics, but the Lord Chamberlain was part of the fabric from which they were woven.

Then, a smile curved his lips. "Do another," he demanded. "Walsingham?"

She stretched her neck so that her chin was tipped to the ceiling, snooty, mimicking the Queen's principal secretary. "You know, Majesty, that the higher the ruff, the closer to God."

Hunsdon let out a bark of laughter and stood. "Remind me, Emilia," he said, "to stay on your good side."

Each night, Hunsdon kissed her forehead, and nothing more. Each day, Emilia wandered through the palatial home with little to do. Sometimes he locked himself in his study, reading. Sometimes he was in his orangery. Sometimes he was at court.

Of all the things the life of a courtesan might be, she had never imagined it would be lonely.

After a month's time, Emilia had befriended the maids in the kitchen and the grooms who cared for the horses. She had asked so many questions of the gardeners that they had to beg her to let them finish their tasks, lest they be sacked.

One morning, she wandered to the mews to find the Baron's falconer taking one of his birds of prey out for a hunt. She had never watched a falcon seeking its quarry, because only certain ranks of nobles were allowed to keep them. "Milady," said the falconer, pulling off his hat when she approached.

John was older than she was, but younger than Hunsdon, with a shock of fuzzy yellow hair that resembled the head of a dandelion. A young bird was perched on his gloved fist, a silk hood covering its head, cropped with a little spray of feathers. "Isn't he beautiful," Emilia said.

"She, beggin' yer pardon, mistress." John blushed furiously. "Falcons be ladies."

She drew closer. "Why must she be kept in the dark?"

"It's what we do, till the game comes."

"So she will hunt today?"

"Aye, I hope," John said. "She been injured and healin'. Broke her wing."

"Poor thing," Emilia murmured, and the falcon tipped her head. "It's all better now?"

"Aye, I imped her. Mended it with a feather from another bird."

Emilia looked at him. "How?"

"You put an iron needle in the new quill, like, and stick the other end into the broken quill, and you bind it up an' hope for the best. Today we'll see how she took to it."

"May I watch her hunt?"

He grinned at Emilia. "Aye. Mayhap she'll want to show off." He shifted position so that Emilia could see silken jesses threaded through John's fingers and fastened to the leather straps wound around his wrist. On one of the falcon's legs was a tiny bell. "You have to loose a hawk agin' the wind, or she won't come back to you," John said, turning in to the breeze. "All right, my beauty," he crooned to the bird, as a small bevy of woodcocks passed overhead. He pulled off the hood.

One black, bright eye focused on Emilia a moment before the falcon was whistled off in the direction of the woodcocks. For a moment, time stopped as the bird raised her wings and bated them before taking to the sky.

One moment the falcon was there, the next, she was a silhouette against a cloud. She reached the pitch, the zenith of her path, and then dove at a blistering speed toward a woodcock, snatching the prey in her talons.

John jogged to the spot where the falcon had dipped, freeing the dead bird from her clutches. "Good girl," he praised, settling her on his gloved wrist and replacing the hood.

"Doesn't she get anything for her hard work?" Emilia asked.

"She be given the head of her quarry," John promised.

Emilia gingerly touched the falcon's wing. "Well done, you," she whispered, and then she looked up at the falconer. "What would have happened if the imping didn't work? If she *couldn't* hunt anymore?"

John frowned. "Well, no use keepin' a girl that can't serve her purpose, is there?" he asked.

That night, Emilia lay on her bed, staring up at the silk rosette, and saw instead a breathtakingly crafted hood.

Reaching for the writing box that Countess Bertie had given her, she slipped a piece of paper free and cut a fresh nib in her quill. She took out the small pot of oak gall ink. Then she touched the quill to the paper, words bleeding from her hand.

My falcon now is sharp and passing empty
And till she stoop she must not be full-gorged,
For then she never looks upon her lure.
Another way I have to man my haggard . . .
To make her come and know her keeper's call,
That is, to watch her, as we watch these kites
That bate and beat and will not be obedient.

130

Was it true? Emilia wondered. Was the falcon content simply to be allowed to hunt? Had she been in captivity for so long that she could no longer remember the feel of freedom?

"Such concentration," Hunsdon said, and Emilia's head jerked up. Instinctively, she took the page, still damp, and slipped it behind her.

"I did not hear you enter, my lord," she said.

"You were lost in your words. Writing a letter, perhaps?"

"A poem."

He tilted his head. "I did not know you wrote."

She opened the lid to her writing box and set the quill and ink inside. "'Tis but a silly distraction."

"Will you share your verse with me?"

Heat crept up her neck. "Not today," she said.

"Ah." Hunsdon nodded. "Then I have something to look forward to." He executed a tiny bow. "Good night, Emilia."

He started for the door, and Emilia found herself pushing off the bed, halfway across the room. "Wait."

He turned, his hand on the doorknob.

"I am grateful for this room, my lord. And this house. And the dresses and the feasts and everything else you have provided for me."

Hunsdon tensed. "But . . . ?"

"But I wonder if you might take me out somewhere? *Anywhere.*"

His eyes lit up. "I did not know how . . . public you wished to be," he replied. "What I mean to say is: It would be my pleasure."

Emilia thought of the falcon, devouring the head of its catch without knowing that, in another life, she might have had the entire meal. She closed the few feet between her and Hunsdon, popped up on her toes, and kissed his cheek.

He clapped a hand over the spot where her lips had been, rolling his eyes and staggering, a pretend swoon. Emilia felt a giggle bubble up inside her, and for a long while after he closed the door behind himself, she stared at the spot where he had been.

The Queen loved a tournament, and in spite of the fact that the knights jousted with lances that were blunted, the combat was still risky enough that physicians would need to stay on the tiltyard. Emilia sat in a grand pavilion on the grounds of Whitehall beside Hunsdon, her arm tucked into his.

She felt so buoyant, released from Somerset House, that she hardly marked the sidelong glances and whispers from nobles who, with a single glance, had correctly judged the relationship between her and Hunsdon. You would have had to be a fool not to — the Lord Chamberlain had dressed in his finest pearl-encrusted black velvet doublet, and Emilia's outfit was a perfect match to his. She was quite literally meant to compliment — and complement — him.

It was a glorious Sunday afternoon, the second day of the competition. The yard was an explosion of color — each challenger had his own brightly colored tent, some embroidered with silver thread, all flying pennants from their peaks with heralds that matched the caparisons draped over their steeds. It looked, to Emilia, like the storerooms of the mercers, bolts of fabric unfurling across workbenches like rainbows.

The two challengers this weekend were the Earl of Arundel — calling himself Callophisus — and Sir William Drury, the Red Knight. Seventeen defendants — some of whom Emilia recognized and many whom she didn't — were also in the competition. Four earls — Leicester, Northumberland, Pembroke, and Worcester — were the judges. The knight who had the highest score after today's exercises would be awarded a golden chain that had been donated by the Earl of Oxford.

Emilia was already imagining the verses she would write when she was home.

Oxford stepped out of a tent of orange taffeta, the sun glinting off his polished armor. He walked to a bay tree that had been gilded from tip to root, so that every leaf and inch of the trunk glittered. Beneath this, he knelt, held his gauntleted hand over his heart, and bowed his head toward Queen Elizabeth.

Then he stood and mounted his horse, bringing it close enough to the pavilion for him to raise his lance and hold it out, begging a favor.

It was a holdover from medieval tournaments, where knights would ask a lady for a token — a veil, a ribbon, a scarf — and tie it to their armor, publicly showing their loyalty.

The Queen looked at him for a long moment — he was still not in her good regard — then directed one of her ladies-in-waiting to give Oxford a silk scarf. The earl's page knotted it around his wrist, over the armor.

"Have a care, Oxford," the Queen said. "You wear my heart on your sleeve."

Oxford directed the stallion so that it faced a dozen golden staves buried one after another in a long row the length of the tiltyard. Then he lifted his lance and kicked his horse into motion. He whipped down the tiltyard in a blur of hooves and dust and glinting light, smashing all twelve of the staves. A roar went up in the pavilion, and Emilia leaped to her feet, clapping.

Hunsdon smiled at her. As the earl dismounted and another challenger readied himself, Queen Elizabeth's voice rang out. "Lord Chamberlain? A word."

Emilia watched Hunsdon make his way to the Queen's side. Two noblewomen sidled closer to Emilia, crows eyeing a feast. Without Hunsdon to shield her, she was suddenly fair game, in a court that was always looking for its next amusement.

There was a reason, Emilia realized, why he was called her protector.

One of the ladies was tall and lithe, her skin painted the same fashionable white as the Queen's. She looked down her long nose, cataloging Emilia's light brown skin and her small frame. "Who thought the Lord Chamberlain might stoop so low?"

"Low?" Emilia shot back. "How low am I, you painted maypole? I am not yet so low that my nails cannot reach your eyes. . . ."

Her words fell into the sudden silence, and Emilia realized the Queen, Sir Walsingham, Lord Hunsdon, and everyone else in the pavilion had overheard her comment.

She suddenly wished that the knight prancing onto the field could run her through with his lance.

The noblewoman raised her thin brows. "Though she be but little, she is fierce."

The laughter that rang out made Emilia's cheeks flame.

Sir Thomas Perrot, the Frozen Knight, trotted toward the pavilion to honor the Queen. But before he could stand in front of the sovereign, Emilia pulled a ribbon from her hair and leaned over the railing, waving the strip of white silk. "A favor for you, sir!"

The Queen rose, vibrating with anger. "Does she wish to make a fool of me, Hunsdon?"

The Lord Chamberlain's face went pale, and Emilia immediately realized her mistake. To distract a knight about to pay court to the Queen was worse than foolish. It was treasonous.

"She is new to our world, Majesty," Hunsdon said. "She does not mock you."

"Then she mocks *you,*" Queen Elizabeth snapped. "You must school her. Indulge her as a child and she shall act as one."

Emilia's fingers tightened in her skirts. It was as if everyone knew her secret: she was meant to be a courtesan, but she was still a maid Hunsdon had not ever touched. She was still every bit the child they thought she was.

By the time she had the courage to lift her gaze, the knight was halfway down the tiltyard. The Queen was seated.

And Hunsdon was gone.

Emilia woke with a start, sitting up in her bed as the lone candle in the room gutted out. She had dozed off waiting for Hunsdon to return to Somerset House. It had been hours, judging from the night sky. She pulled on her brocade wrapper, jammed her feet into slippers, and tiptoed down the hall to Hunsdon's bedchamber.

She had not been invited into it, yet.

She knocked, but there was no response, and when she turned the knob and peeked inside, she saw only the banked fire and an empty bed.

At the feast following the tournament, Hunsdon had been seated at one end of the long banquet table, leagues away from Emilia. She'd made polite conversation with a third son of an earl starting at Cambridge next term. On her other side had been a dowager who fell asleep after the soup course.

She had spoken only once to Hunsdon, briefly, at the close of the meal. He would be delayed going back to Somerset House, he'd said. She should return without him.

Emilia moved through dark rooms, confident of her way. She felt tears thickening her throat. She had mastered Somerset House just in time to be evicted.

The Lord Chamberlain's study door was ajar, and she could hear the scratch of his quill before she even peeked inside. Hunsdon's head was bent over his writing table, papers stacked and spread across every inch. The fireplace glowed like the maw of a devil; a candelabra dripped tallow onto some of the pages near his left hand.

"I could not sleep, either," he said, without looking up at her. His quill struck through several lines of text. "Do you know, sometimes I believe I work best in the dead of the night?"

She stepped into the room, closed the door behind her, and leaned against it.

"This," he continued, as if she had asked a question, "is a play commissioned by Lord Strange's Men. Before they can perform it, the playwright's foul copy is rewritten as a fair copy and sent to me for review." He scrawled a note in the margin. "My role is one of licensing and censorship. Mostly, I make cuts and suggestions. But there have been times I've had to lock a playwright up in the Tower for crafting something problematic."

Emilia took a step forward. "Problematic?"

"Plays that are treasonous. Overly religious. Anti-Christian. Incendiary." He shrugged. "The only text that I cannot censor is the discourse of a clown, as it is usually improvised in the moment by the actor." Hunsdon glanced up for the first time since Emilia had entered. "Speech without thought can be quite dangerous, can it not?"

Emilia felt her breath catch. "I am sorry for my actions today, my lord."

His expression softened. "I know." With a sigh, he drew a line through a bit of dialogue.

She moved closer, across the table from him, until her fingertips could rest on the same sheet of paper. "Why are you so kind to me?"

Hunsdon put down his quill. "What reason have I to be otherwise?"

He is a good man, Emilia thought. This was

not a terrible place to land. She glanced down at the pages fanned across Hunsdon's writing table. Her life could be viewed as a tragedy, or it could be a comedy. It was truly a matter of perspective.

Emilia took another step forward, until she stood on the same side of the table as Hunsdon. She placed her hands on either side of his chair, and then drew her palms up, from the knobs of his elbows to the slope of his shoulders, until she could cup his face. This close, she could see the crepe of the skin near his eyes, the shine of silver in his beard. She leaned forward the way Isabella had taught her, and kissed him.

She felt Hunsdon pull air from her body into his. He did not reach for her, but his fingers flexed hard on the carved arms of his chair. She let her tongue move along the seam of his lips and she twisted until she sat in his lap.

She kissed by the book, imagining herself as an actor in a role, as a woman in love. *Turn here, bite there, now suck.* For a few long, lazy moments, she focused only on his mouth, her fingers sliding against his scalp, until he began to kiss her back with urgency.

Emilia stood, taking Hunsdon's hand. "Come to bed, my lord," she said softly, reaching for the candelabra to guide their way.

He followed her like a shadow to her chamber. Emilia led him to the edge of the bed and set the brace of candles on the nightstand.

She untied her dressing gown, holding the panels over her breasts, pausing until her hands stopped shaking.

All the world's a stage, and all the men and women merely players, she told herself. Emilia knew that at the end of a play the actors shed the skin of their craft and became the truer versions of themselves. It was the same now. The real Emilia, her heart's Emilia, was buried under layers and layers of artifice, but she was not merely an *actor* in this production. Might she write her own story?

It was the most curious feeling, to be part of a scene but not *in* it. Emilia objectively knew she was peeling the robe from her body, that she was standing in front of the fireplace so that the light would outline her silhouette, but she felt as if it were all happening to someone else. As she undressed Hunsdon, she marked the way breath sawed in and out of him in meter, like verse. The curtain fell — her hair — draping them as she straddled his naked body. She touched her hand to his cheek and when she spoke her next line, there was such honesty in it that the boundary blurred between what was real and what was feigned. "There's something tells me — though it is not love," she whispered, "I would not lose you, my lord."

He turned them, so that now he was on top, his cock notched against her. "Call me Henry," he corrected, and he thrust.

Tears sprang to Emilia's eyes. While he rocked — one, two, three times — she stared up at the silk rosette of the canopy. She felt his body stiffen and finish in her, then roll to his side.

It's done, she thought.

"You are well?" he murmured.

How to answer that? Not the *well* bit. She was all right, if a bit raw. It was the first part of the question: the *you.* She wasn't quite sure who she was anymore.

When she heard his soft snores moments later, she let the tears slip down her cheeks. She might have wiped them away, or gotten up to clean herself, but she did not wish to disturb Hunsdon.

So Emilia stayed perfectly still.

Hunsdon became accustomed to coming home from court to find Emilia in his study, engrossed in one of the fair copies of plays sent to him for review. She would give him a synopsis and tell him which works were lazy and which had verse that made her gasp. Sometimes, she told him the story would be better served if a scene were moved from Act IV to Act II, or that a certain character wasn't authentic. To Emilia's surprise, Hunsdon seemed to care for her opinions, and he didn't mind her asking questions.

Theater, like everything else, was a business. Playwrights were commissioned by the company — Lord Strange's Men, Lord Pembroke's Men — to write something to accommodate their roster of actors. As the troupes changed, breaking up and re-forming, plays would be tweaked so that a new actor or set might be featured. Any playwright might be hired to make these changes, not just the original one. The scripts were written quickly and messily for public consumption. In this, she supposed, plays were like traveling coaches. It did not matter what they were made of, as long as they could get you from one point to another.

And yet.

There was a difference between the coach one might hire to get to an inn outside of London, and the one made for the Queen, carved and gilded and festooned with ostrich plumes.

Several months into her new life, the first play that Emilia had read in Hunsdon's study made its way to a stage. As Lord Chamberlain, Hunsdon attended all new performances in London. As the Lord Chamberlain's mistress, so would Emilia.

The Rose Theatre had been built in Bankside, which meant that patrons had to ferry across the river to attend a performance. But the two thousand people pouring into the courtyard of the theater suggested this was not a hindrance. The building was a wooden polygon made of lath and plaster, its roof thatched. At the entrance a woman held a wooden box, a portable office where the groundlings — those who planned to stand — paid their penny each for admission. There were balcony seats, too, and galleries with cushioned chairs, but Hunsdon would be taking Emilia to the private Lord's Box.

Black flags snapped in the wind, advertising the fact that today's play, *Machiavel,* was a tragedy. Hunsdon steered through the crush, past men urinating against the side of the theater, around a woman selling oysters and oranges, skirting a Puritan standing on an overturned crate and lambasting the sinfulness of theater.

When they were situated in their box, Emilia leaned over the railing to get a better view of the stage and the rigging, from which there might be a thrilling flying entrance, or hidden fireworks to simulate battle scenes. When Emilia had read the play in Hunsdon's study, a real cannon burst had been written into the stage directions. The play was about the lengths to which a ruler might go to guarantee the security of his empire — including murder and deceit. It had led to a discussion with Hunsdon about the worst lie each had ever told. He had confessed to telling Leicester years ago that the Queen no longer wished for his company, in the hope that if her paramour made himself scarce it would quash the rumors that the sovereign was having an affair.

Instead, the Queen had pined for Leicester's company and they had reconciled and spent even more intimate moments together.

Emilia told Hunsdon about a time she was tiny and had broken one of her father's instruments, blaming it on her cousin, who received the punishment. It was not truly her worst lie, though. Although she told him she was happy when they lay in bed, she wished for something more.

"Have a care, my dear," he said now, grasping her waist and pulling her back from the rail. "You shall fall three stories, and then what will I do?"

She leaned over and bussed his cheek. "Put me back together, certainly."

Hunsdon stretched his arm around the back of her cushioned chair. He watched her, his own smile broadening with hers. He did that often, she had noticed — brought her somewhere that would delight her so that he could see it fresh through her eyes. "You have surely been to the theater before."

"Yes," Emilia replied. "But the view from up here makes it seem new." She had attended performances with the Countess, and with her relatives, who often provided the musical interludes for plays. In fact, she now spied one of her cousins tuning his lute in the area near the stage where the musicians sat.

Because this was a new play, it had cost twice as much to attend as a revived piece.

"What will happen if the play is a success?" Emilia asked.

Hunsdon shrugged. "Lord Strange's Men will make it part of their repertoire."

She knew that there was no middle ground. If the audience reacted well, the play was a hit. If they started throwing food at the actors or booing the performance, it would never be staged again.

At the strident shout of a woman selling tobacco, Emilia glanced down. There were women hawking concessions, jostling their way through the crowd. There were painted ladies who likely worked at places like the brothel she'd visited, on the arms of men as their escorts. Nearly half the people crammed into the Rose were female.

"My lord," she asked, "we met first at a masque, did we not?"

"A fond memory," Hunsdon said, stroking her arm.

"Why is it that a woman might perform for the Queen — nay, *with* the Queen — but not onstage at the Rose?"

"Because we do not need to give the Puritans more fuel for their fire," Hunsdon explained. "Court is . . . well, a safe enclosure, away from prying eyes." Emilia thought of the man on the overturned crate in the yard, spittle flying from his mouth as he cursed those who chose entertainment over morality. "The Puritans believe every member of the audience here might be better served working or praying to God." He glanced at the groundlings, where a fight had broken out between two very drunk men. "In their eyes, theater already attracts heathens and deplorables. A woman playing a role would be even more indecent."

Well, Emilia thought. In a way, *she* was a woman playing a role, too.

She saw a young boy, likely covering one of the female parts, in the wings of the stage. He thrust a cushion under his skirts, creating a pregnant belly. How charmed a life: to play at being a woman yet take off the costume at the end of the day and go about the world with the privileges of a man.

"My lord," Emilia said. "If it is indecent for a woman to perform in public, might she contribute in private?"

"Some ladies own shares in the companies," he admitted. "And seamstresses create the costumes and headdresses that are used —"

"Yes, but do women ever *write* the plays?"

He blinked at her, and then laughed. "Emilia, you never fail to entertain."

That night, when Hunsdon came to her, Emilia was dressed in a robe she had purchased on his credit from a seamstress who, indeed, worked for a theater. It was diaphanous and had ostrich feathers sewn onto its collar and cuffs. She wore nothing beneath it, and she saw his eyes heat at the shadow between her legs and the dark marks of her nipples. "Your crest features a swan, does it not?" she said, shrugging the gown off her shoulders. "Perhaps I can be Leda, and you can be Zeus."

"Did Leda not snub the swan?"

Emilia smiled. "Then *I* will play the swan, and . . . die in music." She raised a brow, suggestive.

"A *petite mort,* I hope," Hunsdon said, using the Continental term for an orgasm. Which he would certainly have, and she would certainly not, and he would certainly believe otherwise. From his robe pocket he slipped a necklace of rubies set in gold. It easily cost more than her childhood home. "Perhaps if my swan were willing to wear a collar, I could keep her by my side."

"Henry," Emilia breathed. "It's beautiful."

"As are you," he said.

She held the necklace in her hands, the metal warming to her touch. Reaching up, she fastened it around her neck. Then she stepped out of her robe, completely nude, and walked toward Hunsdon. Sometimes, the lack of costume could be a costume.

She touched the necklace, reciting the final lines of a sonnet by Sir Thomas Wyatt, one widely believed to be about his doomed love for the Queen's mother, Anne Boleyn. *"And graven with diamonds in letters plain,"* Emilia said, her voice husky, *"there is written, her fair neck round about: 'Noli me tangere, for Caesar's I am, and wild for to hold, though I seem tame.'"*

Emilia drew her fingers from the juncture of her thighs, between her breasts, to the lowest hanging ruby in the necklace. "Does it fit, my lord?" she asked.

She could not sleep that night, and so found her way to Hunsdon's study, with its ever-growing pile of fair copies of new plays that needed his review. She had dressed in a thick flannel night rail with her heaviest robe, feeling the need to hide herself after being so exposed. She still wore the necklace. It burned like a brand against her collarbones.

Perhaps some reading would make her drowsy enough to forget who she had become.

It was not the sex that made her uncomfortable. Emilia understood now that her body was an instrument. It was her soul that was the melody, and that was hers alone.

She was a talented musician; it ran in her blood. But playing notes in the right order was not the same as being the one who composed them. It wasn't until this afternoon, in the Lord's Box at the Rose Theatre, that she had truly understood the magic of invention, of putting something new into the world that would take root in the ear of the listener. What incredible power it was to create something from nothing.

Today, at some point, she had stopped watching the play and instead watched the audience. She saw the gasps of surprise when an actor revealed himself to be a villain, and laughter when the clown strutted onto the stage to break the tension. She heard shouts of warning when the crowd was so invested in the players that they didn't want harm to befall them. She listened to the muffled weeping when, in the last act, the most virtuous character died.

A playwright had taken a fresh, blank sheet of paper and from it, had made three thousand strangers *feel*.

She glanced down at Hunsdon's writing table. There were four new works. *A Story of Pompey. The Fair Maid of Italy. Abraham and Lot.*

The last was called *The Reign of a Great King.* She picked it up, scanning the first few pages. The writing was stilted, the characters boring, the plot dull. Emilia skipped ahead to see if it got any better, but this felt more tragedy than history, due to the dismal quality of the writing.

Emilia yawned loudly. It would be a terrible play, but it was serving as an excellent tranquilizer.

Even as her eyelids drooped, she was thinking of how much better this story could be if the entire second act were cut; if the character of Edward III was married to Queen Philippa but longed for the Countess of Salisbury, whose castle he must storm.

Now, *that* was a story.

She'd asked Hunsdon if women ever wrote the plays, and apparently they couldn't. But that didn't mean they *shouldn't*.

Emilia picked up the sheaf of papers and shuffled this play to the very bottom of Hunsdon's pile, thinking to protect him from having to read it first thing in the morning. Her glance caught on the lines scrawled across the top of the page — the title of the play, and its author.

I could do a better job than *this* man, she thought. But by the time she reached her chamber, she had already forgotten William Shakespeare's name.

MELINA

AUGUST 2023

Once a month, Melina and Andre blew way too much of their income on overpriced drinks at Sardi's. Originally famous for attracting Broadway glitterati, the restaurant had become a mecca for tourists and the genteel ladies of the Wednesday matinee crowd — until it became so *out* that it actually was *in* again. Melina and Andre would sit at the upstairs bar, drinking dirty vodka martinis and asking for extra blue cheese olives on the side, which functioned as a meal. They'd pretend to be real players in the business — Andre talking about directors he was working with at the casting office and Melina dropping the names of producers who had, in reality, rejected her plays — and see if any eyes turned to them. Meanwhile, they whispered and pointed to Frank DiLella, the suave theater journalist from NY1, nursing a drink across the bar as he checked his phone; or Tom Schumacher, kingmaker at Disney Theatricals, wearing an outrageous pair of red glasses and holding court at a corner table downstairs.

Melina had arrived at the restaurant at four, a full two hours before Andre would join her, which meant she had to nurse a fifteen-dollar martini until he arrived. She had spent the day poring over job postings, patently ignoring her finished play about Emilia Bassano, which had lurked on her computer desktop since the night she decided not to submit it to the Village Fringe Festival. She was sensitive to its constant presence, as if it were leaking radiation.

Finally Andre slid onto the barstool beside her. "Sweet Jesus," he said. "I am more sweat than man." He glanced at Melina. "Why are you not a hot mess?"

"Because I've been waiting here for two hours?"

Andre picked up her diluted drink and took a long sip. "Am I late?"

"Yes, but also I was early."

"Guess what," Andre said, pulling a slightly damp piece of paper from his pocket. "I got you a babysitting gig. It's only for a week, but it's a choreographer with a six-month-old. She has dance auditions and a nanny with Covid."

Melina took the paper from him. "She just . . . took your recommendation that I'm not a serial killer?"

"Oh, no," Andre said, straight-faced. "She specifically wanted a serial killer. After you murder her UPS driver, you can leave your play lying on her nightstand."

"There's no choreography in my play. It's not a musical."

Andre waved the bartender over, laughing. "I *love* that that's the part of the sentence you object to," he said.

It wasn't the baby. That's what Melina told herself, anyway. She had arrived at eight in the morning, because Ulla — the choreographer — wanted to make sure that her daughter, Isadora, took to Melina before she left for work at nine. The first hour consisted of Melina playing with the baby while Ulla stood in the doorway, sipping coffee and scrutinizing every move.

Finally Ulla left, handing Melina ten pages of instructions on how to care for her child. Isadora fell asleep a half hour later, so Melina put her in her crib and started to read the document. In it were notes of all the behaviors Ulla had witnessed on nanny cams that she did not like and therefore did not allow. Some, of course, made sense: *Don't use cellphones while in our home. Do not leave baby unattended.*

But also: *Do not eat in front of Isadora; it is unfair to her feelings. Do not leave baby in her crib while you use the restroom. Do not take the baby into the restroom with you, because there are no cameras in there.*

By the time Ulla returned Melina had to pee so bad she could barely stand. "See you tomorrow," Ulla said, grudgingly.

"Actually," Melina said brightly, "I'm not going to be able to make it. I'm so sorry, but a career opportunity just came through that I can't pass up."

Now, Melina sat on the train back to the city, running through ways to tell Andre she had quit the job he'd found for her. She was hot and tired and smelled like spit-up, and she had less than four hundred dollars to her name. Sighing, she checked the emails on her phone. One was a notification about a delinquent payment for health insurance, which she quickly deleted. Another was an email from Bard's alumni magazine. The cover featured her old thesis adviser, Professor Bufort, with a young protégé who already had a play being produced on Broadway. It was the third time since Melina had graduated that one of Bufort's thesis students — all, wisely, luckily for them, male — had broken into the big leagues.

As if she needed salt rubbed into the wound, the next email she opened was from the Village Fringe. Likely it was an automatically generated response reminding her she had never finished her application process.

She almost deleted it, and then read the subject line. Re: *CONGRATULATIONS*.

Apologies for the late notice — the original

email bounced back to our office and we only just noticed it in our spam folder. Please see below.

Melina scrolled down.

Your play has been selected by Felix Dubonnet as one of five for a staged reading at this year's Village Fringe Festival. Please join us for cocktails at The Place Theater, August 7, 7 PM to meet the other winners. RSVP: regrets only.

What? A mistake, clearly.

She couldn't be a finalist in a playwriting competition she had never actually entered.

Melina read the message again. This time, she noticed the address that her eyes had jumped over before, hurrying to get to the meat of the paragraph.

Mr. Mel Green:

Not Melina. *Mel.*

Mister.

A cold finger of understanding brushed her spine. *Andre,* she thought, *what the hell did you do?*

When Andre got home from work, Melina was sitting in the living room, waiting. "It's so hot out there, I'm sweating like a drag queen at a DeSantis rally. . . ." He trailed off, staring at Melina. "What the hell is wrong with you?"

"What is wrong with *me*?" Melina repeated, barking out a laugh. "Let's see. First, I quit the babysitting job —"

"You what?"

"And because I'm an idiot, I spent an hour on the train thinking, *How am I going to tell Andre without hurting his feelings?* Because that's what friends do, Andre. They own up to their actions. They don't go behind each other's backs —"

"Halt." Andre held up a palm. "Okay, okay. Fine. When I told you that you looked like Mary Berry in that cardigan at the thrift store it was because I wanted it for myself."

"I don't *care* about the cardigan," Melina snarled. "Do you want to tell me why the Village Fringe sent me an email about my play being a finalist?"

Andre's eyes widened. "What? That's incredible!"

"No, what's incredible is that they even knew I had written a play. Considering I didn't submit it. Remember? Prosecco. Felix Dubonnet. Why bother."

"Yeah, yeah," Andre said, waving his hand. "I had a hangover for forty-eight hours."

"Because you were drunk. And drunk people do stupid things."

"I think I would have remembered if I —" Andre's voice broke off, and his mouth snapped shut. "Oh, shit."

Melina sagged like a windless sail. "For fuck's sake, Andre."

"I thought . . . I thought . . ." He sank down beside her on the couch. "I *didn't* think. I just sent the application in."

"Don't sell yourself short," Melina said. "First, you changed my name, so that Dubonnet would think I was male. Congratulations. It worked."

"What are you going to do?"

"Find a new roommate," Melina said. "But first, I'm going to write them back and say there was a mistake."

"Maybe you should wait," Andre suggested.

"Can't. They're having a meet-and-greet tomorrow night at The Place."

Andre turned to face her. "Don't write back," he said. "I have an idea."

Melina raised her brows. "You're kidding, right?"

"I know, I know, but hear me out. Instead of emailing, go to the meet-and-greet and explain the misunderstanding to the artistic director."

"Because . . . I should humiliate myself in front of an audience?" Melina asked.

"That's the point," Andre explained. "If there's an audience, maybe Dubonnet can't say he's changed his mind about the play just because it was written by a woman. I mean, you *do* go by Mel —"

"Only to *you* —"

"Irrelevant," Andre interrupted. "He may have assumed you're a man, but he'll have to keep your play in the festival, or he'll look like an absolute dick." When Melina hesitated, Andre squeezed her hand. "Your play is really good, Mel," he said softly. "It deserves to have that reading. *You* deserve to have that reading. So what if it slipped past a misogynist by accident? You can tell it to the *Times* when they interview you for your Tony nomination."

Melina sighed. "Thank you for being my number one fan."

"Right now I'm your *only* fan, but this could change that."

She met his gaze. "All right," she said finally. "But you're coming with me. You're my emotional support plus-one, and this is all your fault."

"On one condition," Andre said, his eyes flicking over her. "You let me dress you for tomorrow night. 'Cause right now you look like an extra from *Les Mis after* the barricade, and you smell like baby vomit."

Melina leaned back, letting herself be swallowed by the couch. "Coincidentally, *also* your fault." She sighed.

"Shit." Melina rolled her ankle one more time as she chased Andre down the street toward The Place theater. "Andre, wait up."

He glanced over his shoulder. "You have to move faster. We are so late."

Sweating, they reached the building and pushed through the glass doors. Inside, they were enveloped in frigid air-conditioning, soft classical music, and the hum of people making connections.

For a moment, they both paused, scanning the room. There were approximately twenty guests in the lobby. Melina was the only woman, except for the cater waiters passing out mini quiches. "It's like a . . . male harem," Andre whispered.

"There is no such thing," Melina murmured.

"I was trying to think of a place where women aren't allowed."

"A monastery," she offered.

Andre glanced down at her. "A monastery is the opposite of a harem."

Melina's eyes sharpened as she found the artistic director chatting with a group of sycophants. She wondered which of these men was her competition. "Come on," she said, grabbing Andre's wrist.

Before they could approach Felix Dubonnet, however, he looked up and saw them. He glanced at Andre with what seemed to be recognition, grinning widely and making a beeline for them. They both stood frozen. "Why is he —" Andre whispered.

"Don't know," Melina murmured.

Felix Dubonnet was slight and animated. His eyes were sea green and arresting, and his head was shaved. Melina couldn't tell if he was in his forties or his seventies. "Hello, hello!" he called. "The last of our merry band has arrived. I'm Felix Dubonnet." He extended a hand to Andre. "And you must be Mel Green."

The artistic director's eyes hadn't even flicked in her direction.

"There's been a mistake," Andre said. "This is —"

"It's completely normal to have imposter syndrome," Dubonnet interrupted. "Especially, you know, given . . . where you come from."

Andre smiled beatifically at Dubonnet. "Brooklyn?"

If the artistic director realized Andre was calling out his implicit racism, he didn't show it. "Trust me. When it comes to promising young talent, I don't make mistakes. Did you get a glass of champagne?" Dubonnet gestured to one of the waitresses. "Two please, for Mr. Green and his guest."

That, finally, jolted Melina out of her stupor. "Mr. Dubonnet, if we could have just a minute of your time —"

Before he could do more than smile indulgently at her, a skinny young man approached and whispered into Dubonnet's ear. "Ah," the artistic director said. "Duty calls. I must go collect our special guest. More later, yes?" He turned to the crowd, tapping a pen against his own fluted glass. "Friends," he said, "please take a seat in the theater."

The others in the room filed into the auditorium, leaving Melina and Andre with the waiters. "Now what the hell do we do?" Melina asked.

"Obviously he's going to announce the names of the writers and the plays in there — where we can correct him. It's even better, because there's a captive audience, and he won't be able to backpedal."

Melina drained her champagne in one long gulp. She led Andre into the theater, which seated two hundred. Since this was an intimate gathering, however, the attendees were sitting in the first two rows.

A light funneled down in a cone center stage, and Felix Dubonnet entered from stage left. "It is an honor to welcome you all to The Place. The finalists in this year's Village Fringe are the best we've ever had. But before I introduce you to the playwrights, I'd like to announce a little surprise. This year, your plays won't just be staged in a reading. They will also be reviewed in a special column celebrating ten years of the festival, which will be written by the esteemed *New York Times* theater critic . . ."

The room began to close in around Melina.

"None other than Jasper Tolle!" the artistic director finished with a flourish, and at that, Melina Green's nemesis stepped onto the stage.

If there was anything Jasper Tolle hated, other than a lazy jukebox musical, it was being on *this* side of the stage. He much preferred the anonymity of the audience.

He knew what people called him. Jasper *Troll,* Jasper *A-hole.* Though he was routinely accused of having no emotions (how else could he be so surgically eviscerating in his reviews?), this was untrue, because every time he heard one of those names, it stung. There was a difference between having no emotion and having a hard time deciphering the emotions of others, which had been the narrative of his life. As a child, he'd been told he was too blunt (do not tell your mother she looks bad in that dress or announce to your teacher that she has gotten history facts wrong). He had often been put into a time-out to "think about what he said," but when he did, he never wanted to revise his original words. Eventually he learned to guess what people wanted to hear and what they didn't. To him, it had always felt like lying. Wasn't an omission just as bad as an untruth?

Then Jasper had gone to college — Princeton, because he had perfect grades, perfect SAT scores, and was a legacy admission to boot. Unlike his father and his grandfather before him, though, he was not on the crew team and he did not carve his way through the campus with equally athletic friends. In fact, Jasper didn't have any friends. He had a roommate who mostly was high, and who barely acknowledged Jasper's presence. When Jasper wandered into an information meeting for *The Daily Princetonian,* the school paper, he did not immediately realize that he'd found his calling.

He knew nothing about being a journalist. The entertainment critic — who reviewed films playing in town and performances at the McCarter Theatre — had just graduated, and there was a vacancy. *All you have to do, Jasper,* the editor-in-chief had told him, *is write your opinion of what you see.* So he did. The very behavior he'd been scolded for as a child — calling it like he saw it — suddenly became his job.

By the time he left college, he knew he wanted to do this for a living, and he had a portfolio of reviews that got him hired at the *Times.* His stratospheric rise, however, was due not to his competence as a writer but to his brutal honesty. Apparently, readers found it entertaining when he called a show bloated with costumes and scenery "a pavlova" (pretty to look at but leaves you with a stomachache); or when he compared a notoriously off-key Broadway diva to the seagulls that screeched around Chelsea Piers. He said the things everyone was thinking but was too polite to say. Watercooler talk about his columns ranged from whispers about strutting directors who'd been cut down to size by Jasper's words to bets on how long before one of the shows he gutted was forced to close. In 2020, when Ben Brantley retired as the main critic at the *Times,* Jasper had leapfrogged older, more seasoned candidates to get the job. It meant a raise, but it also meant that he was liberated from reviewing avant-garde performances that were far less clever than they thought they were, and from parodies of TV shows playing Off-Off-Off-Broadway *(Fuckcession, the Musical!* And *Bridgertone — An A Cappella Regency Romp)*.

Jasper was a creature of habit. He lived in a co-op on the Upper West Side that had exactly seven live plants because he'd learned that there wasn't enough sunlight to support an eighth; he got his coffee from the same Dominican bodega every day; he bought a Ted Baker suit in several different colors because it fit his lean frame well and why reinvent the wheel? He ate the same thing for lunch every day when he was in the office — a turkey sandwich with goat cheese and sprouts. He enjoyed the niceties his career provided him: a rainbow of silk pocket squares, a frigid Monkey 47 martini, and assigning underlings to review the shows he really had no desire to see.

For all these reasons and more, he did not want to be a part of the Village Fringe Festival. It was not one of the better-known festivals; it was not helmed by an artistic director he liked; and it was in the part of Manhattan outside the grid of numbered streets, which still made Jasper slightly uneasy.

The only reason Jasper Tolle was here

was that he was being punished for a now-infamous review.

To be fair, the actor he'd cited had been serviceable in her part. Jasper had been commenting on the ineptitude of the costume designer. The actual quote was *Since Ms. Ogden is so much larger than the other actresses onstage, one would have hoped costume designer Dante Tigoletti would have dressed her more appropriately.*

Yet instead of readers focusing on the meat of his criticism — specifically, that her costume was a disaster — Jasper became the target of a social media smear campaign. The National Association to Advance Fat Acceptance called him out for body-shaming. His editor, Don, suggested he fall on his sword and publish a retraction, to which Jasper had texted *Over my dead (unshamed) body.*

The next thing he knew, he had been assigned to cover the Village Fringe Festival.

Jasper heard Felix Dubonnet (a preening coxcomb of a director who'd never had an original thought in his life) announce his name. Gritting his teeth, he pushed back the hair that was always falling over his brow and walked onstage to applause. He shook Felix's hand, resisting the urge to wipe his palm on his trousers afterward, and squinted into the light that prevented him from seeing any of the finalists or other attendees. How did actors *do* this every

165

night and manage to connect with humans in an audience?

". . . a few words?" Jasper's thoughts were interrupted by the realization that Felix wanted him to say something inspirational to these novices. He cleared his throat and looked into the blinding stage lights. "Congratulations to the finalists," he said. "I look forward to being impressed by your work." There. That was true, right? Even if it wasn't likely. He glanced at Felix. "Good theater, of course, is subjective — but a good story is *objective.* A good story makes the audience feel something. Do not let the practice of theater get in the way of your storytelling."

He could hear the writers eating up his words as if they were ripe fruit and the playwrights had been starved for months. It was flattering, but it was also bullshit. The very fact that they'd all submitted to this festival suggested they had already drunk the Kool-Aid that was the theater industry. They were looking for recognition and cared more about that than about their craft.

Then again, maybe they just wanted to pay their rent.

He forced a smile. "Since I'll be writing about not just the final products but also the process, I may sit in on rehearsals," he said, "but by all means, pretend I'm not there."

That's what I'll be doing, Jasper thought.

Melina couldn't breathe. She was digging her fingernails into Andre's wrist, but he seemed equally stunned to see Jasper Tolle. "Am I having heatstroke?" he murmured.

She shook her head. Since eviscerating her play at Bard a decade ago, the critic hadn't aged at all, it seemed. He was still tall and angular, with a waterfall of pale hair spilling over his brow and tortoiseshell glasses he pushed up his nose every now and then. Surely it was only her imagination that he seemed to be staring directly at her.

"Rowan?" the artistic director called. "Let's bring up the house."

The houselights warmed. Jasper Tolle was left blinking. As he walked offstage to take a seat, his eyes skated over Melina without any sign of recognition. She didn't know if she was relieved or pissed. How could an interaction that had colored the last decade of her life have been so forgettable to him?

"So," Felix Dubonnet said, clasping his hands together. "An email will be going out to all of you with details, in case you had too much champagne to retain what I'm about to say. But work begins next Monday with representatives from Tara Rubin's office doing the casting. We will have a twenty-nine-hour workshop with the actors, and the writers will serve as directors for their own staged readings. The performances will be held the week of September fifth. Any questions?" He glanced around the room.

"Now, let me introduce you to each other. Adam Levant — where are you?" A man raised his hand. "Adam's play is called *Chimera.*"

There was polite applause. Melina glanced at Jasper Tolle, who was writing in a small black Moleskine notebook.

"Dex McGalpin, whose show is *The Hollow Ocean* . . . Wade Sugarman, *Things My Father Taught Me* . . ."

A calm settled over Melina. She didn't believe in fate, but perhaps there was a reason that Andre, drunk, had submitted her play. There was a reason that Felix Dubonnet had assumed her nickname belonged to a male. There was a reason that Jasper Fucking Tolle was here to write about the finalists. Of *course* the last ten years of her life had been whittling down to this very fine, very sharp point.

"And last but not least, Mel Green, with the play *By Any Other Name.*"

Andre turned, expecting her to stand up and say that *she* was the playwright, but Melina sank her nails into his knee. "Raise your hand," she whispered.

"What?"

"Raise. Your. Hand."

Andre tentatively let his arm creep up.

"And there we have it!" Felix Dubonnet

announced. "Our 2024 Village Fringe Finalists! Huge thanks to our special guest, Jasper
Tolle. And now — back to the champagne in
the lobby."

The audience filed out of the theater, leaving
Andre and Melina sitting alone. "You want to
tell me what's happening in that squirrel brain
of yours?" he asked.

"Dubonnet already thinks you're Mel
Green," she replied. "I need you to pretend
for a little while longer."

Andre folded his arms. "Why?"

"Because of Jasper Tolle. I've spent ten
years crippled by the things he said about my
writing, and now I have a chance to prove
him wrong."

"You can still prove him wrong if you tell
the artistic director *you* wrote the play."

"No, because if Tolle remembers me, he'll
be biased. But if he sees *By Any Other Name*
and raves about it . . . and *then* I tell him I'm
the playwright . . . he has to concede that he
was wrong about my writing."

Andre narrowed his eyes. "I can't decide if
this is ridiculous or Machiavellian."

"Why not both?" Melina suggested.

"You forgot one detail. If I'm Mel Green,
I'm in the room rehearsing the actors . . . not
you."

Melina's face fell. "Fuck," she muttered,
and then she brightened. "I'll be your personal assistant . . . *Andrea*."

He snorted. "Right, because starving writers always have those."

"You're aspirational."

"A damn fool is what I am," Andre muttered, "to even be considering this."

"You wouldn't have to if you hadn't pressed send." Melina raised a brow and mouthed: *You owe me.*

"How am I supposed to get out of work for this?"

"It's twenty-nine hours of rehearsal. You could have the stomach flu," Melina suggested. "Please, Andre. *All occasions do inform against me and spur my dull revenge.*"

"Macbeth?" Andre guessed.

"Hamlet."

He shook his head. "I can't believe you're quoting Shakespeare to convince me."

"I'm quoting *Emilia Bassano,*" Melina corrected.

"Just think, two weeks ago you only wanted a play produced," Andre said. "Now you want biblical vengeance."

"I'm an overachiever," she said.

EMILIA

Why are you here?

MARLOWE

Because most people bore me,
Mistress Bassano. And you do not.

> (snatches her writing, reads
> it)

" 'Fondling,' she saith, 'since I
have hemm'd thee here / Within
the circuit of this ivory pale, /
I'll be a park, and thou shalt be
my deer.' "

> (looking up from the page)

I did not think the Lord
Chamberlain's courtesan's most
seductive body part might be
her brain. Hunsdon's quite the
devil —

EMILIA

> (taking back the paper)

This is not about Hunsdon.

MARLOWE

Do tell.

EMILIA

Venus wants Adonis, but she cannot convince him to stay with her.

MARLOWE

I cannot think of a work of literature where it is not the man persuading the woman.

EMILIA

Don't women have the same urges as men?

MARLOWE

How terrifying to think you lot might be as uncontrollable as we are.

    EMILIA hands THE WOMAN the paper.

    It transforms into the printed poem *Venus and Adonis.*

THE WOMAN
(reading, in a cautionary tone)

"Sith in his prime Death doth my love destroy,

They that love best their

love shall not enjoy."

SOUTHAMPTON enters,
writing.

SOUTHAMPTON

I dreamt of you last night; and then recalled I did not sleep at all. You fill my waking hours.

EMILIA runs to him; they
kiss, dizzy with the taste
of each other.

EMILIA
1588–1592

Emilia is 19–23

As Emilia grew older, she understood what it was like to no longer fit inside your own body. Her legs lengthened; her breasts ripened; she grew into her enormous gray eyes and plush mouth. Those changes were noted — by Hunsdon, by courtiers who lost the thread of whatever conversation they were having when she passed, by noblewomen who glanced at her with jealousy. But nobody seemed to realize that Emilia's mind was also growing. She would stand on the balcony of her bedroom staring up at Tycho Brahe's inconstant stars and wonder how much of the world had to change before you felt the shift in the universe. She could be brought to tears by the flawless blue of a summer sky; she knew that a bed with two people in it could feel emptier than sleeping alone. She felt feral sometimes, wild with conversations she didn't have and dreams she couldn't share.

She was a lord's mistress, a lover, a girl who'd managed to rise above her station and would be lucky to remain there — if she watched her mouth.

Men believed that women were meant to exist on the fringes of their lives, instead of being the main characters in their own stories. But why would God have given her a voice if it wasn't meant to be used?

In public, Emilia played the part of a decorative object. In private, when she felt too full at the seams of her own life, she spilled all that emotion and intelligence and hope onto pages and pages of poetry, fables, and snippets of dialogue. Emilia wrote from the point of view of the bird of prey, delighting in those few moments of freedom before the jesses were pulled. She wrote fairy tales about princesses who climbed down brick towers, rescuing themselves. She wrote female characters who were adored for both their minds *and* their beauty. She wrote witty banter with men who were not afraid of a woman who could think for herself. She wrote of what sex must be like when your soul was as invested as your skin. She wrote love poems, where sometimes love was fire, sometimes it was rote, and sometimes it was agony.

She hid hundreds of pages under her mattress.

She did not write happy endings. As any real poet knows, the best tales are the ones that contain a kernel of truth.

■■■■

Wilton House, the residence of the Earl and Countess of Pembroke, was a massive Tudor estate built on the grounds of a former abbey in Salisbury. Hunsdon had taken Emilia to the country occasionally during their six-year relationship — everywhere except to Hunsdon House in Hertfordshire, where his wife, Anne, spent most of her time, a gesture of respect for the woman who had his name but not his love. Marriage was a business contract; you signed on the dotted line, you produced an heir, and then you got your satisfaction elsewhere.

Emilia's life, too, was a transaction. She was fond of Henry, even if she wasn't particularly attracted to him. She gave him her body, and he gave her security. But he also gave her the freedom to speak her mind, at least within the confines of his home. He solicited her opinions on the plays she read that were submitted to the Lord Chamberlain for review. He did not just applaud at the poetry she shared with him now and then — his whole face lit up with pride, as if he had some hand in her clever rhymes and meter. He was, by default, her best friend.

And Emilia knew that worried him.

Hunsdon was in his sixties; he would not be here forever. Although Emilia prayed he'd settle a sum upon her in the event of his death, he also wanted to make sure there would still be people in his circle who would look upon her with kindness.

That was why they were at Wilton House. Mary Sidney Herbert, the Countess of Pembroke, was not much older than Emilia. She was a great patron of the arts. "I think you have much in common," Hunsdon had told Emilia. "She, too, is a poet."

Mary Sidney ran a literary salon of sorts, and the other guests for the weekend included Edmund Spenser, Michael Drayton, and a young buck named Ben Jonson. Tonight they all sat in a drawing room, a fire blazing in the hearth and casting shadows on the paintings that covered nearly every inch of wall space — portraits of the Earls of Pembroke and their families. A painting of Mary Sidney with her four children hung over the mantel. Emilia sat beside Hunsdon, who was nursing a goblet of claret. The poets had taken turns reading from their works, and it was Spenser now who stood, reciting from an epic poem in progress. He seemed to pluck words out of the air and braid them together, conjuring the Redcrosse Knight, who had been stolen by the fae and raised by them; and his love, Una, betrayed by a wizard who tricked the knight into thinking her unchaste.

There was such magic in language. It could bring you to tears, pull you to the edge of your seat, make you sigh with relief. It could draw you out of the world when you needed to escape, and at other times hold up a looking glass to the world as it was. Emilia was so lost in Spenser's story, in fact, that it took her a moment to realize that Mary Sidney had addressed her. "Mistress Bassano?" she repeated.

Emilia's cheeks burned. "Apologies, my lady. I found myself wandering in the maze of beauty created by Mr. Spenser, much like the Redcrosse Knight himself."

"As were we all," Mary Sidney said. "Perhaps you might take us on a journey as well?"

She felt Hunsdon's hand steal over hers and squeeze. Realizing that he must have told Mary Sidney that she, too, wrote poetry, Emilia felt all her breath dry in her throat. "I could not presume to share my humble words with men who are giants of the craft."

Mary Sidney raised a brow. "Then share it instead with a woman."

Ben Jonson suddenly straightened. He had spent most of the night drinking heavily because Spenser's poem was getting more applause than his own. "Come, Mistress Bassano. We are a friendly lot. We do not bite." Then he grinned like a wolf. "Unless a lady asks."

Emilia clenched her jaw. It was something he'd only have dared say to a courtesan, and it provided the jolt of anger she needed to push herself to her feet. "My verse is not worthy of comparison," she said. "I do not wish to offend with my unpolished lines."

"Every poet must start with a scratch on a blank page," Spenser said kindly.

"Yes," Jonson agreed. "And we will happily offer advice if you wish."

"And even if you don't," Drayton added. Laughter rippled through the chamber.

"Very well," Emilia said. "I have no copy to read to you, only what my mind can recall." She began to recite:

Love comforteth like sunshine after rain
But Lust's effect is tempest after sun;
Love's gentle spring doth always fresh remain
Lust's winter comes ere summer half be done;
Love surfeits not, Lust like a glutton dies;
Love is all truth, Lust full of forged lies.

When she finished, the men were all staring. She wondered what they had expected of her — something pastoral about a maid with a lamb in a field, no doubt.

Jonson arched a brow. "Nicely done, mistress. This is to be an ode to love, then?"

"Not at all, sir," Emilia said. "It is a eulogy. For it describes something that does not exist."

"It is rare to find one so young and so jaded," he replied.

"Jaded," she countered, "or honest? What age must I reach to accept the way the world works?"

"Indeed, a woman is more likely to see the disparity between what one hopes for and what one can achieve," Mary Sidney added.

"A woman . . . or an impoverished poet," Jonson amended.

"Imagine being both," Emilia said. She blushed, afraid she had overstepped. She had become too accustomed to speaking freely in Hunsdon's study.

But Jonson laughed. When he looked at her again, any trace of inebriation was gone. "Mistress," he said, "I think there is more to you than meets the eye."

She did not know if it was a compliment or an accusation, so she simply nodded and took her seat beside Hunsdon. "Well done, darling," he said. "Spenser went on for so long about his Faerie Queen, it's now time for me to retire." Emilia immediately gathered her skirts to rise and leave with him.

"Oh, my lord, you must stay!" Mary Sidney said. "We have only just begun."

"I cannot, but I shall leave the better part of me." Hunsdon reached for Emilia's hand and kissed her knuckles. "Stay," he said softly. "These are your people."

Emilia's fingers tightened on his. He was tired. The execution of Mary, Queen of Scots, had disrupted the relationship with the Scottish king, and Queen Elizabeth had Hunsdon running back and forth collecting information about King James's moves and intentions. Hunsdon had been away from Somerset House for a fortnight, yet upon arriving home had immediately departed to Wilton House . . . for Emilia's sake.

Emilia nodded, grateful. Once Hunsdon had left the salon and more claret had been poured, Spenser turned toward Mary Sidney. "What of our patroness? Might we persuade you to share some of your verse?"

Mary's brother had been a well-known courtier and poet who died on a military campaign. An accomplished translator and poet in her own right, she was finishing the psalter Philip Sidney had been working on at the time of his death.

To Emilia's surprise, however, she did not read that poetry. She crossed to a writing desk and pulled out a small stack of papers. "Since the Lord Chamberlain has retired," she said, "perhaps we may count on the discretion of Mistress Bassano." Mary dropped a small folio, bound with ribbon, into Emilia's hand.

Emilia realized that the others were being given different folios — like the parts players received when a fair copy was distributed to a troupe of actors.

"I have assigned roles based on sex and arrogance," Mary Sidney said, grinning. "I of course shall play Cleopatra. Mistress Bassano, you shall be both Eras and Charmion, my attendants. Spenser, since you held us captive the longest this night, you shall be my Antony."

"A play?" Emilia said. "You wrote this?"

In all the years she had been with Hunsdon, she had never seen a woman's name on a foul copy. She felt her heart thump hard, once, in her chest, as if it were learning a new rhythm.

"Robert Garnier wrote the original: *Antoine*," Mary Sidney explained. "I translated it."

It was not legitimate for a woman to translate work for presentation on a public stage, which was why Mary chose to present this play as a closet drama in her own home. Emilia wondered if Hunsdon would object, if he knew.

"We open on the final day of Cleopatra's life. Antony has been bested by Caesar and knows the honorable thing to do is to end his own life. Cleopatra faces losing both her kingdom and the man she loves." Mary Sidney glanced around. "Shall we begin?"

If the poetry wasn't up to Spenser's level of metaphor, Emilia did not notice. What bled through the pages was the feeling of loss, of entrapment. By the time Cleopatra was begging the tutor of her children to take care of them after she killed herself, it was well past midnight.

Mary Sidney threw out one hand dramatically. "Ah, my heart breaks! By shady banks of hell, by fields whereon the lonely ghosts do tread . . . By my soul and the soul of Antony, I you beseech, Euphron, of them have care."

Mary was staring directly at Emilia — even though Drayton was reading the part of Euphron the tutor. "Let your wisdom let that they not fall into this tyrant's hands," she said, unblinking.

It felt like a secret handshake. It felt as if Mary Sidney had designed this entire evening to culminate this way, and it felt like she was no longer talking about Cleopatra's children.

It felt as though Emilia was being entrusted with something equally precious: a dream Mary Sidney herself would never see come to fruition, a dream perhaps Emilia *could.*

It was nearly four in the morning when Emilia tiptoed upstairs to the chamber she shared with Hunsdon. A maid was sitting outside the door, dozing. She jerked upright when Emilia approached and followed her into the room. Heavy velvet curtains hid the bed from view, but she could hear Hunsdon's slight snore. The maid unlaced her dress so that she could step out of it. "That will be all," Emilia murmured, and the maid bobbed her head and left.

She pulled open the curtain and tried to slip beneath the counterpane without disturbing Hunsdon. She was thinking of the final scene in Mary Sidney Herbert's play, where Cleopatra dramatically kills herself and falls on the body of the man she could not live without. It was not reality as Emilia knew it. In her life, when faced with yet more adversity, a woman straightened her shoulders and said, *All right, I'll take on another burden.* Strength was endurance, not escape. It was looking at a piece of granite and noticing flecks of fool's gold.

She looked at Hunsdon, at the tangle of his hair and the body giving in to gravity. She tried to imagine the kind of love that led to suicide when your lover was no longer in the world.

Hunsdon stirred and curled around her, his arm resting over her waist. His words tickled the shell of her ear. "Did you learn much, my dear?"

"Yes," she whispered. Jonson's words floated back to her. *More to you than meets the eye.*

That night she dreamed of Hunsdon's falcon, hollow-boned and light. Emilia gave the order and watched the bird soar from the gauntlet, trailing her jesses. But the leather unraveled from the falcon's anklet, and Emilia stared at the sky, watching the bird fly away, growing smaller and smaller until it scraped the face of the sun.

The next morning after breaking her fast, Emilia wandered through the warren of Wilton House until she heard a shout. Picking up her skirts, she hurried down the hall and threw open a door to find Mary Sidney behind a long wooden table. The surface was littered with all sorts of glass containers and iron clamps, as well as jars of powders and liquids.

"Ah," she said, looking up. "You may be the first witness to my discovery."

Early morning light streamed through the windows, illuminating a phial suspended over a candle by an ingenious metal arm, contents bubbling.

"The earl allows this?" Emilia asked.

"My husband does not allow it, but he ignores it," Mary Sidney said. "That way he does not have to be upset with me, and I do not have to be upset with him."

Emilia knew that, like Hunsdon, the countess's husband was far older than she was. She wanted to ask Mary if she loved the man, if she believed that affection could transform into passion if the right ingredients were added.

Mary Sidney sharpened a quill and opened a very tiny jar of what Emilia assumed to be ink. She dipped the quill into the jar and scrawled her signature across a sheet of foolscap: *Mary Sidney Herbert.*

"Watch," Mary said.

Before Emilia's eyes, the signature vanished. She gasped. "It is magic?"

"It is *alchemy,*" the Countess corrected. She blew out the candle beneath the bubbling phial. "I call this . . . disappearing ink." She

185

handed Emilia the quill, so that she could test it herself.

Emilia dipped the pen into the special ink and scrawled her own name beneath Mary's. Moments later, the page was as blank as if it had never been written upon.

"What will you do with it?" Emilia asked.

"I am sure someone at court will find a use for it," Mary Sidney said. "And if not, I shall bask in the brilliance of creating something that has not existed before." Her smile faded at the edges as she ran her hand over the blank sheet of paper. "This is how men would prefer it, is it not? That anything written by a woman vanish forever."

Emilia met her gaze. "I did not think you someone who would make it even easier to erase women's words," she said delicately. "You are a great patron of the arts. You are a *countess,* and therefore above reproach. Could you not give your play to a troupe?"

"It is *because* I am a countess that I could not. It would be a scandal. It is one thing to patronize theater. But were I to author a play for performance, my husband would be shamed for it. And *that* he would *not* ignore." She shrugged. "Too many people already know that I dabble as a writer, that I host these salons. It is notoriety that prevents me from being anonymous." She took the quill from Emilia's hand. "For a woman to ever do such a thing, she would have to be invisible."

186

"What does that mean?" Emilia asked. "A woman who makes herself invisible, by definition, gives up her voice. You speak in riddles."

Mary Sidney scrawled the word *invisible* on the paper. They watched it evaporate. "Perhaps one day, Emilia," she said, "you will solve it for us all."

Emilia had, of course, crossed paths with her cousin Jeronimo since he'd bartered her to Lord Hunsdon. She couldn't avoid him at court performing music for the Queen. But she had never again returned to Mark Lane to celebrate the Sabbath.

Instead, she had filched two candlesticks and extra candles from the Somerset House pantry. She cut apart a shift made of the finest linen and hemmed and embroidered it into a head covering. Every Friday night, she would turn her nightstand into a makeshift altar and recite the Hebrew prayer over the candles. She would snuff the flames before it was time to retire, lest Hunsdon discover her. She was not supposed to blow out the candles, but she thought God would understand.

She tried to observe other important Jewish holidays based on the time of year: Rosh Hashanah, the New Year, when the leaves began to turn; Yom Kippur, the Day of Atonement, ten days after; Sukkot, when the apples were ripe on the trees in the Somerset House orchard; Chanukah, just before Christmastide;

Purim, when the daffodils rose from the thawed ground; Pesach, when the hyacinths bloomed.

It was in October, at the end of the Ten Days of Awe, when Emilia fasted for Yom Kippur. Arguably the most important Jewish holiday, these were the days that God wrote the name of the righteous in the Book of Life and condemned the wicked to death. Most people, however, fell somewhere between these two poles, and they used those ten days for teshuvah — making amends. Emilia did not know how God might judge her, living as a courtesan. Since she had not died that first year with Hunsdon, she believed that He found something in her worth preserving.

The High Holy Days were a somber time for Jews, and that mood fit the one at court. Nearly a month earlier the Earl of Leicester had died. Although it had been years since the height of the gossip about him and the Queen, she had taken the news poorly. Plans had been made to distract Her Majesty on October 10, the day that the late earl was to be buried by his widow.

Emilia figured it was just her luck that Yom Kippur — and her fast — fell on the same day as this massive midday feast at St. James's Palace. Because they were at court, she had been trussed into her finery by a maid, her stomach growling as her torso was cinched into her dress. She had managed to avoid Hunsdon all day because he was occupied with the Queen, who was particularly cranky. By the time he came to collect her for the feast, Emilia fought for the self-control it would take to abstain.

The food had been set up on a long table under a bower bright with crimson and yellow leaves that reminded Emilia of the chuppah used in a Jewish wedding ceremony. It was decorated with peacock feathers, on which a birdcage sat with live swallows inside, their beaks and feet gilded. There were platters of veal, stuffed pheasant, a haunch of venison, a civet of hare. There were gravy boats of sauces, rich with herbs and pomegranate seeds. A stack of pigeon pies sat beside dressed capons, a whole sturgeon, boiled eggs, and an aspic with cherries suspended inside.

This was merely the first course.

Emilia heard her stomach rumble. She couldn't sit there for five hours — which was how long it might last — and not draw attention to the fact that she was not eating. She tightened her hand on Hunsdon's arm before they reached the table. "My lord," she said, "I fear I am unwell."

He looked at her with concern. "Perhaps a few bites of food —"

Emilia groaned. "That is the very thing I wish to avoid," she said.

His eyes flew to her abdomen. "You are . . . ill?"

She realized that by feigning nausea, she

had led Hunsdon to believe she might be pregnant. "Merely an upset stomach, my lord," she murmured.

He patted her hand. "I shall make your excuses to Her Majesty."

Emilia fled to the chamber they shared in the palace, trying to distract herself by writing poetry until sundown, when she would be free to eat again. But every metaphor made her hungrier: cheeks as red as apples, words honeyed as mead. Frustrated, she grabbed a shawl and slipped out of her room, heading away from the revelry.

Emilia walked briskly through the park adjacent to the palace, humming to herself. She preferred the wildness of this park to the manicured military regiment of trees that lined the lawn bowling court. In the past when she fasted for the High Holy Days, she had been in the company of others who shared her secret faith. She had rejoiced with her relatives when, at last, they got to break bread and drink wine and celebrate the mercy of God. Being a hidden Jew in England had always been dangerous — but now it was also lonely.

Emilia's slippers kicked black walnuts that had fallen from tree branches, and she stooped to gather a few, making a basket of her kirtle. The husks were so hard that she could not crack them without tools and effort, so there was no risk she'd pop them into her mouth.

She was so intent on adding to her collection of nuts that she almost collided with a young man who was sitting beneath one of the trees, reading a book.

"I beg your pardon." Emilia gasped, dropping her skirt so that her bounty scattered on the forest floor. Her heart was pounding. He was young — barely shaving, if she were guessing correctly — but broad-shouldered and fit, with a long tousle of auburn hair and eyes so blue it seemed the sky passed through him. He was dressed like nobility and was clearly a gentleman — he'd leaped to his feet upon seeing her. But if he were nobility, he should be inside the gates of the palace with the Queen at the feast.

Then again, so should she.

Suddenly, he smiled, and Emilia felt a small tug in her belly. Those eyes. They were not like the sky, she edited. They were the very center of a flame.

"Mistress Bassano," he said, and she took a step back.

"You have me at a disadvantage, sir," Emilia said.

He clapped a hand over his heart. "You wound me. Yet I met you as a butterfly, when I was still in a chrysalis . . . so perhaps it is understandable."

Emilia's eyes widened, remembering the young Earl of Southampton, and how they had met. It was, she realized, the same night she was introduced to Hunsdon. She was now six years older and a hundred years wiser. She calculated quickly; the Earl was sixteen or thereabouts. "You have come a long way from hiding behind the curtains, my lord," Emilia said.

"As have you," Southampton answered.

"Have you been practicing your recorder?"

He laughed, his teeth even and white. "In a sense, but not such that I'd discuss with a lady."

"I have not seen you at court."

"I'm visiting from Cambridge. I've one more year to go in my studies there at St. John's." He crossed his arms and leaned against the bulk of a tree. He stood at least a full head taller than Emilia. "There is no masque at the palace," the Earl said. "What are you escaping this time?"

She could not tell him that she was fasting, but she also found she could not lie, not when he was looking at her as if she were the only other human in the world. "Food," she admitted.

His gaze traveled up and down her body. "You do not seem one in need of reducing. In faith, you seem to be filling out your dress quite —"

"What are *you* escaping?" she interrupted.

"Marriage," he said flatly. "Lord Burghley keeps pairing me with girls still in leading strings." He smiled wryly. "No one like you."

She rolled her eyes. "Like me? You have no sense of what I am like."

"Do I not?" He pushed off the tree trunk, taking a step toward her.

By now, he would know her to be Hunsdon's mistress. She had long ago accepted that role, and as time passed, she rarely bothered to be embarrassed by it. But now, her cheeks flushed deeply. "You forget yourself, my lord," she said.

"As long as you do not forget me," Southampton murmured, and before she could see what he was about, he leaned forward and kissed her.

Almost immediately he reared back. It was difficult to say which of them was more surprised. Emilia felt her insides spinning.

"I should not have done that," he said softly, still staring at her mouth.

"No," Emilia agreed.

She realized that she was the elder here — in age, and in experience. She also realized that although she had been kissed by a man who wanted her, she had never kissed a man that *she* wanted.

Why *shouldn't* she feed a hunger? She was, after all, starving.

Emilia looked at Southampton. "No, you should not have done that." She closed the distance between them. "*That* was a military assault. You should have done *this*." Coming up on her toes, her lips brushed over his like a promise. "A kiss is no soliloquy, but a dialogue." She placed the words in his mouth. "I whisper to you . . . and you whisper back. We are trading a secret between us, like it's a sweet." With that, she touched his tongue with her own, kissing him deeply.

Southampton crushed her closer, using her own knowledge against her. She, who knew the entire choreography of lovemaking, let herself go feral.

Even as Emilia knew that although Southampton was a spark to her straw, carnal attraction was both the start and the endgame. He was fleeing a political marriage that would happen whether he wished it or not; she could not risk losing the protection the Lord Chamberlain had given her. Maybe that was what was irresistible: seeing herself reflected in Southampton's stunning eyes, knowing neither of them had the freedom of choice.

How long they stayed like that, learning the taste of each other, Emilia did not know. But when she shivered, she realized that the sun had slipped below the horizon. The feast would be ending; Hunsdon might come looking for her before attending the nighttime revelry.

"My lord," she said. "I must go."

He stepped back, but still held her hands. "Will you leave me so unsatisfied?"

Emilia raised her brows. "What satisfaction can you have tonight?"

"Wait." She felt him tangle his fingers with hers. They both looked down at their palms, pressed close. "Will I see you again?"

"The odds are excellent, my lord, if you return to court."

"That is not what I mean, and you know it," Southampton said.

Emilia shrugged, pretending indifference. "Who can control his fate?" She pulled free.

"Wait!" the Earl cried again. His fingers circled her wrist. She paused, and he smiled sheepishly. "I have forgotten why I called you back."

"Then I shall stand here until you remember," she said softly.

Oh, Devil take it.

She moved first, or maybe he did, and then they were knotted together again, his hands scattering the pins in her hair and hers seeking the hot skin beneath his doublet. He pressed her against the tree trunk, and she relished the bite of the bark. It was the only thing keeping her tethered to the earth.

When they broke apart, the Earl framed Emilia's face in his hands. "He cannot know," Southampton said.

Maybe he meant Lord Burghley, maybe he meant Hunsdon. Maybe both.

"Your . . ." the Earl's voice faltered. "What do you call him?"

"Henry," she said.

"That is my name, too."

Emilia looked up at him from beneath her lashes. "Yes, my lord," she said deliberately, and she left.

The Queen did not improve in spirits after the Earl of Leicester's funeral — refusing at times to speak to anyone and snapping at those who attempted conversation. Her advisers hovered close by, in part to try to cheer her, and in part because they were terrified of not being at hand when she demanded their immediate attendance. Hunsdon stayed at court day and night, sending Emilia back to Somerset House. As a result, she had not seen Southampton again.

She had wondered if the Earl might send word, and then she became cross with herself. What was the point of a secret correspondence? By now, he was likely immersed in his studies at Cambridge again. Emilia berated herself for fantasizing and told herself to remember her place.

But — after Hunsdon finally returned home, and to Emilia's bed — she found herself doing something she never had before.

Comparing.

Pretending.

Wishing.

She felt even more guilty because the Queen was well enough to have given Hunsdon marching orders once again to Scotland, to smooth King James's ruffled feathers. When

Emilia seemed off, daydreaming and distracted, Hunsdon assumed that it was because she did not wish to be left alone again so soon.

It made Emilia feel worse to know he was thinking the best of her.

Determined to spend their last day together before his travels, he asked her to accompany him to the reading of a play that had been approved by his own hand and that of Edmund Tilney, the Master of the Revels. He knew that she enjoyed readings even more than the actual performances of the shows — being in the room where the changes were being implemented and the characters were honed.

Hunsdon had not been feeling well before they left. It worried Emilia, but he assured her it was just another episode of gout. Unlike most readings, this one was to take place not in a tavern but in a church, because the play was going to be performed for the Queen by a company of young boy actors in London — the Children of the Chapel.

The reading was already under way when Emilia and Hunsdon arrived. Having learned to be unobtrusive when Hunsdon brought her on business calls like these, she slipped into a pew several rows behind the choirmaster, who was directing the boys.

The boy actors were sweet and young, most of their voices unbroken. She had a sudden flash of Henry Wriothesley as a child, his feet sticking out from beneath a brocade curtain. That was followed by a flash of heat so strong she felt an ache between her legs.

The title of the play was *Dido, Queen of Carthage.* She remembered this one because it was a notch above most of the plays that came to the Lord Chamberlain for approval. Written in blank verse, it was a retelling of part of the *Aeneid:* a story in which the goddess Venus made Dido, a North African queen, tumble headlong into love with Aeneas, a prince who had escaped the wreckage of Troy. Emilia often was bored by the prose of would-be playwrights, but this writer — a Christopher Marlowe — was a *poet.* She had gasped in the middle of a page when she came across a rhymed couplet that was split between two characters, as if not just the words but the very structure of the language joined them.

It had never occurred to her to use poetry that way.

They were at the scene where Dido rejected her suitor, Iarbas, and fell in love with Aeneas instead. Emilia listened for her favorite part — that couplet — but before she could mark it Hunsdon limped from the altar back to the pew where she sat. "You are well, my lord?" she asked.

He grimaced. "Not as well as I might be. My joints stiffen; I must stretch my legs." She got to her feet, but he waved her off.

"You shall be my eyes," Hunsdon said, and he hobbled off.

Emilia turned her attention to the altar again. The boy playing Dido was begging Aeneas for his love. "No, no, no," the choirmaster interrupted. "You must be more convincing."

"Were he down on his knees," said a voice, as a man slid into the pew beside Emilia, "his tongue might be more credible."

The stranger was not much older than she was, and handsome in a dangerous way. He had thick black hair that brushed his chin and eyes that were so dark she could not make out the pupils. He was staring at her with a brow raised, as if he were expecting her to faint in a fit of maidenly vapors at his provocative comment.

"Indeed, perhaps young Dido needs a private lesson," the man added. "Who better than the playwright to show him how to shape his lips around . . . the *words*."

So this was Christopher Marlowe.

"If you think to shock me, Master Marlowe," Emilia said, "you cannot." She knew that after performances in public theaters, the boys who played female roles were often visited by male patrons who paid court to them, as if they were actually ladies. She also knew through gossip that Marlowe fancied men, not women. There were rumors of him being a spy for Her Majesty, and also being an atheist. This was clearly not a man who played it safe.

"I am wounded," Marlowe said dramatically. "The lady pricks me, and I bleed."

"I think it is not my prick you seek, sir," Emilia replied.

A smile spread over his face at her wordplay. "You have quite the mouth on you, for a woman."

"Perhaps it is to my ear you should attend."

He leaned back, sprawling on the pew. "You have thoughts on my play?"

"I have thoughts about many things, sir."

"By all means, please share," Marlowe said. He continued to stare at her, but she saw in his eyes the slightest flicker of uncertainty — the same one she had felt when she was brave enough to read some of her poetry to Hunsdon. It was amazing how the slightest splinter of self-doubt could become a lance that ripped through a writer's confidence.

"This is a play about a woman who is too independent, is it not?" Emilia said. "Dido is rebuked by the gods for it. When Aeneas leaves her, she suffers so terribly that she throws herself into a fire to end her pain."

"Yes," Marlowe agreed.

"Why should Dido be punished twice? First by the gods, then by your pen. Is love not already punishment enough?"

He blinked, looking at her as if she were a species he'd never encountered before. "Who the bloody hell *are* you?"

"Someone better placed than you to say what Dido deserves."

A laugh startled out of Marlowe. "You mean a woman with a mind."

"Are you so surprised? Ah, wait. Of course. I've read your work, after all —"

"Your tongue is sharp," Marlowe interrupted, grinning, "but it is the tongue of a writer."

Emilia went very still, all bravado gone. Even when she had been in the company of true poets at Mary Sidney's literary salon — even when they had applauded her short stanza — they had not claimed her as one of their own. "You think me a writer?" she asked.

She watched his face soften. Maybe something in him recognized something in her. He was not a gentleman by birth and had attended Cambridge on scholarship. He knew what it was to claw your way into a society that never wanted you. "I think you someone with much to say," Marlowe replied, "when few are listening."

"My dear."

Hunsdon's voice fell over Emilia like a net. She twisted to face him, a brilliant smile on her face. "Lord Hunsdon." She got to her feet, taking his arm. She knew him well enough to see the flash of pain on his face.

"Apologies, Marlowe, but we must take our leave." Hunsdon waved a hand vaguely to the front of the church. "We look forward to seeing the performance at court."

Marlowe bowed to him and then bent over Emilia's hand.

She could feel his eyes on her as Hunsdon leaned heavily on her to walk out of the church. She had never given Marlowe her name, but now she would not have to. He would know who Emilia was; what role she served for the Lord Chamberlain. Everyone did.

But, for a quarter of an hour, she had simply been herself.

And it had been divine.

It was not the first spell of gout that Hunsdon had suffered, but it was one of the worst. Emilia had him brought to his chamber and elevated his sore foot, wrapping it in wool that had been soaked with boiling water, a remedy thought to bring relief. It was expected that she would care for him, for not only was gout associated with the debauchery of a man as a youth but it was also known to be an aphrodisiac, leaving behind lust that would need to be assuaged.

What was troublesome was that Hunsdon was supposed to leave tomorrow for Scotland again at the behest of the Queen — who did not care if his toe felt like it was being stabbed with knives.

Emilia sat on the edge of the bed, reading aloud to Hunsdon. She had taken one of the potential plays from the stack on his writing table and was performing it as a one-woman show, giving voice to all the characters. When she glanced toward him, his eyes were closed and he was breathing more easily than he had since they'd arrived back at Somerset House. Gingerly, she set the foul copy down on the mattress, only to feel his hand grasp hers tightly. She squeezed back as he smiled faintly. "How do you feel, my lord?"

"Like someone is running a carriage over my eyeballs," Hunsdon said. "It is agony to shift an inch."

"Then do not move."

"Perhaps God will have mercy and take me in the night," he sighed.

A shiver ran down Emilia's spine. "Do not say such things."

Hunsdon gripped her hand more tightly. His eyes opened. "You know, I hope, that I would care for you."

It was the first time they had actually addressed the truth: that she would likely outlive him. He had a wife and a family who would be the beneficiaries of his will. But he was telling her, now, that she would not find herself without means when he was gone. Emilia felt tears crowd her throat. "Thank you, Henry."

Their eyes locked. She had seen his filled with passion, with kindness, with frustration. With a single glance when she entered his office, she knew whether he needed a sounding board or a lover in his lap. "I am glad it was you," he said simply. Whatever unholy barter had begun between him and Emilia's cousin, Hunsdon had not really known what he was getting. As a little girl, with her quick wit and her imagination and her luminous eyes, she had often been *too much* for adults. But for Hunsdon, she was just enough. His mouth twisted ruefully. "It has not been all bad, has it?"

She brought his knuckles to her lips, careful not to jostle him. "Absolutely not, my lord."

There was a knock on the door. "Enter," Emilia called, and her lady's maid, Bess, bobbed, holding a sealed letter. "Mistress," she said, "this come for ye."

Emilia took the letter and pried the wax free.

My humble duty remembered, Mistress —

I dreamt last night of you; and then recalled I did not sleep at all. You fill my waking hours, my every breath. If you think of me a fraction as often as I think of you, end my torment. In Paris Garden at dusk, at the bridge at the millstream where the primroses bloom, I shall wait. This bud of love may prove a beauteous flower when next we meet.

X
Southampton

"Emilia?" Hunsdon said. "All is well?"
Heat flooded her cheeks as she folded the

204

note and slipped it into her *bodies.* "Yes, my lord. It is just . . . unexpected news." She met his gaze. "My cousin's wife is ill. He bade me visit to lift her spirits."

The lies, they flowed from her lips so effortlessly.

Hunsdon closed his eyes, trusting her at her word. "You must go."

The letter felt like an ember caught against her breast. "Yes," Emilia murmured. "I must."

Paris Garden was on the other side of the river in Southwark, which meant Emilia had to take a boat from the Blackfriars landing across to the Paris Garden stairs. She brought a young, flighty maid with her, one that she knew could be bribed with a coin to become distracted at a tavern for an hour or two. Emilia dressed in a plain kirtle, like the ones she used to wear when she visited her cousin's home on Mark Lane, with a voluminous cloak pulled over her head to hide her face.

It was near sunset, and the garden seemed gilded. Emilia wandered toward the bridge that Southampton had mentioned. A man chased a woman over it, laughing. Clearly, Emilia and the Earl were not the only pair looking for privacy. When she felt arms embrace her from behind, folding around her waist, she twisted to find herself looking into the celestial eyes of Southampton. He grabbed her wrist and pulled her away from the bridge to a spot where they were concealed.

Emilia shoved down the hood of her cloak. "What would you have done were it not me?"

"A great deal of explaining," Southampton said, grinning. He stared at her as if she had been the one to fling the stars into the night. "You came."

"I came," she whispered.

His hold tightened on her wrist. She tangled her hands in his hair as he kissed her, lifting her off the ground. She was dizzy with the taste of him, like spirits fizzing through her body at the first sip.

"Why are you not back at Cambridge, my lord?" Emilia asked when they broke apart.

"It's Henry," he corrected, "and why are you complaining?"

She heard voices, and Southampton drew her deeper into the garden, away from the main path and up a small rise. He stopped in the hollow on the other side, where pine needles lay thick on the ground, matted in places where red deer must have slept. "We are not the first to bed here," he said.

Emilia arched a brow. "Is that what we are doing?"

He drew her hand to cover his heart, drumming hale and strong. She let herself think only once of Hunsdon, sallow and stricken, in his bed. "I cannot go back to my studies without knowing your favor lies with me as mine lies with you," Southampton said.

"My favor is not mine to give," Emilia replied.

"I will take a piece if I cannot have the whole."

She smirked. "Shall I guess which piece that might be?"

He took a curl of her hair. "This will do," he said, tugging on it. Then he lifted her hand and kissed her littlest finger. "Or this." He leaned forward, sucking at the spot where her neck met her shoulder until she gasped. "Or mayhap this." Then he pulled back, looking down at her without a trace of the playfulness of his words. "I have never felt like this," he said softly. "I have never imagined I *could* feel like this."

Emilia could not fault him for that, because she felt it, too. Sex had been a ladder to take her from one place to another; it had been a dance for which she'd learned all the steps; it was currency in her pocket. But it had never been a tide, rushing the shore and pulling the ground from beneath her feet. It had never been something uncontrollable and primal.

She also knew that Southampton's father had hated his mother and had taken him from her when he was a young child. He had never seen love modeled. Emilia, on the other hand, knew her parents to be a love match, albeit one that had destroyed her mother when her father died.

She sank down in a sigh of skirts, and Southampton sat beside her. He did not stop touching her — her wrist, her arm, her hair. "I cannot think when you do that," she said.

"Must you?" he asked. "Think?"

He bit her palm as if it were a plum, and she felt it between her legs.

"Henry," she whispered, "we could be discovered."

He looked up at the rise that barely shielded them. "Yes. But where else might we come together?"

"You misunderstand. We could be *discovered.*" She could not — *would* not — shame Hunsdon that way. And she could not fathom the repercussions from Burghley if he found out about Southampton's regard for her. She cupped his cheek — still soft, dear God, barely a man. "There is no happy ever after here," she said gently. "There may not even be a tomorrow."

"All I ask for," Southampton said, "is right now."

It was the only thing Emilia had to offer. She nodded, then kissed him until a fever spread between them. He pushed aside her cloak, his hands everywhere they could reach. "Too . . . many . . . clothes," Southampton gasped, bunching fistfuls of her skirts in his hand.

When she had yanked his hose down enough to take him in hand, he shuddered. She looked into his eyes. "Have you done this before?" she whispered.

Silent, he shook his head.

Emilia felt something roar inside her — not just lust, but power. Southampton was an earl and a peer and not for her, but in this moment, she was the one in control.

"We must be careful," she said. "I take . . . precautions, but you cannot finish in me. You understand?" When he nodded, she straddled him, her skirts pooling around his legs. She guided him inside her, drawing in her breath at the utter youth and strength of his body.

He exhaled slowly and wound his hands in her hair. "You feel made just for me," he said.

At that, she rocked against him. His hips bucked in reflex, and when they began to spasm a moment later, she lifted herself so that he spent between them.

He crushed her tight against him. "I am sorry," he gasped. "I couldn't . . . it was so . . ."

She touched his cheek. "Next time will be better," she promised.

He was already growing hard again — something she had not experienced before — which felt like being given an extra helping of sweets. Southampton slipped an arm around Emilia and gracefully flipped her onto her back. He kissed her, then worked his way down her body until his head was under her skirts. She felt his breath on her, and then a hot press of his tongue. A cry tore from Emilia, her eyes wide with surprise.

Over the crush of her skirts, those fathomless blue eyes met hers and smiled. His words hummed against her skin. "I never said I was *completely* chaste."

This time, when Southampton moved in her, she guided his hand between them — *There. Harder. Now* — until she stopped remembering to be a tutor, and instead let herself learn. This time, before he pulled out of her, she felt herself galloping toward something and finally, finally, soaring, until her ears rang and her vision pricked with black spots and a bubble of pure joy burst out of her throat in a laugh. Although she knew how to give herself pleasure, this was different. *So this is what it is,* she thought, *to give not just your body, but your heart.*

Southampton lay beside her on his back, chest heaving, his fingers still tangled in hers. "You are well?" he whispered.

"I am . . ." Emilia blinked up at the night sky. Even with her vast poet's vocabulary, she could not find a single word to describe how she felt. It was joy that couldn't be contained in a string of alphabet, it was fear of what was yet to come.

I am. She realized, smiling, that this was a complete sentence. An answer, in and of itself.

The maid was waiting for her at the river landing when Emilia returned to Westminster. Another coin paid for her discretion. When they reached Somerset House, Emilia dismissed the servant and tiptoed up the staircase. She gingerly opened the door to Hunsdon's bedroom. A candle burned beside the bed, casting his slack features into shadow. Emilia hesitated at the doorway. She could still smell Southampton on her, and it seemed doubly wrong to enter Hunsdon's bedchamber with the feel of another man still lingering like a bruise on her body.

"You've returned," Hunsdon said, his eyes still shut. "How fares your cousin's wife?"

Emilia blinked, having forgotten her ruse for a moment. "I fear . . . she will be plagued for some time." Her hand flexed on the edge of the wooden door. "Sleep well, my lord," she said.

She looked down on Hunsdon's still form for a moment, trying to imagine Southampton's shoulders narrowing with age, his strong legs succumbing to gout, his flushed cheeks creped with wrinkles. She would not have the privilege of seeing him change that way.

The sooner she remembered that, the better.

In her own chamber, she stripped off her kirtle and chemise and stood naked. She moved her hands from her throat to her breasts, between her thighs. She tried to trace the same route Southampton had. And yet she couldn't set herself on fire the way he had.

Emilia pulled her night rail over her body and unraveled the braid she had fashioned after rolling around the Paris Garden with Southampton. There were still pine needles caught between the strands. Then she reached for her writing desk, cut a fresh quill, and opened her bottle of ink. She stared down at a blank sheet of paper.

She thought of all the poetry she had read about a man seducing a virgin, an innocent.

She thought of her hand wrapping around Southampton and guiding him inside her.

She had never read a poem about a woman who took what she wanted from a younger man.

Emilia closed her eyes and thought of Southampton, a young Adonis, his arm flung over his eyes, the violet light of dusk turning him into a work of art.

Adonis.

He, too, had been loved . . . and lost. With the Countess, Emilia had read Ovid's account of the mythology: Aphrodite had fallen in love with the beautiful young man, a confident hunter certain nothing bad could ever happen to him. When Adonis was gored by a wild boar, he died in Aphrodite's arms.

Emilia dipped the quill into the ink, her

thoughts coming fast and jumbled as she scrawled across the page.

Even as the sun with purple-colour'd face
Had ta'en his last leave of the weeping morn,
Rose-cheek'd Adonis tried him to the chase;
Hunting he lov'd, but love he laugh'd to scorn;
Sick-thoughted Venus makes amain unto him
And like a bold-fac'd suitor 'gins to woo him.

"Thrice fairer than myself," thus she began,
"The field's chief flower, sweet above compare,
Stain to all nymphs, more lovely than a man,
More white and red than doves or roses are;
Nature that made thee, with herself at strife
Saith that the world hath ending with thy life."

She wrote, and she wrote, and she wrote. She crossed out lines and added others. She hid Southampton in Adonis's beautiful countenance, and she buried her own selfish greed for him in Venus — seducing a boy who was younger and more naïve than herself.

She wrote until the dawn outside her window matched the first few lines of her poem.

She didn't finish.

Emilia didn't know yet what the ending would be. She just knew it would not be a happy one.

With Hunsdon in Scotland for several days, it was easier to exchange messages with

213

Southampton without fear of discovery — passionate declarations of love from him, reminders of her station (or lack thereof) from Emilia. But he was wearing down her resistance. She made plans to visit him in Paris Garden again, two nights later.

She spent her time sequestered at Somerset House, wandering in the gardens, watching the falconers train birds, and for hours at a time, sitting beneath a hawthorn tree on a stone bench, adding verse to her poem about Southampton. The more she wrote, letting Venus pay tribute to Adonis, the closer she felt to the Earl. It was as if Emilia herself were creating his smooth chest, his riot of hair, his unearthly eyes.

She was so lost in her imagination that she did not hear the approach of footsteps. "I can only hope that the words that flow from my own pen can create such a blush on the cheek," a voice murmured. Emilia glanced up to find Christopher Marlowe, the playwright, standing in front of her.

"You do not belong here," she said reflexively.

"Such a warm welcome, mistress," he drawled. "Surely this is not how you treat those who come to see the Lord Chamberlain."

"Is that why you've come?"

"What other business might I have here?" He sank down on the bench beside her. "It is of course poor planning on my part, given that Lord Hunsdon is not in residence."

The way Marlowe looked at her suggested that he'd known full well Hunsdon was abroad. If he was indeed a spy for the Queen, Emilia imagined there was little about the Crown's political endeavors that he did not know. "I would not flatter myself, Master Marlowe, to think that you came here with the intent of meeting me," Emilia said.

"Call me Kit. All my friends do."

"Are we friends?"

"Aspirationally," he said. "And you *should* flatter yourself, as my hopes were indeed to find you on the premises."

She turned, meeting his gaze. "Why?"

He shrugged. "Because most people bore me, Mistress Bassano. And you . . . do not. I did not imagine the Lord Chamberlain had a courtesan whose most seductive body part was her brain. Besides, we had not finished our conversation."

"Had we not?"

"I am quite sure you have more to say about Dido's shortcomings," Marlowe offered. "Or my own."

"I am quite sure there are many more qualified than I am to offer you opinions."

"More qualified? Yes. More entertaining? No." He smiled, snaked out a hand, and snatched the poem from her writing desk.

"Stop!" Emilia cried, trying to grab the paper from him.

Marlowe leaped to his feet, reading aloud.

"'Fondling,' she saith, 'since I have hemm'd thee here / Within the circuit of this ivory pale, I'll be a park, and thou shalt be my deer.'" His eyebrows flew up. "Hunsdon's quite the devil."

"You heedless jolthead!" Emilia burst out.

Marlowe laughed, continuing. *"Feed where thou wilt, on mountain or in dale: / Graze on my lips; and if those hills be dry, / Stray lower, where the pleasant fountains lie."* He pretended to fan his face, grinning widely. "You little flirt-gill. It's almost enough to make me wish to partake in the pleasures of a woman's body." Then he winked. *"Almost."*

"This is not about Hunsdon," she gritted out. "Do you write only of what you have lived?"

"I bloody hell hope not," Marlowe said. "Or I am far worse off than even I thought." He tilted his head. "Then what is it you write of?"

"If you must know, Venus and Adonis."

He sat beside her again, handing her the paper. "Do tell."

Emilia sighed, setting her lap desk on the ground. "It is the opposite of your Dido," she said. "When Venus cannot convince Adonis to stay with her, *he* is the one who is killed."

Marlowe's eyes brightened. "How . . . novel."

She drew back, unsure if he was making light of her.

"I do not jest," he said. "I cannot think of a work of literature where it is not the man persuading the woman."

216

Last year, Emilia had read a Marlowe poem, "The Passionate Shepherd to His Love." It was, classically, what one would expect: a man trying to convince a girl to lie with him. "Why shouldn't it be the other way around? Don't women have the same hopes and fears and urges as men?"

"How terrifying to imagine." He laughed. "To think you lot might be as uncontrollable as we are."

"That's the point of my poem: to invert everything. To reverse what we've seen. To suggest that a woman might lust, and a man might be the one to pay the price." She bit her lip. "As in your play, the strong, powerful woman falls in love, and the heroic male dies. But unlike Dido, Venus isn't tossing herself into any fire. She isn't ruined by love. Instead, she ruins love for anyone else." She thought for a moment. *"Sith in his prime Death doth my love destroy, / They that love best their love shall not enjoy."*

Marlowe stared down at the page. "Where's that bit?"

"I haven't written it down yet."

He pushed the paper into her hand. "Well, do. Before it flies from your mind."

Emilia picked up the lap desk and scrawled the line at the bottom of the page. She had barely lifted the quill when Marlowe took the poem back. His lips moved silently as he read. Then he snapped his fingers and held out his hand. "Pen?"

She passed the quill to him and watched him scratch out a line, then write a comment in the margin. "What are you about?"

"Giving notes," Marlowe said.

"Why?"

He did not even glance up, so absorbed was he. "Because," he said, "that is what writers do for each other."

Kit Marlowe may have been a spy and a rogue and an atheist but he was also becoming the best friend Emilia had never had. They wrote each other frequently, although Emilia addressed her notes to Mrs. Padshaw, who was Kit's landlady in Durham House. She was willing to keep secrets, such as Emilia and whatever men he smuggled into his room, in return for a weekly jug of mead. Emilia sent him snippets of her verse, which he critiqued and sent back to her. He asked her questions about plot holes in the play he was writing. They spent borrowed time hidden in the gardens of Somerset House, knowing that when Hunsdon returned, that freedom would be curtailed.

It was this ticking clock that made Marlowe suggest a trial run to spring Emilia from Somerset House without anyone knowing she was gone. He had business at Grocers' Hall and wanted her to accompany him, after which he planned to bring her to a tavern. But Grocers' Hall was on Princes Street, close enough to

Somerset House that Emilia could be recognized. And so, Marlowe had brought her a disguise.

He was waiting for her on Little Drury Lane, as he had promised. When she approached he whistled, and she jabbed her elbow into his side. "I feel ridiculous," she whispered.

"You should feel worried," Marlowe said.

She looked down at her brown doublet and hose and boots, castoffs from a stable-boy Kit had bribed with a coin. Her hair was braided against her head and hidden beneath a feathered cap. She looked, for all intents and purposes, like a young boy. "Why?"

"Because I am far more likely to proposition you when you are dressed like that." Marlowe laughed. "Come, Emile."

She growled as he pulled her by the elbow toward Princes Street. "How do you walk about like this every day?" Emilia asked, gesturing vaguely at her legs. "Do you not . . . chafe?"

He laughed as they walked past drays being pulled by mules and dodged piles of steaming horseshit. Marlowe glanced at her. "You had no trouble leaving?"

She shook her head. No one had even glanced twice at her once she skittered down the servants' stairs and out the rear door. There were boys coming in and out of Somerset House at all times, ferrying food and coal or running messages.

"How goes Adonis?" he asked.

"Still resistant," Emilia replied. She had not finished her poem, because she still did not know how it should end. Well, she knew *what* would happen, but not *how*.

Art imitating life.

"Why do you need to see a grocer?" Emilia asked.

"Because this one happens to perform for Lord Strange's Men," Marlowe replied. "John Heminges used to be with the Queen's Men. But last year, two other actors in the troupe got into it on tour, and one got killed. Heminges married his widow, and I suppose the circumstances were odd enough for him to decamp to Lord Strange's Men."

"It's more incestuous than court," Emilia murmured.

She and Kit already had formed the sort of friendship that engulfed them, fueled by that peculiar sense that each had finally found in the other a missing part of themselves. They were both clever and outspoken and observant — all tools in a writer's box — but more important, they fed off each other's appreciation for those qualities. After only a week, Emilia knew that he detested the color red and pickled herring, that he preferred ale to wine and the city to the country, that his favorite food was gingerbread husbands, and when he ate one he did it with as much sexual innuendo as possible. It had been rumored that he was to go to the Catholic college in Rheims, but he'd confessed he would rather cut out his own tongue than subscribe to any religion — including the Church of England. She knew how Kit had come to university on scholarship and why he admired Walsingham and to whom he'd lost his virginity. The one line he did not cross was telling her about the work he did for the Queen, although he did not deny doing it. In the same way, Emilia told him about her father's death and how she could read music before she could read words and about her cousin trading her to Hunsdon for job security and her lessons with Isabella. She did not tell him her two biggest secrets: her hidden faith, and her feelings for Southampton. The first could have gotten her killed. The second was more complicated. It was hers, alone, now; she feared that speaking the desire into existence would be like a drop of blood in an ocean — diluted until it was as if it had never been there at all.

But most important, she and Kit were bonded by words. After only a week they could finish each other's sentences, not to mention each other's rhymed couplets. It was still a heady feeling, and she knew that Kit valued her mind and couldn't care less about the pretty package it came in.

They had just turned the corner and were about to climb the steps to the guildhall when Emilia suddenly panicked. "What if I am recognized?"

"That will not come to pass."

"Then how will you explain my presence?"

Marlowe smirked. "Darling, it would be considered more shocking for me *not* to be in the company of a young man."

After years with Hunsdon, Emilia knew there was a pipeline of sorts from the livery companies to the theater companies. The young boys who played the roles of women often came from livery companies, where they were bonded in service to drapers, goldsmiths, grocers, or tailors. Many of the boy players went on to become hired adult actors.

Heminges was a portly man with a face like rising dough, and when Emilia and Kit were directed to him, he was deep in conversation with another man. This one was slighter, with a receding hairline and a weak chin badly camouflaged by a dark beard. "I shall make the introduction," Heminges said, "but I make no promises."

Marlowe stepped forward, smiling widely. "A man who promises no promises is one who cannot disappoint anyone but himself. Well met, Master Heminges."

"Marlowe," the grocer said, nodding.

"Marlowe?" The other man turned. "I saw your *Tamburlaine.*"

"If you have chosen to speak to me, instead of turn tail and run, I shall hope that you found it agreeable."

"This is Master Shakespeare," Heminges said.

Shakespeare. Emilia stood mute, a step behind Kit, trying to remember why she knew that name.

"Will," the man corrected, nodding at Kit. "I, too, write for the stage."

Oh, *yes.* Emilia remembered the plays he had submitted to Hunsdon. *Badly,* she thought.

"May I introduce my . . . friend. Emile Hammersmith," Kit said, his hand pushing between Emilia's shoulder blades. She blushed a furious crimson but didn't dare open her mouth. If she spoke, the ruse would be up. "Emile is . . . mute," Kit said, smiling. "Which means if I disappoint him, I never have to hear complaint of it."

Emilia smiled sweetly and kicked Kit surreptitiously in the shin.

"Master Shakespeare's father is a glover in Stratford," Heminges said, "and has of late been in the wool trade as well. He would like to contract some of his apprentices to Lord Strange's theater company."

Marlowe smiled politely. "What a happy coincidence," he said. "Heminges, I thought perhaps you could mention to Henslowe at the Rose that I have a new play circling in my thoughts, should he care to be the one to commission it."

"I, too, would like to offer my plays," Shakespeare interjected.

Kit slid a glance toward Emilia. "Huzzah," he said.

"May I ask the title, Master Marlowe?" asked Heminges.

The Jew of Malta, Kit answered, and Emilia startled.

He continued chatting, but Emilia could only hear the blood pounding in her ears. When Kit finally ushered her out of the hall, it took a few moments before she could focus on his rambling words. ". . . not surprising he wants into the theater business. Shakespeare's *pater* got into trouble as a wool brogger, and he wound up in court for selling without a license. I'm quite sure young Will wants to carve a path as far away from his father as possible. Why *not* theater," Kit mused. "Everyone else and their brother seem to feel they have a skill for it."

"He doesn't," Emilia said, the world rushing back into place. "I read one of his plays."

Kit laughed. "Good. Less competition for me."

They were on the street again, the bright sunlight making her wince. "Your new play," she said carefully. "It's about a Jew?"

"Yes, Barabas. He's the villain — a rich Jew whose wealth is at risk, because the governor of Malta wants to extort money from his kind to pay the Turks."

"He's the villain," Emilia repeated.

Kit glanced down, bemused. "Yes, yes, keep up," he said impatiently. "Barabas, of course, refuses, and the Christians take his money anyway and turn his house into a nunnery. So he decides to get vengeance on them all — including his daughter's Christian lover, and his daughter, whom he poisons." He whirled, walking backward on the street so that he could look at Emilia as he continued. "Finally, he sets a trap and winds up falling into it himself, dying in a boiling cauldron that was meant for the Christians. Brilliant, is it not?" He paused. "You hate it," he guessed.

"No, I . . ." Emilia bit her lip. "I am a fan of tragedy. But is it not already tragic that Jews are treated as they are?"

Kit scoffed. "You speak as if you know so many of them."

What could Emilia say to that? "What I mean to say is that mayhap villains are made, not born. Mayhap it is the treatment of Barabas as a Jew that teaches him to treat others so unkindly."

Marlowe jammed his hands into the pockets of his coat, mulling. "All religion is a fiction," he said. "All of it is evil. That's the whole point." He slung an arm around her narrow shoulders. "Come. Instead of drowning in fictional despair, let us drown ourselves in ale." He peered in the general direction of St. Paul's. "Mermaid Tavern, that way."

"I do not like ale," Emilia muttered.

"No? How can you even call yourself a writer?" Kit joked.

She stopped walking. "I *can't,* Kit."

For a long moment Marlowe just stared at her. He understood what it was to keep secrets one couldn't reveal, to wish for lives one would never have, to play multiple roles — hired hack, libertine, hidden agent of the Crown. He chucked her under the chin. "Go to, Mouse," he said, trying to cheer her. "You are still a writer, even if the words you put to paper have never been read by another. I look forward to the day when you pen *your* play about this aggrieved Jew."

She looked at him. "Mayhap, one day, I will."

In the middle of the night, Emilia heard something strike the window of her chamber.

She leaped from her bed, lit a candle, and approached the window. In the garden behind the house a cloaked figure bent in the pouring rain, scooping pebbles from the walkway. Even before he threw back the hood of his cloak to reveal his bright hair, she knew it was Southampton.

She struggled with the window latch, opened it, and leaned over the threshold. "What are you doing here?" she hissed.

He threw his arms wide. "Letting my eyes drink in the —"

"Sshh!" Emilia interrupted. "Are you mad?"

"Yes! Mad for you . . ."

God save her from inebriated men. Emilia closed the window, jammed her arms into a robe, and flew down the stairs to the doors leading out to the gardens. Southampton stumbled toward her, and she dragged him into the shadows.

He buried his face in her unbound hair and breathed deeply. His arms were wet and cold around her. "I've missed you."

Emilia shoved him away. "You *cannot* be here."

"Love, you cannot break a heart that's already been broken. Why have you not answered my letters?"

"Because it was unsafe to do so," Emilia said. Even as she held him at arm's length, even as she panicked about whether any staff had seen him or had witnessed her flight to the garden, her body bowed toward his. "Hunsdon will be home any moment."

"Then let me have the moments he has not claimed," Southampton said. "I cannot return to Cambridge without one last kiss."

Emilia pushed back her sodden hair and stamped her lips against his. "There. Now, go." But even as she spoke, he caught her close.

She melted into him, and everywhere his

hands roamed she felt fire lick her skin. She nearly expected the rain striking them both to turn to steam. Her fingers twined in his hair and his mouth fell against her throat, and just like before, there was a devil whispering to her: *Why can't you have this one small thing?*

"What you do to me," Southampton breathed against her, his hand finding the split of her robe and sliding inside. "Tell me you feel it, too."

"It does not matter if I feel it," she sighed.

He cupped her face. "It matters. It is *all* that matters."

The rain ran down his cheeks and spiked his eyelashes. "Not here." Emilia grabbed his hand and pulled him along the dark walk between the hedges, until the peaked frame of the orangery came into view. She opened the door and hurried in, sealing the storm outside.

In the dark, the shapes of the plants seemed monstrous. Through the glass, moonlight pooled. Southampton peeled off her robe and then pulled her drenched night rail over her head. She stood before him, silvered.

He untied his cloak as her hands worked buttons through the swollen fabric of his doublet. When he was naked, too, she wrapped her legs around his waist, allowing him to hold her up while he pivoted and set her on the edge of a potting table. As he thrust into her, she tilted her face up to the glass roof, where the rain pelted as if the world wept for them.

Afterward, they lay on a canvas beneath a small grove of potted orange trees, Southampton's body curled around Emilia's. "This is our Eden," he murmured into her shoulder. "I am Adam, and you are my Eve."

She turned to face him. "And there is no escaping the tree of knowledge."

"I will find a way," Southampton vowed.

Emilia had never felt so old, nor had Southampton ever seemed so very young. What must it be like to be rich and privileged and to believe with utter conviction that obstacles would clear themselves from your path?

"My lord," she said softly, "some stories are meant to be tragic."

"Not ours," he insisted. "I will write you, every day."

"You will not. It is too dangerous."

Just then, she heard her name being called. Emilia jerked upright, yanking her night rail over her head. She tossed Southampton's clothes at him. "Dress," she whispered fiercely. "There is a rear door that way." She pointed, hoping that he would spy the latch in the wall of glass panels.

"Emilia?"

"My lord?" she called, hearing the door at the front of the orangery scrape open.

Hunsdon struck flint and lit a candle, which must have been doused by the storm. It illuminated a circle where he stood, with the orangery door still open and the rain hammering outside. As Emilia stepped toward him, his face creased into a smile. "Is this an apparition or an angel?"

She realized that in her voluminous nightwear, with the glow of the flame in front of her, she must indeed look otherworldly. "Which would you prefer tonight, my lord?" she asked, dimpling.

She imagined Southampton, mere yards away, listening to this exchange. She felt her cheeks burn in shame, and hoped Hunsdon would see it as passion. He reached out a hand, and she placed hers into it. "I did not expect you so late," Emilia said.

"Our carriage broke a wheel," Hunsdon replied. "I came to find you in your chamber, but you were missing." He glanced over his shoulder. "I have the staff turning the whole house out in search of you. What brings you to the orangery past midnight?"

She turned the words over in her head, inspecting them for accusation but finding only concern. "It is the strangest thing," Emilia said. "I must have walked in my sleep because I found myself in the gardens without knowing how I'd arrived there. And then, when it began to rain, I took refuge here."

Hunsdon rubbed his hand over the night rail. "We must get you dry," he said, just as there was a clatter in the rear of the glasshouse. "What's that?" He took a step toward the noise.

"Likely some small creature seeking shelter, as I was," Emilia answered quickly, putting her hand on his cloak. "You are soaked, too," she said, lowering her lashes. She wound her arms around Hunsdon's neck, kissing him as she maneuvered so that his back was facing the spot where Southampton must have knocked over a pot. "So wet," she murmured as she pushed him up against his worktable, dropped to her knees, and tugged down his hose. "I have missed you, my lord," Emilia said, and she closed her mouth over him.

She felt his hands on her head like a benediction. As Hunsdon moaned, she saw Southampton, dressed now, step into the aisle. She met his eye over Hunsdon's hip.

This is who I am, she silently willed. *You need to know.*

As Southampton whirled, silently padding out the rear door of the glasshouse, Emilia closed her eyes. She wasn't an angel, and she wasn't an apparition.

She was a wraith, and every chamber of her heart was haunted.

Emilia did not leave her room the next day or the day after, pleading a headache. While Hunsdon was at court, reporting to Her Majesty, Emilia wrote.

She tore apart her love poem and put it back together.

She found the words to kill off Adonis, and to let Venus grieve for him. Because no matter how she had delayed, that was the way it was always going to end.

She dedicated the poem to Southampton.

Then she copied it clean and sent it to Marlowe's landlady folded inside a simple missive:

Help me, it read.

That was how Emilia revealed one of her secrets to Kit Marlowe, who answered her summons for aid in all the ways she had hoped he would — as an editor for her poetry, and as a shoulder to cry on. She met him weekly at the Falcon Inn in Southwark, a different day each time, so that Hunsdon would never become suspicious. She had given the young maid so much coin for her continued silence that at this rate, the woman would probably be able to afford a house on the Strand.

Months passed without word from Southampton, which Emilia had expected after the manner in which they'd parted. She told Kit how she had finally managed to drive Southampton away, to which the poet had no reply, but he opened his arms and held her while she sobbed.

A year went by, and although she still thought of Southampton, Emilia buried her memories. The handful of times she heard that the Earl was to be at court, she made sure to feign illness. She decided to consider herself lucky to have had one grand love in her life, and over a decade of comfort with a kind man who had become a friend. She distracted herself by reading plays for Hunsdon — including Kit's *Jew of Malta*. She started another poem, this one based on a tale from Ovid's *Fasti* about a woman who was raped by her soldier husband's best friend after her husband boasted about her. It was dark and devastating and tragic, which was always her mood these days.

The Falcon Inn wasn't very crowded, but then it was just early afternoon. A barmaid carried tankards to patrons, and in the corner of the room, a man played a lute and sang. It was unclear to Emilia if he had been hired to do so or was merely drunk.

"You know," Kit said. "You *used* to be fun."

Emilia had pillowed her head on her folded arms. "Pray continue," she said. "I will try to pretend I am interested."

Just as Emilia had spent months grieving the loss of Southampton, Kit had spent months stirring up trouble. He'd moved house, and after he and the poet Thomas Watson had gotten into a deadly fight with his neighbors in Norton Folgate, he'd spent a fortnight in Newgate Prison. Only a month ago Kit had been in the Netherlands, caught up in a counterfeiting scheme tied to Catholics who were still vying for the throne. He'd been sent to Lord Burghley, the Queen's treasurer, but hadn't been charged or jailed. When Emilia had asked him directly if he was an agent of the Crown, he laughed and said, "I am simply an agent of chaos." It seemed to Emilia that they both had deep, endless caverns inside them that they tried unsuccessfully to fill — Emilia's days spent writing poetry dedicated to the object of her affections and nights spent servicing Hunsdon; Kit's days spent drowning in ale and his nights rife with brawls and secret missions that could get him killed at any moment. They were, Emilia thought, a sorry pair — always reaching for the fruit on a branch too high, instead of finding satisfaction in the things within their grasp that could sustain them.

The lute player finished his song and, spying Kit, launched into a ballad based on one of his poems. Kit groaned and waved to the barmaid for another drink.

He was reading a pamphlet that Robert Greene had just published, *Groatsworth of Wit,* in which Kit (and other writers) had been referenced through allusions. "What rot. He's contending George Peele's work is on a par with mine. I have *far* more talent than Peele."

"And so much more humility." Emilia smirked.

Kit ignored her. "Ah, this bit's more interesting. He says actors are only as good as the words we writers give them — so they owe us. And he warns of one untrustworthy actor, an *upstart crow* who's pretending he's a writer and passing other people's material off as his own."

"Who?"

Kit shrugged. "He calls him *Shake-scene.*"

"Shake-scene," Emilia repeated. "Didn't we meet him once?"

"That was Will Shake*speare,*" Kit corrected. "He does act now, for the Queen's Men. But he's a nobody. This is likely a reference to Ned Alleyn, chewing up the scenery in my *Tamburlaine.*"

Emilia picked up the Groatsworth pamphlet, leafing through it. "Well, whoever it is, it seems that if actors are trying to write for themselves, they need more playwrights."

A long finger hooked over the page and tugged it down. Kit's dark eyes were on hers, dancing.

"No," she said.

"You don't even know what I am going to ask."

"I don't need to. I can tell by the look in your eyes."

"Why not you, Mouse?" he asked.

Emilia winced. Her head hurt from the ale they'd been drinking, her heart hurt from Southampton, and she didn't really give a fig about this stupid pamphlet that had Kit's hose tied in knots. "Why not me *what*?"

"Why don't you write a play?"

"If you do not know the answer to that, you are more cotton-headed than I believed." She looked down at her boy's clothes. "Or perhaps you have forgotten what's beneath this doublet."

But when Kit caught tail of an idea, he could not let it go. "*Everyone* collaborates," he said. "Indeed, it would be unnatural for a playwright to not have a friend's quill in his inkwell."

"Is that a sexual pun?"

"Maybe. But it's also true. Why, a week ago, Fletcher and Beaumont were at a tavern discussing a play they were writing together about killing a king. They were discussing the murder scene and who should take which part, and they got arrested for treason, because someone assumed they were plotting regicide."

Emilia narrowed her eyes at him. "Do not jest."

"I am not. I'm telling you that it's perfectly normal for more than one writer to have a hand in a play. Kyd and I share rooms, and he's helped with my plays when I reach a spot that makes me wish to tear out my hair. If Lord Strange's Men wind up with a new apprentice playing a maiden's part, they might come to me and ask me to add a soliloquy for a play of Nashe's. Sometimes a clown is added, sometimes one is taken away. It's all good coin. A play is a living thing, and it grows and shrinks with time. This is why the best playwrights work with each other. And by the best of us, I mean me."

"I cannot write a play, Kit."

"You cannot put your *name* on a play. That is not the same thing."

Despite herself, Emilia found that she was leaning forward. Kit was the first person to ever take her writing seriously, as more than a hobby. He spent precious time working on her verse with her, and he solicited Emilia's opinions on his own. He treated her the way he would treat any male writer. "I . . . I don't know *how* to write a play."

"Mouse," Kit said gravely. "You are an accomplished writer. Words are words. A play is merely a different shape."

Even considering this felt like stepping to the edge of a cliff. Emilia could feel the roar of the wind and the spray of the sea and knew that, with one step, she might fall. But, then again, maybe she could fly. "You would aid me?"

"There is little I would not do for you," Kit said, smiling. "Now. We need a plot." He rapped his fingers on the table, thinking.

The lute player began another broadside ballad, this one sung to the tune of "Fortune or Foe." *"Ay me, vile wretch, that ever I was born . . . Making myself unto the world a scorn: And to my friends and kindred all a shame, Blotting their blood by my unhappy name."*

237

Kit smacked the table. "That's it! Do you know this tune?"

Emilia nodded. "Is it not about a murder of a husband?"

"Yes. Thomas Arden, killed by his wife, Alice, because she wanted to be with her lover instead. Happened in Kent forty years ago. She hired two accomplices to commit the murder, but it took five tries before they succeeded. Eventually Alice was burned at the stake for her crimes." Kit grinned. "It's perfect. Who doesn't love bloodshed and murder onstage? And since you are forever telling me I cannot write tragic women well, this is your opportunity to educate me."

"What if she was not tragic?" Emilia asked.

"Go on."

"Marriage is a business and has little to do with love. For a woman to have status, she must be married. Yet a married woman loses everything — her name, her body, her property, her money. It all belongs to her husband. A widow, on the other hand, is given back all that rightfully belongs to her." Emilia shrugged. "It is a wonder there aren't more husbands murdered."

Kit shuddered. "You terrify me sometimes."

"Because I speak truth?" Emilia said. "Who knows why Alice Arden wanted to kill her husband, or what happened behind their closed doors? Was she foolish to try to break free . . . or impossibly brave?" She turned to the lute player, no longer singing in poor Alice's voice but in that of a narrative chorus warning others not to behave as she did.

"Love is a god," Emilia said. "Marriage is but words."

Kit clinked his tankard of ale against hers. "That's my girl." He flipped the *Groatsworth* pamphlet to its blank back and signaled for the barmaid again, this time to ask for a quill and ink. "Now," he said. "Where will you start?"

MELINA

SEPTEMBER 2023

Melina felt as if she were looking into a mirror. The woman staring back had green eyes, not silver, but tears were shining in them, just like in hers. Her voice spoke words that Melina knew before they were uttered. It was just the two of them in the room, and everyone else had fallen away — the other performers, the artistic director, the audience.

The actress playing Emilia Bassano spoke the last lines of Melina's play:

It does not matter if they know you. It only matters that they heard what you had to say.

Melina wondered if this was what Emilia Bassano had felt, watching one of her plays performed, surrounded by people who did not know that she was its author. It was so strange for Melina to find herself now in the exact same situation her protagonist was.

The vacuum created by the art suddenly was unsealed, and Melina's senses were flooded with the thunder of applause, the bows of the actors, the squeeze of Andre's arm around her shoulders. "Listen," he murmured in her ear. "That's for *you*, Mel."

Almost immediately, people came over to pump Andre's hand and congratulate him. Melina knew that this was supposed to be the moment where she revealed herself as the author of *By Any Other Name,* but she couldn't muster the energy to get out of the chair. She felt sapped, boneless. The twenty-nine-hour workshop had been intense. She hadn't had time to process the changes to her play, and whether they had been improvements.

Gradually she became aware of Felix Dubonnet talking to Andre about the brilliance of a device used in the play where a sonnet became a child loss poem. A bolt of anger sizzled through Melina: it wasn't a *device;* it was a possibility. Her play about Emilia Bassano's life wasn't meant to be a fiction; it was meant to be the resurrection of an erasure, like the reveal of Mary Sidney Herbert's invisible ink. Just the fact that history books hadn't included this version of events didn't make it untrue; it merely underscored who'd controlled the narrative.

Side conversations blossomed around the room.

Did you ever hear of this Emilia person before?

You know her, Melina thought. *You memorized her words long before you knew she wrote them.*

241

Only crazy people question Shakespeare's authorship. . . .

And yet you are entertaining the notion, Melina mused.

And one woman, gesturing wildly to her male companion: *It was so . . .* real. *You have no idea what it's like to talk and know no one's listening to you.*

The man: *What?*

"What I found most impressive," Felix continued, "is the question of whether the art is more important than the recognition. This piece stands on the shoulders of Sondheim and Lapine, John Logan . . . Yasmina Reza."

"Shouldn't that be the other way around? Since Emilia Bassano came first?" Andre yanked Melina's arm until she was standing. "Speaking of art and recognition . . ."

"Mr. Green," a voice interrupted, and Melina turned to see Jasper Tolle standing with his hands clasped behind his back. "Might we speak in private?"

Andre darted a glance toward Melina. "I would like that very much."

Felix Dubonnet patted Andre on the back, ignoring Melina. "I'll let you two talk. Good work, lad. Good work." He caught the eye of someone across the theater and began to weave away through the aisles.

Jasper seemed unreasonably crisp in a linen suit. His ubiquitous Moleskine was held tight in his palm. His eyes were neither blue nor green but some strange, seascape combination of the two, and Melina realized she had never been close enough to him to notice that. She could see, too, a patch on his jaw that he had missed while shaving, and a few threads of silver at his temples. It made him so human that, for a second, she forgot how much she despised him.

This is my moment, Melina thought. *This is where I tell him the truth.*

But first, she wanted to hear his feedback.

Jasper led Andre toward the stage, where a stagehand was setting out the ghost light now that the performance was finished. Melina followed at their heels.

"I'm not going to beat around the bush," Jasper said. "I love your play."

Andre glanced at Melina. "Thanks, but —"

"I don't think you understand how rarely I say those words," Jasper continued. "And I've never said what I'm about to say now: I want to help this show transfer."

Melina froze, stunned. Andre, too, stood speechless. "It is truly exciting to me to see a man write from the female point of view so clearly, and to eloquently explain what it feels like to be sidelined because of gender," Jasper said. "It certainly calls into question the debate that only those who've lived an experience should create art about it."

"No one has ever stopped a man from writing about women," Melina blurted out. "But when their hot takes on what it means to be a woman fill up slots in theaters that could instead be given to female playwrights, it's problematic."

Jasper blinked. "I'm sorry . . . *who* are you?"

Andre opened his mouth, presumably to introduce Melina as the actual writer of the play Jasper was raving about. But in that moment, Melina realized two truths. The first was that Jasper Tolle did not recognize her as the student whose work he had savaged at Bard College. The second was that if Jasper knew she had written the play instead of Andre, he would no longer champion it.

Melina stepped — hard — on Andre's foot and stuck out her hand. "I'm Mel's assistant. Andrea."

Jasper frowned. "So . . . I should contact *you* to set up a meeting to talk further about next steps for the show?"

Melina glanced at Andre, who still seemed paralyzed. "Yes! I'm the one who keeps Mel's schedule." She smiled, all teeth. "Creative types. Too lost in their art to pay attention to a calendar, am I right? I'll give you my contact information. I'm the best way to reach Mel. He . . . isn't on social media and he usually keeps his phone turned off so it doesn't interfere with his . . . process."

"I do?" Andre said.

Melina ignored him, taking Jasper Tolle's phone and typing in her own contact information under the name ANDREA WASH-INGTON. "There!" she said brightly. "Look-ing forward to hearing from you!"

Jasper looked back and forth between Me-lina and Andre, as if he couldn't quite figure out this relationship. Then, he leaned closer to Andre. "I hate these public things, too," he said, apparently deciding that Andre's dis-comfort was social anxiety. Jasper took back his phone. "I'll be in touch."

Andre and Melina watched the critic lope up the aisle. Through his teeth, Andre hissed, "What the actual *fuck* was that, Mel?"

"He wants it to transfer. *Transfer,* Andre. Can you imagine *By Any Other Name* at a *real* theater? Earning *real* income? When am I going to get this opportunity again?"

"Well, *you're* not, because apparently *I'm* the one who is getting the opportunity," Andre exploded. "We agreed on this! You were sup-posed to come clean after the performance."

"That was before I knew he wanted to help *produce* it!" She softened. "Please, Andre? You're my best friend, and I really, really need this break. I know I'm asking a lot. But it's just a few more weeks."

"And then? When are you going to tell him? When it earns out? Transfers to Broadway? Or will you wait for the Tonys?" Andre shook his head. "I can't keep playing a role for you, Mel. I have a *day job.*"

"I know. It's why you never have time to

finish your own plays. But if Jasper Tolle gets this to a real theater, it means I'll get paid . . . something. You can have the money, and use it to take a few weeks off from the casting agency to write."

He considered this; she could see him softening at the thought of having the luxury of time *and* money. "Your name won't be in the *Playbill,*" Andre pointed out.

"It doesn't matter. My play would be *out in the world,*" Melina said. "I can worry about getting credit later."

"Friends don't let friends fuck up their lives with *I Love Lucy*–type schemes that are bound to fail," Andre argued.

"Friends don't let friends down when they need them most." Melina turned a beseeching gaze on Andre.

He pursed his lips. "Fine."

Melina threw her arms around his neck. "Thank you. *Thank you.*"

"You're welcome," Andre sighed, peeling her off. "Now go get me a coffee."

"Get your own damn coffee."

"Best watch that tone, *Andrea,*" he said, grinning. "Good personal assistants are a dime a dozen in this town."

When Melina was young, her mother had been diagnosed with cancer. She would come home from school and sit on her mother's bed, waiting for her to wake up from her exhausted sleep, or whatever cocktail of chemicals had been pumped through her system to try to eradicate the disease. When her mother did stir, she never asked Melina, "How was your day?" Instead, she would say, "What do you wish you'd done today?"

At the time, Melina's answers ranged from the mundane to the esoteric — *I wish I'd clocked Jimmy Faraday in the nose when he called me Pizza Face during recess; I wish I was a mermaid and I could swim around the world.*

As her mother's illness raged and ebbed, Melina turned the question back on her. Her mother's answers were a list of the things she no longer had the stamina to do: ski on a day so cold that when you breathed in, your nostrils stuck together; do a back dive into a clear, cold pool; read an entire book in one sitting.

Melina knew that her mother's failing health wasn't really because cancer was winning but because, after so long, her mother was done fighting. One weekend, when Melina was sixteen and doing her English homework, she looked up to find her mom uncharacteristically alert. "I wish," her mother said, "I could see the northern lights."

"We will," Melina said.

Her mother shook her head. The words she wasn't saying filled the space between them.

"Melina," her mother asked. "Will you take me out for some air?"

She put down her books and pulled the

wheelchair over to her mother's hospice bed. But after she had pushed the chair to the wildflower garden outside the facility her mother said, "Keep going."

"Where?"

"The parking lot," her mother said. "Your car. You're breaking me out of here."

"Mom," Melina said, "I cannot break you out of hospice. What if you —"

"Die?" her mother interrupted. She reached for Melina's hand. "Let's go see the northern lights."

Melina had a provisional license that wasn't legal outside the state. She had no idea where you could see the northern lights that didn't require boarding a plane. "Okay," she said softly.

With her mother manning the GPS, Melina drove north. She was exhilarated and terrified, and kept sneaking glances at her mother in the passenger seat.

They did not reach Canada. They didn't see the northern lights. Instead, Melina's father caught up to them at a rest stop just over the border in Vermont, having tracked her phone on their family mobile plan. "Melina," he said, furious. "What were you *thinking*?"

Melina's mother held up a hand. "It was my idea, Matthew."

"Do you have any idea how dangerous this is? You could have cut weeks off your life —"

"It's still *my* life," Melina's mother said. "Don't take that away from me, too."

At that, her father had choked on a sob, and then he was kneeling beside the wheelchair and embracing her mother, and once again, Melina felt, for a moment, utterly excluded.

They pushed the chair to the edge of the parking lot, a hilly rise with the roar of the highway somewhere behind it. Melina and her father sat on a quilt streaked with bike grease from the back of his trunk. They watched the stars burn holes in the fabric of the night. Melina, who had barely seen her mother awake these past few weeks, was amazed to find her attention unwavering. She reached out her hand so Melina could take it.

Melina felt the knobs of her mother's knuckles, the skin stretched thin over her palm. She thought about how strange it was that at some point when she touched her mother, it would be the last time. She looked away, because she was afraid she might start to cry, and blinked up at the sky.

There weren't any northern lights, of course.

"I'm sorry I couldn't make your wish come true," Melina said.

Her mother turned, her gaze brushing over Melina. "You will," she said, "and then some."

Three days after the reading of *By Any Other Name,* Melina woke to a text from Jasper Tolle.

Producer interested — 3 PM, Glass House Tavern bar, will meet Mel there.

She leaped out of bed and began pounding on the bathroom door. Andre appeared, a towel wrapped around his waist. "What's a girl got to do to get some privacy around here," he grumbled.

"You have a meeting. *We* have a meeting. Today," Melina babbled. "With a producer."

He pushed past Melina in a cloud of steam. "Okay."

"It's at Glass House Tavern." Melina followed Andre into his bedroom, watching him disappear into his closet and begin throwing clothes on his bed. "At three."

"Great."

She narrowed her eyes. "You're being awfully amenable."

He popped his head back out. "That's because I'm not going."

Melina crossed her arms. "You have to go. You're Mel Green."

"Actually, *you're* Mel Green, but I can see how this is confusing," he said. "Look, I promised I'd pretend to be the playwright, but I said nothing about taking meetings in the middle of a workday."

"What am I supposed to tell the producer?"

"That you're Mel Green?" Andre suggested. At Melina's murderous look, he shrugged. "You're a writer. You'll think of something."

Six hours later, Melina was stepping off the

subway when her phone dinged with another text from Jasper.

Unable to join — work emergency. Will check in with Tyce later and report back.

Tyce? Melina typed, her stomach sinking.

D'Onofrio. Sorry — that's the producer.

She knew Tyce D'Onofrio. She'd met with him last year, after sending him one of her plays. She'd bought him a ten-dollar venti Starbucks concoction. In return, he'd said the main character in her play was unrelatable, because she made questionable choices. At the time, he was producing a revival of *Sweeney Todd,* about a barber with anger-management issues who murdered his patrons.

Melina made her way into the Glass House Tavern, heading toward the bar. This time of day, the restaurant was empty. There were only two men at the bar, both on their phones. Her mouth was cotton dry. "Um," she said. "Tyce? I think you're waiting for me."

He glanced up and smiled, getting off his stool. "You are definitely not Mel Green," he said, not a single glimmer of recognition in his eyes.

Melina sucked in a breath and smiled brightly. "Guilty!"

"Jasper said Mel would probably bring his assistant along. Is Mel on his way, then?"

"He is not," Melina said slowly. "He had . . . a work emergency."

"Paper cut?" He laughed, toothy. "Because he's a writer . . ."

"Yeah, I got that," Melina said.

"What's your poison?" Tyce asked, gesturing to his drink and taking a seat.

She turned to the bartender. "Grey Goose martini. A double." She sat on the barstool beside the producer. "Mel asked me to keep the meeting so that I could answer any questions you have," Melina said. "I — um — *he* is truly grateful for your interest in the show. So . . . what is it about *By Any Other Name* that excites you?"

Tyce shrugged. "Well. I mean, where do I *start*? I just think it's something that's really been missing from the theatrical landscape, you know? Men like me don't think about what it might be like to be erased from history, because we haven't been. But a work of art from a man that forces you to look through the eyes of someone who hasn't been given a lens of her own — well, it's good allyship, right? It's pointing out one's privilege and decrying it simultaneously." He popped a handful of cashews into his mouth, speaking around them. "I also think having a Black playwright speaking to the plight of women is fascinating — you know, it takes one marginalized person to recognize another one, and all that." He hesitated. "That's probably not something I should say out loud."

No, Melina thought. *It is not.*

The bartender passed Melina's martini to her and she drained half of it in a single swallow. "You know, we've met before."

Tyce D'Onofrio squinted at her. "Really?"

"We had coffee. I had sent you one of my plays."

"Ah!" Tyce said, the way people signal remembering when they really don't recall a thing.

"You told me my main character was hard to relate to," Melina replied, smiling pleasantly. "I think you used the words *emotionally unapologetic*."

"Good on you for getting a job as Green's assistant," Tyce said. "Never hurts to have a mentor with the same interests."

"Just out of curiosity — for my own personal growth, of course —" Melina said, "what was it Mel's play had that mine was missing?"

Tyce didn't hesitate. "Jasper Tolle's recommendation. If he likes it, it's going to be a hit." Then he pushed the little dish of cashews closer to Melina. "Nuts?"

She looked down at them. "Yes," she agreed.

All newscasters could talk about was the heat wave that had engulfed the city. Melina had slept fitfully, naked on top of her sheets, letting her oscillating fan blow hot breath over her skin. Like everyone else who did not have the privilege of air-conditioning, she only wanted to find a place to spend the day that

253

was cool and did not charge twenty bucks or multiple lattes for admission.

She headed for her usual go-to place, the Manuscripts and Archives room of the New York Public Library, where she had done most of her deep-dive research on Emilia Bassano. She had found precious few primary sources that mentioned Emilia — the most notable being the client records of an astrologer named Simon Forman, whom Emilia had visited after several miscarriages. Emilia was also present as a footnote in the lives of more famous Elizabethans, like Henry Carey — Lord Hunsdon — and the long line of Bassanos who were court musicians for Henry VIII and Elizabeth I. Then there were the spotty, incongruous records of Shakespeare's life, where Emilia had not been mentioned at all, yet where blatant holes in the time line seemed to take on her shape.

The secret that most New Yorkers did not know was that even if you were not in the reading room to get access to a rare book, you could sit in its cool, quiet space.

Today she had brought a novel from home — a romantasy Andre had been trying to get her to read for a year so that they could discuss the twist at the end — and she planned to remain in the air-conditioned room until her stomach started growling and she had to venture out for food.

She pulled her T-shirt away from her chest, fanning it as the cool air of the library worked its magic. She had no sooner cracked open her book than her phone dinged with a text. Immediately six pairs of eyes snapped to Melina, and she cringed. "Sorry," she whispered, setting her phone to silent.

D'Onofrio onboard, Jasper Tolle had messaged. *His office will get rehearsal space. Would like to set a meeting with Mel about casting/schedule.*

Melina's thumbs scrolled over the screen. *Will get his avails.*

Somewhere behind her, another patron's phone pinged. Well, at least she wasn't the only one.

Then she added: *Mel wants to know if you have a theater in mind.*

Another ding. "Sir," a librarian said, pejorative. "This is a *quiet space.*"

Melina's phone buzzed in her hand. *Cherry Lane.*

A cold finger of awareness pressed between her shoulder blades. She whipped around in her seat and found herself staring into the shocked eyes of Jasper Tolle, who sat one table away, a laptop open in front of him.

She found herself standing, moving toward him. "What are you doing here?" she whispered.

"Reading," he whispered back. "It's a reading room."

"Nobody knows about this spot," Melina said, frustrated.

"Clearly," Jasper said, glancing around, "that is not the case."

A woman to his right narrowed her eyes at him. "Sssh."

"Did you follow me?" Melina said.

"Why on earth would I *follow* you?"

"I've been coming here for years and I've never seen you here before."

"How flattering to know you were looking," Jasper replied drily.

"Miss," a librarian said, her voice a knife. "And sir. I'm afraid if you want to have a conversation, you'll have to do it elsewhere."

Neither of them looked at the librarian. Instead, Melina focused on Jasper Tolle's unfathomable eyes and the line of his jaw. He, likewise, coolly regarded her. Then he closed the top of his laptop.

Melina whirled to stuff her book into her backpack and sling it over one arm. She exited the room, feeling Jasper Tolle just a step behind her.

Neither spoke as they passed through the grandeur of the Rose Reading Room, through the catalog room to the rotunda. It wasn't until they were at the staircase leading to the Fifth Avenue entrance that Jasper said, "For the record, the reason I like the Manuscripts and Archives room is because it's too crowded everywhere else."

She glanced at him from the corner of her eye. "Same."

"When I was little, I wanted to live in a library. Everything seemed so loud in my head, and libraries were always quiet," Jasper said. "It was devastating to learn that the librarians didn't actually sleep overnight in the stacks."

"Did you know that the New York public libraries used to have apartments in them for the caretakers?" Melina said. "The one in here was seven rooms. The guy who lived in it had once been a designer for Thomas Edison. The library made him move out in 1941 because they needed to renovate the space into a telephone switchboard and a smoking room."

Jasper's eyes gleamed with interest. "How do you know that?"

"I *read,*" Melina said. "In the *reading room.*"

"Did *you* know," Jasper said, "that the library has over four million books, but also Charles Dickens's favorite letter opener, Jack Kerouac's crutches, and a letter Columbus wrote in 1493 announcing that he'd discovered the New World?"

"Discovered," Melina scoffed. "Fucking Columbus."

Jasper laughed. "Fucking Columbus indeed." He slid a glance toward her. "I, too, read."

They walked through the front doors of the library, smacking into an oppressive wall of heat. "So," Melina said. "Cherry Lane?"

Jasper nodded. "If Mel agrees, of course. What did you think of Tyce?"

"He's . . . enthusiastic," Melina finally said.

"He's a moron," Jasper said cheerfully. "But he gets the job done. What did Mel think of him?"

"Mel wasn't there," Melina said.

Jasper stopped dead on the street. "I thought he wanted his play to actually transfer."

"We do! He does! He just . . ." She cast around for a lie that would sound like the truth. "He's finishing a new piece. Creative types, can't be disturbed when the muse strikes . . ."

But Jasper, still unmoving, narrowed his eyes. "You are lying to me," he said, "and you truly do not have to."

Melina had thought she could not possibly sweat more in this infernal heat than she already was.

"Most new playwrights have to hold down day jobs," Jasper continued. "There's no shame in figuring out how to support your art with a second career."

"Yes!" Melina gushed. "Exactly."

"What does he do?"

She couldn't say that Andre worked at a casting agency, because Jasper knew too many people in the theater world. So instead, Melina blurted the first thought that landed in her mind. "He's a nanny," she said. "That's why he needs me."

Jasper turned the corner. "It's counterintuitive

to have to pay someone else a salary when you're starting out."

"Oh, he doesn't pay me. I do it for room and board."

Jasper raised his eyebrows.

"Not like that. God!" Melina said, horrified. "We knew each other in college." She took a quick, sharp breath and decided to jump off a cliff. "I'm a playwright, too."

Jasper's face was blank, still completely devoid of recognition of who she was or what he had done to her. "And Manhattan is expensive, so you took the job instead of running home to Mama."

Melina struck back like a viper. "My mother's dead," she said flatly.

They were still waiting for the walk signal. Jasper looked at her, then nodded.

"This is where you say you're sorry for my loss," Melina said, incredulous.

He flinched. "I didn't know her, and I don't like lying."

The signal changed, and Jasper stepped off the curb. When Melina didn't follow, he turned. "Coming?"

She started walking. "You know, you're kind of an asshole," she muttered.

"So I've been told."

She realized that they were headed to Bryant Park. Jasper stopped at a kiosk and ordered a coffee and a croissant, then turned to Melina. "What would you like?"

"Oh, I don't —"

"Milk or sugar?" he interrupted. "Gluten-free?"

"Milk and sugar, please. And all the glutens."

He handed her a coffee and asked for a second croissant before continuing across the great lawn of the park, near the mainstage where the Broadway in Bryant Park performance ran on Thursdays. He sat at a round table with two chairs, beside a large metal tablet on the ground. "Do you know what this is?" Jasper asked.

Melina read the dedication to the benefactors of the park, including mayors David Dinkins and Ed Koch. "A commemorative plaque?"

"Yes, but it covers up an escape hatch. The library stacks are under there — eighty-four miles' worth — and there had to be an emergency exit."

Melina broke into a delighted smile. "How did you —"

Jasper shrugged. "I like learning about things that are usually overlooked."

"So do I! It's why I started researching —" Melina broke off abruptly, realizing that she had almost blown her cover.

"Listen," Jasper said, "I know you had a great deal of input into *By Any Other Name.*"

"You . . . do?"

"Personal assistants don't usually have quite as candid an opinion as you do about their

260

boss's work. So what if you researched Bassano for Mel? It doesn't take away from the beauty of his actual writing. And you shouldn't hide your contribution. After all, theater has always been collaborative." He smiled, handing her a croissant from the takeaway bag. "I wrote my thesis on Shakespeare and the theatrical code of conduct. That's likely why *By Any Other Name* spoke to me. Why did it speak to you?"

"Because Emilia Bassano is my ancestor, on my mother's side," Melina said.

"Your late mother," Jasper repeated. His brow pinched. "I'm sorry for your loss."

Melina's gaze snapped to his, to see if he was making fun of her, but he seemed tentative, nervous — as if he still wasn't sure he was saying the right thing at the right time. It was almost as if . . . he was waiting for *her* approval.

She felt a knot inside her give the slightest bit. What had he said before? He didn't like to lie. But Melina was starting to realize that he *couldn't* lie. What you saw, with Jasper Tolle, was what you got. It might be blunt and it might be devastating, but there was something refreshing about cutting through all the bullshit in this business and speaking truth instead of platitudes.

She may not have agreed with the truth he dropped on her ten years ago. But it also occurred to her that she had run away instead of standing up for herself.

For so long he had loomed large as Melina's nemesis. She had grown him to monstrous proportions, and he'd taken up an outsize amount of her emotional and intellectual energy, seeding so much doubt that it crowded out space for anything else.

She'd been one of the people calling him an asshole.

What if she'd been wrong?

Jasper often felt like he had been dropped into a life-size board game without anyone giving him a set of rules. If he knew what was expected, he could memorize it and act accordingly. Otherwise, he invariably made a misstep. And it wasn't just constantly having to recall social cues that were second nature to most people, like a stock response you were apparently supposed to give upon hearing that a near stranger's relative had died. It was constantly wondering if the things that were interesting to him were also interesting to the person caught in the web of his conversation, or if he was just boring them to death.

He'd taken a gamble, leading Andrea to the emergency exit hatch in Bryant Park. But she seemed to be a collector of odd information about the New York Public Library, too, so he'd dragged her to see the plaque that hid the entrance to the bowels of the hidden stacks.

He wasn't quite sure why he wanted or needed to impress a woman who was easily ten years younger than he was, in an entry-level job that involved getting coffee and keeping someone else's schedule. He also didn't know why he, who barely registered important information like which subway line went downtown, knew that Andrea Washington had silvery eyes the color of lightning flashes.

She was smart, that was evident — too smart to be wasting herself as a personal assistant for a young playwright. "You said that theater has always been collaborative," Andrea mused. "Didn't it make you ask, when you were writing your thesis, why Shakespeare was a one-man wonder?" While she ate, she leaned her elbows on the rickety metal table, which delighted Jasper, because that was a rule that he had broken hundreds of times as a child, too.

She went on: "Marlowe collaborated. Middleton. Kyd. Beaumont. Now, everything is copyrighted and licensed and God forbid a word gets changed. Back then, a play was a living thing, getting revised all the time. They wouldn't even bother going back to the original playwright! An author never thought that the work was ruined if it got revised by another writer. In fact, it would have been really, really strange for an Elizabethan playwright *not* to collaborate. But Shakespeare — who had a full-time job, by the way, as an actor — managed to write almost forty plays by himself? That's not just impressive, it's fantastical."

"Well," Jasper countered, "there are scholars who think he collaborated with George Peele on *Titus Andronicus,* and we know he worked with John Fletcher on *Two Noble Kinsmen* —"

"That's if he wrote anything at all," Andrea said. "Shakespeare's will was incredibly detailed. He gave his property to his daughter Susanna, a silver-gilt bowl to his other daughter, Judith . . . twenty-six shillings and eight pence each to three of the actors he worked with so they could buy mourning rings. He gave his clothes to his sister, a sword to the son of a friend, ten pounds to poor people in Stratford, and his second-best bed to his wife — but he didn't bequeath any unfinished manuscripts or works. When Shakespeare died there wasn't a single play with his handwriting on it."

"Not true," Jasper said. "He left behind additions to the play *Sir Thomas More* —"

"All we know is that he edited it. We don't know that he wrote it. His name isn't even *printed* on a play until 1598. There are plenty of documents putting him in Stratford at that time — just not in London's theater world."

Those silver eyes of hers were molten; Jasper found himself leaning closer. "The Henry plays and *Titus Andronicus* have been traced to the 1590s," he said.

"Yes, but not to Shakespeare, specifically. They were performed at the Rose Theatre. The owner, Philip Henslowe, kept meticulous notes of the plays he bought — he had a diary with the names of twenty-seven other playwrights who sold him works, and he wrote down the Henry plays and *Titus Andronicus* — but with an anonymous author. Shakespeare doesn't even appear as an actor on a *pay stub* for the Lord Chamberlain's Men until 1594."

Jasper leaned back in his chair. "You know most of the anti-Stratfordians are utter crackpots," he said.

"Not all of them. A Supreme Court justice — John Paul Stevens — thought there was reasonable doubt that Shakespeare was the true author of the plays. So did Mark Twain, Helen Keller, Sigmund Freud . . . and Malcolm X!"

"Don't get me wrong — you know I love Mel's play. But ultimately, it's still just a hypothetical," Jasper said.

"I'd argue that it's a bigger fiction to say that Shakespeare was the greatest playwright of all time and that he worked alone," Andrea said. "What made him decide out of the blue to write a whole bunch of Italian wedding comedies? Why did he use Italian in his plays, colloquially, though he didn't speak the language? Why do his plays have more allusions to music than any other works from the time, when he didn't even play an instrument? How did he write about court when he was never a courtier, or law when he wasn't a lawyer?"

"Books," Jasper countered.

"But he couldn't just mosey over to the New York Public Library to check them out — and he also didn't have any books in his will when he died." She looked at Jasper, almost sheepish. "The real thing that got me thinking were his female characters. Beatrice . . . Rosalind . . . Viola . . . Portia. They were feminists long before there was ever a women's movement. But Shakespeare, in real life, had two daughters that he never educated. They didn't even know how to write their own names." Melina shook her head. "I just can't believe a man who created such iconic women in his plays wouldn't want his daughters to have the same rights."

Jasper folded his arms. "On the other hand, Emilia Bassano was the first published female poet in England."

"In her forties," Andrea said, reaching across the table to take the second half of Jasper's croissant. "It's rare for a writer to just appear out of nowhere, right? Much more likely that she was writing before that, but not using her own name. Plus, she was highly educated, Italian, came from a family of musicians, and was the mistress of the guy who controlled all theater in England. She was a Jew who had to hide her religion. Every gap in Shakespeare's life or knowledge that has had to be explained away by scholars, she somehow fills."

"The one fact I remember about writing my thesis was that often Shakespeare's name was hyphenated in texts from the era," Jasper said. "It could have been a printing press thing. But hyphenating back then also traditionally signaled a make-believe name."

Andrea considered this, and then shook her head. "I don't think it was a pseudonym, because we know that William Shakespeare existed. There are documents I read — in the Manuscripts and Archives room, as a matter of fact — that showed him selling malt at a great markup in Stratford during a famine. Another document shows a restraining order put out against him, and others show him defaulting on his taxes. The actual proof we have of Shakespeare shows that . . . well . . . he was *not* a great guy."

"You can be 'not a great guy' and still be an extraordinary playwright," Jasper pointed out.

"Then you'd think someone else would have mentioned it," Andrea said. "His son-in-law, John Hall, kept a diary —"

"Which you read in the Manuscripts and Archives room —" Jasper interjected.

She grinned. "Yes. And Hall never mentioned his father-in-law wrote plays. His cousin, who wrote with Shakespeare about land enclosure practices — which were really shady business dealings to get them more private property — never mentioned him as a playwright. We know that all the other great writers at the time were connected because it was an incredibly small world — God, Marlowe was roomies with Thomas Kyd — but none of them ever mentioned Shakespeare as a playwright. And when he died, no one wrote about the loss of a great writer." Andrea met his gaze. "Do you know who Francis Beaumont is?"

"No. Should I?"

"He was a relatively unknown playwright that died seven weeks before Shakespeare and even *he's* buried in Westminster Abbey with Chaucer and Spenser in Poets' Corner." For a moment, her attention was drawn by a toddler who fell, and a mother who swept in like a hawk to carry her away. Then she shook her head. "It just doesn't make sense," Andrea said softly. "How can a brilliant genius with empathy and moral imagination be the same man who's documented for his crooked business practices and dubious character? Either he had multiple personalities . . . or there's another explanation.

"That's what I . . . what *Mel* wanted to get across in the play. I think Shakespeare let people see what they wanted to see, and only a handful of people knew he was not the actual writer. He was just fronting plays for others who used his name. I think the theater community was in on it. When they saw a play with the name Shakespeare on it, it was an inside joke. But over four hundred years later, we've forgotten the punch line."

268

Andrea stopped abruptly, as if she realized how long she'd been talking. She glanced down at the table and her cheeks flooded with color. "Shit. I ate your croissant, didn't I?"

"It's fine."

"Sometimes when I talk about Emilia, I get carried away."

Jasper looked at her. He could remember, as a little boy, being fixated on trains. Adults, thinking they were engaging a child, would ask him about the model set he had set up in the basement, and he would chatter about track and rolling stock, about a sixty-foot Pullman-Standard bulkhead flatcar and code 55 flex track and a Bachmann forty-foot wood reefer, until their eyes glazed over and they drifted away. He knew what it was like to be obsessed with a topic and to think there was no one else in the world who might be as interested.

But when Andrea spoke so passionately about her ancestor, Jasper would have listened forever.

She shifted nervously, spinning her empty coffee cup. "What's that look for?"

"I'm wondering how much I'd have to pay you to be *my* assistant," Jasper said.

"Not gonna happen." Andrea smirked.

"I hope Mel realizes how lucky he is."

"I doubt that's the adjective he'd use."

Their eyes met. Jasper's breath caught in his throat. He wanted to say, *Tell me more. Keep talking. Don't leave.*

He could absolutely understand how she'd compelled Mel Green to write about Emilia Bassano.

"What time is it?" Andrea asked, breaking the spell.

Jasper looked down at his watch. "Three."

Her eyes went wide, and she began to gather up the empty coffee cups and the napkins, the detritus of their conversation. "I'm sorry. I had no idea it was so late — I need to — Mel's expecting me."

"Let me at least walk you . . . where? To the subway?" Jasper said.

"I'm fine. I'm good. I'm *great*." Her voice came out unnaturally high.

He stood, slipping his hands into his pockets as Andrea turned away, her arms full of garbage. "Thanks for lunch," she said.

"Thanks for the company," he replied. "You'll get me a list of times that are good for Mel, for a meeting?"

"Of course. Yes. Because that's my job." She nodded, hurrying away, only to take a few steps before turning to face him. "Will you be at rehearsals?"

Jasper had not planned on it. He had simply wanted to be a matchmaker: to get Mel a decent director and producer, set the show up at a theater, and then to step back.

But he found himself looking at Andrea, his mind buzzing in a way it had not done for years. "Wouldn't miss it," Jasper said.

EMILIA

Remind me why we trust him, then?

KIT

Because you have something he
wants . . . talent.

> THE WOMAN as SERVING
> WENCH enters carrying a
> tray with goblets of
> wine. EMILIA and KIT
> follow her.

THE WOMAN AS SERVING WENCH
(serving the wine)

He did not rise to his feet
when Emilia entered, which meant
either he was not a gentleman, or
he did not consider her a lady.

KIT

Will! This is Mistress Bassano.

EMILIA

Well met, sir.

SHAKESPEARE

Mistress.

                    (takes a drink)

I hear you have a business
proposition.

          KIT
          (exiting)

I'll leave you to it.

          EMILIA

Mr. Shakespeare. You wish to
write, but you cannot.

          SHAKESPEARE

I beg your pardon . . . ?

          EMILIA

Your plays, sir. They have not
found favor.

          SHAKESPEARE

I did not come here for insult —

          EMILIA

I, too, wish to write. But *I*
cannot.

          SHAKESPEARE

And you believe I can help you?

          EMILIA

I believe we can help each other. You wish for everyone to know your name. I wish for no one to know mine.

They clink glasses.

EMILIA
1592

Emilia is 23

Overnight, it seemed, the Puritans had multiplied. Led by Philip Stubbs, always wearing stark black, they were an unkindness of ravens on a crusade to make the Church of England even more authentically Protestant. One of their missions was to shut down the dens of iniquity known as theaters. Their campaign was taking its toll on Lord Hunsdon. He had to not only assuage the fears of the theater companies about these existential threats but also give small concessions to Stubbs and his devotees to mitigate their incessant attacks.

The Puritans claimed that if you attended the theater, you would not be able to tell the difference between what was fiction and what was real. A man might look at a boy actor dressed in the clothes of a woman and think him an actual woman. A person who witnessed a murder onstage might leave the theater with bloodlust and repeat the act, this time in a tavern with a real knife. A morally upright woman might leave a performance depicting infidelity and become a strumpet. Theater also stole time away that people could be using to worship God.

Emilia understood the true motivation: a play might make its viewers *think.* And when people *thought,* instead of blindly following the Gospel, they escaped from your control.

She did her best to make the Lord Chamberlain forget the Puritans, but it was difficult when they congregated outside performances, shouting their vitriol and passing out pamphlets. It was hard, too, to argue against a group that claimed to have God's will on their side. She found herself putting on the best performances in all of London, in her bedchamber for an audience of one. Like Scheherazade, she would weave escapist stories for Hunsdon as she stroked his hair and massaged his temples. Sometimes she removed her clothing piece by piece. Other times she simply played dice with him, using grapes as currency for bets. But no matter what she did to divert Hunsdon's attention, it was not enough, and he carried his frustration with Stubbs into court, into his interactions with servants, and into their bed.

It was one night after she lit her hidden Sabbath candles that Emilia came up with a strategy to help the Lord Chamberlain. She found him in his study, plays scattered across his writing table. There were dark circles under his eyes, and he did not look up when she entered. Silently she slipped around to the back of his chair and dug her fingers into the tight muscles of his shoulders.

Hunsdon sighed and closed his eyes, covering her hand with one of his own. "You are too good to me, my dear."

"I do not like seeing you this way. You are near dropping from exhaustion."

"Ah, well." He removed his spectacles. "There are so many hours in a day and Her Majesty believes all of mine belong to her. And yet the Puritans claim I am too decadent to do any meaningful work."

"That is precisely the reason for my errand," Emilia said. "I wish to invite Philip Stubbs to dinner."

"To poison him, dare I hope?"

She smiled, slipping onto his lap. "No, to win him over." When Hunsdon opened his mouth to respond, she placed her fingers over his lips. "He cannot hate that which he knows, my lord. What better way to convince him that you are not a heathen than to invite him to your own home, quote the Word of God, and ask him to preach the Gospel at your own chapel on the Christian Sabbath? Then, over a meal that is plain and humble, you can convince him that the messages you allow onstage are meant solely to inspire and reinforce godliness in the theatergoer."

She reached into her bodice and pulled out the cross she wore around her neck — to Emilia, essentially costume jewelry. "Naturally, I shall be at your side as your dutiful helpmeet."

"That is a spirited idea, my sweet," Hunsdon said. "Perhaps some good could come of it, yet . . ."

Emilia waited. "Yet . . ."

He sighed. "I do not think a Puritan will consent to crossing the threshold of a man who shares his bed with a woman who is not his wife."

Emilia felt her cheeks blaze. Ten years with Hunsdon had made her complacent about the origins of their relationship. "Of course," she managed.

"Emilia —" Hunsdon grasped her hand.

"It was but a foolish thought." She pulled away, unable to meet his eye. "Beg pardon, my lord," Emilia said, and she fled the room.

As Emilia had been working on the play *Arden of Faversham,* she told Marlowe that there was only one thing she would not compromise on as they collaborated: that Alice, the murderous wife, must have more lines than any other figure in the play. She told Kit it was because Alice had the most to explain to an audience . . . but it was more than that. It was as if the character she brought to life on a page must be able to speak freely in a way that Emilia herself couldn't.

The plot was based on the real-life murder of Arden. After several abortive attempts to kill him, Alice and her lover, Mosby, hired two former soldiers — Black Will and Shakebag — to do the deed, but they bungled the job, too.

That afternoon Emilia sat at the Falcon Inn beside Kit, begging him to read aloud a scene she had been struggling with. Empty tankards, mostly Kit's, sat between them. Buying one round after another helped him (he said) get into character. He was reading the role of Alice's lover, Mosby, as Emilia read Alice. Act III began with a soliloquy in which Mosby talked of their scheme to do away with Arden. But then his discontent turned to Alice, supposedly the object of his affections. *"'Tis fearful sleeping in a serpent's bed,"* Kit read. *"And I will cleanly rid my hands of her."* He reared back, turning to Emilia. "Now he wants to murder his ladylove, too?"

"Yes," Emilia confirmed. "Just go on."

He continued reading Mosby's part until the character of Alice entered, holding a prayer book ("Dramatic irony," Kit praised), repenting her affair and her violent thoughts.

"It is not love that loves to anger love," Kit read.

"It is not love that loves to murder love," Emilia replied.

He feigned shock, as Mosby would, thinking Alice had read his mind. *"How mean you that?"*

"Thou knowest how dearly Arden loved me."

"And then?" Kit said.

"And then . . . conceal the rest, for 'tis too bad, Lest that my words be carried with the wind, And published in the world to both our shames."

Kit pushed down the paper. "Are you still acting as Alice, or was that Emilia's voice?" He chucked her under the chin. "Second thoughts about our project, Mouse?"

She did not know what to say. Was it foolish to think that she might get away with writing a play that might one day be performed in public? Or was she tempting fate, like the character of Alice, trying to change an implacable set of rules and expectations?

Emilia knew that Kit thrived on skating at the edge of impropriety. He would probably welcome a scandal. But he was a man, and he would weather it, and go on to write a new play.

On the other hand, Emilia would be shunned. It would not matter if she created a masterpiece. It would only matter that she had dared to create it in the first place.

She did not understand why a woman's accomplishment had to come at the price of a man's worth — as if there were a finite amount of success in the universe, as if letting another into that sacred space meant someone already there would be evicted.

For once, she could not find the words to respond to Kit — so instead, she skipped down the paper and borrowed Alice's. *"A fount once troubled is not thickened still. Be clear again, I'll ne'er more trouble thee."*

Kit wrapped an arm around her. "You should not worry so." He flattened his hands on the table. "Now, why do you waste your time? I cannot stand the thought of this scene remaining unwritten. How shall I sleep not knowing if Mosby and Alice will keep arguing or if they will strengthen their resolve to commit murder?"

Emilia laughed. "Mayhap both?"

He yanked at the back of her chair so she was forced to stand. "Mouse," Kit commanded. "Go home and write."

For months Emilia and Marlowe had worked out a system of communication, by which notes telling her when and where to meet were concealed within other notes and dispatched from seamstresses, milliners, and other merchants who might have business with the lady of Somerset House. She received what she thought was another missive from him one morning — until she cracked the wax seal and saw a familiar, elegant hand that made her heart start to pound.

If thou cry war, there is no peace for me; I will

do penance for offending thee. Paris Garden, dusk.

Emilia spilled the cup of ale she had been drinking.

"My dear?" Hunsdon said, looking up from a sheaf of documents.

"Just a mercer," Emilia lied, "telling me that the bolt of fabric I ordered has arrived."

"It must be quite the color if that is your reaction," he mused. "I look forward to seeing you garbed in it."

It had been almost three years since Emilia had last seen Southampton, or rather, three years since his last sight of *her* servicing Hunsdon.

"Shall we?" Hunsdon asked, standing and holding out his arm for Emilia.

It was Sunday, so they made their way to the small chapel at Somerset House. Emilia knew how to go through the motions; it was just another part to play. The Anglicans believed that man was wicked by nature, and that no matter what good you did in the world, you were always going to be a sinner. The only way to salvation was to ask for God's grace.

It seemed strange to her to think of existence as a pit you could never crawl out of.

Then again, maybe these Christians had it right. Because as she sat, listening to a priest read from the Book of Common Prayer, she was thinking about the Earl of Southampton.

In that moment, she understood fully what

made Alice Arden kill her husband. Love was a religion all its own, one that could damn you or save you or turn you into a zealot.

Emilia glanced down at the hymnal on her lap and thought of Alice entering with a prayer book in the scene she had read with Marlowe. She thought of Southampton's note, and her mind started composing.

> *If thou cry war, there is no peace for me;*
> *I will do penance for offending thee.*
> *And burn this prayer-book, where I here use*
> *The holy word that had converted me.*
> *See, Wriothesley, I will tear away the leaves,*
> *And all the leaves, and in this golden cover*
> *Shall thy sweet phrases and thy letters dwell;*
> *And thereon will I chiefly meditate*
> *And hold no other sect but such devotion.*

If Southampton wanted to see her, it did not mean he loved her still.

Then again, it didn't *not* mean that.

Although Emilia had been worried about how to slip away from Lord Hunsdon that Sunday evening, he was summoned to court by the Queen, so it turned out to be easier to leave Somerset House than she'd expected. She took a servant along and paid coin to have the maid meet her back at the Paris Garden landing on the Thames three hours after sunset. Then she hid herself deeper in the voluminous folds of her cloak and crossed to the bridge where she'd met Southampton years before.

She almost walked right past him.

He caught her arm, and the motion caused her hood to fall back from her face. "Mistress," he said.

Southampton was no longer a green boy of sixteen. He was nearly twenty, wide-shouldered, a full head taller than Emilia. But oh, his hair still tumbled over his brow in auburn waves; his eyes glittered like the sun on the sea.

"I did not know if you would come," he said quietly.

"I did not think that you would ask," she replied.

The memory of their last encounter flooded her with shame. Nothing had changed since then. She was still a courtesan. Southampton was still a peer who would take a noble wife.

They stood inches away from each other, and miles apart.

The Earl released her and clasped his hands behind his back. "Will you walk with me?"

"Of course, my lord." Emilia fell into step beside him. "How go your studies?"

They crossed the bridge, stepping into the marshy fields of the garden. "Well. I am to accompany Her Majesty to Oxford," Southampton said.

"What an honor," Emilia replied, but her blood beat out a different response: *He is*

leaving, when we have only just been reunited.
She could feel his gaze. "The days have been temperate, have they not?" she said, staring forward.

"Emilia." Southampton stopped moving. *"Emilia."* He waited until she faced him. "Is this what we are to be to each other?"

Her throat was dry. "What would you have us be?"

He touched her cheek. "Not acquaintances who talk about the weather. I know how you taste. I know the sounds you make when you —"

She pulled away from him. "Nothing has changed."

"There you are wrong," Southampton said. *"I've* changed." He smiled ruefully. "Suffice it to say I am a bit older, and perhaps a bit wiser." He looked down at the ground between them, and then met her gaze again. "You cannot promise me a future and I will not ask for that which you cannot give. But we are both here, and I have missed you, Emilia, so bloody much."

They crashed together. Southampton's hands were in her hair, pulling the pins free. Her palm flattened against his chest, holding his heartbeat. Their kiss was a collision. He tasted of mead and despair.

"Not here," Southampton groaned, wrapping an arm around Emilia's waist and pulling her deeper into the garden. The dark settled around them with a sigh, and he guided her down onto a thick carpet of moss.

For long moments, they lay on their sides, her skirts ballooned over Southampton's legs, his hand stroking the curve from her ear to her collarbone. Emilia drank him in, marking all the changes three years had wrought. When she felt herself drowning in regret, she pulled him closer and stole his breath into her lungs.

Finally, when they spoke, their voices tangled and they both laughed. "I am sorry," Emilia said. "For how we ended."

He brought her fingers to his lips. "I am sorry, too . . . for forcing your hand." Southampton's eyes caught hers.

She nodded.

"I also cannot claim that I have been chaste," he said.

As much as that felt like a blow, Emilia had hardly expected otherwise. "I cannot claim that I have been chaste, either," she said, with a smile.

He grinned, and his dimples deepened. Emilia flung herself onto her back, arms wide. "Is something amiss?" he asked.

"No," she said. "I am just . . . happy."

He rolled on top of her. "I could make you happier," he said.

Emilia wrapped her arms around his neck. "Challenge accepted."

She turned and sat astride him. She had

forgotten how, in their lovemaking, she had often taken the lead — not just because she was the one with more experience, but because Southampton was secure enough to allow and enjoy it.

Emilia tried to memorize the angle of his jaw, the temperature of his skin, the silk of his hair in her hands. Being in his arms felt both familiar and fresh, like she was reliving a memory and making a new one at the same time.

After, with her heart still racing, she lay on her back looking up at the night sky, her fingers tangled with Southampton's. The moon made a marble statue of him, a knight in immortal repose on a tomb. In another place and another time, maybe, they would have been able to live together. To marry and have children. He would have been holding her hand when she took her last breath and exhaled the truest statement of her life: *I have loved you most.*

Without opening his eyes, he said, "I can *hear* your mind churning."

"I shall try to think more quietly, my lord," Emilia murmured, smiling faintly.

Southampton rolled to his elbow and touched a finger between her brows. "What do you think on that makes you frown so?"

"Death."

"Mine?" He buried his face in the curve of her neck. "Then let me try to please you better. . . ."

"Mine," Emilia corrected.

"Then mine as well, for there is no life without you."

They both knew it was not true, but she played along. "When I die, then, we shall cut you out in stars, and you will make the face of heaven so fine that all the world will be in love with night."

He kissed her. "I do not need the adoration of the world," Southampton said. "Just yours."

Emilia believed that somewhere deep within her, there must be a fatal flaw. How else to account for the fact that, even though she resided in the luxury of Somerset House and had the favor of one of the most important men in the country, it was not enough?

Lord Hunsdon pulled off his spectacles and rubbed his eyes. "These playwrights," he mused, "never seem to write in a good hand. I shall go blind reading this."

Emilia frowned at the paper on her lap desk. "I fear I am no cleaner with my pen."

"What do you write tonight, Emilia?" Hunsdon asked. "Another poem?"

She was working on her play, but she nodded.

His eyes twinkled. "Might this old man be the subject?"

She glanced down at the lines she had just penned: *Frown not on me when we meet in heaven; in heaven I'll love thee, though on earth I did not.*

It was Alice's line, after her lover finally murdered her husband. Or maybe it was just Emilia's conscience.

She looked up at Hunsdon. "Yes, my lord. You are my muse."

He got to his feet and held out his hand. "Let us retire then, that I might inspire you." Hunsdon pulled her into his arms and kissed her. For a moment, Emilia went still. It had been so long. As he grew older, he'd been less interested in sexual intimacy.

He drew back. "Is aught amiss?"

She cupped his cheek. Love was not always passion — it was fondness, too. "Not at all," Emilia said, and she followed him to her chamber.

Hunsdon undressed her slowly in front of the window. Then he turned Emilia, thrusting into her from behind. She stared at a pane of glass in the window, thinking of how it held only the last fingerprint that had been pressed against it, erasing whoever had touched it before.

One day, a note from Southampton arrived that asked Emilia to meet not at their secret spot in Paris Garden but at a new address, in Cheapside. She arrived on Gutter Lane, where a door swung open to reveal a man with wild curly hair, garbed only in a loose white shirt and trousers. "Mistress Bassano," he said. "Come in, come in."

She drew back. "I am not in the habit of entering the homes of strangers, sir," Emilia murmured. Just then, Southampton's bright hair appeared over the man's shoulder.

"This is no stranger," he said, smiling.

The man executed a small bow. "Nicholas Hilliard at your service, mistress."

"The painter?" Emilia asked. Hilliard had captured the likeness of the Queen many times, but Her Majesty had never recognized him as the royal portrait painter. Court gossip suggested that without the Queen's favor he'd never attained a certain stature, and was always in need of funds. He had a rare talent, but anyone who could afford to pay three pounds could commission one of his miniatures.

Emilia looked at him appraisingly. Disheveled attire or no, she felt a strange kinship with this man, who was doing what he had to to survive.

"You bring me a gift," Hilliard said, bowing over Emilia's hand. "My art can only approximate beauty such as this."

"I don't understand," Emilia said.

"I wish him to paint a miniature of you," Southampton explained, and then he lowered his voice so only she would hear it. "I already carry you close to my heart," he said. "I hoped to carry your likeness there, too."

She had never sat for a portrait. Artwork had decorated nearly every surface of the Countess's home, as well as Hunsdon's and the Queen's palaces. But the people who were commemorated in paintings were titled, wealthy, important. Not poor wards, courtesans, or illicit lovers.

It was one thing to meet Southampton secretly and to leave Paris Garden without any record of their coupling except a patch of crushed grass and a memory. It was another thing to create a tangible token of their love; it left them exposed to anyone who might find her portrait tucked into Southampton's doublet.

She would not risk humiliating Hunsdon that way.

"Henry," she said softly. "I cannot."

Southampton met her gaze. "If I cannot have you," he murmured, "will you deny me this substitute?"

God help her, she was selfish. There was a part of her that wanted to lay claim to Southampton even when they were apart. She bit her lip and nodded. "All right," she conceded. "But you leave me at a disadvantage, then, with no likeness of *you*."

To her surprise, he blushed. "I have taken a liberty," Southampton admitted, "hoping that you might wish for that very thing." He drew her deeper into Hilliard's home, to a room with light streaming through the open shutters. Another painter was mixing colors on a palette as they entered. "We shall sit together, and Master Hilliard and his apprentice shall each paint a miniature."

The second man inclined his head. "Isaac Oliver at your service, madam," he said.

"Let us start," Hilliard said, "before we lose the light."

As if, Emilia thought, that was all they stood to lose.

A month later, when Emilia finished her draft of *Arden of Faversham,* she sent Marlowe the foul copy in its entirety, hidden inside a pamphlet from the Puritans that Hunsdon had discarded. She spent a week pacing the halls of Somerset House, waiting for Kit's feedback.

She wandered the prayer labyrinth on the house's grounds, her thoughts running in circles.

She visited the falconer and fed mice to the hawks.

She attended a play at the Rose with Hunsdon.

She visited the milliners at the Royal Exchange and purchased a headpiece she did not need.

She sat in the solar, embroidering distractedly, and more often untangling knots of thread.

During that time there were messages from Lord Burghley and Sir Robert Cecil, and one from Emilia's old friend Isabella. She was no longer the mistress of the Baron but lived in relative comfort from the settlement he gave her upon their parting.

Finally, one morning, a message came from Kit, instructing Emilia to meet him at the Falcon Inn at half past six.

Emilia left word that she was visiting her cousin, then dressed in her borrowed boy's clothes, tugged a cap low on her brow, and exited through the servants' door. She picked her way through the tangled streets of London, past vendors hawking damsons and garlic, fine bone lace and silk garters, starch to clear one's complexion. By the time she reached the Falcon Inn, Kit was well into his cups. He was flirting shamelessly with a young apprentice. "Emile," he drawled. "I feared you had forgotten me." He plucked a goblet from the table and poured from a bottle of wine. He handed it to her, then pulled from his coat the sheaf of pages she had sent him. "Drink up, darling. You're going to need it."

Emilia's heart sank, and she swallowed the entire cup. "Is it terrible, then?"

"On the contrary," Kit said. "It's *excellent.*"

She swatted him. "Why did you make me drink, then?"

"Because now you have to actually *do* something with it."

"I thought *you* were going to do something with it. That was the point of collaborating."

Kit drained his own goblet. "The point of collaborating was to give you confidence in the talent you naturally have. If I bring the play to Henslowe at the Rose, he will assume I wrote it."

"So?"

"So I can *already* get a play published. This is about *you* getting a play published." He slid his glance toward her. "If only, say, you had the ability to slip an anonymous foul copy onto the desk of the Lord Chamberlain."

Emilia paled. She could just imagine what would happen if Stubbs, the Puritan, learned that the mistress of Lord Hunsdon was also a playwright — it would confirm his every theory about the moral corruptness of theater.

"I cannot do that, Kit," she whispered.

If Hunsdon ever discovered that this was Emilia's writing, the scandal would have repercussions that would reach all the way to the court. At the least, she'd be turned out without a penny. At the worst, she'd be imprisoned by the Queen for writing about a wife's murder of a husband.

She took the manuscript back and began to rewrap it in the folds of the Puritans' pamphlet. REPENT, its title screamed. "This was a terrible idea," she said.

Kit took the pamphlet from her hand. "What is this?"

"You are drunk," Emilia accused.

293

"And you are brilliant." He smacked her with the pamphlet. *What is this?*"

"Rubbish from the Puritans."

"Only if you're looking at the outside." Kit raised his brows. "Mouse," he said. "All you need is a cover."

When Southampton could, he sent for Emilia. The more frequently they met, the more varied their rendezvous spots. Sometimes they sat on their mantle of moss in Paris Garden; sometimes they met at the bearbaiting pits packed with throngs of spectators; once he brought a bottle of wine and bread and cheese and they picnicked in Pike Gardens, watching the freshwater fish swim in lazy circles in the ponds. They walked; they dreamed; they laughed; they coupled. Whenever Emilia boarded the ferry to cross the Thames after one of their illicit trysts, she told herself it was likely the last time. She pretended that this would prepare her for disappointment.

She knew that he was never without the miniature Hilliard's student had painted of her. It was pinned inside his doublet, and she felt its sharp filigreed edges when she pressed her body close to his. The artist's apprentice had painted Emilia against an indigo field, her dark hair piled high above an elaborate collar of lace, a strand of Italian Murano glass beads wrapped around her throat.

Southampton had asked Hilliard not to

paint him on his signature field of blue but instead on a background of black. His hand was inside his open shirt, covering his heart, as if he could keep it safe for her. On the back of the painting, flush against its ivory casing, was a tiny image of the six of hearts — the soulmate card, the symbol in cartomancy of a love you were destined to have . . . and to lose.

Southampton had not just given Emilia his likeness — he'd given her the entire story of their bittersweet relationship. She could not risk hiding the miniature of Southampton in her own *bodies* but instead had cut a slit in her mattress and kept it hidden inside — where it was the first thing she looked at when she woke, the last thing she touched before she went to sleep.

One night as Southampton was helping her restore her clothing in Paris Garden after they'd made love, he paused in the act of tying up her laces. "What if we spent the night together?"

"We spend many nights together."

"I have often said good night to you," Southampton said. "But never good morning."

They made a plan. She merely mentioned to Hunsdon that Isabella had fallen ill and did not have anyone to look after her, then dressed in a simple kirtle and walking boots. As directed by Southampton, she went to Gray's Inn, one of the Inns of Court where lawyers trained, and found a horse that was tied to a post, stamping impatiently beside a hostler. It was not until the man turned that she saw it was the Earl, outfitted in rough homespun instead of silk and velvet, his face hidden by a brimmed cap. "I almost did not recognize you," she said.

"That, darling, is the point." He grinned, taking her small satchel and securing it before giving her a leg up. He swung into the saddle behind her, and the horse set off into a trot.

When they reached the Great North Road, the gelding lengthened into a gallop. The buildings gave way to fields, some grazing sheep and others untamed, thick with gorse and wildflowers. Mud flew up from the hooves of the horse, spattering their legs. Emilia had learned to sit a horse when she was a child at Grimsthorpe, but she had been only competent at best. Now, she let herself rock in the cradle of Southampton's body as they rode for several hours.

He sang to her in a lovely baritone — was there anything about this man that was not beautiful? He told her stories about how an acrobat visiting court had taught him to ride while standing on the saddle when he was a teen. He told her how, as a child, he'd fallen from a tree and broken his arm and now always knew when it would rain by the ache in his elbow. He would *not* tell her their destination. When they finally stopped at a coaching inn called The Bull, Emilia couldn't feel her bottom and she slipped off the horse into Southampton's arms. Through the open doorway she could hear other travelers in the tavern, having a meal or a respite. "Have we come here for the ale, my lord?" Emilia teased.

"Not your lord," he said quietly. "Just your husband."

At his words, her belly clenched. He pulled her through the doorway, where he approached the innkeeper. "Have you a spare room for the night for my wife and me?"

"Aye, sir," the man replied. He pocketed the coins Southampton offered and led them up a narrow set of stairs. He opened a door, revealing a small bed, a small table and chairs, and a banked fire.

"Very good," Southampton said. "Might we have a tray brought up for supper?"

Emilia wondered how the innkeeper could not tell that Southampton was a peer. It was in the timbre of his voice, his bearing, his confidence. When the innkeeper left, promising to send his daughter up with some food and ale, Southampton unfastened her cloak and set it aside on a chair.

"Is this our destination, then?" she asked.

"No," he said. "Like everyone else here, we are in the middle of a journey."

"To where?"

He kissed her. "Not where, but when. A moment in which I am just Henry, and you are just Emilia."

They broke apart at a knock on the door, and Southampton answered it to take the tray. He set it on the table and came back to her, looping his arms around her waist. "Shall we not eat?" Emilia asked.

"I am hungrier for my wife."

She smiled. "Ah, but your wife is so tired from keeping your house, mending your clothing, and cooking your meals. She deserves to dine like a fine lady, does she not?"

He tumbled them onto the bed in a flurry of laughter and limbs. Emilia valued this more than anything else — his playfulness — since she had never had the luxury of a childhood. "How foolish of me," he agreed. "You are near run ragged by our brood."

Something inside Emilia softened. "We have babes?"

"Aye," Southampton said. "A little girl who looks just like her mother."

She framed his face with her hands. "And a boy with eyes like the sea."

As he peeled off her clothing and she unraveled his, Emilia realized that they had never been truly bare in each other's company. When they met for their trysts, they were still in public places, coming together furtively and fast. Yet this disrobing went beyond their bodies. Stripped of their titles and their roles, they could start fresh. They could belong only to each other.

It was not until afterward, when Southampton's thumb wiped away her tears, that
she realized she had been crying. "What is it,
sweet?"

Emilia forced herself to smile. "It is just that
I am happy. So much so that it has nowhere
else to go."

It was only a half-truth. This was not happiness she felt. But emotions *did* have a way of
spilling out when they could not be contained
in your heart. You could love someone even
when you were apart. You could grieve before
you lost him.

Marlowe met Emilia at the Bear Garden,
where their conversation would go completely
unnoticed by the hordes of spectators who
had come to see the bearbaiting. After Kit had
placed his bet, they sat on a granite bench,
watching a beast famous for its longevity and
strength — the bear named Sackerson — led
into the pit and chained to a stake by its leg.

"Oxford has been writing plays for a while
now," Kit told her.

"The Earl of Oxford?" Emilia said, shocked.

"See? You are not the only scandalous author, Mouse. Anyway, he manages a small
group of writers who all wish to remain anonymous for various reasons."

"Like whom?"

"If I told you that, I wouldn't be very
good at keeping secrets, would I?" Kit said.

"It's almost like a scriptorium from ancient times — they all collaborate, but they cannot sell the work under their own names, so they have someone else front the plays for them."

"Who?"

"A businessman-cum-actor who works with Lord Strange's Men, who is always looking to make a quick profit. Apparently, he has delusions of being a writer but isn't particularly gifted. Still, Oxford pays him to sell the plays to various theater owners. Since he's a real person, working in that industry, it seems less fishy." He turned his attention to the ring as a huddle of bulldogs appeared, ready to be unleashed to torment the bear. "His name is Shakespeare."

"Shakespeare," Emilia repeated. "We met him. At the guildhall."

Kit considered this, frowning. "So we did. Well, clearly he was unremarkable. Which means he's probably perfect for Oxford's aims." He glanced at her. "Perhaps you could become part of Oxford's stable of writers. I could set up a meeting."

Emilia blanched. She did not need an introduction to the Earl of Oxford; he knew exactly who she was. The Baron was distantly related to him, and she had sat across from him at Somerset House when he'd dined there.

And it was Oxford's daughter that

Southampton had refused to marry.

"It could get back to Hunsdon," Emilia said. "It's too risky."

From the bear pit came an unholy roar and the frantic barks of the bulldogs as they tore at the chained animal. "Well then," Kit replied, "I suggest we go straight to the source."

"Shakespeare?"

"He's agreed to broker other people's plays. Why not yours?"

"Other *men*," she qualified.

"From what I have heard about this fellow, coin shall speak more loudly than all else."

One of the bulldogs drew blood, and the bear swiped at him. The crowd surged.

"If you wish to hide your femininity," Kit said, "Shakespeare seems the perfect choice. The name already sounds like a pseudonym, does it not? *Shake spear.*" He beat his chest. "How very phallic."

By now, the bear had killed two of the bulldogs and the rest were whimpering at the far end of the pit. Sackerson would live to fight another day. Kit cheered, standing up to collect his winnings. He turned back for a moment, to where Emilia still was weighing his suggestion. "Come now, Mouse. What have you got to lose?"

Emilia watched the bear — wounded, bleeding — being led out of the pit, still in chains. She looked up at Kit. "Yes," she said. "Let us meet."

Emilia's palms were sweating. She was dressed as befitted a lady, which she had never done when meeting Marlowe. This was not their usual haunt, but the White Hart. She stood under the eaves of the building, protected from the pouring rain, in a cobbled courtyard where plays were sometimes performed. Kit was somewhere inside with William Shakespeare, and when he was ready, he would come out and get her.

She wiped her hands on the silk of her skirts. She had not worn any jewelry because, Kit said, rich people have no leg to stand on in a negotiation. But she wished she had her glass beads, if only to fidget with.

The door opened and Kit appeared, rolling his eyes. "This one's a beef-wit. If I have to listen to any more of his pribble, I shall impale myself on my own dagger."

Emilia smiled, feeling a swell of gratitude for her best friend, who — she knew — was trying to make her less nervous. "Remind me why we trust him, then?"

"Because you have something he wants," Kit said. "Talent." He pulled her into the inn, away from the stares of those drinking in the main hall and toward a smaller, private room he had secured in the back. "Remember. You will give him a cut for the use of his name, but since you're providing the product, you are the one with the upper hand."

Emilia nodded, swallowing. She walked through the door as if she were being presented at court — head held high, shoulders back. At a table, drinking from a goblet of wine, was Shakespeare.

She hadn't paid much attention to him the last time they met, but now she let herself mark his dark, deep-set eyes, his too-thin brows, his ever-receding hairline. He had a shrub of a mustache and a few wispy strands aspiring to be a goatee. He wore a lace collar at the top of his doublet, but it was stained with what looked like gravy. He did not rise to his feet when she entered, which meant one of two things: he was not a gentleman, or he did not consider her a lady.

"Will," Kit said, "this is Mistress Bassano. The playwright."

"Well met," Emilia said.

"Mistress," Shakespeare replied, inclining his head. "I hear you have a business proposition."

He was direct; she would give him that. And he might have been a buffoon in his writerly pride, but that didn't mean he wasn't a shrewd negotiator.

Kit clapped his hands together. "Splendid! I leave you to it." Behind Shakespeare's back, he gave Emilia an encouraging smile, and then he left, closing the door to the private room behind him.

Her pulse raced. Was it utter foolishness to put her trust in a man she did not know?

"Marlowe speaks highly of you," Shakespeare said, and she caught the flash of jealousy in his eyes.

Emilia nodded. "He is a good friend and a better teacher."

"You are fortunate, then, to stand in his shadow."

"I prefer the shadows, sir," she confessed.

He smiled. "You speak as one who has never taken a bow in front of a fulsome audience."

"I was raised in a family of performers. Fame is fleeting, in the moment. True art is creating something that lingers in the minds of the audience."

"Indeed, it is why I aim to be a playwright *and* a player."

Emilia met his gaze evenly. "I have read some of your work, Master Shakespeare."

For a moment, they just stared at each other.

"You wish to write," she continued. "But you cannot."

His eyebrows rose. "I beg your pardon?"

"Your plays, sir," she said softly. "They have . . . not found favor."

Shakespeare started to rise from his chair. "I did not come here for insult —"

"I, too, wish to write," Emilia interrupted, "but *I* cannot."

She did not have to explain why; it was obvious. "I believe we can help each other," Emilia said. "You wish for everyone to know your name; I wish for no one to know mine."

Being a playwright was not a prestigious career, but regardless, fame was not the point. It was the work that mattered. Male playwrights who wrote women — Kit included! — didn't give them the nuance that Emilia could. She believed words written by a woman about women might allow audiences to see them more fully, to realize that they had thoughts and dreams and worth.

The fact that she had to borrow a man's name to do that was a small price to pay.

"If you front my work, you can claim authorship," Emilia offered. "In return I receive half the profit."

"A play may sell for forty shillings," Shakespeare answered. "I would give you ten."

"Twenty."

"Fifteen," he said. "It is, after all, my name on the cover, should it not be a success."

A shilling could buy one a loaf of bread — or a maid's silence, when you were sneaking to Paris Garden to meet an earl.

"It is a deal," she agreed.

"Not quite yet," Shakespeare hedged. "I should like to test the merchandise before I hawk it."

"I do not understand, sir."

"You give me a play . . . I shall try to sell it

anonymously. If it proves popular, then the next shall bear my name."

It seemed fair. "We are agreed, then," Emilia said.

From the satchel she carried, she removed the foul copy of *Arden of Faversham*. Handing it to Shakespeare felt unnatural, like she was cutting away a piece of her own flesh.

She thought of her mother, on the day Emilia had been handed over as a ward to the Countess. Her mother had pushed her toward the noblewoman and had walked away without a glance. Emilia had felt pain at this lack of emotion — but perhaps her mother had only been forcing herself to be stoic, as Emilia was now.

She recalled Mary Sidney's advice — that to be successful as a woman, one would have to be invisible.

Emilia thrust the manuscript toward Shakespeare before she could stop herself. "What is the subject?" he asked, scanning the first few pages.

"A woman who kills her husband so she can be with her lover," Emilia said.

"Does she get punished?" Shakespeare asked.

"Yes. With death."

"Hmm," he said. "People will like that." He stood, folded the papers inside his doublet for safekeeping, and walked out of the small room.

Only then did Emilia let herself exhale. Her hands, which had been clenched tight in her lap, shook like aspen leaves.

The door flung open and Kit strode toward her. "Well?" he demanded.

Emilia opened her mouth . . . and vomited at his feet.

The first death in London from plague that year came in August, but it was not the first time the disease had ravaged the city. As in 1563, the Queen and her court left London in September for Hampton Palace. The rich escaped to country homes. The poor died.

Thirty years earlier the position of Saturn in the night sky — passing through parts of the constellations of Cancer and Leo — had been credited as the cause of the disease. Now, the same pattern was in the heavens, and no one believed that London would escape unscathed.

The theaters had been shut down since June because of a riot, but they were to remain closed because of fear of infection. As a result, the players and the playwrights toured through the countryside, hoping to avoid getting sick and to find audiences. Hunsdon was busy late into the night dealing with the chaos as theater companies broke apart and re-formed, doing whatever it took to stay financially sound. He planned to take Emilia to Hampton before the end of the week.

She'd found him in his study, ink blotting his hands and the sleeve of his shirt, as he signed paper after paper granting charters to these new, amorphous theatrical groups. "Henry," Emilia said softly. "Rest a while."

"In a bit," he muttered.

"You will grow weak, and fall ill," she chided.

He lifted his quill and stared bleakly at the mess before him. "What if they are in the right?"

"Who?"

"Stubbs, and the Puritans," Hunsdon said. "They claim the plague is the rot from theater infesting the city."

The pious saw the rampant illness as a punishment from God. But it was hard to follow that logic when priests — who were often among the only ones who would attend someone sick or dying — found themselves infected as well.

There was a scratch at the door, and Emilia looked over her shoulder to find Kit standing beside a servant. "Begging yer pardon, milord, but the gentleman insisted on seeing you."

"Marlowe," Hunsdon said. "I'd have thought you gone by now."

"I leave tomorrow, my lord," Kit replied, sliding a glance toward Emilia. "Mistress."

Emilia nodded, pretending, too, that they were strangers. But she felt sick with the thought that Kit was leaving. She had sent missives to Southampton without hearing anything in return and feared for his health. She couldn't stand the thought of losing everyone she loved.

"It is only due to my imminent departure that I took the liberty to come to you in private," Kit said. "It is my hope that my newest work might pass the censor's eye in time for it to be staged as soon as the theaters reopen."

"A new work?" Hunsdon asked, leaning back in his chair.

"I call it *Doctor Faustus.*"

Emilia had read multiple drafts of the play as Kit was writing it. It was about a man who made a pact with the Devil. Her editorial suggestions made him focus not only on Faustus's ambition but on the cost of sin — which would catch up to you no matter how you tried to evade it.

She should know.

"I shall leave you to your work, my lord," Emilia said, dipping a slight curtsy to Hunsdon and exiting. But instead of heading to her chamber, she slipped out the front door of Somerset House and waited in the shade beneath a line of trees, knowing that Kit wouldn't leave without seeing her.

The Strand was eerily quiet; searchers had already begun to comb through the homes of London to find the sick. They were older matrons, dispensable, who earned about five

309

pence for each plague victim they identified. Then the house's door would be marked with a red cross and sealed with the sick and still healthy inside until the plague had passed, or everyone was dead. Some of the very ill were taken to the pesthouse or hospitals, but if you were admitted there, you were likely to exit as a corpse. Streets that had been full were now deserted, for fear of contagion.

In less than a quarter of an hour, Kit appeared. "Your business is finished?" Emilia asked.

Kit snorted. "I might have sent him the foul copy by messenger, Mouse. My business was with *you*."

Her expression softened. "Must you really leave?"

"Not all of us get to escape in the company of the Queen," Kit joked.

"But it could be ages until I see you again."

"I know. Which is why I came." Kit slid his hand into the fastenings of his doublet and pulled out a printed pamphlet. He passed it to her.

The Lamentable and True Tragedy of M. Arden of Kent.

She gasped, covering her mouth with one hand. "Kit," she breathed.

Her eyes read the rest of the title page. *Who was most wickedly murdered, by the means of his disloyal and wanton wife, who for the love she bear to one Mosbie, hired two desperate ruffians, Black Will and Shakebag, to kill him.*

Wherein is shown the great malice and dissimulation of a wicked woman, the unsatiable desire of filthy lust, and the shameful end of all murderers.

She looked up. "They gave away the ending."

Kit laughed. "*That's* all you have to say?"

"This is . . . this is real?"

He smiled down at her. "Edward White printed it. Which reminds me." He fished in a pocket for a small leather pouch and dropped it into Emilia's hand, the coins jangling inside. "Here's your pay."

Emilia took the money but could not take her eyes off her play. *Her play.*

"Strange's Men are headed out to the countryside, too," Kit said. "Shakespeare will not be able to meet again for a while."

She looked at Kit, sobering. "Promise me you will not take ill while you are traveling."

"I am far too churlish for Death to take." He kissed her knuckles. "Until we meet again, Mouse," Kit said, and then he frowned. "I fear I cannot call you that any longer, as you have found your voice."

Emilia grinned. "Then what shall you call me?"

"*Playwright* has a nice sound to it, does it not?" Kit winked, then walked off whistling a bawdy tavern song, leaving Emilia behind.

311

"Mistress," a maid said. "Will you be wishing to take the Turkey carpets?"

Emilia looked at the small woven coverings on the oak table. "Yes, please," she said, and the woman bobbed a curtsy and disappeared.

The house was a hive of activity, servants packing trunks that would accompany Hunsdon and Emilia to Hampton. She was being dressed for court by her lady's maid, which was an hours-long process. She was already overheated and she had not yet been corseted into her outer layer. Perspiration ran down her back between her shoulder blades and Bess's chatter was making her head throb.

"Mistress!" another servant asked. "The gentleman of the horse wishes to know if His Lordship wishes to ride in the carriage or astride?"

"You shall have to ask him," Emilia said, wincing as a second maid pulled at her hair, braiding it into loops.

"Mistress, beggin' yer pardon, but the steward wishes a word with His Lordship before —"

"Mistress, should we put the holland sheets over the furniture in the dining parlor?"

"Mistress, is it the silver salver you wished as a gift for Her Majesty, or the tureen?"

Mistress.

Mistress.

Mistress.

"Emilia!" Hunsdon's voice cut through the buzzing of the others. She whirled around to face him so quickly that one of the pins Bess was using pricked her breast.

"My lord?" she answered, and then everything went black.

It was not just that she had fainted. For several days, she'd had an upset stomach, and had been overtired. She kept falling asleep in her chair while reading the foul copies of Hunsdon's plays.

Hunsdon had sent word that they would be delayed going to Hampton. They could not risk Her Majesty falling ill. The Queen was fastidious about sickness; during the last bout of plague she had erected a gallows and instructed her staff to hang visitors who had not expressly been invited.

From her bed, where she had been sequestered, Emilia heard the maids whispering. No one said the word *plague,* but the syllable rang in her ears. She did not have the telltale bumps on her neck or under her armpits, but she was feverish and logy and unable to keep food down. She had been given tisanes with treacle and gunpowder in the hope of sweating out the disease. She had been made to eat a plate of butter, because it rid the body of poisons. She had promptly cast up the contents of her stomach after that. Tobacco, which had been brought to England by Sir Walter Raleigh only recently, was burned in her chamber with the windows shut tight, because the smoke could choke out the foul smells that carried illness. Everything smelled like fire and char, and each time Emilia drew in a breath, she coughed uncontrollably. With the intention of sweating out the sickness, she was denied food and water, and she vacillated between utter exhaustion and delirium.

On the third night of her confinement, she woke to find Hunsdon sitting beside her bed, holding her hand and praying.

How useless it would be, and how fitting given the arc of her life, for Emilia to die before her play might be performed for the public. Every time she had allowed herself to hope, she had found herself cast into the gutter of reality again.

On the fourth night, she dreamed of her father. He sat at the end of her bed playing his recorder. When she opened her eyes, he handed her the instrument. "The music, *piccolina*," he said. "You must play." She obediently fitted the wood to her mouth, but it was closed at the bottom end, and there were no finger holes. No matter how hard she tried, she could not produce a single note.

On the fifth night, she woke to a monster holding her down on the bed. She gasped and struggled, only to hear Hunsdon's voice. "Ssh, Emilia, calm yourself." The monster pressed into the soft tissue of her neck, her breasts, as Hunsdon watched.

She realized she had been mistaken: not a monster, but a man in a leather mask with a long pointed beak.

The bird-man spoke. "Perhaps you might give us some privacy, my lord," he said.

After Hunsdon left, the man drew up her night rail and held her legs apart. "This will take but a moment," he said behind his mask, as his fingers probed inside her.

No, she screamed, but she had become the recorder, and she did not make a sound.

When Emilia opened her eyes, she knew she was dead.

She could hear birdsong, and there was fresh air pouring into the chamber. The sky was the blue of forget-me-nots, smudged with clouds.

"Where . . . where am I?" she whispered, and when the legs of a chair scraped across the floorboards, she turned to find Hunsdon sitting beside the bed. His eyes were bloodshot, and deep grooves bracketed his mouth.

"You are here. You are well." He reached for her hand and then, at the last moment, flattened his on the counterpane a few inches from hers. "You did not have the plague."

She thought of her nightmares, of the birdman, and realized that he had been a plague doctor, called to examine her. But . . . she was alive. She was not ill. Surely that was a relief?

Yet Hunsdon did not smile at her. In fact, he looked as if he had received the worst of news.

Emilia swallowed, her throat as dry as muslin. "My lord," she managed. "Are *you* well?"

At that, Hunsdon closed his eyes and gave a small shake of his head.

She threw back the counterpane, intent on getting out of bed.

He shook his head. "Emilia," he said softly, stilling her motions. "You will not be going to court."

His words were ragged, the voice of someone grieving a loss.

She stilled. Perhaps she did not have the plague, but that didn't mean she wasn't riddled with some other fatal disease — smallpox, the wasting disease, the flux. She remembered, shamefully, the man's hand reaching between her legs, and thought of other illnesses Isabella had taught her about. *What had the doctor discovered?* "Henry?" she whispered.

You will not be going to court. Not *we.*

The Lord Chamberlain pushed back his chair, putting inches between them. In his eyes, she saw an ending. "You do not have the plague," Hunsdon said. "You are with child."

MELINA
SEPTEMBER 2024

"All I'm asking," Jasper said, as they whizzed down the Jersey Turnpike, "is for you to take the meeting with an open mind."

Andre sat beside him in the front seat of Jasper's spotlessly clean Audi. From the backseat, Melina could pinch Andre when she thought he needed to respond. Like now.

"Ow," Andre yelped, twisting in his seat. "Should we consider finding a female director?" This was the one point Melina had drilled into him as they stood in the kitchen that morning eating Lucky Charms, before Jasper came to pick them up.

"You're right," Jasper said. "The optics would be better. But the three women I've reached out to already have other projects."

Melina muttered, "Surely there are more than three female directors. . . ."

Jasper's eyes met hers in the rearview mirror. "Yes. But if Tyce is going to get investors for *By Any Other Name,* it needs heat. Some new graduate from Pace who's directed her

317

first black box show isn't going to convince anyone to part with their money."

"Shakespeare isn't enough name recognition?" Andre asked.

"Not when you're saying he didn't write his plays," Jasper said. "On the other hand, attaching someone like Raffe Langudoc makes the industry take note."

Raffe Langudoc had been nominated for two Tonys in the early 2000s, but he hadn't had a show on Broadway since 2010, and his current project — in Melina's opinion — seemed questionable. He was directing a show that traveled like a circus, playing at gun shows across America. *Tucker Everlasting — The Fox Newsical* starred Scott Baio. Kid Rock had composed the songs. Politics aside, Melina just didn't think that theater concessions should include M&M's, box wine, and rounds of bullets.

"Raffe is the perfect fit," Jasper insisted. "He needs you as much as you need him."

Comp seats for the sixty-minute performance were waiting for them at the box office. Melina tried to follow the plot, which included a literal sword fight with an actress playing Greta Thunberg and an anthemic conclusion with bald eagle puppets and red-white-and-blue confetti cannons. The crowd went wild, clapping and whistling.

They remained seated while the audience exited. After a few minutes, Raffe Langudoc jogged across the sawdust stage, zeroing in on Jasper. "My man," Raffe said, clapping him on the shoulder. "Thanks for coming."

"My pleasure. Raffe, this is Mel Green — he's the playwright I was telling you about. And his assistant, Andrea Washington."

Andre and Raffe shook hands. The director was middle-aged, with a buzz cut and a cross earring, and the long legs of someone who used to be a chorus dancer. "So? What did you think?"

Andre opened and closed his mouth like a fish. "The audience *loved* it," he finally replied.

Raffe smiled. "I just think it's really important, now, when we're all so divided, for everyone's voice to be heard, you know?"

"Did you have a chance to read the script I sent?" Jasper asked.

"Indeed," Raffe said. "I have to admit, it excites me to unring the bell that is the Shakespeare juggernaut."

"It'll certainly raise some hackles," Jasper agreed.

Melina interjected, "That's because if you're a Shakespeare scholar and someone casts doubt on the subject, it doesn't just invalidate Shakespeare — it invalidates you, too. English literature didn't even exist as a field of study until Shakespeare was already basically canonized."

Raffe's head snapped toward Melina, surprised.

319

"As you'll see, Raffe," Jasper said, "Andrea's quite an *active* assistant."

He managed to make that sound like an insult.

"Your script reminded me of this show, actually," Raffe said, turning to Andre. "*By Any Other Name* is truth born from doubt. Climate change deniers, Covid deniers, Flat Earthers — they're all questioning authority. Same thing with your play."

Melina felt her cheeks burn. Asserting her ancestor's authorship was very different from refuting science.

Wasn't it?

It made Melina understand, for the first time, why those fusty old Shakespeare scholars thought of anti-Stratfordians as upstarts.

It also made her look at Raffe Langudoc in a different light. Maybe he was not the clown she had thought he must be, choosing a project like *Tucker Everlasting.* He was fucking *smart,* because he was thinking of who bought tickets, and why. There were clearly some theatergoers at *Tucker Everlasting* who loved this story, who'd *lived* this story. There were others who considered it satire. It was like *The Book of Mormon,* which had won raves from atheists and Mormons in equal measure. Good theater had something for everyone. Perhaps Raffe thought he could shape a production so that it attracted both an audience that doubted Shakespeare's

320

authorship and an audience that was assured of it.

Was this what Jasper meant when he'd said to be open-minded?

She caught Andre's eye and nodded. He turned to Raffe. "I think you'd be a great fit for *By Any Other Name*," he said.

"I'm glad, because I have been having ideas about this show since I read it," Raffe gushed. "Like . . . what if we went full Elizabethan? We perform with a fully male cast."

Melina didn't need to pinch Andre to get him to speak up this time. "You want Emilia Bassano to be played by a man?" he asked. "You don't think that might be . . . counterintuitive?"

"Counterintuitive, provocative. Po-*tay*-to, po-*tah*-to." Raffe shrugged. "It was just a thought. I have dozens. Hundreds." He lowered his voice. "I contain *multitudes*."

Melina felt the weight of Jasper's gaze on her face. He seemed to be waiting for her approval, which would be ridiculous. Surely it was more important what the playwright — or the alleged playwright, in this case — thought.

"I think," Andre said carefully, "that as long as we all remember this story should be told through the prism of what it's meant to be labeled *the weaker sex,* then no idea is a bad idea."

Melina wanted to hug Andre. She wanted to high-five him.

"We haven't discussed schedule," Jasper

said. "Rehearsals begin next week, and because we're filling a slot at Cherry Lane for a show that dropped out, it's intensive. Two weeks till tech."

"I can make that work," Raffe said. "Who should my agent contact?"

It struck Melina that they had assembled an entirely male creative team — and an angel benefactor, if you included Jasper Tolle — to tell Emilia's story. But Melina knew that was the only way a show like hers would succeed so quickly. When you were a novice male playwright, you got the benefit of the doubt. When you were a novice female playwright, you had to prove yourself before anyone would take a risk on you.

They said their goodbyes and walked back to Jasper's car. "So? Thoughts?"

"The play is terrible," Andre said.

Jasper laughed. "I was writing a hypothetical review the whole time: 'It's true that some of the songs in *Tucker Everlasting* are catchy. So is chlamydia.' "

Andre slid into the passenger seat. "But I guess it can't hurt to have a Tony-nominated director interested in *By Any Other Name.*"

Jasper headed toward the highway again. "I'm glad you feel that way. This was always about you being comfortable with him. It was a given that he'd want the job."

"Because of the material?" Melina asked, with no small amount of pride.

"No." Jasper gestured to the empty traveling stage, growing smaller in the rearview mirror. "Because he clearly needs the money."

On the day rehearsals began for her play, Melina woke up at dawn. She cooked scrambled eggs and toast and made coffee for herself and Andre, and finally, at six-thirty in the morning, she pounced on his bed. "It's the first day of schooooool," she sang.

"This is my vacation," he moaned. "Go away."

"It's not your vacation. It's your fake job, and I'm your fake PA. A faux pa," Melina said, smiling widely. "Get it?"

"Am I dead?" Andre said to the ceiling. "Is this hell?"

To get three weeks off from the casting agency, he had said that his father was having surgery, and he took family leave without pay. Andre and Melina had argued about that excuse, which Andre felt was tempting fate, but ultimately he agreed that Darnell would be tickled to have the leading role in a ruse.

As agreed, Melina had signed over the three-thousand-dollar check addressed to Mel Green for writing the work. Any further potential income would be royalties — a share of the box office — provided people actually came to see the show, and it didn't close as quickly as it opened.

"I made you breakfast," she coaxed.

From beneath the pillow, Andre grunted. "I've eaten your cooking," he said. *"Hell."*

She sat down on the bed, all playfulness gone. "Andre . . . today, a bunch of legit actors are going to sit at a table with a Tony-nominated director and rehearse my play. Rehearse. My. Play."

Andre pulled the pillow away from his face. "Yeah, they are," he said, grinning. "Big-ass day, Mel."

"That's what I've been trying to say."

"You could have said it an hour later," Andre said. "We don't have to be there till nine-thirty."

But Melina's excitement was contagious. Andre showered and dressed and they ate breakfast together, looking at pictures of the cast so that they could memorize everyone's name. "We need a signal," Melina said. "So I can tell you when I have a note for the actors."

"Why can't you just whisper it?"

"I'm supposed to be an assistant. I'll sit somewhere you can see me, but not at the actual table." She mulled. "What if I pull my earlobe like Carol Burnett?"

"Who's Carol Burnett?"

"You're a Philistine. She's a legend."

"Beyoncé's a legend," Andre corrected, then paused. "You can wear pearls, like she did in Houston on the Renaissance tour, and if you want my attention, just twist them."

"I don't have pearls."

"Then wear mine." Andre shrugged. "Or better yet, just sit next to me. We'll say I'm dyslexic and you type for me."

It could work, Melina reluctantly agreed. When they finished eating, he stuffed Melina's laptop into his messenger bag and looped his arm through hers. "Come along, *Andrea,*" he said.

The tiny rehearsal room felt both energized and claustrophobic — possibly the worst imaginable combination. A gruff stage manager named Elaine led them to their table. Melina sat shoulder to shoulder with Andre, the laptop illuminating her face, the script open and ready for tweaks. She looked around the room at the actors, who were buzzy and excited to be there; at the stage management table with little baskets of pencils, Post-its, and Hershey's minis.

Conspicuously absent? Jasper Tolle.

"Where's Jasper?" she whispered to Andre.

"Why do you care?" he whispered back. "Isn't it less stressful when he's not here?"

Before she could answer, the stage manager said they were ready to start. Raffe stood up from the table, where he'd been in deep discussion with his own assistant. "Hello, family. I use that word intentionally, because we *are* family, for the next few weeks and for as long as this work of art remains at the theater."

The door opened, and Jasper and Tyce

entered with a whiff of strong coffee. They slipped to the back of the rehearsal room, attempting to pretend they hadn't just interrupted the director.

"You know what?" Raffe said. "Let's all stand. Circle up." He gestured at Andre, then at Jasper and Tyce. "You, too."

Andre grabbed Melina's wrist. "I'm not doing this alone," he murmured, yanking her to her feet.

They made a small, uneven loop. "Let's go around the circle," Raffe said. "Tell everyone your name, your role in the show, and a fact no one knows about you. I'll start: I'm Raffe, the director . . . and my fact is that I was born in France and only became a U.S. citizen in 2019."

The baton passed to other actors: *I'm Josh, I'm playing Willie S. One time I took the wrong train and I was too embarrassed to get off and go backward so I went all the way to Buffalo. . . .*

I'm Daya, I have the honor of playing Emilia, I have a pet hedgehog named Quillary Clinton.

That led to a round of snaps. Everyone turned to Andre. "I'm . . . Mel Green, the playwright," he said. "And I never in a million years thought I'd be standing here."

Everyone in the room *awwwwed*, except for Melina. "I'm Andrea Washington," she said. "I'm Mel's assistant, and, um, I'm actually related to Emilia Bassano." She paused. "And

326

also, apparently, to Ted Bundy and Rasputin, so don't be too jealous."

The last person to share was Jasper. "I'm Jasper Tolle," he said, "and I have a photographic memory. If you give me a date, I can tell you what the headline was in *The New York Times* that day."

"No way," said Josh. "November fourth, 1964."

"Johnson Swamps Goldwater," Jasper said immediately.

"That's like a superpower, dude," said Tyce.

He shrugged. "How do you think I convinced the paper to hire me?"

Everyone laughed, and an actress said, "I know what your day job is, *obviously,* but why are you at rehearsals?"

Jasper's gaze skimmed over Andre before settling on Melina. "That's easy," he said. "I'm Mel Green's number one fan."

At first, Melina was so caught up in rehearsals that she forgot to give Andre notes, astounded to hear her words morph from two dimensions into three. It felt like a magician was pulling a colorful strand of sentences and soliloquys from her mind with a flourish.

Every now and then she would shake the wonder off her shoulders and remember to kick Andre under the table. He would lean toward her, as if he were the one delivering the note, when in fact she was the one who spoke: *That line shouldn't be delivered in anger . . . more in desperation.* Or: *I want to try swapping the order of those two scenes.* Or: *Shit, I just realized she can't interact with Southampton there because he's supposed to be on a military mission.*

By the second week of rehearsals, Raffe had gotten everyone off book and on their feet. He'd also hired a lute player to cover the transitions between scenes, which — Melina had to admit — was a nice touch. True to his promise, Jasper dropped in and out of rehearsals without interfering. Most of the time, Melina was so focused she didn't even notice when he was there.

Okay, that was a lie. She knew. She felt it in the way goosebumps rose on her arms, as if he were an unwelcome winter wind. She had begun this swapped-identity escapade to enact revenge on him, and she still wanted his comeuppance — but there were huge swaths of time when she forgot that. He'd make an incisive comment about a scene that wandered off the rails and she would have to admit to herself he was right, it was stronger with the cut. She'd find him staring so intently at her sometimes that she wondered if he knew who she really was and was just waiting to punk her. The only other reason he could possibly be so invested in this show was that he truly believed in it — and that was orthogonal to the ogre she'd cast him as.

Melina had taken to reading Jasper Tolle's old reviews where a particularly savage phrase had tanked a show: "The most positive thing I can say about seeing this musical is that I never have to see it again," and "The least wooden actors onstage were the puppets."

His comments on *By Any Other Name* could be just as brutal. He'd told the costume designer that the plague doctor looked like a goth pelican; he told the actor playing Marlowe he needed to be less RuPaul and more Oscar Wilde. But Melina had spent a decade being flattered emptily by people who had no intention of producing her plays, and that had been more painful.

Today the cast wore bits and pieces of their costumes. Daya was in a petticoat so that she could get a sense of how to move in it across the stage. Tommy — their Southampton — was in a doublet and jeans. The bulk of the morning had been taken up by an intimacy coordinator, who was working with the two actors on a love scene in Southwark, in which they would have to gracefully attack each other with passion, maneuver to the ground, and simulate sex. It led to a lot of giggling, a broken prop, and a minor injury: stage management had been required to file an incident report when Tommy tripped over Daya's skirt and landed hard on his wrist.

At one point, Raffe had pulled Andre aside. It wouldn't have been appropriate for Melina to hover on the fringes of the conversation, but she felt itchy every time she looked up and saw Raffe and Andre deep in discussion. *You trust Andre,* she reminded herself. *You* asked *him to do this.*

After twenty minutes of watching Raffe and Andre huddled together over *her* computer while Daya and Tommy ground against each other with a Pilates SAD ball trapped between their groins, Melina distracted herself by scrolling through TikTok. She was watching a performance of *Pride and Prejudice* done by cats when they moved on to a new scene — the first business meeting between Emilia and Shakespeare.

Daya and Josh waited for stage management to set a prop table and chairs so that they could sit. So far, Daya had nailed Emilia — there was a restlessness to her delivery that felt organic. It also felt right to have a Puerto Rican actress play Emilia, who — as an Italian Jew — did not blend seamlessly into the milky white landscape of Elizabethan England. And Josh had managed to give his Shakespeare a hunger for validation that made him less of a buffoon, and more a man so self-important that he wasn't self-aware.

"All right," Raffe said. "Let's just read through this first and see what we have."

Andre was still standing near Raffe on the other side of the room as Daya slipped into character and lasered her gaze on Josh. "You want to write," she said slowly. "But you can't. *I* want to write . . . but I can't." She frowned, glancing down at the script. "Wait. So Emilia is going to give this no-talent loser her work just so it gets seen?"

"No-talent loser?" Josh said, heated. "What if he has a family he's trying to support and that's why he signs on as an actor for the troupe, and just doesn't have the time *she* does to write?"

"Are you suggesting," Daya shot back, "that Shakespeare's struggles as a man are anywhere near comparable to Emilia's as a woman?"

Raffe held up his hands in a time-out signal. "I'm loving this passion, but let's stay focused, hmm?"

Daya disappeared into the character of Emilia. "If you front my work, you can claim authorship."

"And what do I get out of it?" Josh scoffed.

"The praise you seek." Daya broke character again and turned to Andre. "I'm sorry, that just doesn't *feel* right. I think Emilia would call him out. I think she'd say *Bank.*"

Melina could think of a thousand reasons why Emilia would not say *Bank* in response to Shakespeare's question, beginning with the fact that the term was anachronistic.

"I don't tell *her* how to act," Melina said under her breath, just as she realized Jasper Tolle had arrived at rehearsal, and was

331

standing behind her. She could smell his shaving cream — a bite of soap, with no spice and no flowers.

"If I had a dime for every actor that made a suggestion that actually made it into the final script . . ." Jasper murmured, "I'd be able to buy a coffee. A *coffee,* mind you. Not a latte. Tell Mel he's the one with veto power. *He's* the playwright, and nobody else."

Melina cleared her throat. "I'll make sure he knows."

"Knows what?" Andre said, throwing himself into the seat beside her and passing her the laptop.

"I'll tell you later," Melina murmured, trying to telepathically alert him to the fact that she didn't want to elaborate within Jasper's range of hearing.

Andre lowered his voice. "Raffe has thoughts about the ending," he said.

"What kind of thoughts?"

"Oh, also, your dad is texting you nonstop. Keeps popping up on your computer message app. Which was a *whole* ball of fun when Raffe wanted to know who calls me cupcake."

"From the top," Raffe said.

Daya started to recite her lines before abruptly breaking off. "I'm sorry, I'm still having a really hard time finding the motivation for Emilia to just *give away* her writing."

The director looked at Andre, waiting for him to give the actress an explanation.

"What other options did she have?" Andre asked.

"Well, that's part of the problem. I don't buy that Marlowe would encourage her to do it. As a writer himself, he knows better. It feels like *such* a breach of friendship."

Andre froze. "I'm sure he had his reasons."

"Daya," Raffe sighed. "I so appreciate your commitment to Emilia's character. But I think this really will resonate with theatergoers — seeing how far women have come since then."

Melina nearly fell out of her chair.

Before she could open her mouth, Andre grabbed her hand in a death grip. "We're going to be late," he said pointedly, then turned to Raffe apologetically. "Eye doctor's appointment. Totally slipped my mind." He turned before the director could object, pulling Melina with him.

She stumbled behind him until they stepped out of the rehearsal room into the hallway. "What's with the hasty exit?"

"It is time," Andre said, "for you and me to have a chat."

Andre took her to a bar and ordered martinis. "Why are we doing this?" he asked, as he sat down and pushed a glass toward Melina.

"Day drinking?"

"This whole . . . scheme. I feel like an idiot — you're a ventriloquist and I'm your dummy."

He took a long sip of his drink. "Daya was right, and I'd rather kill a puppy than admit that. A best friend would not encourage you to put someone else's name on your work."

"First, you didn't encourage me. I begged. Second, it's not someone else's name. It's my name. Sort of."

"I know you thought this was a good idea at the time, and I was stupid enough to agree with you," Andre said. "But the reality is different, isn't it?"

Melina looked down at her cocktail napkin, which she'd begun to shred into pieces. "Okay, you're right, it's different than I thought it would be. But this all still feels worth it . . . for Emilia. I can't really explain it better than that."

"All the more reason you should be recognized as the playwright," Andre said.

In the darkest corners of night, when she couldn't fall asleep, Melina had rehearsed in her own mind what it would be like to come clean. She thought about the reactions of the actors, and Raffe, and, yes, Jasper; imagined the narrowing of their eyes, the tightness of their mouths. The closing of ranks when they realized they'd been duped.

The odds of everyone treating this as a madcap lark were far less than the odds that Tyce D'Onofrio would pull funding and shut down the production.

"I can't undo what I've already done,"

Melina said. "But I'm not the first author to pretend to be a man just to get traction in her career. The Brontës did it. George Eliot. George Sand. J. K. Rowling."

"Maybe *that's* why she doesn't understand gender," Andre muttered. "But the point is, Mel, we all know who those writers are now. They eventually revealed themselves. You . . . you're erasing yourself."

"I'm in the room. I'm just . . . playing a role. If I was Melina Green, I wouldn't have been chosen for that fringe festival. I wouldn't have had Jasper Tolle at the reading. He wouldn't want anything to do with this play. You heard him — it's not the subject matter of Emilia Bassano that intrigued him. It was the fact that *you,* a *man,* could write well about her experience." Melina shook her head. "At least now I have a seat at the table. You have no idea what it's like to be a woman in the theater business," she said.

Andre's brows rose to his hairline. "Are you really saying that to a gay Black man? You want to know how many white kids fresh out of college have been promoted at my agency, when it took me three years to get a cost-of-living raise? Or how many times some white producer comes in and gives me the Starbucks order instead of assuming I'm a legit casting director? As a matter of fact, do you know how few Black casting directors there even *are*?" He flattened his hands on the table. "The only reason *I* have an invitation to this particular party is because I'm pretending to be the person who wrote the play. It's the words that matter, Mel, and you're the one who created them. You don't see anyone clamoring for me to quit the casting agency and write."

"That's your own fault," Melina snapped, "because you're too afraid to even try!"

Immediately, she knew she had gone too far. She clapped her hand over her mouth and Andre reared back, as if she had struck him.

"Okay, then," he said softly. "At least I know how you *really* feel."

"Andre —"

"I can't do this, Mel," he said, and he walked away, slamming the bar door open on its hinges.

Melina hunched her shoulders, pressing her cheek to the cool wooden table. She was an idiot, and worse, she was a terrible friend.

She pulled out her phone, where Andre's contact was not his name but the emojis queen and bee. *I'm sorry,* she typed. *If you want me to tell everyone the truth tomorrow, I —*

Her phone buzzed with an incoming call: DAD.

"Hey, Dad," Melina said, holding the device up to her ear. "Sorry I didn't answer your texts."

"It's fine," her father said. "I was . . . to . . . you know."

"Sorry, you're breaking up —"

"Oh, the service isn't good in the hospital."

"The *what*?"

"Hang on . . ." She could hear him moving, and voices swelling around him. Then he was speaking again. "It was just a little procedure. Beth brought me."

Who the hell was Beth? "Dad," Melina said, "what is going on?"

"Nothing. I just missed you, is all."

"I may have something good to report," Melina said. "But I don't want to jinx it."

She could hear her father's smile in his reply. "Fingers crossed."

"Dad," she said, a chill skating down her spine. "You'd tell me if you weren't okay, right?"

"Cupcake," her father answered, "why would I lie to you?"

They talked for another ten minutes, then hung up after Melina promised to call him soon. By the time Melina headed back to the theater, she'd completely forgotten to send her text to Andre.

Andre was not at the theater. Melina made up an excuse about conjunctivitis and spent the rest of the workday putting Raffe's notes into the script and getting new pages to the actors. Later, she expected him to be at their apartment, sulking. "Andre?" she called out, wandering through the small

337

space, only to realize that he had likely never come home.

A part of her was relieved.

She scrawled a note on a Post-it — *Let's talk. Wake me up whenever* — and stuck it onto his bedroom door.

Melina was about to strip out of her sweaty clothes and shower and order sushi when her phone dinged with a notification. LILLYS.

Fuck.

The Lillys had been created in 2010 by a handful of female theater makers who wanted to celebrate the work of women in the business, and to push the industry toward gender and racial parity. Named for Lillian Hellman, the outspoken playwright, they gave out awards with the most fantastic names — and often with cash prizes: the Stacey Mindich "Go Write a Play" Award, the Daryl Roth Creative Spirit Award, the Giant in Theater Award, the You've Changed the World Award.

Melina had always wanted to go to the awards ceremony, and she had finally figured out a way in: she'd applied to be a cater waiter. She couldn't afford a ticket, but the next best thing was handing out champagne to actual women who had achieved actual success in the industry. You never knew who you'd strike up a conversation with.

The bad news was that she had completely forgotten she was due at the venue in forty-five minutes. This year the May ceremony had been rescheduled after there had been a burst pipe at Playwrights Horizons, which was why she'd lost track of the date. She washed under her arms at the sink, twisted her hair into a topknot, and pulled on black pants and a white shirt.

At the site, she was given an apron and a tray and instructions, and guests began to mill in the lobby. She spotted Theresa Rebeck and Lynn Nottage and Kristen Anderson-Lopez. It took all of Melina's self-control to walk up to each of them and offer a glass of champagne instead of peppering them with questions about how they'd gotten started, how they persevered, and how they stayed gracious in a business so heavily dominated by men.

There were more male producers and directors there than she'd anticipated. She circled between the kitchen and the lobby, retrieving empty glasses and receiving trays of full ones. She was just approaching a small tangle of people — *Oh my God, was that Suzan-Lori Parks?* — when she felt a tap on her shoulder. She turned to see two men standing there. "Welcome to the Sour Grapes Awards," the first man said to his companion, and he plucked a flute off Melina's tray. "Care for some . . . *whine?*"

"People in glass houses, Jack," someone behind her warned. "That was quite a tantrum you threw when the Local 802 union picketed your show for using prerecorded tracks instead of live musicians."

The man's face went crimson, and he muttered something before slinking away. Melina turned, shocked, and confirmed that it was indeed Jasper's voice she had heard.

She wasn't sure who was more surprised: herself, when she realized that Jasper Tolle was the owner of the voice; or Jasper, seeing her in a waiter's outfit at the Lillys. "I can only assume," he said, "that being Mel Green's assistant doesn't cover groceries."

"The two-day-old bread at the bodega down the street is pretty cheap, and it only *sometimes* has mold on it," Melina quipped. "What are you doing here?"

"I don't have a choice," he said, without a trace of irony. "It's part of the job."

"I *took* this job just to be here," Melina countered. "It's an honor to be here with these women."

He rolled his eyes. "No one likes award ceremonies. They're all too long and dreadfully boring."

"Says the person who goes to the Tonys every year."

A chime rang, calling the audience to their seats. Jasper made no move to go into the theater. "I went to our reading room today," he said.

Our reading room. Melina felt a little zip of electricity run down her spine.

A small smile played over his lips. "Don't you want to know what I was reading?"

The lights flashed, twice.

Melina hurried toward the theater. She set her empty champagne tray on top of a trash can and slipped into the auditorium to stand along the rear wall. In the dark, she felt the movement of Jasper filling the spot beside her, even though he obviously had a seat.

Marsha Norman, who'd won a Pulitzer and been nominated for a Tony for *'Night, Mother,* welcomed everyone. "When we started the Lillys in 2010," she said, "we wanted to shine the spotlight on women."

Jasper leaned closer. She could smell the soap on his skin. "I learned today that the *Tragedy of Mariam* was the first play written and published by a woman in England," he whispered. "Elizabeth Cary."

"Not true," Melina murmured back. "*Arden of Faversham* was published twenty years earlier. It just didn't have Emilia Bassano's name on it."

"You can't prove she wrote *Arden*."

"No, but I can show you how Cary's historical book on Edward II was published as her *husband's* work, and only recently attributed to her."

"No one needs permission to make theater," Marsha Norman continued from the stage. "But you do need support. And that's what the Lillys hope to do. Since we began The

341

Count, female writers of new plays have increased from 14 percent to 39 percent. That's progress, but it's not equality."

"Just because Elizabeth Cary is the first woman whose name appears on a published play doesn't mean other women weren't writing for the theater," Melina whispered fiercely. "Eighty percent of the plays from the 1580s were recorded without the names of their authors, so the belief that every one of those was written by a man is nothing more than an assumption."

Marsha Norman finished her speech. "The fact that stories of women told by women are still rare onstage is insupportable. When women's stories aren't told, it suggests that women's lives don't matter." She looked around the room. "You know what does matter? Women lifting up other women."

In the thunderous applause, Jasper leaned toward her again. "So it's like the way Emilia published the first country house poem in *Salve Deus* in 1611 — but Ben Jonson gets credit for being the first, in 1616."

Melina turned, about to respond, when she realized what he'd said. "You read Emilia's book of poetry?"

"Manuscripts and Archives, ma'am," he said, inclining his head. "I'm halfway through."

In the half-dark, she could see only the curve of Jasper's jaw and the light in his eyes. He had not just surprised her with his

342

intellectual curiosity about Emilia Bassano. He'd upended her.

He tilted his head, studying her just as carefully as she was studying him. "I know you came here to see the ceremony," he said, "but is there any chance you would . . . duck out and go somewhere with me?"

This was, by far, the best awards ceremony Jasper had never attended. He sat across the table from Andrea in a booth at his favorite diner. They were sharing a plate of French fries and chocolate milkshakes. "Mary Wroth," she was saying, as they continued to banter about the female writers who'd been lost to history. "She wrote mostly poetry, but there was a closet drama in there somewhere. And Ben Jonson even wrote a sonnet to her, saying her writing made him a better poet. He wasn't afraid to give credit to a woman, even if the rest of society wouldn't."

Jasper found himself looking at her midnight hair and those intense silver eyes — mirrors that made him see himself more clearly. He was a guy who was too nervous to stop fidgeting; a man who was acting more like a boy, trying to impress a girl who was out of his league. Andrea Washington might be ten years younger than he was, but she was smart and passionate and didn't give quarter.

Most of all, she wasn't scared of him.

He had cultivated a persona based on his

caustic reviews. People assumed he was a dick because of the acerbic columns he wrote; he didn't correct them. To be honest, the assumption kept others at a distance, which was usually the way he liked it. But Andrea didn't hesitate to debate with Jasper, to counter his arguments, to tell him he was wrong. It was . . . liberating. Refreshing.

Amazing.

He had the urge to reach for her hand but he was not that suave, and besides, they were business colleagues and that was a terrible idea — not to mention a form of harassment, since she was a lowly assistant and he was, well, who he was. So instead, he tried to impress her with his knowledge of female authors. "Mary Sidney," he said.

"That's cheating. You know about her from the play."

"Fair," Jasper said. "Katherine of Sutton."

Andrea's face was blank. "Who?"

Triumph! "A Benedictine nun. She wrote and directed Latin liturgical dramas in the fourteenth century that were performed at Barking Abbey."

"I call BS," Andrea said. "Barking Abbey?"

"I kid you not," Jasper said. "Even better, the nuns played *men* onstage. One of them was Jesus."

Andrea shook her head, laughing, and Jasper watched some loose curls unravel from her topknot. They danced along the nape of her neck and the curve of her shoulder and he could not look away.

He'd last had a girlfriend two years ago. All had been relatively smooth until Yvonne moved into his apartment. Jasper had had such anxiety from seeing her clothes in the same hamper as his and her toothbrush touching his own that he found excuses to stay away. After three weeks, she moved out and broke up with him.

"If I didn't know better, I'd think you were a professor, not a critic," Andrea said. "Did you study English in college?"

"No. Theater." He looked up from beneath the fringe of hair that was always falling in his face. "I never wanted to be a critic," he confessed. "I wanted to be a director."

"What happened?"

"Guess that got lost, along the way."

"So instead of making theater, you pick holes in the way other people make theater."

Jasper leaned back against the banquette. "That's one way to look at it. The other is that people have limited time and money, so I help guide them to what's most worthwhile."

"But that focus is only with your lens," Andrea pointed out. "If a play isn't your cup of tea, should you be allowed to crucify it? Should *any* critic be allowed to do that, without ever writing or directing a play himself?"

"How is what I do different from tourists

talking about a show they've seen on the walk back to their hotel?"

"You have the power to close a show with your opinion, and Joe from Iowa does not," Andrea said. "And your taste is biased by your experience. Things that appeal to you might be different from subjects that appeal to someone Black or nonbinary or female, because you haven't lived their lives. There aren't many Black or nonbinary or female theater critics — they're mostly white men."

"Being a white man doesn't mean I can't recognize good work when I see it," Jasper argued.

"No, but it does mean that if you don't like something, you might not realize it wasn't *meant* for you to like."

Jasper felt as if someone had shot a gun next to his head. His ears were ringing, and he couldn't quite focus. Was he that blind? Had he ever dismissed a play that "didn't speak to him" not because of a flaw in the execution of the show but because it didn't resonate with his personal experience?

That couldn't be true. Off the top of his head he could name ten plays by playwrights of color and LGBTQ writers that were masterpieces. But by the same token, he could remember a show by a Black writer that he thought was "bitter." A musical about the AIDS epidemic that he called "melodramatic." A play by a woman he'd called "cloying and emotional."

Had the fault lain with the material, or with his own distance from it?

"In spite of what the critics say," Jasper pointed out, "you have to admit that theater's gotten more diverse lately."

Andrea grimaced. "I don't know about that. Okay, yes, there are more Black playwrights getting produced. But are they really given the same platform? Pretty much every Black-written show since 2020 has gotten a bad slot in the Broadway season, no publicity, no attempt to find an audience."

Jasper's jaw dropped. "Is that what Mel thinks, too?"

She hesitated, then swallowed. "I think Mel would tell you," Andrea said carefully, "that there's still work to be done. And I think he'd agree that when it comes to other minority groups — like, say, *women* creators — they're barely getting onto the field. That's not real change. It's tokenism."

"In the past five years, three women have won the Pulitzer for theater," Jasper said.

"Of those three, not a single one got a Broadway theater for her Pulitzer-winning play," Andrea said. "But the two *guys* who won did. In fact, since 2002 only Lynn Nottage and Suzan-Lori Parks have won the Pulitzer *and* had commercial productions. But nearly every man who's won it did."

Jasper thought back through the winners: James Ijames, Michael R. Jackson,

Lin-Manuel Miranda, Tom Kitt, Tracy Letts, David Lindsay-Abaire.

Shit.

She was right.

Andrea looked directly at him. "It's not your fault that you were born in that body, or that you had the upbringing you did. But all the decision makers and tastemakers are white men." She folded her hands and rested her chin on them. "You know who buys tickets to shows."

Jasper nodded. Nearly seventy percent of seats sold on Broadway were bought by women.

"Then why are there so few female critics and producers and theater owners and writers? It's not like playwrights haven't known forever that catering to a female audience is wise," she said: *"I fear, / All the expected good we're like to hear / For this play at this time, is only in / The merciful construction of good women; / For such a one we show'd 'em: if they smile, / And say 'twill do, I know, within a while / All the best men are ours; for 'tis ill hap, / If they hold when their ladies bid 'em clap."*

His brows pinched together. *"Henry VIII?"* he guessed.

"All Is True," Andrea corrected, giving the original title of the play Shakespeare and John Fletcher allegedly collaborated on in 1613.

"Six of one, half dozen of another," Jasper said, smiling ruefully. "Well, it makes me even more proud that *By Any Other Name* is transferring," he said. "And patently ashamed that I dragged you away from an awards ceremony for women."

She smiled. "You didn't abduct me, I went willingly. Although I'm pretty sure I won't get paid since I ditched before cleanup."

She glanced out the window as a carriage horse clip-clopped down Eighth Avenue. "Where do they sleep at night?" Andrea wondered absently.

"On Fifty-Second Street, near Eleventh Avenue. They have a stable."

Andrea turned, surprised. "How do you know that?"

"Because I wondered where they slept at night, too, and I followed them once."

She twisted to look out the window again as the horse moved out of view. "I had a date once, in college. The guy took me to a sushi place near Central Park. It was around eleven-thirty at night and a horse and carriage went by just as the light changed. The horse spooked, and bolted, and a taxi clipped it."

"Oh my God," Jasper said. "That's *awful.*"

"Yeah, it was. I watched the whole thing through the window of the restaurant."

"What happened?"

"The horse didn't make it," Andrea said. "Neither did the relationship."

She hesitated, her quicksilver eyes meeting

his, as if she were gathering the courage to tell him something important, and falling short.

"Jasper," she began, just as he said, "Naturally —"

They both broke off awkwardly.

"You go," Jasper said.

"No, you."

His hand grazed hers as he reached for his water, and they both froze. "I was just going to point out that it would have been impossible to overcome a beginning that tragic," Jasper offered, smiling. "What were you going to say?"

Andrea's fingers slid away from his, and then so did her gaze. "I can't remember," she said.

>   Their kiss is a collision.
>   EMILIA's hands flatten on
>   his chest, holding his
>   heartbeat.

SOUTHAMPTON

My love.

>   (draws back, parting her
>   cloak, shocked to find her
>   pregnancy)

Is it mine?

EMILIA

I do not know.

>   It begins to snow.

THE WOMAN

The snow made him sparkle, as
if enchanted, and Emilia wished
it were so — that he might wave
a wand or cast a spell and take
them far away.

SOUTHAMPTON

I hope it is.

EMILIA

To what end, Henry? Where is this fairy-tale world where we might live?

SOUTHAMPTON

We shall make one. I will buy you a home and —

EMILIA
(interrupting)

I am married.

SOUTHAMPTON

How . . . how could you?

EMILIA

To whom should I complain, did I speak of this? No one would believe me.

SOUTHAMPTON
(swallowing)

Do you love him?

EMILIA

I will never love anyone as I love you.

THE WOMAN

He skated his hand over the baby inside her, staking a claim and a wish, no matter the truth.

SOUTHAMPTON

Do not say that. He will be as
greedy for your affections as his
father.

EMILIA
1592–94

Emilia is 23–25

All anyone could talk about was the elephant.

It was the perfect antidote to the dire whispers about the plague outbreak. King Henri IV of France had heard that Queen Elizabeth wished to see one, so he had procured an elephant to be shipped to England. A Flemish elephant handler and his wife would accompany the animal on a London-bound vessel and get it accustomed to English weather in return for charging a fee to curious Londoners who wanted to see the animal.

The Queen, however, did not want an elephant. *If I said I wished to see the moon, would someone rope it down from the sky?* she had groused. It had fallen to Lord Hunsdon to remedy the situation, which involved rehoming a massive creature and making sure Her Majesty did not have to hear about it ever again.

It was a convenient excuse for him to spend all his time away from Emilia.

Being the courtesan of a man of status meant being discreet, and pregnancy was not part of discretion. It was Emilia's responsibility to avoid falling pregnant, though no herb she took was ever going to be foolproof. It was surprising that it had not happened before in the ten years she had lived with him. But for all that Hunsdon had flouted society by parading her around at court and allowing her to act as hostess at Somerset House, there was a line he would not cross, and that was humiliating his legal wife with a second family.

The conversation between them had been awkward and brief. "You will be taken care of," Hunsdon had told her, after she learned she was pregnant.

"Thank you, my lord," she had said.

Here are all the things she did not say aloud: *What did being taken care of actually* mean? *Where would she live?* *Who was the father of this child?*

Although she had been intimate with Hunsdon once in the time period that would account for the pregnancy, she had been intimate with Southampton far more often.

At that thought, tears had sprung to her eyes. "I am so sorry, Henry," she had whispered.

Hunsdon had folded her into his embrace. "I am not," he replied. "One small moment cannot poison a decade."

But it could and would end their arrangement.

She gripped his wrist, suddenly terrified of what was to come. Emilia had been plucked out of homes and dropped into others four times already in her life, but she had been lulled into a false sense of security with Hunsdon. She had known that he was older and would not live forever, but she had not foreseen that *she* would be the reason this relationship ended. "Will you be in London when I leave?" she asked.

Hunsdon had nodded, but that was the last time she had seen him, and now he was off dealing with the elephant. In the meantime, word had clearly been given to the staff. Servants who had acknowledged her as the lady of the house were now unable to meet her eye. She would enter her chamber to find a maid packing her dresses into a trunk. She was left to her own devices — which in the past would have been a boon — but with Marlowe away and no word from Southampton and a plague raging through London, she had nowhere to go.

She simply had to wait until she was told where she was going, or shoved out the door, she supposed.

So Emilia channeled her emotions into her pen. She wrote poetry that she discarded as too maudlin, and started plays she tore to pieces when she realized she had killed off every character by the second act. She wrote letters to Kit (which she sent) and to South-ampton (which she burned).

And then, she felt the quickening of her baby — the tiniest flutter in her abdomen, like the shimmy of a silverfish.

This time, at least, she would not be alone.

To my dearest friend Kit,

After my heartiest commendations, I wished to share that nothing has been the same since you left. I find myself in a delicate state and know not how to share my predicament. Yet I trust you to read what I cannot put into words here, and to let you know that when you return you shall not find me at Somerset House. I would give you my address but it remains a mystery to me; I feel like a poor actor just waiting for the playwright to provide the lines for the next scene.

Is it overwrought to think of oneself as a message in a bottle — surely important to the sender but unknown until it washes ashore? Is anything written even real, until it is read by another? It puts me in mind of an ink I once saw, imperceptible until it was held over the heat of a candle.

Mayhap this heat I find myself in will make me impossible to overlook, too.

Your friend,
E.

As the season changed, those who were unable to leave London had contracted the plague in droves. Emilia would not venture near the city walls or Fleet Prison, which was heavily infected. But in a last-ditch effort to carve out a future for herself, she contacted her old friend Isabella in St. Helen's Bishopsgate.

She had no way of knowing if Isabella had already escaped a festering London, or if she would welcome a visit from a friend whose communication had been sporadic. But Emilia had spent a a few weeks now at Somerset House being ignored by servants and staff, and she was starting to feel like a ghost. She wanted — no, she *needed* — to be seen.

When Isabella wrote back, Emilia immediately put on her walking boots and headed through the empty streets of London, even though it was nearly dark.

Emilia wound a scarf around her face, her eyes her only visible feature. The homes with infection were marked with red paint and sealed shut from the outside. She passed a watchman setting food into a basket lowered from the second story of a quarantined house. The woman at the window was pale as the moon, with dark circles under her eyes. A death cart pulled by two sleepy horses stood in front of one building. Emilia watched two men carry out a body and drop it on top of others already in the cart. At the end of their rounds, near dawn, they would throw all the corpses into the Great Pit at Aldgate. She could not imagine the extra alcohol ration these workers were given made up for the risk of being that close to death all the time.

Emilia skirted the dray as the men went back inside to fetch more of the dead. The woman they'd carried out was not much older than Emilia. Where the shroud of her blanket had fallen away, Emilia could see that her throat and arms were covered with lumps that oozed pus and blood. Her empty eyes stared up at the sky.

Just then, a young man scrambled from behind a stack of barrels and nearly knocked Emilia down in his haste to climb into the death cart. He rifled through the pockets of the dead, finally holding up a small ring that caught the light of the moon before he jumped off the wagon and ran away.

Emilia hurried off, winging a quick prayer to her God and the Christian one that everyone she loved would be spared.

She had barely knocked at Isabella's door before it opened and she was yanked inside, not by a servant but by Isabella herself. Emilia found herself pulled into the tightest embrace. "I do not let just anyone cross that threshold, *cara*," Isabella said.

"You are well?" Emilia asked.

"As well as one can be, in the midst of a plague." She plucked at the ties of Emilia's cloak to remove it. "Come. Sit."

But as soon as the velvet fell away, Isabella's brows rose. "Oh, Emilia," she sighed. "How far along are you?"

Emilia looked down at her flat belly. "How did you know?"

"Your breasts," Isabella said. "That dress is barely holding them in."

Emilia felt her eyes well with tears. "I don't know how it happened."

Isabella smiled wryly. "I imagine you know quite well." She took Emilia's hand and led her upstairs to her chamber, still beautifully appointed with cushioned benches and the largest bed Emilia had ever seen. Isabella poured two large glasses of wine and handed one to Emilia. "Now," she said. "Tell me."

"I took the tea every morning — the herbal one, like you showed me — and I guess . . . I guess it did not work."

"By my count it worked for nearly ten years," Isabella said. "What did Hunsdon say?"

"That I cannot stay with him."

"Well, it would not be seemly for the Lord Chamberlain to be living with the mother of his bastard child," Isabella mused.

Emilia swallowed. "It may not be his child," she confessed.

A smile curled across Isabella's face. "Well,

well, look at my little protégée. Will you tell me who, then?"

"Southampton," Emilia said.

"You do not dream small when you dream, do you, *cara*." Isabella laughed. "He will not have you?"

"He does not know. But even so, he could not if he wished it. You know that people like you and me . . . are not meant for people like him."

Isabella's gaze touched on the beautiful paintings that hung on the walls and the thick tapestries covering the tables and the silk counterpane that lay still as a pool on the bed. The Baron had left her well appointed. "Hunsdon will not provide for you?"

"He will," Emilia said carefully, "but he isn't offering up details of his plan."

"You should be delighted there *is* a plan. Many men would have turned you out on the street. And right now, Emilia, you do not want to be without a safe home."

Emilia thought about the death cart workers. "Which is why I have come to you. We are friends of a sort, are we not? Perhaps we might grow old together."

Isabella narrowed her eyes. "You are twenty-three, Emilia. I am twenty-eight. Neither of us is in our dotage."

"No, but . . . I could pay you for lodging."

As soon as she said the words, Emilia recognized her mistake. She had no guarantee that Hunsdon was settling a sum on her. She did have William Shakespeare circulating her play, but even that pipeline was broken by the plague . . . and she could hardly admit that was her source of potential income.

"*Cara,* you know this is not just my home, but a place of business."

Oh. *Oh.* Emilia had not realized that Isabella had taken a new protector.

"It is a comfort to have this residence, yes. But the deed to a house will not put food on the table or wood in the fireplace. I am still in need of support."

"I . . . I'm sorry —"

"Do not be. He is good to me. A lordling, third son of an earl. He wants someone to find him fair of form, to comment on his shoulders and his legs and not his immense belly. I have always been a good actress," she said.

"I would not stand in your way," Emilia begged. "I would leave before he arrived."

"I do not even know when he will choose to visit me — how could *you* predict it?" Isabella gestured to Emilia's midsection. "And it is bad for business, *cara,* if a man comes to his mistress's home and is confronted with the reminder that his visit could end with a bastard child."

Emilia nodded, deflating. "Of course."

"You know I will do anything I can to help you."

Anything else, she meant.

Emilia tipped up her wineglass and drank the contents. She could feel the heat of Isabella's gaze. "All will be well," Isabella said brightly. "Hunsdon is a good man, yes?"

Something about those words dissolved the knot in Emilia's chest. "He is," she said quietly. "He did not deserve this."

Isabella took Emilia's hands in her own and squeezed. *"Cara,"* she said, "neither did you."

Dearest Mouse,

I, who despise the very tenets of faith, have faith in you.

Vermin survive when little else can.

(I refer only to your sobriquet, not your personality.)

(I also hope that made you smile.)

Your servant,
Kit

One day when Emilia returned from a walk through the gardens in a misty rain and went up to her chamber to tidy her hair and change her boots, she found her room stripped entirely of personal effects. Her hairbrush and her perfume and her lap desk were gone. The carpets that covered the oak table, missing. The clothing press, devoid of dresses. Even the bed had been stripped down — the linens and counterpane removed, the feather bed rolled away to expose the bare wool-stuffed mattress.

Emilia blinked, backing out of the room for fear that she had lost her mind and entered the wrong chamber. She nearly collided with the lady's maid who had served her for a decade. "Bess, where are my belongings?"

"Why, packed up tight, mistress, like His Lordship asked. The carriage, it's ready."

In a daze, Emilia followed her downstairs. The servants milled, but they were not lined up in rank the way they would have been for a true lady. Some of them — the maid of the kitchen, the groom of the great hall, the yeoman of the buttery, the chief cook — looked at Emilia with true pity, but they did not say goodbye or acknowledge her. She followed Bess to the front door of Somerset House, stopping at the threshold as if she had been struck by lightning. "Where am I to be sent?"

No one replied.

"Where is Hunsdon?" she asked, hearing the raw stripe of desperation in her voice.

He'd promised.

Lifting her chin the way she had seen the Queen do hundreds of times, Emilia sailed out the front door of Somerset House as if it had been her own choice.

"His Lordship said I could go with ye," Bess chattered, oblivious to how stiffly Emilia sat in the carriage.

"His Lordship said he would be here when I left," Emilia murmured.

Weeks later, Bess — who fancied the yeoman of the horse at Somerset House — would learn from him that on the day Emilia left, Lord Hunsdon had sent a note for her that had been delayed by the messenger, who had been quarantined in a plague household and unable to deliver it. The yeoman eventually gave the missive to Bess, who — now — gave it to Emilia.

Hunsdon wished her well in her new endeavors. He had hoped to say goodbye in person but could not leave Hampton Court because the Queen was still annoyed about the elephant.

It was, Emilia realized, an even bigger problem than *she* was.

The carriage that bore Emilia away from Somerset House stopped in front of a small, familiar doorway. Her cousin Jeronimo's home was just as she remembered it, even if it had been a decade. When the door opened and a young man stared at her, it took Emilia a moment to realize that this was her littlest cousin — now older than she had been when she first was sent to Hunsdon. "Cousin Emilia," he said without surprise, which was how she knew they'd been expecting her.

Hunsdon had, once again, brokered a deal with her family.

Alma, Jeronimo's wife, pulled Emilia into her embrace. "It will be all right," she whispered in Yiddish.

Emilia struggled to hold back her tears. Whatever monetary boon Hunsdon had offered would still not make it possible for Jeronimo and Alma to squeeze two more people into their tiny household.

She watched as Jeronimo helped stack her trunk and Bess's small satchel precariously inside the doorway, along with her writing desk and the carpets that had covered the tables in her chamber. It all looked ridiculous in this space — like putting a crown on an urchin. Bess stood uneasily behind her as the carriage pulled away. "This will not be permanent," Emilia vowed to her cousin. "Your obligation to me should not exceed your comfort —"

Before she could continue, Jeronimo interrupted. *"Piccolina,"* he said. "We will have none of that. You are family."

He kissed her on both cheeks. Emilia felt herself soften just the tiniest bit. She had started to believe that she would only ever be a burden. If her cousin could take her in like this after the way she had purposefully avoided him for so many years, then she, too, could bend.

He gestured vaguely behind him, and Emilia realized that there was someone else in the room. The man stood in the shadows near the hearth. He was slight, and not much taller than Emilia herself. He had red hair and pock-marks on the part of his face his beard did not cover. But he had the same dark eyes that her father and uncles had, and familiarity tickled the back of her neck like a hot breath. "Hello," he said, pulling his cap into his hands. "It is good to see you again."

"Again, sir?" Emilia questioned.

Jeronimo clapped him on the shoulder. "Have you forgotten our cousin?"

She had a brief recollection of a little boy stealing her favorite sky-blue marble when she was not more than a toddler. Jeronimo's sister, Lucretia, had married Nicholas Lanier — and this was their son, Alphonso. "Yes, of course. I do hope you've learned how to share."

"I suppose we shall see," Alphonso said. For the quickest moment, his eyes dipped to Emilia's stomach.

Once, when Emilia had been younger and living with Countess Bertie, she had been with her Latin tutor at lessons and suddenly the whole room seemed to shrink to the size of the head of a pin. The air sawed in and out of her, and stars swam in her vision, and she knew — she just *knew* — something terrible was going to happen. The next moment, her tutor leaned forward over the table and the candle sputtered and caught his long hair. Within moments his entire head was wreathed in flame as he shouted and beat at himself to put out the flames, but not before his skin blistered and melted in front of her eyes.

She had never had a moment of foreboding like that again, until now.

Once again, Jeronimo had decided Emilia's future.

"Emilia," Jeronimo said, marking the look on her face. "You need a husband."

"What I *need*," she seethed, "is to be asked, *for once,* what I want."

"What you want hardly matters when you have little choice," Jeronimo argued.

"I only have little choice because of the *first* decision you made for me!"

They were inches away from each other, screaming. Alma and Bess cowered against the wall. Her young cousin was pretending to be fascinated by the grain of the wooden table. And Alphonso? He turned his cap in his hands like the wheel of a ship. "I rent a home," he said. "Just a few streets from here." He swallowed. "We have much in common."

"Like what?" Emilia asked.

"Our . . . family."

"Who I would rather not be related to right now. What else?"

He frowned. "Our faith."

"It is hard to believe in a God that would force this on me."

Alphonso's face flushed. "God did not force you, from what I am told. You spent a decade flaunting his wealth with pleasure."

She reeled back as if she had been slapped. She had not expected such vitriol from the meek man before her. "How much?" she asked evenly.

He blinked at her.

"How much did Hunsdon pay you to marry me?"

Alphonso looked at Jeronimo, who nodded. "Seven hundred pounds. And an appointment in the court recorder consort."

Because she had been acting as Somerset House's de facto mistress, Emilia had been privy to the accounts. She knew that seven hundred pounds was slightly more than what the Lord Chamberlain had paid last year for a handful of doublets and three cloaks.

She nodded, then walked out of her cousin's house.

Seven hundred pounds. At least now she knew what she was worth.

On October 18, 1592, Emilia Bassano married Alphonso Lanier in St. Botolph's Aldgate. The groom was drunk. The bride wore black, and a scowl.

As Emilia stood before a priest reciting a blessing to a God she didn't believe in, she told herself that this was a sham. And yet, legally, she knew it wasn't. The moment this farce of a ceremony ended she would belong to Alphonso Lanier, like his lute and his pocket watch. The seven hundred pounds that

Hunsdon had settled on Emilia — ostensibly enough to last a commoner a good long time, if one was careful — was no longer hers, but Alphonso's.

She remembered how Isabella had explained the difference between being kept like a courtesan and being owned like a wife.

Despite Hunsdon's attempts — to, well, assuage his guilt with money, she supposed — she now had less than she'd had when she arrived ten years ago at Somerset House. She had lost her freedom.

Jeronimo and Alma were their witnesses, and after the ceremony they returned to Mark Lane to find an unruly group of Bassanos, Alphonso's passel of brothers and sisters, plus other relatives by marriage. No sooner had Alphonso crossed the threshold of Jeronimo's small home than he was subsumed into a knot of cousins, plying him with more to drink.

Emilia stood abruptly when Alma passed her. "I should like to leave," she said quietly, and her cousin-by-marriage frowned.

"But you cannot," Alma said.

Emilia glanced over her shoulder at Alphonso, who was dancing some kind of sloppy jig while his father played the recorder. "He need not accompany me."

Before Alma could reply, Dr. Hector Nuñez entered the little home. He, too, lived on Mark Lane, and he was the de facto head of the Portuguese Jewish community there, who — like the Bassanos — attended church religiously but also maintained Jewish rituals within the walls of their own homes. To those who knew him in London, Dr. Nuñez was a physician. But to the residents of Mark Lane, he was the closest they had to a rabbi.

Dr. Nuñez took a length of silk from his doublet, pointed at four of Emilia's relatives, and positioned them in front of the hearth. Alma slipped an arm around Emilia, drawing her to the fireplace. Alphonso staggered beside her, gripping her arm for support. The four men chosen by the rabbi lifted the silk, creating a chuppah — the canopy under which a traditional Jewish wedding took place.

Emilia froze. It had been one thing to say words she did not mean in a Christian church. It would be another thing entirely to make a mockery of her own religion's rites.

And yet. Wasn't this already a mockery?

There should have been a *kiddushin* — a betrothal — where the groom paid *kessef* to the bride, some money or the equivalent. Instead, Alphonso had received funds to solve the problem Emilia had become.

She froze as Alphonso took her hand and put a ring on her right index finger. It was too large, clearly a ring that belonged to a man, and she wondered from whom he had borrowed or bought it.

Ke'dat Moshe ve'Yisrael, Dr. Nuñez was saying.

According to the laws of Moses and Israel.

Her hearing fuzzed as the rabbi recited the seven bridal blessings. She drank mechanically from the cup of wine that was thrust before her. It was not until she heard the shatter of the glass under Alphonso's foot signaling the end of the ceremony that she suddenly felt immersed in the action, instead of an observer. Her relatives shouted *mazel tov* and clapped Alphonso on the back.

The next step was for her to be sequestered in a room alone with Alphonso for *yichud,* symbolizing the consummation of the marriage. Instead he grabbed her hand and to the cheers of the others, dragged her out of her cousin's home and yanked her down Mark Lane to another dwelling.

He opened the door so forcefully he startled Bess, who was standing in the entryway with wide eyes. "Mistress?" she said, taking a step forward, but Alphonso shoved past the maid to the rear of the house, a bedroom. Emilia registered her hairbrush set out on a table and her writing desk tucked into a corner before Alphonso tossed her down on the bed. His hands went to the fastenings of his hose and Emilia struggled to a sitting position. "Cousin," she said.

"Husband," he corrected. He fell on top of her, pinning her against the straw mattress.

He smelled of wine and sweat and anger. With one hand he yanked up her skirts, and Emilia felt tears spring to her eyes.

"Please," she begged. "Not like this."

She flailed as Alphonso took himself in hand and stabbed between her legs. A cry tore out of her throat, and he pressed his palm over her mouth and nose.

Emilia couldn't breathe. She shook her head, but it only made him push down harder as he rutted into her. Her vision went black at the corners and she thought: *This is how I die.*

She bit him, hard.

Alphonso swore and shifted, and in doing so, came into contact with the hard, round reality of her belly. Her pregnancy was slight, but it was *there* — solid where her flesh should have been soft, curved where she had once been slender. She saw his eyes fall to the swell of her abdomen, and suddenly he went flaccid, slipping out of her body.

Emilia didn't move. She just stared at his cock, shriveled and small.

He rubbed his hand up and down it, but nothing happened. The irony, of course, was that Emilia had tricks up her sleeve for just this circumstance. Isabella had taught them to her; she had employed them as Hunsdon aged.

She would not give Alphonso the satisfaction. Literally.

He knelt on the bed again and smacked her

so hard across the cheek she tasted blood. *"Puttana,"* he hissed. *Whore.*

She rolled to her side, cradling her face, testing her jaw gingerly. She heard the door slam, and a key turn in a lock.

Slowly, Emilia sat up. She smoothed her skirts and swung her legs over the side of the bed. Shaking, she pushed to her feet and began to walk around her new chamber. It had no paintings or rugs. The furniture was sturdy and functional. The tester hanging above the bed had no curtains. It was the chamber of someone who had to work for a living, not someone who was born to wealth.

Her trunk had been set at the foot of the bed. She opened it, plunging her hands into the velvets and brocades of her gowns. She pushed aside her shifts and robes, the ribbon-tied stacks of correspondence, the trappings of her former life, until her fingers closed around a small wooden box.

Inside was her necklace of Murano glass, a pair of gold hair combs Hunsdon had given her, and her miniature of Southampton. When she knew she was leaving Somerset House, but didn't know quite when, she had taken it from her mattress and slipped it in here, so it would come with her wherever she was headed.

Holding back a sob, she pressed the miniature to her lips. Then she used a small

374

penknife to cut through the seam of the feather bed ticking and pinned it to the fabric just beneath where her head would lie.

She knelt again in front of her belongings, fishing through them until she held her most prized possession: the printed copy of *Arden of Faversham*. Alphonso could lock her up, he could beat her, he could squeeze the air from her throat, he could even kill Emilia — but there was one thing he would not be able to do.

Silence her.

My dearest Kit,

I am married.
*   I would describe to you my husband's fine attributes, but I do not like to lie.*

Yours,
E.

As the year turned, the death count from the plague rocketed. Emilia accustomed herself to running a household with only one servant, which meant she had to share in the work. Since she had never learned to cook, she left that to Bess, and instead she would clean and sweep and beat a batlet against Alphonso's clothes in a buck basket, attempting to remove the stains. The baby inside her grew, taking up so much of her breath and her energy that she sometimes had nightmares it would pry her ribs open to escape.

She did not mind, because the bigger she got, the less Alphonso wanted to do with her.

He drank spirits the way others breathed air. He had been put on probation from the court recorder consort after he arrived at the palace so inebriated that he vomited moments before the Queen entered. As a result — determined to find a new, more lucrative career — he had gambled on investments that had failed, bought shares of cargo ships that sank, and in a matter of months, had squandered three hundred pounds of Emilia's settlement.

Emilia sold her hair combs first, then her Murano beads. She needed income, a stash of her own money, which she could hide from Alphonso. She had tried several times to get Kit to find where Lord Strange's Men were performing in the hope of getting word to William Shakespeare, who had proved untraceable.

So Emilia decided to capitalize on misfortune. She visited the apothecary from whom she'd purchased her contraceptive herbs. There she bought dried plants believed to prevent illness, and from these she made teas to protect against the plague. She and Bess sewed the crushed herbs into sachets: yarrow and tansy and featherfew. Emilia would walk the streets between Mark Lane and Spitalfields, trading her preventatives for pence.

She had no idea if her remedies worked. She just knew that if they didn't, the dead would not come back to demand a refund.

A woman approached, face pinched and hands shaking in the cold. "Have you one to keep a child healthy?"

Emilia nodded, feeling her baby kick, as if to punish her for her fib. "Yes, but it costs a groat."

The woman counted out four pennies in her hand, and Emilia handed her a slightly larger packet of rue, briar leaves, elder leaves, and sage. "Steep these in wine, add ginger and the thickest treacle you can source, and have the child drink the tisane at sunrise and sunset."

"Thank you," the woman breathed. "God bless you."

Emilia stamped her feet and blew onto her fingers. A cold sleet had begun to fall. She moved along the buildings, which loomed over her, using the uneven walls for support so that she didn't slip on the slick cobblestones.

By the time she reached Mark Lane and Alphonso's home, her teeth were chattering. She unwound the scarf she kept wrapped around her face when she went out selling to find Bess wide-eyed and nervous. "Mistress," she said, "there be someone here for you."

Over Bess's shoulder she saw an unfamiliar, well-dressed man. "Mistress Bassano?"

"Lanier," she corrected. "I find I am at a

disadvantage, sir, as I do not know to whom I speak."

"Apologies, mistress. I am Edmund Greaves, solicitor."

For a moment, her heart stopped. *He's gone and done it,* she thought. *Alphonso has drunk himself to death, and this man is here to tell me I'm a widow.*

The man rose. "I represented Mistress Isabella Lucchino's interests."

Emilia's mind snagged on a single word. *Represented.* Past tense.

"I regret to inform you that Mistress Lucchino has died of the pestilence," Greaves said.

Emilia felt her knees give way. After her wedding, when she had visited Isabella, Emilia had sobbed in her arms, confessing what happened when Alphonso came home drunk enough to ignore her belly but not drunk enough to be impotent. Telling someone had been a relief. Isabella had known that Emilia hadn't come for advice or help, only to have someone else know what she suffered. Now, Emilia thought of Isabella's deep laugh and her perfume, musk and roses. She thought of how tightly she hugged. She remembered Isabella teaching her to straighten her spine when the world was beating her down.

The solicitor held out a small black pouch. "In her will, Mistress Lucchino requested that you have this," he said. "I remain sorry for your loss."

Emilia heard Bess opening the door for the solicitor as he left.

Isabella had left her the triple strand of pearls with the ruby clasp that she had been wearing the day the Baron dropped Emilia off at her residence. Unwarmed by Isabella's skin, the pearls were cold and hard.

Emilia carried them in her palm to her chamber, leaning down to see her reflection in the looking glass. Pulling her hair over one shoulder, she fastened the pearls around her throat. She pressed the necklace down hard enough on her skin to leave an impression.

Then she unlatched the clasp and set the pearls back into their pouch. Tomorrow, she would take the necklace to a jeweler and see how much money he would give her for it. Isabella would understand. In fact, it was probably why she had bequeathed the pearls to Emilia.

By the time she left the chamber, the skin of Emilia's chest was smooth and unblemished, as if the pearls had never rested there at all.

My dearest Kit,

I am more globe than woman, in truth. Were you to see me, I should be a laughingstock, and you doubled over with mirth. Myself, I cannot double over at all, and I take no lev-

ity in the situation. In faith I am melancholic and cannot disclose if this is because of where I find myself, with whom, or without whom.

I wish I could keep this life inside me for a little longer. The world is not kind to those who have no weapons to fight.

In sooth, I know not why I am so sad. It wearies me.

Has there been word from Shakespeare? From news as such, I should take joy.

Yours,
E.

Six weeks before her baby was due, Emilia was expected to go into confinement. She would not be able to leave the house to make the meager income she had from selling her teas. She would still be expected to work with Bess and ensure Alphonso had a clean house and mended clothes and food on the table when he deigned to come home. Windows would be shut to keep out the bad humors that might affect the child, and tapestries hung to block out the light, because too much of it could damage her eyes. The house would become as dark and silent as a womb.

She wondered what it was that made men fear women who were heavy with child — so much so that they did not even want to cross paths with them in public. Was it because so many women died in childbirth, and it was uncomfortable to be reminded of that? Whatever the reason, it was cruel to make a woman sit in silence for weeks with thoughts of her own mortality.

During the week before she went into confinement, Emilia made a list of the errands she needed to run. She rolled wool stockings up her legs and let Bess draw the kirtle over her head. She couldn't bend down to tie her boots anymore, so Bess did that for her, too. "I could come with ye, mistress," Bess offered, but Emilia shook her head. This was something she had to do on her own.

Her first stop was All Hallows Staining, the church at the northern end of Mark Lane. She sat in the pew listening to the service, waiting for the moment when she could rise and take communion. It was true that she did not believe in a Christian God, but like any soldier in battle, she would hedge her spiritual bets. However, most important, she had to be seen receiving communion by others in the community, because it was during birth that women were believed to be most susceptible to witchcraft, and Emilia would not let herself or her child be branded as pagans.

With the wafer still dissolving on her tongue, she lumbered toward London Bridge, where the mercers had shops. It took over an hour on foot, in the whistling wind that licked up her legs and frosted her eyelashes. But just as merchants near her home had closed their businesses during the plague, so had the merchants who traded in linens and fustian and silk.

The shutters were drawn, shop after shop. She pounded on one door . . . a second . . . a third . . . and no one answered. Emilia felt tears spring to her eyes. It was possible that these mercers had fled to the country, just as nobles like Hunsdon had.

She had not thought of him much. She didn't let herself, because there was no point. He had not contacted Emilia, nor had she expected him to. He had provided for her, or so he believed. And yet she wondered if he thought about this child, which he likely believed to be his.

Emilia brushed away the tears that were freezing on her cheeks and moved to the fifth door. This time when she knocked, it swung open. A small man with a badger's pointed nose and spectacles perched upon it took one look at Emilia. "We are not open for business," he said.

"Please. I have coin."

"No." The man started to close the door in her face. "Come back another time."

"But I cannot come back!" Emilia said, her voice breaking.

"John," a soft voice called from inside. "Hold." The man fell back to reveal a woman balancing a small child on her hip. She took one look at Emilia's swollen belly and patted the mercer's arm. "I shall take care of this customer," she said.

Her husband fell back, muttering.

"Thank you," Emilia said. "I am in need of . . ." The words stuck in her throat. "A winding-sheet."

She was not the first pregnant woman to buy her own potential shroud, the sheet in which her body would be wrapped should she die in childbirth.

The woman nodded, and an entire conversation passed between them in silence. "Wait here," she said.

Emilia stamped on the ground to keep her toes from going numb. When the woman returned, she was no longer carrying the child but held a parcel wrapped in paper and tied with string. "Two shillings," she said.

Emilia began counting out her pennies with shaking fingers. Twelve . . . fifteen . . . nineteen. She turned the pouch inside out, but she did not have the twenty-four pence that the sheet would cost. Her face burned as she met the gaze of the mercer's wife.

"I am mistaken, mistress," the woman said gently. "It is discounted in price." She counted out twelve pence from Emilia's palm and folded her fingers over the rest of it. "God be with you," she added, handing Emilia the package before she closed the door.

To His Lordship the Earl of Southampton,

My humble duty remembered, I hope in the Almighty of your health and prosperity and do beseech Him long to continue.

And yet I am vexed often, awake in night, having had a vision of you — skin pale, chest still — asleep for eternity in a crypt. I pray that this pestilence skips over your home and that God keeps His eye fixed on you.

I fear I am not long for this world, either.

Wait for me on the other side, love. It is the only place we shall be as equals.

From this residence in Mark Lane, I remain yours always,
E.

Emilia knew that when noblewomen went into confinement, they sometimes wrote letters to their unborn children with messages of love and advice for the future. In the common event that the woman herself did not survive the birth, her child would still have something of her voice. And if, by God's grace, the woman did survive . . . the note was thrown into the fire, because of the bad luck it might attract.

Emilia spent days trying to think of what she should put in a note to her baby. She was convinced she was having a daughter, and it seemed even more important to impart the wisdom she had accumulated in her years.

I may not live to see you, she began, *so here is what I wish you to know about me.*

But then, she got stuck. Did she want her child to know that Emilia's own mother had relinquished her — that this was somewhere in her bloodline? Did she want to speak of how poetry and prose could transport you? Did she want her baby to know that she had loved her father — whichever of two men he might be? Did she want to warn her daughter to fade into the woodwork and move silently, lest Alphonso take note of her?

That which Emilia most wanted to say she could not, for fear that this letter would be found and read when she was gone.

My darling — I was a published writer.

My words were spoken onstage by men who were no wiser.

My body was given to the keeping of a gentle, kind man. My troth was sold to a monster.

The one choice I made for myself was to love someone who loved me, for a little while.

Truth be told, I did not want you, at first. Now I cannot imagine a world without you in it.

And if I am not alive to hold your hand and lead you through this maze of what it means to be a woman in a man's world, promise me this: you will not blame yourself for arriving just as I left. Your existence did not come at the expense of mine.

Indeed, you are the poem I penned from heart, and like lines that are never forgotten, you were meant to outlive me.

She started and stopped her note many times.

What more would she want the child to know, if she were not around to impart that wisdom?

That she was not inferior because she had been born female.

There would be a day when her daughter felt stifled by her sex, and so Emilia decided to start there — to describe the weariness and frustration and maybe even the forbidden relief of facing your own death when the world was a battle every day.

When, in disgrace with fortune and men's
*   eyes,*
I all alone beweep my outcast state,
And trouble deaf heaven with my bootless
*   cries,*
And look upon myself and curse my fate,
Wishing me like to one more rich in hope,
Featured like him, like him with friends
*   possessed,*
Desiring this man's art and that man's scope,
With what I most enjoy contented least . . .

Emilia read what she'd written.

Perhaps she had been asking for too much.

Perhaps dissatisfaction was relative, and this

baby was all she needed to fill the emptiness inside her. Maybe Emilia did not have to tell her stories to the world; she only had to tell them to her child.

Let us both stay healthy, God, she prayed silently, *and I will stop wishing for what I cannot have.*

She picked up her quill again and addressed her unborn child.

*Yet in these thoughts myself almost
  despising,
Haply I think on thee, and then my state,
(Like to the lark at break of day arising
From sullen earth) sings hymns at heaven's
  gate;
For thy sweet love remembered such wealth
  brings
That then I scorn to change my state with
  kings.*

Emilia had just finished the sonnet when there was a scratch at the chamber door. Bess poked her head inside, carrying a note with a wax seal. "Mistress, the man what brought this said it was urgent and he awaits your reply."

Emilia took the folded missive and broke the seal. It had been nearly a year since she'd seen Southampton's handwriting, or received a request to meet.

Alphonso was not playing at court tonight.

He would stagger home at some point from the stews, and if he found her missing, she would pay for her recklessness.

Emilia looked up at her maid. "Tell him yes," she said.

When Emilia had met Southampton before, it was not Bess who had accompanied her from Somerset House, so she first had to ensure her maid's discretion. She had no sooner set Bess down to beg her silence than the servant gripped her hands. "Mistress, since you became a wife, I have washed your cuts and put poultices on your bruises. If you were to leave when I was occupied, say, I could not be expected to report on your whereabouts."

Emilia had thrown her arms around Bess's neck and hugged her tight. "Thank you," she said, and moments later, when Bess went to take the baking bread from the hearth, Emilia wrapped herself in her warmest cloak and slipped out of the house.

With the few pennies she had left, she hired a hack to take her to Water Lane and the Blackfriars Stairs, where she could catch a ferry to Paris Garden. Unlike the last time she had met Southampton there, it was deserted.

She saw him standing at the bridge near the tidal millstream and began to walk faster, impeded by her girth. As if he could sense her, he whipped around a moment before she reached him.

"My love," he whispered, and his hands were in her hair, drawing her lips to his. She drank from him as if he were an elixir.

Emilia could not get enough of him — his rosemary and woodsmoke scent, the heat in his hands and his eyes, the sense that she was exactly where she was meant to be. She wriggled closer and felt Southampton's arms close around her. Only then did she remember what was wedged between them.

He drew back and parted her cloak. The sphere of her belly stretched the rough homespun of her kirtle.

Southampton met her gaze. "Is it mine?"

She shook her head. "I do not know."

For a long moment they stared at each other. It had started to snow, flakes sparkling in his hair as if he were enchanted, and Emilia desperately wished it were true — that he could wave a wand or cast a spell and take them so far away they would never be found.

Gently, he settled his hand over her abdomen. "I hope it is."

It took all the strength Emilia had to step backward. "To what end, Henry? Where is this fairy-tale world where we might live?"

He gripped her hands tight, his fingers running over the calluses she had developed washing and mending. "We shall make one," he vowed. "I will buy you a home and —"

"I am married," she blurted, and the words fell between them like a blade.

The shock on his face nearly drove Emilia to her knees. "How . . . how could you let that come to be?"

"To whom should I complain, did I speak of it?"

He looked away. "I tried to reach you before I left the city. But my messenger was told you were ill . . . and then, when he returned a second time, that you no longer lived at Somerset House."

"No," she whispered.

"I have been frantic with worry, Emilia. It was as if you had completely disappeared from the world. I thought you were . . ." His voice broke. "I thought the pestilence had taken you. Until you wrote and mentioned Mark Lane." Southampton hesitated. "Why did you not send word sooner?"

"To what end?" Emilia challenged. "The deed was done."

He nodded, swallowing. "Do you love him?"

She would have laughed, but she was too near tears. She cupped Southampton's cheek with one hand. "I will never love anyone as I love you."

He leaned in to kiss her. "Do not say that," he murmured, skating his hand over the baby inside her, staking a claim and a wish. "He will be as greedy for your affections as his father."

"She," Emilia countered, smiling against his lips.

She closed her eyes and forced herself to say what she had come here to say. Yes, she had needed to see Southampton healthy and hale, so that she could stop tormenting herself with the worst imaginings. But she had also needed to give them both the opportunity to say goodbye.

"Henry," she began. "We cannot —"

He pressed a finger to her lips. "We can. We *can*." He took their joined hands and pressed them to her belly. "Is it not a miracle, what love has wrought?"

She felt the baby shift in her, a slow roll, as if it, too, needed to get closer to Southampton. And Emilia realized she did not need him to make magic.

They already had.

When Emilia's water broke, she told Bess to go to Jeronimo's house en route to the midwife. She was to ask Alma to come immediately, so Emilia would not be alone.

She was strangely calm considering that, within hours, she might be dead. Pain arrowed down her spine and banded around her abdomen, making her drop to her knees. It took three tries for Emilia to reach her bedchamber, and by then, Alma had arrived. "I am here, sweet," she soothed, offering her arm to Emilia as a hard contraction gripped her. "Let's get you on the bed."

"No," Emilia panted. "There is . . . a parcel . . ."

"I will get it for you when you are settled," Alma said.

Emilia shook her head. "The linens . . . change them."

Alma hesitated, and then took the parcel from the table where it rested. She tore at the string and unfolded the pristine linen, while Emilia slid down the wall.

How did women do this?

How did *anyone* survive?

Alma laid the sheet on the bed and then helped Emilia to her feet. "Shroud me in it," Emilia gasped.

"No one is dying today." Alma tugged Emilia's kirtle off, leaving her in her shift. She handed Emilia a shard of jasper. "Take this. It brought me luck and health with the boys."

Emilia nodded, palming the charm. Laboring women had all sorts of superstitious amulets — bits of tin, cheese, butter — meant to calm them.

By the time Bess returned with the midwife, Emilia was soaked with sweat and twisting on the new bedsheet. The woman was short and squat, with eyebrows that met in the middle of her brow and a hairy mole on her chin. She looked, to Emilia's tired eyes, downright witchy, but like other midwives in London she would have taken an oath to not steal the umbilical cord or placenta or anything else that might be sold to a practitioner of magic. "All right, dearie," the midwife said, "let's take a look, shall we?" She bent Emilia's knees and probed between her legs, murmuring to herself. "How long have ye been laboring?"

Alma answered on Emilia's behalf. "Since midday."

"Dear Lord," the midwife said, "look down on Mistress Lanier and touch her womb. Give her an easy delivery and protect the life of her babe. Saint Margaret, pray for her. Amen."

"Amen," Emilia and Alma said, and then exchanged a look.

Time passed in a blot of pain that spread to the edges of Emilia's body like spilled ink. Bess brought her caudle, an eggy alcoholic brew meant to ease the agony. By sunrise, Emilia could not stand without her legs collapsing beneath her, and she dozed between the aches that were ripping her apart. When the band of fire inside woke her again, she heard Alma and the midwife whispering. "There's an unnatural presentation," the midwife said. Emilia was barely conscious as she felt strong arms come beneath her own and start bouncing her up and down as if the baby was meant to be shaken out of her.

No, she thought. *Stop.*

She could smell wild thyme suddenly and saw the midwife rubbing the ointment on her own arms and fingers. Only a moment of confusion passed before the woman jammed her hand between Emilia's legs.

Emilia could not even recognize the sound of her own scream. She had never made a noise like that. She was being split in two. Her hand scrabbled for Alma's.

The pressure changed and suddenly there was a burning between her thighs. "That's it, mistress," the midwife said, hauling Emilia into a crouch. She felt a gush of hot fluid, and then a slick of flesh as the baby slipped out of her body. A moment later, there was an aggrieved cry.

Emilia toppled backward, staring at the ceiling. Her vision swam.

Alma helped her sit up, and the midwife placed a small, wrapped bundle in Emilia's arms. "Mistress Lanier," she said. "Ye have a fine, strapping son."

A boy.

A boy?

"Oh, Emilia," Alma cooed, pulling away the blanket from the baby's face. "He's so beautiful."

Emilia glanced down. The baby's hair was damp, but it was red.

Hunsdon, before he had gone gray, had ginger hair. Southampton's curls were auburn.

Well.

She knew a baby could not have two fathers, and yet maybe this one could be the exception to the rule. She hoped that Hunsdon might have blessed him with compassion and that Southampton might have given him spirit. He would share a name with *both* of these men.

"Henry," she whispered, and the baby opened his eyes and stared directly at her.

They were silver, like hers.

Emilia had forgotten that her son might have some of her *own* attributes as well. She touched her finger to the soft moon of his cheek. She hoped that she had bestowed on him endurance, so this baby, like her, would be able to survive whatever obstacle was thrown in his path.

When the door of the house slammed open in the middle of the night, Emilia startled. Her movements woke Henry, who had fallen asleep in the crook of her arm after nursing, and she rocked him tightly. She could hear Bess's voice and Alphonso's louder, slurred one. There was a crash and a squeal and then heavy footsteps.

The bedchamber door opened and Alphonso stood in the threshold, rubbing his eyes as if he could not believe what he was seeing. Bess scrambled to squeeze in beside him. For a skinny slip of a thing, she was fiercely protective of Emilia. "Master Lanier," she said nervously, "what a fine son the mistress has delivered!"

Emilia had never expressly told Bess why she had been sent from Somerset House.

She imagined the maid now knew; she could count months like anyone else. But the truth of the baby's paternity was never spoken aloud, and the expectation had always been that Alphonso's acceptance of the marriage (and the money) meant he would raise the baby as his own.

Yet even if he presented the child as his in public, that did not guarantee how he would treat the baby in private.

Emilia saw his eyes grow damp, and for a heartbeat she thought: *Mayhap this will change things. Mayhap this will change* him.

"Alphonso," she said softly. "Would you . . . would you like to see him?"

He walked slowly to the side of the bed and stared down at the baby. He reached out one finger as if to touch the tiny fist, and then pulled back as if he did not trust himself.

The baby started to cry. Emilia tried to soothe him by holding him to her breast, but he did not want to nurse. He was damp through his blanket.

Bess sprang toward the bed. "I will wrap him in a fresh swaddling cloth," she said, taking the infant. "And then he will wish to eat, mistress." She hurried out of the room, leaving Alphonso standing beside the bed.

He seemed to be chewing on his words. "You are well?"

"I am," she said. "Although it is not an experience I care to repeat." She realized her mistake immediately, even before Alphonso's dark eyes flashed.

The baby's cries grew more urgent as he was cleaned by Bess in the adjoining room.

"What did you name the bastard?" Alphonso asked.

Perhaps it was his use of the slur, or the spirits on his breath. Perhaps it was her anger at being bound to Alphonso as tight as the baby was in his swaddling. Emilia looked him directly in the eye. "Henry," she said.

She should have seen it coming. The fist struck her on the side of the head, snapping her sideways. The second blow crunched her jaw. She curled away from Alphonso's beating, but not before she heard the sickening crack of bone in her nose and tasted blood running down her throat.

After that, she didn't feel anything.

Dearest Kit,

I need you. Please come home.

Because public houses were still closed, when Kit sent word for Emilia, they could not meet at the Falcon Inn. He sent her the address of his lodgings in Norton Folgate.

If Kit's landlady was surprised to see a woman holding a baby on his doorstep, she didn't say anything. Emilia had a cloak pulled over her head, her face deep in the shadows.

She bounced little Henry in her arms, but he was a good baby, as if he'd been born knowing that attracting attention invited disaster.

A moment later, Kit himself was in the doorway, and tears tightened her throat. "Mouse!" he cried, embracing her, momentarily flustered by the small bundle of human caught between them. "Now, what is this I hear of you being needy? If this is advice about finding a wet nurse I should inform you that I stay as far from a woman's breasts as —"

His irreverent chatter faltered as Emilia pulled the cloak back from her head, revealing her face. Her broken nose had healed, but she still had two deep black eyes, a tender jaw, and a healing gash on her forehead. His face was a one-man play of emotion — shock, pity, fury. When he took her shoulders in his hands and she cried out — one of the most tender bruises still bloomed there — she thought he would rear back and put a fist through the plaster wall.

"I shall kill him," Kit said evenly.

She smiled a little. "Mayhap we could not have this discussion on the street."

Kit seemed to notice the open doorway for the first time. He gently drew her into the building, gesturing for her to precede him up the stairs. Emilia knew that Kit had lived with Thomas Kyd there; she hadn't realized that he'd held on to the rooms when he left for the country. If Kit still had a roommate, he wasn't home. The small residence was surprisingly tidy and spartan, without any of Kit's oversize personality. She thought about his alleged secret work for the Crown and wondered if the nondescript decor was intentional.

There was a fire blazing in the hearth; the rooms were warm. Emilia tried to unfasten her cloak but couldn't manage it one-handed. She thrust the baby toward Kit, who held Henry like he was laced with gunpowder. He stared down at the infant's tiny features, the russet fluff of his hair. "What is his name?"

"Henry," Emilia replied, shrugging off her cloak. "He is named after his father."

"Hunsdon?" Kit asked. "Or Southampton?"

"I do not know," she said.

Kit swore and handed the baby back to her. "All right," he said. "Tell me everything."

For three-quarters of an hour, she did. From time to time, Kit seemed to forget to breathe, and once he even growled, but he did not interrupt her.

She began with the moment she learned she had fallen pregnant and ended with the gash in her forehead that Bess had stitched up hours after childbirth. When she was finished, Kit poured her some ale. The baby awakened and she unbuttoned her dress so that he could nurse. "Is that all of it?" Kit asked.

She blinked. "Is it not *enough*?"

"I will kill him," Kit repeated.

"Alphonso? You cannot."

"Then I will take you away and hide you." He glanced at the baby. "Both of you."

"Kit," she said, "I am his *wife*. Legally, he owns me."

"As if I've ever cared a fig about the law," Kit scoffed. He began to pace, running his hands through his hair the way he did sometimes when he had written himself into a corner and had to figure a way out of it. It was so familiar it made Emilia want to weep. "I will bring you here and you will live with me."

She smiled. "I am sure a squalling infant will be music to the ears of your young lovers."

He fell to his knees in front of her, so that they would be at eye level. "Do you think you matter less than my love life?" Kit said fiercely. "Do you not believe that you are closer to me than my own sisters?"

She touched his cheek. "I believe it. It is why I asked for you. I cannot do this on my own."

"Tell me," Kit begged. "What do you need?"

"Money," Emilia said bluntly. "I need my own income, which my husband cannot touch, so that he cannot bankrupt me."

"Would that I could, Mouse, but I am far from a wealthy man. Would Southampton deny you funds?"

The color drained from Emilia's face. "I was a courtesan, Kit," she said. "Never a whore."

Chagrined, he nodded. "Then how can I aid you?"

She met Kit's gaze. "Find Shakespeare."

■ ■ ■ ■

By April, the epicenter of the plague was Fleet Prison, which the disease had ripped through like a fire. A month later, the weather grew so hot the entire city reeked. London was giving Hell a run for its money.

Emilia spent her days taking care of Henry and writing whenever he was asleep or quietly laying in his crib. She spent her nights avoiding Alphonso. Southampton was stuck at court; the Queen had refused to let her courtiers leave for fear they'd bring the plague back through the gates of the castle. Although Kit had promised her that he would track Shakespeare down, she had known it would take some time. She marked this in milestones: Henry's first smile, the first time he held up his own head, the day he rolled from his belly to his back.

Bess had become Emilia's strongest ally. She didn't know the contents of the notes that came for Emilia from Kit or Southampton — she could not read — but she always brought messages to Emilia rather than Alphonso, so that Emilia could siphon off the missives meant for herself. She took care of Henry without Emilia ever having to explain why she was gone for several hours at night. She never asked why Emilia wrote so furiously for hours, when most ladies had only minimal correspondence to complete. She had tended to Emilia's injuries after Alphonso beat her. So on the day Kit finally sent word that Shakespeare would be coming to Norton Folgate, Bess did not question why Emilia wished to wear one of her old court gowns instead of her rough kirtle, or why she had an appointment that would require her to be apart from Henry all afternoon.

Emilia took the entire stack of her work in progress and slipped it into a leather satchel. She kissed Henry on the brow. "Be a good boy for Bess," she said, and she hurried into the street.

By the time she reached Kit's apartment, Shakespeare had arrived. He and Kit were drinking, and had been for a while, from the looks of it. Emilia felt a flood of gratitude for Kit, as she was certain that the very last thing he would have chosen to do was form any kind of social bond with Shakespeare, who toadied up to him and wanted to claim association with Marlowe in the hope that fame would rub off on him like gilt.

"Ah," Kit said. "Mistress Bassano has at last arrived!" To Emilia, in a whisper, he added, "And not a moment too soon. I was considering strangling myself with my ruff."

Her lips twitched. "Master Shakespeare," she said. "Well met."

Shakespeare got to his feet and bowed. "Good day, mistress."

She sat and slipped her writing out of the satchel. Her breasts ached, reminding her she had only a finite amount of time before her milk would leak and stain the fine damask.

"When last we met, we agreed to provisional terms," Emilia said. "Yet with the sale of *Arden of Faversham,* I have proven that my writing is a profitable commodity." She let her gaze slide to Kit, who nodded at her, encouraging. "I would like you to hold to your end of the deal."

"I know not what that means, mistress," Shakespeare replied.

"You told me you would broker my writing in return for the use of your name," Emilia said. She lifted a stack of pages. "I have been working on a play about marriage and obedience — it's called *Taming of a Shrew.* It's a comedy —"

"I cannot sell a play," Shakespeare said. "The theaters are closed."

"Are you not even now performing with Lord Strange's Men in the countryside?"

"Aye, but older repertoire. No theater manager will risk the cost of new material while the very business itself is in peril. It is why I am reduced to making my coin as an actor."

Emilia rather thought that he was reduced to acting because his writing was pedantic and plodding, but she knew insulting him would not do her any good right now. She smiled prettily. "I imagine that must be devastating for you."

"Indeed, the Rose was in the midst of my Henry VI historicals when the edict to close theaters was handed down," Shakespeare said.

Kit winked at her. Those historical plays had come from Oxford's scriptorium of writers. But she could not be angry at Shakespeare for so seamlessly taking credit; was that not exactly what she wished him to do with her own writing?

"I am sorry, mistress, but I am not in the market for plays right now."

"If only there were entertainments that could be enjoyed in the privacy of one's own home, safe from pestilence," Kit smoothly manipulated. "Did Mistress Bassano fail to mention she is an accomplished poet?"

Emilia gaped at Kit as he shuffled through her stack of papers and pulled free the *Venus and Adonis* poem she had written for Southampton.

Shakespeare reached for it. "Is this true? This is also your work?"

"Yes, sir," Emilia said.

He fanned through the pages, his eyes roaming over her handwriting. "A poem will not fetch the same price as a play. Maybe twenty shillings."

"She will honor the same split she did for *Arden,*" Kit said.

Shakespeare smoothed his wispy goatee. "There is something to be said for keeping my relationship with printers in a time when product is scarce. You have read this poem, Marlowe?"

"Indeed," Kit said.

Emilia bit her lip. "I could give you a fair copy —"

"No need. The printer will set it." Shakespeare crossed to a small table on the other side of the room. He lifted a quill lying on a piece of paper — something Kit must have been working on — and leaned closer to read the prose in progress. With a scowl, Kit snatched the paper away, and Shakespeare shrugged, dipping the quill into the inkwell. Then he scrawled his name beneath the title of *Venus and Adonis.*

"I shall take Master Marlowe at his word," Shakespeare said to Emilia. "As you have pointed out, your work is a known commodity to me, and therefore any topic you expound upon should sell, should it not?"

Emilia nodded, not trusting herself to speak.

"I shall be in touch after the sale," Shakespeare said.

"You can leave word with my landlady," Kit injected. "She will know how to reach Mistress Bassano even if I am not in residence in London."

Shakespeare reached for his cloak and hat, then picked up the poem and strode from Kit's apartment.

"Kit," Emilia breathed. "What were you *thinking*?"

"That my Mouse needed money, and that I wasn't going to let him leave here without

405

taking something of yours to sell." He hesitated. "But also, truly, that if he'd stayed in my rooms another quarter of an hour I might have pitched him out the window."

"The poem you gave him is the one I dedicated to Southampton."

"I know."

"It is also about a woman seducing a younger man. It's quite . . . erotic."

Kit shrugged. "I repeat: I know."

"Shakespeare put his name on it without allowing me to alter the dedication."

"Southampton's a patron of the arts. Others dedicate work to him."

Emilia frowned. "Yes, but when people see Shakespeare's name on this — in tandem with this particular subject matter — will they not make the assumption that he might have . . . *carnal feelings* for Southampton?"

Kit raised a brow. "Darling, *my* tribe does not want to lay claim to that vapid, vainglorious half-wit. Your kind can keep him. Although I do look forward to everyone questioning Shakespeare's sexual preferences once the poem starts circulating."

Emilia set her hands on her hips. "You gave him that poem on purpose."

Kit's eyes gleamed. "A gentleman never tells," he said.

The last week of May, Bess smuggled two missives in one day to Emilia. The first was from Kit, letting her know that Shakespeare had given him her earnings to pass along and inviting her to Norton Folgate later that week to celebrate her newfound success as a poet.

The second was from Southampton, asking her to meet on the same day.

She hadn't seen him since before giving birth to Henry, and even as she pulled a fresh sheet of paper from her writing box for the reply, she knew she would be sending her regrets to Kit.

Alphonso, however, was underfoot. The same fear of plague that had kept Southampton sequestered with the Queen had led her to deny court musicians entry to the castle. This meant that Emilia had to find an excuse to slip away without her husband becoming suspicious.

In the end, she bartered with the only tool she had: her body.

Since their first abortive consummation on their wedding night, Alphonso had mostly left Emilia untouched. The bigger she had grown with child the more he'd avoided her. But now, Henry was almost three months old. Her body had healed. So days before she was to meet Southampton at the Paris Garden stairs, Emilia served Alphonso his supper — but rested her hand on his shoulder as she did. Hours later when nursing Henry, instead of covering her breast, she let her shawl slip and watched her husband's eyes flick toward her.

The night before her meeting with Southampton, she waited for Alphonso to enter the bedchamber. "Mayhap it is time for a real marriage, sir," she said meekly.

It was all he wanted: her submission. He did not realize she was orchestrating the entire experience. He did not know, as he grunted and thrust into her, that Emilia was nowhere to be found, locked so deep in her mind that she was untouchable. Instead, she imagined Southampton's touch, Southampton's mouth, washing away the stain of Alphonso.

The next morning, Alphonso strutted like a crow. Just as she had anticipated, he could not wait to share with his closest friends how he had tamed his shrew of a spouse. "Wife," he announced, "I have people to visit. I know not when I'll return."

"Of course, Alphonso," Emilia said softly. "You need not make me aware of your comings and goings."

He jerked his chin in assent. "It is good that you have seen the error of your ways, Emilia. I prefer this version of you."

As soon as Alphonso closed the door behind himself, Emilia thrust Henry into Bess's waiting arms. "I prefer this version of me, too," she muttered, pulling her cloak on so that she could conceal her face in its hood. She kissed the baby's brow, and slipped outside.

She hurried to the ferry landing because it had taken her husband longer to leave the house than she anticipated. Even as the boat pulled up, she could see the Earl — tall and broad, silhouetted by the sun as if the shape of him needed to be filled in with color and light. Emilia found herself laughing, joy spilling from the seam of her lips. He caught her around the waist and spun her, the hood falling back from Emilia's face as he kissed her.

"You are well?" she asked, framing his face with her hands.

"It is I who should be asking that," Southampton said. "The babe . . . ?"

"Is so beautiful," Emilia breathed.

"I had thought you might bring him."

She could not read, from his tone, if he was disappointed. Indeed she had considered taking young Henry to meet him, but the truth was that she was too selfish. She had so few moments with Southampton, she could not bear to share them, even with her son.

"He is very demanding right now," Emilia said.

Southampton slipped a hand beneath her cloak and squeezed her arse. "Is he now," he murmured.

They crashed together again, stealing each other's words and breath, parting only when he grabbed her hand to pull her into the garden. When Southampton brought her to the mossy banks of the stream where they had first made love and spread his cloak on the ground, Emilia lay on her back and stared up at a sky as vivid as his eyes. Between long, lazy kisses, they filled in the empty spaces in each other's lives — Emilia telling him that Isabella had died of plague; Southampton sheepishly admitting that he'd been nominated as a Knight of the Garter. Neither of them mentioned Alphonso. "Tell me about my son," Southampton said.

Emilia considered before she spoke. Whatever bits she offered could not have any barbs that might, upon later reflection, hurt to recall. "He has red hair," she began. "And he sometimes sleeps with his arm up in the air, as if he is performing the galliard." She rolled on her side to face Southampton. "When he nurses, he makes little sounds, like an old man so captivated by his meal he cannot help but hum while he devours it."

Southampton laughed, nuzzling the rise of her breast over the edge of her dress. He began to peel down the fabric, but she stilled him with her hand. "I am . . . not the same," she said, suddenly nervous. She had silver lines on her belly. Her breasts hung lower. Sometimes, they leaked.

He met her gaze. "You are exactly the same. You are mine. No matter the package that comes in."

She kissed him then, and his hand slipped beneath her neckline, pinching her nipple. He pushed up her skirts, frothing the satin between them. She took him in hand and guided him, throwing her head back and crying out in a way she never had before when they were together. Let them be seen; let them get caught. If other people saw their love, it would only affirm it — evidence that this connection had been real, should there come a day when it was nothing but a memory.

After, she lay in Southampton's arms, her hair streaming over his chest like ink. "You are leaving again," she guessed.

"For Titchfield, in the morning." His grasp tightened on her. "How did you know?"

It wasn't something she could put into words. It had simply felt like Southampton was not giving himself to her but trying to anchor himself instead.

She imagined confessing it all to him: that her husband broke her body and sometimes her spirit; that she did not know if Henry was his but wished so with all her heart; that there was a poem circulating with a dedication to him that she had penned.

He sat up, rummaging about in his cloak. She was so lost in her thoughts that she did not realize, for a moment, that he was pressing a small velvet pouch into her palm. She felt the shift and jingle of coins inside. "If I cannot be with you, with *him,* then —"

Emilia sat up, dropping the pouch as if it contained a viper. "I will not take payment for what I give freely, my lord."

"It is not payment, Emilia —"

"Then I will not take charity." Bright spots of color burned on her cheeks. Much had been taken from her, but her pride was still intact.

Southampton let the coins rest between them on the ground and curled his fingers around hers. "I am trying to do the right thing, love," he said softly.

"As am I," Emilia replied.

He was the one who looked away first. "If ever you . . . if were you to find yourself in need . . ." His voice broke. She knew he was trying to offer a safe harbor, but she could barely stomach the thought of showing up at his ancestral home in the country in her plain clothing with a baby in her arms and being shown around to the servants' entrance for charitable leavings from the master's meals.

Southampton seemed so defeated that Emilia relented. She squeezed his hand and tried to lighten the mood. "Were I to find myself in need, I suppose I could appeal to you through a poet's dedication. . . ."

He blushed and raised a brow. "You have read it? *Venus and Adonis?*"

"Who has not," she said diplomatically.

"I know not this Shakespeare fellow," Southampton said. "But the turn of phrase — it's quite good. Do you agree?"

What she wanted to say: Yes. *Yes.*

I am the poet; and you are not the patron, but the subject.

And: *Did you like it? Truly?*

Instead, Emilia met his gaze. "Apologies, my lord. I should not have snapped at your kindness," she said softly.

"And I should have thought before I spoke. I swear to you, I meant no offense."

"I know." She drew in a breath. "Do you ever feel as if every moment of your life is a transaction? As if you must trade away parts of yourself to keep what makes you . . . you?"

His eyes snapped to hers; she knew that he understood completely.

"I fear that I'll give too much away," Emilia confessed, "and I won't remember who I am."

"Then I shall remind you," Southampton promised, kissing her. With each brush of his mouth she felt her melancholia lift, her tears dry as if her cheeks had never been damp.

"Love comforteth, like sunshine after rain."

She did not realize that she had spoken a line from *Venus and Adonis* out loud until Southampton drew back to look at her, quizzical. "You have *memorized* parts of that poem?"

Emilia smiled against his lips. "I might have done," she said.

Dearest Kit,

Come now, it has been a week. You cannot still be holding a grudge because I could not meet you.

413

I remain indebted to you, presuming you still hold my purse.

Yours,
E.

It was Jeronimo who told her what had happened, and it wasn't even meant for Emilia's ears. They were gathered at Alma's table for a secret Shabbat dinner, and Alphonso had asked what news they'd had from court, which was currently residing at Nonsuch. "Her Majesty is mulling a move to Windsor," Jeronimo said, "but will not allow entertainers to join her until the pestilence clears."

"Nor will she pay for tunes we do not play." Alphonso speared a bit of meat with his knife. "What is the point of being a court musician if there is no music at court?"

"Yet the talk is mostly of Marlowe's death," Jeronimo added, as if he were speaking of the weather, as if he hadn't just sucked all the air out of Emilia's lungs.

"What?" she managed.

"The playwright," Jeronimo said. "You know of him?"

She forced her chin to bob.

"Stabbed. Last Sunday in Deptford Strand, over payment for a shared meal."

Emilia saw black stars at the edges of her vision. She braced one hand on the wooden table, clutching Henry closer. Kit had been

414

killed on the afternoon that she had been lying with Southampton on the mossy expanse of Paris Garden, quoting her own poetry.

Something tells me your little death was better than mine, Mouse, he would have said.

If he'd been here to say it.

No.

Nonononononono.

She pushed away from the table, hearing Alma's concerned voice, and passed the baby to her cousin's arms before staggering outside. She pressed the heels of her hands to her eyes and took great gulps of air. She could not imagine a world without her best friend in it.

"Baruch dayan ha'emet," she mouthed silently, God is the true judge, as she tore the neckline of her kirtle. It was the traditional way Jews said goodbye to the body of someone who died while acknowledging that the emotional bond would last.

She could not say how much time had passed before she simply started walking down Mark Lane — without a cloak, without a clear head. Eventually she heard boots on cobblestones as Jeronimo caught up to her. "Cousin? Are you well?"

"I met Marlowe . . . with Hunsdon," she muttered. "I must pay my respects."

"He was buried the next day, after the coroner reported that the fatal blow was made in self-defense. Awfully rushed, if you ask me," Jeronimo said, his voice lower. "The gentlemen he was with, they weren't playwrights but government agents. You know there were whispers that Marlowe worked secretly for the Crown . . . but I wonder if the argument was about him being an outspoken atheist." Her cousin raised a brow. "A good reminder for all of us about what we choose to show the public, and what we do not."

Emilia faced him, her eyes red and her face scarred with tears. *I did not get to say goodbye,* she thought.

Jeronimo looked at her with surprise. "You enjoyed his work, then?"

"Loved," she said fiercely. "I loved him."

For a week, Emilia grieved without letting anyone know she was grieving. Sitting shiva in plain sight was impossible, but when she could, Emilia sought out the most uncomfortable seat in the house, a reflection of the pain in her heart. She recited the mourner's Kaddish, holding the words of prayer on the bowl of her tongue in silence.

She could not help but feel responsible.

If only she had postponed her visit with Southampton and had met Kit instead at his apartments — then he would not have been in Deptford Strand and he would not have dined with agents of the Crown and there wouldn't have been a fight.

If only, when Kit had asked what he could do to help her, she had not told him she

416

needed money. If she had said, *Keep yourself safe,* maybe he would still be here.

Needless to say, she would never be paid for the sale of *Venus and Adonis.* But she did not miss the coin. She missed Kit.

With Southampton in Titchfield and Kit dead, Emilia became a wraith. She lost weight she could not afford to lose, and her milk dried up, requiring Bess to find a wet nurse for Henry. She rarely spoke and for days at a time did not change her clothing or brush her hair. Alphonso did not seem to notice. The biddable wife who did not bother to talk back, just stumbled in the direction in which he pushed her, seemed to be the one he'd hoped for. Sometimes he rutted on her at night. If there was any solace to being so numb, it was that Emilia barely cared.

In October more gossip arrived from Windsor Castle: Dr. Rodrigo Lopez, Her Majesty's physician, had been condemned to death for plotting to kill the Queen. Emilia had been introduced to him at court when she was with Hunsdon and had pretended not to know him, but in fact, she had met him years earlier at her cousin's *bris* ceremony, where Dr. Lopez served as the *moyel.* The rumor was that Dr. Lopez had made an enemy of the Earl of Essex by telling others that he'd treated the nobleman for syphilis ("A night with Venus, a lifetime with mercury," Kit used to say, which only brought Emilia to tears once again). But regardless of the source of the accusation, having a Portuguese converso Jew accused of conspiring to kill the Queen cast Mark Lane, and all its residents, under a microscope.

In November, a page at Windsor Castle contracted the plague and died. Since Her Majesty had removed herself to Windsor to escape the disease, it sent everyone there into a panic. None of this interested Emilia, except that the dead page had served Lady Scrope — the daughter of Hunsdon and his wife, Anne.

In early December, Emilia dreamed of Kit.

In her mind's eye, she was the size of a rodent. She shimmied down the bedsheets and had a heart-pounding run-in with a house cat before she managed to squeeze through a crack in the floor. There was a white rat there, with a pink twitch of a tail and red, inebriated eyes. *Mouse,* Kit said, *it took you long enough.*

You do not look like yourself, Emilia replied.

You're one to talk.

I don't know how to not *feel this way,* she admitted.

Of course you do, Kit said. *You give the feeling away to a character.*

Having tasted success, she didn't know if she could go back to writing without anyone ever reading her words. Before she could admit this, however, the rat smacked her with its tail. *Send the coxcomb a message. You're lucrative now.* He *will come to* you.

When the sun rose, Emilia startled to find

418

Alphonso still snoring beside her. She dressed in fresh underthings for the first time in days and pulled her hair away from her face. She wrote a letter to Master Shakespeare in care of Lord Strange's Men, informing him of her lodgings and reminding him of the need for great discretion. Then she sealed it and paid a messenger to deliver the note in the countryside.

Within a week, she had arranged to meet him at the Falcon Inn Stairs.

"God be with you, Mistress Bassano," Shakespeare said. "And my condolences for the loss of our dear friend."

She gritted her jaw tight. She would not reply and let this man presume that Kit meant to him even a fraction of what he'd meant to her. "To be blunt, sir, I wish to continue our partnership." She pulled another long-form poem from her satchel — *The Rape of Lucrece.* "When it sells," — *when* — "you may write me at the address I last gave you, and please continue to refer to yourself as a glover with a delivery."

This time, Shakespeare scanned the title page. "Southampton again?" he said wryly.

"He is an unparalleled lover," Emilia replied, "of the arts."

By the time 1594 dawned, Emilia's poem had sold. Shakespeare had also given her a piece that he'd been penning — *Titus Andronicus*

— and asked her to revise it. Emilia did not enjoy reworking someone else's plays, particularly this one about a Roman general, but money was money. She needed it more than ever since Alphonso had no work. As a result, Emilia treated the revisions like any other drudgery, from laundering clothes to emptying chamber pots. She leaned into the theme of revenge and raised the body count to fourteen gruesome, creative deaths — severing heads and hands and baking two rapists into a pie. She wrote in bawdy jokes. As a way of leaving her fingerprint on the text, she added characters named Æmelius and Bassanius.

She could imagine Kit grinning at that.

Rewriting *Titus,* however, made her itch to craft her own plays again.

In the early days of her marriage, she'd written *Taming of a Shrew.* She decided to revisit her initial draft. A character she'd originally called Alphonso became Baptista — the name of her father — instead. The character Emilia became Bianca. She changed the setting to Italy, peppering it with a hundred allusions to music, and false identities.

The plot was simple: when a suitor became attracted to the sweet, compliant Bianca, her father said that her elder sister — intractable, brash Kate — had to be married first. A man named Petruchio took on that challenge, and the entirety of the play showed him trying to break his willful fiancée.

420

On a hot midday in late July, Emilia sat at the oak table in their home, writing the end of her revised play as Alphonso entered. "Where is the dinner meal?" he asked. "I am famished, truly."

She no longer hid her writing from Alphonso, who either believed she wrote correspondence in blank verse or truly did not care.

"Indeed you must be, husband," Emilia said without glancing up. "A man as strong as you must needs have his sustenance."

"Is this not what I said?"

From the larder, Bess peeked around the shelving.

"It is why I have planned a truly special dinner for you, sir," Emilia continued.

Alphonso stepped closer. "A special meal?"

"What say you to a piece of tripe finely broiled?"

"I like it well enough," Alphonso said.

"Nay, 'tis choleric. What say you to a piece of beef and mustard?" She continued to scrawl on her page as she spoke.

"A dish I do love to feed upon —"

"Ay, but no . . . the mustard is too hot."

"Why, then," Alphonso said, "the beef. And let the mustard rest."

"Nay, I could not live with myself if I served a man as fine as you beef without the mustard to dress it. That would be as if to admit that my own lord and master does not tower head and shoulders over them in all things, that he might be satisfied with such trivial repast," Emilia said.

"Just so," Alphonso blustered.

"Which is why I cannot bear to serve you your midday meal."

He blinked. "But —"

She beamed at him. "Perhaps Jeronimo has extra from his table?"

With a growl, Alphonso slammed out of the house, presumably to his cousin's.

In the larder, Bess giggled. "Mistress, he will beat you for that one day."

"Very likely," Emilia agreed.

She flipped to the end of her play, which was the height of absurdity.

After vowing to tame Kate — his shrew of a wife — Petruchio finally wore her down to the point where she displayed her utter obeisance in front of others. When Petruchio called, she came.

But when Kate's sister Bianca — the rule follower — was called by her new husband . . . she resisted.

Bianca, who was — in her prior draft — named Emilia.

She liked that, even if she was the only person who would know such a thing.

She thought about Alphonso, crowing to his friends about his submissive wife. She thought about how she outwitted him daily, as just moments before.

I am ashamed that women can be so simple-minded as to declare war when they should be surrendering for peace, Emilia wrote, giving words to Kate. *Or that they want control, supremacy, and sway, when they are bound to serve, love, and obey. Why would our bodies be soft and weak and smooth — unsuited to toil and trouble in the world — unless our soft characters and our hearts should match our external parts?*

She paused. What else would her husband most wish to hear?

My mind used to be as arrogant as yours, my heart as great, my reason perhaps even more. I used to exchange word for word, and frown for frown. But now I see our swords are only straws, our strength is weak, our weakness beyond compare so that we seem to be most what we are not.

At that, Emilia gave a little grin. It was her hint for the audience to read between the lines.

So lower your pride — there's nothing you can do. Place your hands below your husband's foot. This duty my hand is ready to do, if he wants me to.

There could be nothing more ridiculous than a wife putting her hand on the ground for her husband to tread upon, so that his tender sole would not have to touch the ground. Except, perhaps, for reading such a line as earnest, instead of utter sarcasm.

And for those who were truly paying attention — the speech in which Kate declared herself well and duly silenced was the longest monologue in the entire show.

What was it about a woman's voice that was so terrifying to a man? Was it the thought that a lesser creature might have intelligence or agency?

Or was it simpler than that?

If she took herself seriously, others might do the same.

Other women.

Scores of women.

And that just might erode the power men had always effortlessly held.

"Mistress?" Bess asked, breaking her concentration. "What shall we serve for supper, then?"

Emilia grinned. "Who cares?" she said.

In 1594, London was reborn. Cases of the plague trickled and then stopped. Taverns and theaters reopened. Little Henry was walking and talking now, a good boy who happily sat at Bess's feet gumming a twist of bread while she prepared meals. The boy had the calm assurance of Hunsdon, and the joyful disposition of Southampton. Emilia spent hours trying to catch a reflection of Southampton's smile in her son, or the intelligence of Hunsdon's eyes when young Henry asked her why the sky was blue. But mostly, when she looked at him, she saw his wary gray gaze — a silver mirror of her own — learning how to be quiet when Alphonso was loud, how to be invisible in plain sight.

Shakespeare sold her play to Philip Henslowe, the theater owner who was now working with the newly formed Admiral's Men and the Lord Chamberlain's Men. He planned to present *The Taming of the Shrew* at Newington Butts — a theater in Southwark — in a season that would also feature Emilia's edited version of *Titus Andronicus.* Shakespeare himself had become a shareholder in the Lord Chamberlain's Men, which meant — if the venture was successful — he'd have a greater stake in the profits than an ordinary actor. "I thought you would be happier," Shakespeare admitted, taking a swig of his ale. They were meeting at the Falcon Inn, the old haunt where Marlowe had introduced them years earlier, and it held ghosts for Emilia.

"I am happy," Emilia said. "It will be the first time my work will be on a stage. It is only that I do not have the means to see it performed."

He frowned, gesturing at the small pouch of coins in her hand — her cut of the payment. "You have more than a penny," he pointed out, the price of admission to watch the performance from ground level, standing.

"It is not so easy for a woman, sir," Emilia said.

Shakespeare leaned forward. "You know," he said, "*I* could accompany you."

"Sir," she said primly, "we are both married."

He covered her hand with his own. "We work so well together. It would be interesting to explore the bounds of that, would it not?"

Emilia would rather fuck the ancient barkeep than this vain mammet. She slipped her palm from beneath his. "I do not mix business and pleasure, sir. And given my need for anonymity as a playwright, it would not seem wise to attend the theater together."

"Oh, you needn't worry about that," Shakespeare said blithely. "No one would ever imagine *you're* an author."

A tight smile ached across her face. "How fortunate for me," she murmured.

After she and Shakespeare had parted ways, Emilia walked home considering who might accompany her to the performance at Newington Butts. She could ask Jeronimo, but he'd likely ask her why she so badly wanted to see a performance that was a mile south of the city when there were more accessible diversions. She could take one of her young cousins, but they would report back to Jeronimo. She would have asked Kit, and they would have gone in glorious disguise, and the thought that this would never happen again made her chest hurt so much she had to pause in her journey.

In the end, there was really only one man

who could take her, and even though Emilia had no desire to spend any time in the company of her husband, she began to forge a campaign of obedience so different from her usual self that it caught Alphonso off guard.

She did not know if it was the food that she instructed Bess to make for him, or her own ministrations in bed, or even just agreeing with every idiotic statement that fell out of his mouth, but when Emilia asked Alphonso if they might attend the theater, he agreed.

A few weeks later they entered the courtyard of the theater with hundreds of others attending the afternoon performance, pulled in by the buzz and the chatter of entertainment. Alphonso did not balk at paying the entrance fee, but to her surprise, he gave extra coin so that they would be on a higher level of the gallery and could have cushions on their seats. She was touched by this, until she realized that he had done it not for her but because he wanted others to see him as more prestigious than the groundlings.

When the performance started, Emilia let her gaze slide from the actors on the stage to the raucous audience. Soon, they were whooping with laughter.

They like it, she thought, letting out the breath she had not known she was holding.

Nay.

They love *it.*

When Katherine and Bianca, the sisters,

entered with their father, and Kate began flaying suitors with her sharp tongue, Alphonso leaned toward Emilia. "That is the shrew," he explained.

"Ah, thank you for pointing that out, Husband."

"And ho, her father's name is Baptista, as was yours!"

She did not take her eyes from the gallery. "A remarkable coincidence, indeed."

She had not anticipated what it would feel like to hear words of her own creation in the mouths of others, to see the effect her writing had on the crowd. She found herself waiting to see if a joke landed, if a turn of phrase elicited a sigh, if the crowd was reading sarcasm where they were meant to. The show, for Emilia, was not what was happening onstage — it was in the way the men in the theater laughed when Petruchio snatched a gown away from Kate as a means of subjugating her — and the way the women recognized their own frustration on Kate's face. It was comedy, but maybe when these couples left the theater, it wouldn't be. Perhaps the husbands would realize that wives were not meant to be housebroken. Perhaps the wives would believe they mattered more.

The Taming of the Shrew was not a play about how women should be biddable. It was a comment on how fragile men were, that they could not countenance the thought of a woman who was an equal in wit and strength. It was the headiest feeling, to think you might change the world under the guise of entertainment.

Emilia realized that this was the true reason for the Lord Chamberlain's position, and for appointing a Master of the Revels. Plays must be vetted so that they were not espousing any radical ideas.

At that thought, she glanced up, feeling the heat of someone's gaze on her cheek. Across the gallery, a level higher than where she and Alphonso sat, was Hunsdon.

He looked a bit thinner, and his hair was white now instead of simply silver. Beside him was a peaked, pearl-encrusted woman — his wife, perhaps? He put a hand over his heart and gave her a small smile.

She smiled back at him. *I am well,* she tried to convey. *I miss you.*

Two things happened at the same time: the woman beside Hunsdon leaned closer to whisper to him, and Alphonso noticed Emilia looking at the Lord Chamberlain.

Emilia felt her husband grab her wrist with such cruelty it made her cry out. "You will not look at him," Alphonso hissed.

"I am not —"

"I will not let my wife cuckold me. Think you I'd make a life of jealousy?"

The scene onstage was eliciting laughter from the gallery, enough to hide the argument between Emilia and Alphonso. Petruchio was pointing at the sun and calling it the moon, browbeating Katherine into agreeing with him.

Alphonso yanked Emilia out of her seat. He dragged her from their row, as other audience members shouted at the disturbance. Emilia tripped over feet and skirts and made her apologies as her husband pulled her down the stairs and into the mostly empty courtyard.

"Do you not wish to see how the play ends, sir?" Emilia murmured.

He looked at her, incredulous. "The play," he said, "is over." Then he smacked her so hard across the face she spit blood.

She fell into the mud as Alphonso kicked her in the gut and then gripped her throat, smacking her head on the ground. *Help*, Emilia called out, or she thought she did. Yet even if she had been able to speak, who would have come to her aid? It was within the rights of a husband to discipline his wife for whatever infraction she had committed.

By the time Alphonso gave up and left her lying in a puddle outside the Newington Butts playhouse, Emilia was exactly the kind of wife he wanted: silent and unmoving.

When she had regained consciousness, the play was over and the crowd was leaving. Emilia dragged herself to the side of the yard. Her mouth was crusted with blood, and searing pain ran down her leg. She was forced to beg passing gentry for a coin for the ferry, imagining the reaction if they knew she'd penned the play they'd just seen.

On the far side of the river, she paused to consider her next step. She thought about young Henry. Even if Emilia did not return home with her husband, she felt certain that Bess would lay down her life for the boy before she let Alphonso near him. Putting her own needs before her son's felt like a blade to her heart, but Emilia knew that she would be no good to Henry as she was. She needed strength and a plan, and she could find neither alone.

Emilia had never been to Southampton House. It was not far from Somerset House, on the northern side of a square with gardens and greenery laid out in the pattern of a cross. She limped to the servants' entrance, keeping her eyes downcast as she knocked. A barrel of a man answered, sniffing in disdain at the sight of Emilia. "The broken meats are gone for the day," he said.

"Please," Emilia said softly. "I know your master."

The usher scoffed. "*Everyone* knows my master," he said and closed the door.

She had not thought ahead to what might happen if she were not allowed entry into even the servants' quarters — she had been too busy swallowing her pride. She shuffled toward the street, only to be nearly mowed down by a carriage. As the conveyance stopped, South-ampton burst out. "Emilia?"

The moment he reached her, she collapsed against him. "Dear God," she heard him whisper as he swung her into his arms. He pulled her into the carriage, shouting a direction to his coachman. Emilia drifted in and out of consciousness, finally awakening on a narrow bed with a rough wool blanket. She gingerly touched her swollen throat. A fire leaped in the hearth, and Southampton was sitting on a chair beside the bed. On a small table was a bowl of water, pink with blood, presumably from tending to her wounds. "Where are we?" she rasped.

"My hunting lodge," he replied, taking her hand. "What happened?"

The moon was already rising. "I must get home to Henry —"

"I sent word that you would be detained."

She did not even want to imagine what excuse he had given. "If I am not there, he will take his anger out on the boy —"

Southampton's eyes seared hers. "I will eliminate him before that happens."

"You cannot kill my husband."

A muscle ticked in his jaw. "It would not be the first time a peer has evaded the noose."

"If you were capable of murder," Emilia said quietly, "you would not be the man I love."

"I would ask what brought on his wrath, but I do not believe there is any just cause."

Emilia lifted a shoulder. "We crossed paths with Hunsdon. Jealousy is a green-eyed monster that mocks the meat it feeds on."

"You were promised away as a child," Southampton replied, incredulous. "Surely he cannot blame you for an arrangement you had no hand in making."

"The only choice I have ever made for myself," Emilia said, "was you."

He gently brushed his lips against hers, pulling back when she winced. "Forgive me," Southampton said. "I did not mean to hurt you."

She pulled him closer. "You are all that heals me."

The next morning Emilia insisted on returning home, because she could not put Bess in danger by making her remain there alone to protect little Henry. Southampton compromised by saying he would let her go only if he could return her in his carriage and see her again later that week. He would go to Gray's Inn and discreetly ask the legal minds there for a way to protect her within the constraints of a marriage contract.

He also told her that while she slept the night before, he had penned a note for his coachman to deliver to the Earl of Oxford, unequivocally stating that he would not marry his daughter Elizabeth — not two years ago, when the match had first been suggested, not now, not ever.

"I want you," he'd said simply. "And if I cannot have you, it will be because *you* turn your back on me . . . and not the other way around."

It hurt too much to hope, so Emilia did not say anything in response.

She returned to a quiet, placid house. Henry was playing with river stones on the hearth, stacking them until they fell. He clapped when she entered, running into her arms, and asking why her neck was purple. Bess didn't ask; she didn't need to. Emilia turned to her maid. "Where is he?"

"He never come home last night, and good riddance, I say." Bess spat.

Perhaps he'd gone out drinking or playing dice after leaving her in the mud. Perhaps he'd gotten caught cheating and was knifed by his opponent or tossed into the Thames. With any luck she was a widow and did not yet know it.

Her throat was still a necklace of blackberry thumbprint bruises a day later, when Alma brought word that Alphonso had angered Jeronimo by quitting the court recorder consort unexpectedly, determined to make a name for himself as a warrior so that he might be knighted. He was shipping out to Brest with a battalion at the behest of the Queen to aid King Henry IV of France in his fight against the Spaniards. "He may be gone for months," Alma said, allowing her eyes to skate over

Emilia's injuries. "Should you need food, aid, you must turn to me for assistance."

Relief washed over Emilia. Getting money and food was a problem she had solved before. She and Henry would be physically safe.

And she could work.

After all, now that William Shakespeare was a shareholder in the Lord Chamberlain's Men, he'd be even hungrier for content.

The late summer of 1594 was to be among the happiest of her life. Emilia was mistress of her own household. Her wastrel husband was (she hoped) getting himself run through by a Spanish sword in a harbor in Brittany. She met Southampton once or twice a week, making love beneath a palette of stars, often letting herself doze in his arms until dawn had broken and she could sneak back home before her son awakened. She and Bess took little Henry to Paris Garden, where the maid let him toddle around in his leading strings as Emilia wrote feverishly.

The play was a storm in her head, like the one she'd experienced so many years ago on the ship crossing to Denmark. It funneled, picking up thoughts and words and growing stronger until it seemed Emilia lived more in her mind than in the real world. She thought of who she had been when her cousin had presented her to Lord Hunsdon as a fait accompli. She thought of Southampton, and how she lived on sips of him, as if that might be enough to nourish her.

She was going to write a romance. The grandest, most terrible, doomed romance. The heroine, like Emilia, was going to be thirteen when the story began.

The heroine, Juliet, had parents who knew she was too young to be married. When her suitor, Paris, claimed, *Younger than she are happy mothers made,* her father countered, *And too soon marred are those so early made.* When Juliet's mother asked if she'd consider Paris's suit, Juliet protested: *I'll look to like, if looking liking move, but no more deep will I endart mine eye than your consent gives strength to make it fly.*

But when it became clear to Juliet that she was going to wind up married without her consent, she did the most radical thing of all.

She fell in love with the one person she could never be with.

Instead of a class chasm, Emilia wrote a family feud. She borrowed memories from her love affair with Southampton. She drew Romeo in his image, and let Juliet's devotion spill from her own heart onto the page. Written in this play were all the private truths she could never say — that she would give up the rest of her life for another five minutes with Southampton; that it had been not sex that made her a woman but love; that the world would never allow them to be together.

On the day Emilia finished the play, she asked Bess to return home with Henry so that she could run an errand. The streets were hot and fetid as she made her way to the apothecary shop that Isabella had brought her to years ago.

The woman who emerged from the back of the shop had the look of the former apothecary, but younger — perhaps her daughter? "Mistress," the woman said, wiping her hands on her apron. "How can I help?"

Emilia picked her way beneath the dried herbs swaying from the ceiling beams. She cast about for something unexceptional. "Have you lavender?"

"Aye," the woman said, leading her to the pale purple stalks.

Emilia gathered a handful, willing her hands not to tremble.

"Will that be all ye need?"

She met the young woman's eyes. "Have you anything to . . . urge the terms?" This last she whispered. It was, after all, a sin.

Emilia had known for some time now. Her breasts were tender, her stomach broadening. She had not been able to abide the smell of cooking meat.

This baby could not have any father but Southampton, because Alphonso had been at battle — and absent — for months. Which also meant that there was no way to fool her husband into believing he had sired this child.

The apothecary looked at Emilia without judgment. She pulled a small wooden box from a shelf. "First make a pessary of this stinking gladdon," she said, holding up the petals of an iris. "Then boil this juniper with wine and drink it down."

Emilia dumped a few coins on the worktable and slipped the herbs into the pocket of her skirts.

"Mistress," the woman said, as she turned away, "God be with you."

For two days she bled and cramped and sweated. When she could stand, she bundled her sheets and helped Bess wash them. When she couldn't, she rocked Henry on her lap, imagining what his little sister might have looked like, with strawberry ringlets and silver eyes.

Southampton, uncannily, asked to meet her the night she aborted his baby. She sent word that she was indisposed. She did not tell him why, and she never intended to.

On the third night, she dreamed of the daughter she would never have. She smiled, thinking that the child would kiss her brow, or let Emilia kiss hers. Instead, the girl opened her tight little fist to reveal a branch of juniper, and she shoved this down Emilia's throat until she screamed an entire forest.

On the fourth day, she felt well enough to meet William Shakespeare at the Falcon Inn with her completed manuscript of *Romeo and Juliet.* She noticed, absently, that he was better dressed than he'd been before. Well. So this arrangement was working out for him.

"You are not yourself," he remarked.

Emilia looked at him wanly over her cup of ale. "It is the heat," she said.

"Ah." He thumbed through the play. "What is this one about?"

"It's a love story," Emilia told him.

He frowned at the title page. "But it is subtitled *A Tragedy.*"

She thought about seeing her play performed in person. She remembered the feel of Alphonso's fingers squeezing the breath from her throat. She grieved for Juliet, for Romeo, for Southampton, for herself.

"Yes," Emilia said. "Precisely."

MELINA
SEPTEMBER 2024

After dinner with Jasper, Melina returned to her apartment at midnight ready to end her argument with Andre, but he was still gone. The next morning, she padded to Andre's bedroom door to find the Post-it she'd left there undisturbed. The thought of having to mend their friendship at the theater, in front of others, made her queasy.

It was the first day that Andre and Melina had not arrived at rehearsal in tandem. Instead, Melina arrived alone, feeling imbalanced. The sound designer was in the theater, as was Raffe's assistant. The deputy stage manager gave the fifteen-minute call, and actors began to dribble down from the greenroom, or in from their commutes. Raffe arrived. There was still no sign of Andre.

When Jasper entered the theater, he made a beeline for the row where Melina sat. *"Salve Deus Rex Judaeorum,"* he announced, sliding into the seat beside her. "Explain to me how the same person who wrote that book also wrote some of the most beautiful soliloquys in the English language."

"Good morning to you, too," Melina said, but she could feel her lips twitching, as if he were pulling the smile from her. "I'm guessing you couldn't sleep last night, if you were up reading Emilia's poetry?"

"Well, I couldn't very well go to sleep with half of it unread, could I?" Jasper scoffed. "If I had been reviewing it, I'd call it stylistically flat. So patently different from the language used in the Shakespearean plays that it almost blows Mel's entire hypothesis in the play."

Melina closed her laptop. "There are scholars who've run *Salve Deus* and the Shakespeare plays through a computer to see if there are any parallels," she said. "There are phrases in the book of poetry that don't exist anywhere else — except in the plays. The words *hoary frost,* for example — they're in Emilia's Cooke-ham poem, but also *A Midsummer Night's Dream.* Or the mention of Dictima the Moon Goddess in the patronage letter in the front of *Salve Deus* — the only other mention of her in all of English literature is in *Love's Labour's Lost.*"

"Authorship studies are notoriously suspect," Jasper said.

"Yeah," Melina agreed. "Particularly because they never include women's writing in their database, right?"

"Look, there's just no getting around the

441

fact that Emilia's poetry is at best pedestrian. It's nowhere near as elegant as even the worst Shakespeare play." Jasper shrugged. "If Emilia truly was the author of the plays, why would her writing deteriorate? Why stamp her name on a collection that's run-of-the-mill?"

Melina turned in her seat. "First, let's put a pin in run-of-the-mill. Emilia was a woman in Elizabethan England, so she gets major brownie points for having her name printed on anything. And maybe the writing style wasn't untrained . . . but completely intentional."

"You're saying she dumbed down her own poetry?"

"Hear me out," Melina said. "Let's say you decided to write a mystery novel all of a sudden, but you didn't want anyone to know you were the critic who wrote scathing reviews for *The New York Times* — would you use the same voice you use when you're critiquing a show?"

"I'd make sure it didn't sound the same."

"Exactly," Melina said. "And before you say the poems are pedestrian, remember the risk Emilia took in writing about Jesus's crucifixion, since she was a hidden Jew. If that's not dangerous enough, she says that Christ's bros failed him, and the women in his life had his back. That's not just scandalous . . . it's heretical. So is her take on the Fall from Eden — that it wasn't Eve's fault."

From the corner of her eye, she saw Andre

enter the theater and take a seat as far away as possible. She waved, trying to capture his attention. Andre turned as if he hadn't seen her.

Jasper, of course, saw the whole thing. "Uh-oh. Did you get Mel's coffee order wrong?"

"No," Melina said. "It's nothing."

It was *everything.*

"Writers," Jasper said, making the word sound like a swear. "You were saying?"

She dragged her attention back to Jasper. "In *Salve Deus,* Emilia literally uses the patriarchy's own bullshit to underscore how ridiculous men's expectations of women are. Which she did before, in a play . . ."

"*Shrew!*" Jasper guessed.

She nodded. "*Shrew.* When Petruchio is taming Katherine, he isn't violent — although he could have been. Men were legally allowed to beat their wives as long as the stick they used wasn't wider than their thumb. He starves her, he slights her."

Melina's phone began to buzz with a call, but she silenced it.

"Again," she said, "the language in *Salve Deus* may be less inspired, but her choice of content is still radical — whether it's finding mercy for a Jew, or letting a woman lawyer save the day, or tearing down the patriarchy."

Her eyes darted to the rear of the auditorium, where Raffe and Andre were in conversation. Then Raffe jogged down the aisle, calling the actors together to give some notes.

Andre followed him, and as they passed by Jasper and Melina, she reached out to tug at his sleeve. "Do you have a moment, *Mel*?" she asked.

Andre stared at her, impassive. "I do not."

Melina's phone began to buzz again. She glanced down and saw DAD flash on the screen.

"Excuse me," she murmured, taking the call.

"Is this Melina?" a woman said.

She turned away from Jasper and Andre, trying to create a cocoon of privacy. "Yes . . . ?"

"I'm Beth. I'm your father's . . . um, friend. He's had a heart attack."

Melina's fingers froze on the phone. She heard the woman say something about texting her the hospital address. Melina ran the last conversation she'd had with her father through her mind: He had been at the hospital for a procedure. He'd said it was nothing.

"Andrea? Are you all right?" Jasper held one hand on her shoulder.

"My father . . . he's in the hospital," Melina managed.

"You should go."

She swallowed. "Mel . . . can you spare me?"

Andre met her gaze. *Say it,* he telegraphed silently. *Tell the truth.*

But now wasn't the time.

His face was unreadable. "It's not like you're

the playwright," he said, permission disguised as an insult, and then he turned away.

If Jasper was surprised that her boss was behaving like a dick, he kept his opinion to himself. "What hospital?" he asked Melina.

She glanced down at the text on her phone. "St. Mary's. It's in Litchfield, Connecticut."

Jasper stood. "I'll drive you," he said.

When she thought of her childhood, Melina didn't remember a time when her mother wasn't dying. In her first memories, her mother was weak from chemo, with a bright scarf wrapped around her bald head. She remembered the day her father had shaved his head in solidarity, leading her mother to laugh at the misshapen potato of his skull. Her father had said, *Well we can't all be as beautiful as you are.* She'd pulled him down for a kiss and they had completely forgotten that their young daughter was in the room, too.

After her mother died, there had been an awkward year of high school during which she and her father found themselves adjusting to being a family of two. They'd had to forge their relationship from the ground up, feeling more like strangers in each other's company than soldiers who'd come through a war together.

He'd tried to fill in the blanks for her while also making sure she knew her mother's history.

She learned that he'd lived in Alaska for a year after college, before he met her.

She learned that they'd met while her mother was dating his roommate.

She learned that her mother's breast cancer diagnosis had happened when she'd gone to the ob-gyn because she'd just found out she was pregnant with her second child. But she couldn't have chemo and keep the baby, so she had terminated the pregnancy, and they'd told themselves there would be time to have another child once she recovered.

Except, there never had been time.

Melina had wondered how different life would have been with a sibling, if she hadn't turned inward for companionship, but outward. If, when her father and mother had sealed themselves off from her, she'd had someone, too.

It was fitting, Melina thought, that her father was an optometrist, since what she knew of him came with twenty-twenty hindsight.

There was still a hint of distance between them. Her father had patched it with silly texts and fun facts from history or genealogy, and Melina had dutifully told him curated stories about living in Manhattan. But there was a hell of a lot Melina *didn't* tell her father — mostly about her career, or lack thereof. She didn't want him to think she was a failure. She didn't want to be one more person he had to take care of.

Now, she realized there was likely a great deal that her father hadn't told *her*, either.

"Are you and your dad close?" Jasper asked, from the driver's seat.

Melina jumped. They had been traveling for an hour in silence, and she'd been relieved he didn't need to fill the quiet with small talk.

"That," she sighed, "is a complicated question. When I was a kid, my mom was really sick." Melina turned to look out the window at the traffic zooming past. "I love my dad. He laid down his life for my mom when she was losing hers. But I think parents have, like, a shelf for their emotions, and only so much fits on it. There were times my dad just didn't have the room for me."

Jasper glanced at her, then back at the road. "You don't have to make excuses for him."

"I'm not," Melina said. "It's just the way it was."

He was quiet for a moment, and then he said, "My dad wanted a son who would go fishing with him and who didn't get freaked out when his hands touched a worm, or when fish guts got on his sneakers. He also liked being the expert on, well, everything. When he lectured on manly things like hockey or driving or grilling meat, I'd go read up on it and come back with even more information, which just pissed him off. I used to think that I was the problem."

447

"What about your mom?"

"She wanted a daughter," Jasper replied, shrugging.

Melina did not like knowing these things about Jasper Tolle. It made him so . . . human. "Right now I'm just worried that I should have spent more time with my father."

He didn't tell her she would have plenty more moments with her dad in the future. Jasper had said, from the start, that he didn't like lying.

"I bet he's sorry he didn't spend more time with you, too," Jasper offered, and he reached across the console to squeeze her hand.

Melina stared at the spot where their palms touched. It felt like they were holding a small sun between them.

Then he pulled his hand away and set it tight on the steering wheel, as if he realized, too, that this was skating the edge of propriety or that he didn't know her well enough to offer physical comfort,

But for a long time, Melina could still feel the heat of his skin.

When they reached the hospital, Melina had exploded into the lobby in a cyclone of guilt. The information desk directed her to a surgical waiting room on the third floor. While she approached the receptionist, Jasper hung back, giving her privacy. She was told that her father had been in open-heart surgery for two hours and was expected to be there for several more.

At that, Melina had stilled. A heart was such a small organ; how much could be wrong that would require such a long procedure?

She turned to find a hummingbird of a woman with a bleached pixie haircut and nervous hands. "I . . . overheard you asking about Matty."

Matty? Melina blinked. Her mother had only called him Matthew.

"I'm Beth," the woman continued. "I brought your father in."

Melina gave a jerky nod. She wanted details, but she didn't want to admit this stranger might know more than she did about her father's condition, so she kept her lips pressed tight.

Suddenly, Jasper was beside her again. "I'm Jasper," he said, holding out his hand.

Melina turned. She had forgotten he was there. "You should go," she said. "You heard them — it's going to be a while."

"I have my computer. I can write a column anywhere." He crossed to an empty row of chairs in the back of the room, as if he knew that Melina needed space.

Beth was saying things about blockages and stents. "Were you with him?" Melina asked, swallowing. "When it happened?"

Beth nodded. "This . . . isn't how I thought we'd meet."

It burned, the confirmation that her father had kept secrets, too. Melina wondered where Beth and her father had met. If Beth had kids, an ex, a story. "Well, I'm here," Melina said. "You can go home now."

Beth looked at her for a long minute. "If it's all the same to you," she said, "I'll stay."

An hour later, Melina had read every old magazine in the waiting room and was bouncing her knee beside Jasper as he typed. "You're annoying me," he said, without looking up.

"Then distract me. What are you working on?"

"A review."

"Of?" Melina asked.

"I could tell you," Jasper deadpanned, "but I'd have to kill you." He rolled his shoulders, cracking his neck. "Just kidding. It's the new Shakespeare in the Park."

Melina frowned. *Hamlet?*

"Yup." He closed his laptop and pinched the bridge of his nose. "I am winging it."

"Why? Did you not go?"

Jasper shook his head. "I went. But instead of paying attention to the performance, I found myself noticing for the first time how Hamlet spends a lot of literary real estate explaining how to play the recorder, like the Bassanos did. And how Hamlet lies about the subject of the play-within-the-play by saying it's about someone named Baptista . . ."

450

". . . which was the name of Emilia's father," Melina finished.

"I used to *like* Shakespeare, you know?" Jasper mulled. "Now I'm second-guessing everything. I know the authorship question has been around for centuries, but somehow it didn't matter until *By Any Other Name* made it not about whether Shakespeare deserved the accolades, but about whether someone like Emilia deserved to be deprived of them. Mel Green is a wizard."

"Yeah," Melina said, her voice thready. "He is."

Suddenly Jasper sobered, as if remembering why they were there. "I'm sorry. I shouldn't be talking about myself. How are you holding up?"

Melina looked down at her hands in her lap. She was jittery and leaden all at once, and she could still feel Beth sneaking glances at her from across the room. "Walk with me?" she asked.

Jasper stood, slipping his laptop into his messenger bag. "Coffee," he pronounced. "Coffee makes everything better."

They wandered through hallways past the stages of life: women being wheeled out cradling their newborns, a teenager on crutches, elderly men shuffling into a urology clinic. In the cafeteria, Jasper bought them both coffee and pudding because, he insisted, if the coffee didn't improve her state of mind, pudding certainly would.

Melina, who had insisted she wasn't hungry, ate her entire cup of pudding. Jasper asked, "Are you worried he'll die?"

She blinked at his directness — rudeness, really — and realized that Jasper just wanted to *know.* So she nodded. "I keep thinking about it. If I'd have to pick out a casket. Why I never asked him where he keeps his important papers or his passwords. What I'd say in a eulogy."

"Well," Jasper said practically. "You've thought about it. Now stuff it away, like a box of T-shirts in the winter, and don't take it out again until you know you need it."

Melina suddenly thought about a time when her mother had been feeling well enough to spend a day at the beach. There were tide pools everywhere, and her mother sat with her scarf around her bare head. Melina had played at her feet, watching hermit crabs that had outgrown their homes scurry like tiny extraterrestrials to the next best thing.

She'd wondered if they felt naked without those shells.

She wondered if, before the crabs lost their shells, they'd even realized they were wearing shells.

"Do you think it's worse to have decades to say goodbye to someone," Melina asked, "or to not get the chance to say goodbye?"

Jasper opened his mouth to respond, but her phone buzzed between them on the table.

She looked down at the text. "He's out of surgery," she said.

When the doctor came out, both Melina and Beth stood. Melina found herself listening for key words: *blockage, two arteries, full recovery.* She did not realize that Jasper was standing behind her until the doctor was finished. All the adrenaline leached out of her and she stumbled, only to find his hand at her elbow.

A nurse took her to the ICU to see her father. She had been cautioned that he would be unconscious, with a breathing tube still down his throat and wires attaching him to various machines; but the warning in no way prepared her to find him so still and pale. Melina hesitated at the doorway before going inside and pulling a chair closer to the bed.

Since arriving at the hospital, she'd been thinking about how her mother had always been front and center in Melina's recollections — possibly because memories of her were all she had left. Now, however, Melina was imagining the same moments, but from another camera angle. Her father had been present for most of those memories, too.

The winter that she was ten, they had gone to Mohawk Mountain, a ski hill in Connecticut. Melina remembered how the sun sparkled on the snow like a spray of diamonds, and how her mother had sat by a window in the lodge where Melina could wave to her from the bunny slope. What Melina *hadn't* remembered, until she was sitting at her father's hospital bedside, was how he taught her to ski. Her father had been the one who coaxed her down the little slope. "The only rule," he had said, over and over, "is that you are not allowed to get hurt."

She'd been knock-kneed and shaky and terrified of falling. The only rule! As if safety was something she could control.

Sitting at his bedside, Melina took her father's hand in her own. "The only rule," she said aloud, "is that you are not allowed to get hurt."

At some point, Beth asked if she could see *Matty* for a bit, and Melina left the room and went searching for Jasper. He was buried in his computer again, and she stood over him for a moment, watching his long fingers dance across the keyboard.

When he looked up at her, he said, "Oh, it's you." He pushed his glasses up the bridge of his nose. "How is he?"

"Still asleep," Melina said. "Jasper, you should really go back to the city. I'll stay at my dad's house tonight, and Uber to the hospital tomorrow. I'll take the train back in after he's discharged."

"Did you tell Mel?"

"I, um, will," Melina replied. "Later."

Jasper closed his laptop. "Right. Obviously

not a priority." His gaze slid away from hers. "I know you have a good excuse, but I hope that you can make it back before the first preview with an audience. There's . . . so much of you in it."

She knew that he was referring to the research he believed she had done, and the fact that Emilia was an ancestor. Little did he know.

Melina realized she *wanted* to be honest with Jasper. His behavior in the last twelve hours alone had been so different from the critic who had flayed her alive when she was in college. Back then she had been angry that Jasper had misjudged her so completely; now, she had the objectivity to admit she had done the same to him. *It's kind of a funny story,* she would begin, except it would not be funny, and she didn't have the emotional bandwidth right now for that conversation.

When I get back, Melina promised herself. *I'll tell him the truth.* "It was really, really kind of you to bring me here."

He flushed and looked down at his lap, jerking a tight nod. "Okay," he said, gathering up his things and standing.

"Drive safely."

Jasper scoffed. "What's the alternative?" he said, and he turned and walked out of the surgical waiting room.

Melina laughed softly. To a stranger, that exchange made Jasper seem like an asshole.

But she was no longer a stranger.

Several hours later, Melina's father was awake. His voice was still scratchy and weak after the respiratory team had extubated him. She sat down on the side of his bed, and he said, "I know what you're thinking."

"That if you hadn't nearly just died, I'd want to kill you for keeping this from me?"

"No," her father sighed. "That there are easier ways to get you to come visit."

She reached for his hand. "I thought I was going to lose you, too."

"You know the problem with bodies," he said. "They're a constant betrayal."

Melina knew that he was thinking of her mother. She swallowed. "Dad, I should have been here."

"You absolutely should *not* have been here. If you were, it would mean I'd have failed as a parent. You have a life now, and you're supposed to be living it."

"Then I at least should have —"

"Nothing you did or didn't do would make a difference, Melina. Believe me. I've been there. If only I'd gotten the radon in the house tested earlier, if only I'd fought her when she said she didn't want to do chemo a second time . . . would that have changed the outcome? Even if you still lived at home, you wouldn't have known there was a time bomb ticking in my chest. Hell, *I* didn't know." He

456

struggled to push himself up higher on his pillows. "What I do know is that my mouth feels like something died in it."

Melina poured some water from a plastic pitcher into a glass with a straw and watched her father drink. She vowed to not be so focused on what came next that she neglected what was happening right now. It was the collateral damage of ambition, but she'd force herself to reset the stopwatch, starting now.

Her father had the most blissful expression on his face. "There's nothing like that first sip when you're really thirsty," he said. "I would have missed this."

Melina curled up at his side on the bed. "I would have missed you," she said.

When Beth came to drive Melina back to her father's house, he'd said, "This is Beth," and that was that. Once she was home, Melina had eaten a bowl of cereal and taken a shower. The only clothes in her dresser were from high school, so she pulled on a Fall Out Boy T-shirt and a pair of sweats with her high school mascot, a dragon, on the butt.

She wondered if Jasper had gotten home yet. It was good that he had left while her dad was still in the ICU, because if he'd met her father, she'd have had to explain why Jasper called her Andrea. And what if her father recognized the name of the critic who had derailed her in college?

Melina scrolled through her texts until she found Andre's name. *Dad's okay. Out of surgery,* she typed.

Immediately three scrolling dots appeared.

Melina waited. And waited.

The three dots vanished, and a thumbs-up emoji pinged beside her text.

She curled on her side and fell asleep waiting for a longer text from Andre that never came.

Melina spent the next six days shuttling back and forth to the hospital, cataloging her father's slow improvement. After those six days, he was discharged, and Beth drove them both home. When she left to go to the grocery store, Melina sat down beside her father on the couch. "Can we talk about the elephant in the room?"

Her father raised his brows. "Beth? She wouldn't like being called that."

"Where did you meet?"

"On a dating app," he said.

Melina's jaw dropped. "You're on a dating app?"

"Aren't *you*?"

"No!" she said.

"Oh. Huh. Well, she's widowed, too. Her husband died in 2020 during the first wave of Covid. I think that's why we clicked." He glanced at Melina. "Theoretically you know that loving someone means you'll lose them, or they'll lose you. But until it happens and you're the one left behind, you don't really get what that means."

Melina felt her throat tighten. "I'm glad you found her. . . ."

"But she isn't your mother."

She nodded, relief gusting out of her lungs.

"That's why I didn't tell you. I didn't know how." Her father rubbed his hand over his jaw. "God, I loved your mother. But she was very, very sick. And even so, I wouldn't have traded a single moment of the time I had with her. Not even when she was throwing up or when she cried herself to sleep. Love isn't Hallmark movies, Melina. It's *Jeopardy!* but with categories so narrow only two people in the whole world know the answers. *Have you seen my reading glasses?* and *Do I have a tick on my back?* and *Will you be there for me when it's time for me to go?*" He shook his head, laughing ruefully. "Mind you, when people say this is what your mom would have wanted for me, I don't believe a word of it. Your mother would have come at me with a hatchet at the thought of me with some other woman. But . . . I also think she'd forgive me." A small smile ghosted over his face. "Because that's what best friends do."

That's what best friends do. Suddenly Melina needed to talk to Andre.

Her father was recovering brilliantly and would be in good hands with Beth. Melina had some bridges to rebuild, and some confessions to make.

"Dad," she said, "I'm going to go back to the city."

"It's about time," he agreed. "You shouldn't be here when Beth gives me a sponge bath."

Melina shuddered. "Never utter those words again."

She hugged her father. "One of my plays is going to be produced," Melina whispered, the first time she'd said it out loud. "You have to get better so you can come." She pulled back, meeting his eyes. "Bring Beth."

The night before the first official audience preview of *By Any Other Name,* Melina's train arrived at Penn Station at 8:00 P.M., so she went straight to the dress rehearsal. She slipped into the back of the theater and sat in the last row. As her eyes adjusted to the darkness, she could pick out Andre and Raffe sitting behind a makeshift table — a piece of plywood balanced over a row of chairs, with a small reading light shining down on its surface. The costumer and set designer were in the front row taking notes. Jasper was not in the theater.

The actors were onstage, costumed and miked, and for a moment, Melina could barely breathe. It was like watching a dream take shape in three dimensions.

She knew, from the dialogue being

performed, that they were near the end of the play.

Emilia walked with Marlowe, both dressed entirely in white versions of their costumes. Behind them, in a line, were all the people who had sanded the edges of Emilia Bassano's life: Countess Bertie, Mary Sidney, Bess, Hunsdon, Southampton, Henry, even Alphonso. Everyone of note, except Shakespeare.

Melina had intentionally omitted him. When Emilia gave her final monologue, explaining that her writing would long outlive the writer, Melina had not wanted Shakespeare present. It was the smallest gift she could give her ancestor: letting the audience leave with Emilia's face in their minds for once, instead of his.

She leaned forward, her lips soundlessly mouthing Emilia's final lines.

Except the actress was saying the wrong thing.

Instead of what Melina had written, Emilia was stating the opposite: that words *didn't* matter more than the wordsmith. "Why must it be one or the other?" Daya recited. "Why not both?"

Then the line of actors in the back of the stage split to reveal Shakespeare, the only actor dressed in a costume with vibrant color. The lights narrowed to a pin spot on him as Emilia — in darkness — said, "There once was a girl who became invisible so that her words might not be."

The stage went black. Melina felt herself rising out of her seat, powered by outrage.

How dare he.

How *fucking* dare he.

House lights came up as Raffe clapped. "Nicely done, all! Get out of costume, and let's reconvene here in fifteen. Josephina, why is stage left still too dark for me to see the actors' faces?" As he jogged toward the lighting booth, he passed Melina. "You're back! Mel told me about your dad. I hope he's doing all right."

She didn't trust herself to speak, so she nodded and plowed past the director until she reached Andre. "Can I have a word? she said tightly.

He looked at her. "Sure. But it better be *thanks.*"

She cocked her head toward the doorway. When they reached a fire exit that led to an alley behind the theater, she pushed through it, plunging them into the heat of the night. "That is not the ending I wrote," Melina accused.

"You weren't here," Andre said.

"My father was in the *hospital!*"

"I *know*! And I am sorry about that. But you disappeared for a *week*. You were the one who wanted me to be Mel Green, so don't get pissed at me for doing what you asked."

They were toe to toe now, and her voice was rising in pitch and volume. "I never asked you

462

to change my play. In fact, I trusted you *not* to change it."

Andre folded his arms. "It wasn't working."

"So you changed it without asking?"

"You. Weren't. Here," Andre spat out. "Emilia Bassano is buried in an unmarked pauper's grave. You really think she'd be cool with the fact that nobody knows who the hell she is? Because *I* don't. Raffe doesn't. Daya doesn't. The character *you wrote* wouldn't."

"Wow. Thank you for mansplaining my play to me," Melina said.

"You do not get to play the marginalized card," Andre said, his voice quiet and lethal. "Not unless I get to play one, too. Spoiler alert: It *does* matter that you get credit for your work, Mel. You want to know why I'm so sure? Because I've been sitting here for three weeks, pretending to be *you,* when I can't get a play produced as *me.*"

Melina swallowed, her eyes glittering. "Change it back."

"*You* change it back," Andre said, "because *I* quit."

"You can't quit," Melina breathed, her heart hammering in her chest. "You're supposed to be my friend."

"You were supposed to be mine, too." There was a hint of something in his voice — regret or disappointment — like a flavor in a dish you couldn't quite place.

He shoved past Melina, walking out of the

alley. Her brain was working in slow motion. "Andre," she said, spinning around. "Andre!"

She ran after him but was waylaid by a group of women staggering around with a bride-to-be, barhopping for a bachelorette party. Melina looked left and right, but Andre had disappeared.

She was going to have to go back inside and explain to Raffe that Andre was gone but that he wasn't Mel Green — *she* was — and the show opened in a matter of days.

The house of cards she had built began to collapse around her. Her scheme had started as a need to justify her talent; it had morphed into ambition.

How fucking Shakespearean.

She had tried to be someone else to teach Jasper Tolle a lesson, and instead she'd learned that the real Melina Green was not someone she was particularly proud of anymore.

"Andrea?"

As if she had conjured him, Jasper was standing a foot away.

He took one look at her face and frowned. "Is your father o—"

Before Jasper could finish, Melina burst into tears.

Jasper had been thinking about Andrea that day, after a week of absence, and then she'd appeared like a figment of his imagination. He'd wanted to call her to see how her father was, but he analyzed and overanalyzed whether that was appropriate in a business relationship and eventually talked himself out of it. Besides, she was busy. She didn't need to be distracted from taking care of a sick parent.

He missed her. It really was that simple. He liked the way she argued with him and he liked the way, when she smiled, the left half of her mouth quirked up before the right. But right now she wasn't smiling at all. She was a sobbing, shaking mess, and he had no idea what to do.

He'd offered to take her to her apartment, but she shook her head violently. At the mention of sitting down for a moment in the theater to calm down, she started shaking so uncontrollably that Jasper grabbed her hand and pulled her into the nearest subway station.

And that's how he wound up with Andrea sitting on the couch in his apartment. He had given her a box of Kleenex and now handed her a shot of whiskey.

"I don't like whiskey," she said.

"I don't, either," Jasper admitted, "but in the movies it's what you give someone who won't stop crying."

She wiped at her eyes again. "You must be thinking I'm insane."

He shook his head. "I'm thinking that my apartment is really . . . gray." He glanced at the gray couch, the paler gray walls, the monochromatic kitchen. Andrea, with her primary-colored Fall Out Boy T-shirt and red face, stood out like a hothouse flower.

"I," she announced, "am a fucking mess."

Jasper disagreed. Tears only made her eyes even lighter, a pale and gleaming silver. He sat down on the coffee table (also gray) in front of the couch so that he was facing her. "I mean, the Fall Out Boy shirt is questionable — go Coldplay or go home — but . . ."

"I am a fucking mess," Andrea repeated, "on the inside, too."

"Do you . . . want to talk about it?" Jasper knew this was the right thing to say, because he had been in plenty of situations before where he *hadn't* said this and realized too late he should have. *Please don't want to talk about it,* he silently begged.

"I don't want to but I have to," Andrea said, a hitch in her voice. "I'm not who you think."

He blinked, his mind racing to the extraordinary: *She's in the witness protection program. She's CIA.* And: *I should have poured myself whiskey, too.*

"I'm Mel Green," Andrea continued.

He frowned, wondering if she was off her meds, or high as fuck, or if she'd hit her head before he ran into her.

"Melina, actually," she corrected. "My name is Melina Green. And I wrote the play you liked so much that you wanted to help it transfer."

Jasper tried to spool backward to their first meeting. The name of the playwright had been given to him by the artistic director of the Village Fringe. Given how competitive it was to succeed in this business, why would she not have claimed ownership of the play?

"It was an accident," Andrea — Melina? — *fuck* — began. She explained how she'd tried to get a play produced for ten years, and how her best friend had drunkenly submitted it to a festival with a notoriously sexist artistic director. How they'd planned to reveal Melina as the true playwright in a public setting, so that Dubonnet would have no choice but to keep her as one of the winners. But then Jasper had been introduced.

"Why would that make a difference?"

"Because," Melina replied, "you and I had met before."

Jasper blinked. Given the visceral tug in his gut every time she was in proximity to him, he found it impossible to believe he had crossed paths with her before and didn't know it. "I think you're mistaken."

She laughed softly. "Oh, no. I am most definitely not. Do you remember where you were in May 2013?"

He had been working at the *Times,* still wet behind the ears. She was too young to have been part of the theater business back then. Had she been a waitress, and had he forgotten to tip? A journalism student who'd written him a letter to which he'd never replied?

"You judged my play at Bard College," Melina said, "and — to put it mildly — you found it lacking."

He vaguely remembered the competition he'd adjudicated. He'd had two martinis beforehand to take the edge off his stage fright. But he'd also never questioned that everyone wanted to hear his unedited thoughts. He could not remember what her play was about, or what she had looked like back then. If he'd even taken the time to look closely at her.

"You said my play was small," Melina continued. "And that I was too emotional to handle criticism. You called me difficult."

With each comment, he flinched. "That sounds . . . like something I'd say," Jasper managed.

"Well, I definitely took it to heart. I spent the next ten years thinking I wasn't good enough to be a writer and getting rejected enough to back that up. Then came the Village Fringe. When Dubonnet announced that you'd be reviewing the readings, I thought I could get vindication. I knew my play was good. I wanted you to rave about it, and then I was going to have a big dramatic reveal where you learned that the person you said would amount to nothing a decade ago was actually talented." Melina's gaze slid to the floor, her eyelashes damp and spiked. "When we finally

468

met face-to-face, you didn't even bat an eye. I had spent ten years hating you, *blaming* you, and you . . . you didn't even recognize me."

Jasper found himself doing the very thing that had gotten him into this mess: he acted without thinking first. He bridged the distance between them, lifting Melina's chin. Those eyes, like mercury, met his. "I cannot imagine not recognizing you," he said quietly. "Because you are unforgettable."

And then he kissed her.

Melina had felt the truth rip out of her, an aching tooth being pulled, and had closed her eyes against what she was sure would be an onslaught of pain. Jasper Tolle did not like lying. He wielded language the way other people used knives, and she had put him in a position where he would have to publicly admit that he had been duped.

Not to mention the fact that they had spent countless hours in each other's company, hours when Melina could have confessed.

This was where he told her grown women who wanted to be playwrights didn't play games.

This was where he called Raffe and Tyce D'Onofrio and told them they had a problem.

This was where, instead of calling *By Any Other Name* brilliant and incisive, he called it emotional and saccharine.

This was where the playwright's flaws overshadowed the play's merit.

But none of that happened. Instead, his fingers curved around her chin, and then his mouth was on hers. She felt the pressure of his lips and the sweep of his tongue and the taste of him: wintergreen, lemon, want. His kiss was a series of questions: *Can we . . . ? Let me . . . ? Will you . . . ?*

It was Melina who slid from the couch practically onto his lap. Her hands pushed into the cornsilk of his hair as she fought to get closer.

But just as suddenly as it had started, Jasper pulled back. His eyes snapped to hers, enormous behind his glasses. "Is this okay?" he said.

Okay? It was exactly what she needed. After tonight's fight with Andre she'd been completely lost, and Jasper was like a north star. If he wanted her, she had to be worth something. Her hands were still tangled around his nape, her pulse raced under his thumbs. She shifted, and he groaned.

"Isn't it obvious?" she joked, pressing closer.

But Jasper did not laugh. "No," he said, completely solemn. "Not to me."

Melina's hands slipped from his neck, over his shoulders, off him. "Oh," she said. And then, as it became clearer: *"Oh."*

It made sense: his indifference when his reviews were seen as cruel, his blunt manner, verging on rudeness. It wasn't detachment or disinterest; it was a disconnect.

"Sometimes," he said, haltingly, "it's like

470

there's a blurry window between me and the rest of the world. I can't see them clearly, and they can't see me. Neurodivergent. That's the label, anyway."

Jasper, ironically, understood exactly what it felt like to be misunderstood by everyone. Melina threaded her fingers with his. "I'm really sorry you've felt that way," she said.

He brought her hand to his lips, and Melina marveled at the fact that someone who was so skilled with prose could be so eloquent in silence, too.

"Who *are* you?" she murmured.

"You know who I am," Jasper said.

"I don't mean your name." Melina rubbed her temples. "For ten years I thought you were just some asshole. And it turns out you're . . . well, not that. But that doesn't mean I know who you actually are."

"What do you want to know?"

"Anything," Melina said. "Everything."

"My favorite ice cream is mint chip, but the white kind, not the green. I know every word of the first Guardians of the Galaxy movie. I've broken my collarbone three times in the same spot — once playing soccer, once in a car accident, and once during a bar fight."

"You were in a *bar fight*?"

"I don't have any siblings," Jasper continued, "but I used to have an imaginary friend named Todd. I say I'm allergic to hamsters, but I'm really not, they just creep me out. I didn't learn how to swim until I was in college. I'm terrified of heights." He took her hand again, and this time, he placed it over his heart. "So please, Melina," he said softly, "don't make me fall alone."

Melina wasn't sure who moved first — Jasper or herself — but she was in his arms, plastered to him, her hands pulling his dress shirt away from his trousers and sliding up his smooth back. He grabbed a fistful of her hair, tugging her closer, and skated his hand beneath her T-shirt. "Fall Out Boy," he scoffed against her mouth, and his lips curved against her own in the shape of a smile.

When he fumbled with the clasp of her bra, she thought she would incinerate, and a second later she was stretched out on the living room floor beneath him, one of his hands pinning hers overhead while his breath feathered over her stomach. His teeth caught at the tie of her sweatpants. "Bedroom," he muttered, as if he was trying to convince himself, but she shook her head, crossing her legs behind his back to cage him. She yanked his shirt over his head, thinking it was a crime this body was hidden beneath the trappings of a desk job, as he skimmed her sweats down her legs.

"It isn't Wednesday," he said, looking down at the loopy script on her panties.

"It was the only clean underwear I had in Connecticut," she managed, as he closed his mouth over the fabric, breathing her in.

"It's confusing," he murmured.

"I'll remember that for next time," Melina gasped, as the last barrier between them was peeled away, and that mouth, that abrasive, keen tongue of his, moved on her.

"*Next time,*" Jasper repeated with wonder, as if they were words that had just been born into the world, and he was the first to hear them.

There *was* a next time, during which Jasper cracked his head against the coffee table, which was why for the *next* next time, they relocated to his bedroom. After, Melina slipped out to use the bathroom and raided his kitchen cabinets, finding disappointingly healthy food and one glorious sleeve of Thin Mints buried behind the granola and kale chips. She brought it back to bed and watched Jasper fight with himself to not comment when she crawled under the covers to eat them there. "You look," she said, "like you're about to have a limb amputated without anesthesia."

He had taken off his glasses, and it made him look unfinished. "Crumbs."

"What if I'm careful?"

"What if you're a barbarian?"

"Ooh." Melina lit up. "That means I can plunder."

"Pirates plunder," Jasper said. "Barbarians . . ."

She rolled on top of him, dropping the

473

cookies in the sheets. "Barbarians conquer," Melina said.

Melina woke to find the dawn seeping into the sky and Jasper propped up on one elbow, glasses perched on his nose, watching her. "Hi," she said, shyly.

"Hi."

She could not remember the last time she'd had sex three times in a single night. Actually, she could not remember the last time she'd had sex. The string of condoms that Jasper had retrieved from his bathroom snaked over his nightstand, behind his shoulder. She found herself reaching out to trace the line of hair that arrowed from his chest to the parts of him still covered by a blanket, but he loosely grasped her wrist before she could get very far. "Do you want to talk about it?" he asked.

"About this?" Melina asked, gesturing between them. "Or about the show?"

"Both?" He tangled his fingers in her hair. "You could have told me who you were. It wouldn't have made a difference."

She raised a brow. "Wouldn't it? Would you have been as impressed by the play if you thought a woman had written it, instead of a man?"

"Good work is good work —"

"But even a name carries bias," Melina argued. "Be honest. If you had seen Emilia's

474

story and knew it was written by a female playwright, would you have dismissed it as another feminist rant? Would you have wanted it to transfer? Or was it the novelty of a *man* writing about this stuff that made you think it was so insightful?"

"When I review a play, I look at the writing, not the gender of the playwright."

"But you don't *not* look, either," Melina said gently. "You're already influenced by what society thinks."

"You aren't making sense," Jasper said.

"When I created Emilia, I made her opinionated and manipulative and sexual even though I've been told by men that women like that aren't *relatable.* But what it really means is that women like that make men uncomfortable, and above all else, we can't let that happen. So stories about complicated, wholly realized men get put onstage and stories about complicated, wholly realized women *don't* . . . which reinforces the belief that men, and their experiences, matter more. It becomes a cycle." Melina glanced at Jasper. "See?"

"See what?"

"You're all . . . blotchy. You're angry being called out for behavior you'd never bother to question."

"I'm not blotchy," he insisted. "I just think that you're painting with a very broad brush when it comes to what gets produced and what doesn't. The answer shouldn't be an identity politics quota . . . but who can tell the best story."

"That is exactly the kind of thing a straight white man would say."

"What's *that* supposed to mean?"

"Someone is always willing to listen to you," Melina explained. "When the only stories told are by straight white men, it becomes the norm. People assume that the only stories that will turn a profit are stories about that particular experience — when in fact there are whole untapped audiences who would love to see their lives replicated on a stage. Do you know how gratifying it would be for more women or Black or Latinx or Indigenous or trans or disabled people to see themselves represented in theater? The answer is *no, you don't* — because you've *always* seen yourself reflected there."

She waited for him to tell her that she was wrong — which, of course, would be proof of everything she was alleging. But instead, a small crease formed between Jasper's brows. She could see him mentally creating a profit-and-loss sheet of how he had benefited from being born in the body he was in.

Then, suddenly, he grabbed her by the shoulders and branded her with a kiss. "You're brilliant."

"That," Melina said, "was not what I expected you to say."

His eyes glowed. "Two birds, one stone. You

476

reveal that you're the actual playwright of this piece, and we get positive media attention for it." Jasper leaned against the headboard, drawing the sheets with him as Melina sat up, too. "All you have to do is let me help you."

She narrowed her eyes. "How?"

"In the *Times*. I promise I can write a nuanced piece about gender and theater. It will talk about Emilia and how nothing's changed in over four hundred years — as proven by the fact that a talented, magnificent, gorgeous female playwright — that's *you* — had to hide her gender to get a play produced about this very topic. People read me," Jasper said. It was a statement rather than a boast. "This could start a conversation the business needs to have." He kissed her again. "And yes, I do realize the irony of a male theater critic getting the rest of the world to pay attention to something female writers have been saying for years."

Melina chewed on her lower lip. It was possible that Jasper was offering this from a place of justice. It was equally possible that Jasper did not want his reputation to implode if *By Any Other Name* was canceled by a producer who did not like being a pawn in a revenge scheme. Even if she gave Jasper the benefit of the doubt, there was something about hiding behind his name and influence that felt defeatist.

"Trust me," Jasper said softly. "The only

people who can really criticize theater are theater insiders. After George Floyd's murder, the theater world got called out on their lack of diversity, so they made room for an extra seat. One measly seat . . . when what they *really* needed to do was build a bigger fucking table."

What if, Melina wondered, this was how change began — one mind at a time? What if the linguistic sword Jasper brandished in his columns was used not to vanquish but to protect? What if, this once, instead of assuming she was in this fight alone, she accepted help?

"Okay," she said. "I trust you."

Jasper left Melina sleeping, her black hair wild on his pillow and her hands fisted in his sheets. He knew that when she woke, she would be stressed about next steps — not just this new relationship, but the play itself, and her argument with Andre. She'd told him, in a quiet interlude last night when they were just holding each other, that her apartment lease was in Andre's name, and she wasn't sure she was ready to confront him to get her clothes or books or even a toothbrush.

She could read Jasper's whole library from cover to cover, and he'd buy her a toothbrush. As for clothes, he wouldn't mind if she never got anything to wear and stayed naked in his bed.

He crept out of the bedroom, snagging a

robe (also *gray,* for God's sake) and wrapping himself in it. He was afraid to wake Melina by grinding coffee beans, so he made himself tea from a tea bag of dubious age, and he hated tea. It was a clear indicator of how quickly he had been overwhelmed by this woman.

Then he sat on a stool at the kitchen counter, opened up his laptop, and started to type.

Since 2020, Broadway has faced a reckoning about inclusivity and diversity. Although there have been slight gains for some marginalized groups, with more BIPOC and queer playwrights being produced, women have been left behind. In the presence of gains for these other deserving writers, female creators are understandably reluctant to say they've been leapfrogged — once again — because doing so reinforces the stereotype that they are whining.

But I *can say it.*

Jasper hunched over the keyboard, writing furiously. He talked about the review he'd written body-shaming the actress, and how he'd been banished to reviewing a fringe festival. He talked about seeing, and loving, *By Any Other Name.* He talked about Mel Green, or who he thought was Mel Green at the time, and his young female assistant. Then he flashed back to Bard College ten years earlier, and their first interaction.

He wrote about the real Emilia Bassano, and how it was possible that for over four hundred years her plays had been credited to someone else. He talked about how society had made it impossible for Emilia to write publicly unless she hid behind the name of a man.

He wrote about Melina Green, who had been advised the subjects she wrote about were too small in scope, too mawkish, too limited in commercial appeal — told this, in fact, by Jasper himself — the same critic who loved her play when he didn't know it was written by a woman.

He admitted to his own unconscious bias and, in doing so, invited the rest of the theater community and its audience to admit to their own.

Finally, Jasper uploaded his column to his editor. He added a note: *Not my usual, but fucking timely. Can we run ASAP?*

As if on cue, Melina appeared in the doorway of the bedroom, deliciously rumpled, his sheet wrapped around her body like the peplos of a Greek goddess.

Everyone knew that the birthplace of theater was Ancient Greece. *Drama* came from the classical Greek word δρᾶμα — *deed* or *act* — which had in turn evolved from δράω: *I do.*

I do.

Jasper could not stop the lightness in him, a second sun rising. It drew him off the stool, floating closer to her. "There you are," he said, as if he had been waiting for ages.

Entering, EMILIA finds
ALPHONSO at the table,
surrounded by her letters
from SOUTHAMPTON and
SHAKESPEARE. Beside him
sits an empty bottle of
gin.

ALPHONSO
(eerily calm)

Where is your lute? You were
tutoring music, were you not?

EMILIA
(well and truly caught)

I . . .

ALPHONSO
(reading)

"I am lost without you. Yours, S."

A glover? The only thing being
gloved here is his prick.

(throws a printed copy of
Venus and Adonis at EMILIA)

How careless, Emilia. Poetry, with
his name *printed* on it?

THE WOMAN AS BESS

He had conflated the letters.
He did not realize S stood
for Southampton; he assumed
she was having an affair with
Shakespeare — and had saved his
poem. But worse — she had stored
the letters in the wool of her
mattress, along with the money
she'd made with her writing. And
now, it was his.

EMILIA

Alphonso, wait —

THE WOMAN AS BESS

He threw her to the ground as
she sucked at the sudden air,
only to lose it when his booted
foot caught her gut over and
over. She tried to crawl away
from him, blood running down her
chin.

EMILIA
(sobbing)

Please —

(to THE WOMAN AS BESS)

Make sure Henry does not come in.

THE WOMAN AS BESS leaves.

ALPHONSO

I will fuck him out of you.

ALPHONSO rips open the
placket of his trousers,
pinning EMILIA to the
ground. He rucks up her
heavy skirts as she

EMILIA
1596–1604

Emilia is 27–35

Emilia lay on her belly on the edge of the stream, with little Henry beside her. "Like this, Mama?" he asked, picking a tiny white stone from the sediment of the bank in Paris Garden.

"That is a perfect one, my darling," she said, kissing his copper hair where the sun crowned him. "Where shall we place it?"

"On the queen's throne," Henry said. "Because the king is so naughty."

She gently nudged the stone into position in the little tableau they had created. It was a faerie garden like the ones she used to make when she was little.

There were times like this — when the city was not its usual gloomy gray and when she and Henry could pass an afternoon eating cream biscuits and making up stories — that Emilia could let herself imagine another life. If her family had stayed in Bassano del

484

Grappa, would she be married to a musician she'd known since birth? Would she never have entertained the thought of writing?

What if the Countess had not remarried but had encouraged Emilia to keep learning? Would she chafe even more than she did now?

What if she had never gotten pregnant, and was still living with Hunsdon, a nightingale in the loveliest of cages?

She watched her son reach into the water again with his chubby fist. Well. She knew exactly what she would be missing, if that had been her lot in life.

"Why would the king make his queen love someone else?" Henry asked.

He was quiet and wise for his years. "Because sometimes the only way to value love is to lose it first," Emilia said.

She had spooled forth the old story she'd told her little cousins a decade ago, about the faerie king who wanted to play a trick on his queen. But Emilia had added four lovers in the woods, entangled in the same errant magic, so that two men now fell for the same woman.

Henry rolled onto his back. "But it's silly to love a donkey."

Bess, who'd been hovering nearby, slid a glance at Emilia. " 'Tis true, little master, that it's no easy thing being wed to an ass."

Emilia bit her cheek to keep from laughing. It was easy to joke about Alphonso while he was away on his far-flung military campaigns. She did not know how he was faring and she did not care. And in his absence, she had fashioned a different kind of family.

"When you are in love, young Henry, there is nothing silly about it," a deep voice said behind her. She turned to see Southampton striding toward them. "What your lady looks like doesn't matter, as long as you can lay eyes on her. Where she comes from doesn't matter, as long as she is headed toward you."

He knelt beside Emilia, twining his fingers with hers in the folds of her skirt. They were careful with physical affection around Henry, because he was a child and could not be trusted with secrets — but Southampton had been introduced as Mama's good friend. When he could, he joined them in the gardens.

"My lord," she murmured, smiling. "Do you compare me to a donkey?"

He squeezed her hand. "Only if I am the burden of such a beast." He hunkered down beside Henry. Sometimes Emilia caught the similarities of their profiles, sometimes she believed she was looking too hard for meaning where there was none. In the end, it did not matter. Southampton was the father figure Henry deserved, no matter how it had come about.

"Sir, have you seen the bears?" Henry asked Southampton. The boy was craning his neck to watch the throngs of people heading into the bear pits not far away.

"I have indeed."

"Mama says I am too little."

"Your mama is right. They can be dangerous. Why, once I saw a man go in and then come out again . . ."

"That doesn't sound dangerous . . ." Henry pouted.

Southampton grinned. "He was being pursued by a bear."

She watched Henry's face light up as Southampton told the story. The bear and bull gardens were far from the only entertainment. The new theater, the Swan, was in its finishing stages — built by Francis Langley, who'd erected it on the site of the old Paris Garden manor house.

In another life, she and Southampton would take in a performance in the sumptuous new building. Perhaps, after she watched emotions play across his features in reaction to sentences she had penned, she would confess that she was the one who had written them.

It was just as outlandish and impossible a thought as any other. Southampton was a tremendous supporter of the arts, having racked up far more dedications than just the ones in the poems she had given Shakespeare years ago. He and Emilia often talked about plays, but she had never admitted that she had written some of his favorites. If Southampton recognized himself in the character of Romeo, he'd never mentioned it.

She made a mental note: a story about faeries and lovers and a man with the head of an ass was too particular to be coincidental; if Southampton ever saw it performed he might be suspicious. Emilia would have to make sure to change the story she told her son, so that it wasn't identical to the play she would eventually provide to Shakespeare.

"Master Henry," Southampton asked, "might I borrow your mother for a moment?"

Her son was dropping pebbles in the stream and seeing how fast they sank; with a nod to Bess, Emilia let the Earl help her to her feet. She watched her maid crouch beside Henry, taking a leaf and sailing it like a little boat, to his utter delight.

She walked beside Southampton for a while, until they were out of sight. Then he caught her up in his arms and kissed her, fitting himself against her like the key to a lock. "I did not think to see you today," Emilia breathed. He was supposed to be at court. "It is the best of surprises."

"You will not believe so," Southampton murmured against her temple. He held her a little tighter. "He is dead, Emilia."

Her first thought: Alphonso. She felt herself starting to float, tethered only by Southampton's arms, but he braced her against him. "Hunsdon," he said.

Emilia stilled. The Lord Chamberlain was an old man; this was not unexpected — but it did not make it any easier. The list of people who had known and cared for her was thinning out. She wondered how long it would be before she could count only on herself. "May his memory be a blessing," she whispered.

"I wanted you to hear it from me."

She touched her hand to his cheek. "Thank you," she said simply, and he nodded.

"Let me escort you home," he offered.

She shook her head. He always offered, and she always said no. In the first place, an earl wandering down Mark Lane would be too conspicuous. In the second, it was Alphonso's home, and he might arrive unexpectedly at any moment.

Ever since Southampton had turned down the Earl of Oxford's daughter, other potential brides had been suggested to him, or thrown into his arms on dance floors. She imagined he extricated himself from every snare with the grace and charm for which he was known, so that the lady in question did not even realize she was being dismissed. She did not know how long he could avoid marriage, however. The Queen would want him to have an heir.

In another life, young Henry . . .

She would not even let herself think on that.

Emilia knew Southampton did not see it this way, but she was the stone dragging him down, and it was only a matter of time before he either freed himself or sank. Here he was trying to save her from sorrow, and she could do nothing but cause him eventual heartache.

"I think I would like to be alone for a bit," she said. "Would you tell Bess?"

She turned toward the Thames, approaching the Swan worksite. It felt right to pay homage to Hunsdon here, at a place of theater. Emilia listened to the ringing of hammers and she imagined the quiet cocoon of Hunsdon's study, the rustle of pages on his desk, the way he would sometimes hum as he struck a line through an objectionable phrase. She remembered how proud he was when he grew a potato from a root brought back by Sir Francis Drake, and how they'd tried the delicacy boiled in prunes and soaked in wine and crusted in ashes and finally had to declare it fit only as chicken feed. She imagined Hunsdon's hands on her — not taking her virginity but helping her out of a carriage as if she were a true lady, and sponging her brow when she was feverish. He had paid for her body, but he'd valued her mind. More important, he'd made *her* value it, when it would have been so much easier to believe that she was worth only the pleasure her flesh could bring a man. He was not a father figure and not a lover but something in between. And he had been kind.

She turned away from the clatter of the construction site, brought her hands to her kirtle, and she tore the neckline of the fabric. Just two months ago she had lit what would have been a yahrzeit candle for the anniversary of Kit's death.

Grief was the tax of having something precious.

By the time she reached the unlikely group of a maid, a common boy, and a courtly earl blowing maple seeds across the stream with gusts of their own breath, Emilia had wiped away her tears and boxed up her memories of Hunsdon. She sat beside Southampton, whose astute gaze fell to the rip in her clothing. "What happened?"

"A branch," she lied.

Southampton had told young Henry that there was nothing silly about love — but there was: its untested arrogance.

He could love only the parts of her he knew about. But she would never tell him she was a hidden Jew. A playwright. That she had conceived, and aborted, his child. And if he didn't *know* those things, did he truly love Emilia, or just the person he thought she was?

Southampton walked them to the Paris Garden stairs to take the ferry across the Thames. He ruffled Henry's hair and kissed Emilia's hand, his teeth scraping against the inside of her wrist and his lightning eyes searing hers as he helped her onto the boat. A wind whipped out of the north, chasing off the temperate day and bringing a thunderstorm that shook the flatbed of the ferry. Henry, frightened, hid in the folds of her skirt between her legs.

It was a rainy walk back to Mark Lane, and by the time Emilia opened the door, she, Henry, and Bess were all soaked to the skin.

Canted back in a chair, with his dirty, bare feet propped on the oak table, was a barely recognizable Alphonso. His hair was shorn close to the skull and he reeked of liquor, evident even from a distance. A pile of rags — a uniform? — was puddled on the floor in front of the hearth, which he had not bothered to light. When a smile oiled over his face, she saw that he was missing a tooth. "Hello, Wife," he drawled. "Did you miss me?"

Emilia had not realized that when your landscape was missing a piece of scenery for months you could convince yourself it had never existed. "Alphonso," she said. "How good to see you."

She realized her mistake immediately — she had greeted her husband as if he were a stranger in his own home. He stood, swaying. "What you mean is: how good of me to let you remain in *my* lodgings while I was abroad."

"Yes, of course," she said, scrabbling in her pocket for a coin. She pressed this backward, blindly reaching for Bess, who would know what to do. The last thing she wanted was for Henry to set out in the driving rain again, even if it were to purchase a sweet or whatever bribe Bess could afford with the coin Emilia had given her, but —

No, actually. The last thing she wanted was for Henry to bear witness to what was going to happen.

She heard the door shut behind her, and she breathed a sigh of relief. "You . . . are on leave then? From battle?"

"You could say that. But permanent, like." He stumbled, knocking over the bottle of alcohol, which dripped from the table onto the rushes on the floor. "They couldn't even prove it was me who was poaching. It was dark enough, I made sure of it."

Emilia closed her eyes. "You were poaching? From the lord you were supposed to be serving under?"

"It was a fucking *rabbit*," Alphonso said. "If they gave us more to eat, I wouldn't have had to do it."

She wondered how much of her settlement Alphonso had scrubbed through. She wondered how long ago he had been discharged from the Queen's service. But she could not figure out a way to ask either of those questions without angering him further.

His eyes locked on her face as he moved closer, and instinctively, she backed up against the door. "Is that any way to treat an English hero?" Alphonso asked.

"You must be exhausted."

"I'm hungry."

She edged past him toward the larder. "Let me see what we have to eat."

"Not for that." He snatched her hair in his fist before she could reach the shelved alcove. He pushed her down so that her cheek rested in the puddle of alcohol on the table and lifted her skirts. "You haven't forgotten how to do this, I hope."

No.

Emilia did not realize she had said the word out loud until Alphonso pressed down harder on her temple. "What did you say?"

"No," she whispered.

She might have been answering his question. But they both knew that was not the case. His answer was to push himself into her, sweating and grunting against her back while she closed her eyes, pinned by his weight. It was over in seconds. She felt her skirts skim the backs of her calves again, and then her legs gave out and she slid to the wet floor.

"The whores that followed the camp don't act like they're carved out of marble," Alphonso said. "They couldn't wait to lie with me."

"They were *paid* to lie with you," Emilia murmured.

She thought he would strike her, but Alphonso just laughed. "As I was paid to lie with *you,*" he pointed out. "No wonder the old prick couldn't wait to get rid of you." Then he straightened, throwing his arms akimbo. "Welcome home, Alphonso," he announced to nobody, and left her steeped in a mess of his making.

Master Shakespeare,

May the Almighty preserve you in good health.
I humbly ask if we might hasten our next transaction for gloves. It has become a matter of dire importance.

Thus indebted to you,
Mistress Lanier

Mistress Lanier,

I fear I cannot accommodate your request for gloves as I have returned to Stratford indeterminately. My son Hamnet now sleeps with angels.

The rest is silence.
Thus I commit you to God's protection.

Wm. Shakespeare

For a long time, Emilia stood in her chamber, rereading Shakespeare's missive. She knew he was married, and that his wife lived apart from him in the country, but she had not known he had children. If she had, she would have wondered at his ability to choose a career that required him to stay away when there was so little time to watch them grow.

She thought about the little redheaded girl she sometimes dreamed of, still, who never would be. This was the first time Emilia felt anything for William Shakespeare that resembled compassion.

She admired Shakespeare for his singular passion for making money. She was uncomfortable at the ways in which he did that. Recognizing her limited choices, she accepted their partnership.

When Alphonso entered the chamber, she turned her back hastily. "What have you there?" he asked, and she shook her head, the note already stuffed between her breasts.

"Just the linens," she said, pulling them off the bed in a cloud, bustling past her husband to the washtub outside.

From the corner of her eye, as she left, she saw Alphonso lift up the mattress, searching.

Over the next few weeks Emilia learned that Alphonso had squandered nearly all the money that Hunsdon had settled on her — gathering the materials he needed to become part of the Queen's army and then, after being ignominiously sacked, nursing his feelings in France before returning home. He seemed to want nothing to do with Henry, for which she was grateful, but he would come to her and demand his conjugal rights if he were still conscious after a full day at the tavern. He claimed that he was doing business, trying to foster connections to new nobles who might sponsor him for knighthood. He also was looking for information on lodging since he could not maintain the rent on Mark Lane anymore.

Emilia had heard once from Southampton and sent word that it was not safe for her to see him.

She had not received any further message from Shakespeare. She feared that if she did not find a way to make money soon, she and her son would be put out on the street.

She found herself, these days, thinking about Christine de Pizan, the scholar whose work the Countess had made her study when she was young. Emilia had memorized the start of *The Book of the City of Ladies,* but it wasn't until now that she truly understood it. "I could scarcely find a moral work by any author which didn't devote some chapter or paragraph to attacking the female sex," Pizan had written. "I had to accept their unfavorable opinion of women since it was unlikely that so many learned men, who seemed to be endowed with such great intelligence and insight into all things, could possibly have lied on so many different occasions. . . . Thus I preferred to give more weight to what others said than to trust my own judgment and experience."

Emilia wanted to even the balance a bit, to create a female character whose mind — as Pizan claimed — was as capable of legal thought as a man's. Emilia had already written a tragic heroine — Juliet. She'd written a faerie queen duped by her own husband. Now she wanted to create a woman who saved the day.

She began on a sunny Wednesday. On the banks of the river with other laundresses, Bess had been soaking the household linens and undergarments in urine and had poured lye and potash over them. While Henry sat at their feet, drawing in the mud with a stick, Emilia helped beat out the stains and rinse and scrub. After, the women stretched the linens out on the grassy slopes of the bleaching grounds to let them dry.

It took time, and you could not leave your belongings without risk of them being stolen, so while Bess took Henry home for a nap, Emilia stayed behind. She set her writing box on her lap and cut a fresh quill, glancing down at her hand.

Her skin was red and raw from the lye. As always when she scrubbed laundry, she had taken off her wedding ring. This time, though, she left her finger bare instead of restoring the ring to its place. It felt like the smallest act of resistance.

She dipped the pen in the ink: another act of resistance.

Emilia used, as a starting point, a story she'd read in the original Italian: *Il Pecorone*. She wrote of her own liabilities — female, intelligent, Jewish — and distributed them among the characters who were most likely to be judged for those traits. She gave her maiden name to the character Bassanio, who wanted to marry Portia, an heiress, but didn't have the funds to do so. Bassanio asked his friend Antonio for money, but Antonio's funds were tied up in a shipping venture. Hoping still to help Bassanio, Antonio approached another moneylender — the Jew, Shylock — for a loan. But Shylock held a grudge against Antonio. He agreed to lend the money but demanded a literal pound of Antonio's flesh in exchange if the loan wasn't repaid.

As Emilia wrote her, Portia was a fierce, smart, independent woman frustrated because her father's will prohibited her from picking her own husband. Instead, Portia's suitors would choose from three caskets — gold, silver, and lead — one of which held her portrait. Whoever claimed the casket that concealed her portrait would have her hand. Two princes picked the caskets made of precious metal and were dismissed. But Bassanio picked the lead casket, which contained the portrait and which — like Portia herself — was more than met the eye. When a letter arrived from Antonio saying that his ships were lost at sea and he would have to face Shylock in Venetian court, Bassanio left immediately. Portia's money would be his after marriage, and he hoped Shylock would take that for repayment, rather than Antonio's flesh.

Emilia began to write furiously, in Portia's voice.

But now I was the lord
Of this fair mansion, master of my servants,
Queen o'er myself; and even now, but now,
This house, these servants, and this same
  myself
Are yours, my lord's. I give them with this
  ring,
Which, when you part from, lose, or give
  away,
Let it presage the ruin of your love,
And be my vantage to exclaim on you.

Emilia drew her wedding ring from her pocket.

That little band was imbued with so much power.

Without thinking twice, she pitched it into the Thames, and did not even bother to watch it sink.

Suddenly she knew how she wanted her play to end. As a woman, Portia was powerless to help save Antonio. As a man, however, Portia had a voice.

Disguised as a male lawyer named Baltha-zar, Portia told Shylock he was well within his rights to demand the payment of a pound of flesh . . . he just could not extract a single drop of blood while doing so. When Shylock backpedaled, asking for the money instead, Portia insisted it was his own reliance on the face value of the law that had led him to this moment. Shylock's wealth was stripped from him, because he'd threatened a Venetian, and he was forced to convert to Christianity.

Since that, of course, was what the audience would see as a happy ending.

She wrote Shylock as if she were still having a conversation with Kit about his *Jew of Malta.* She made her Jewish character vengeful — holding a grudge against Antonio — and she made him reviled for his faith, like Dr. Lopez had been before his execution by the Queen. But she also made him human.

I am a Jew, she wrote, and even putting those words on paper sent a shiver down Emilia's spine.

Hath not a Jew eyes? Hath not a Jew hands, or-gans, dimensions, senses, affections, passions?

If you prick us, do we not bleed?

If you wrong us, shall we not revenge?

It was exhausting — for Shylock, for Por-tia, for Emilia herself — constantly trying to be more than society believed you to be. If you were condescending, if you acted above your station, if you lashed out — it was only because you'd received that treatment from others.

The villainy you teach me I will execute, Emilia wrote in Shylock's voice.

By the time the sun was setting, the linens were dry enough to be folded. Emilia brought the corners to her chest, aligning the pleats and setting the bedsheets in the empty basket. As she worked, she mentally sketched out the last scene in her play. As payment for legal services, Balthazar/Portia would demand that Bassanio give her the very wedding ring he vowed he'd never remove. When he returned home without it, Portia scolded him for giving his ring away and claimed he had therefore given up his right to her bed and her body. In fact, *she* was now entitled to share a bed and her body with the very person to whom he'd given that ring. Eventually she'd reveal that she and Balthazar were one and the same . . . but not without making Bassanio sweat. Because what was the point of a wedding ring — a symbol — if the vow behind it was specious?

When she entered her home, Bess was serving dinner. Henry sat like a perfect little gentleman, his face lighting up to see hers. At the head of the table was Alphonso. "Apologies," she said, blustering inside. "It took longer than I expected for the linens to dry."

Alphonso cut a bit of mutton with his knife. "We did not think to wait for you."

"I would not have wished you to," Emilia said. "How was your day, Husband?"

"Fruitful," he replied.

She moved past him to set the linens in the bedchamber, but Alphonso grabbed her wrist, pulling her off balance. The basket fell to the floor, and she toppled onto his lap. "Have you no welcome kiss for me, then?"

Dutifully, she leaned forward and pressed her lips to his cheek.

His hand tightened painfully on her wrist. "Where is your ring?"

She glanced down at her hand as if its absence was unexpected. "I know not," she answered.

"You stupid cow," Alphonso spat, dumping her off him. "We could have sold that for a month's lodging."

"You are right, Alphonso," she said, her eyes cast down. "What punishment shall I have by your hand? Let me choose it, for my own brainlessness. By heaven, I shall never come in your bed until I once again see that ring."

"Indeed," Alphonso agreed, and then his features pinched with confusion. "But —"

"Husband, it is no more or less than I deserve." She picked up the basket of linens and, with humble chagrin, trudged up the stairs to the bedchamber. There, she closed the door behind herself.

She knew her reprieve would be fleeting,

that he could demand access to her body whenever he wished it.

But still.

Emilia smiled.

Good Mistress,

I pray this letter finds you in good health and calm spirits as I wish not to offend you by denying your wishes.

If you cannot deliver your response in person I beg for your thoughts and words to know that your days remain as empty as mine; a void that could only be filled with one the shape of you.

I am lost without you; what other explanation could there be for why you have not found me?

I remain,

Yours.
S.

Emilia refused to meet Southampton, because the danger of being caught by Alphonso was too great. But when Shakespeare finally corresponded, she took the risk of an encounter, because she needed money to pay for food.

She paced in front of a brothel quite far from their usual meeting spot, wondering why on earth Shakespeare had wanted to meet her here. It was not nighttime yet, but

Emilia feared being seen by one who knew of her through Alphonso, or by Alphonso himself. It was overcast, an autumn day with the teeth of winter. Emilia drew her shawl closer and clutched her satchel more tightly. Inside it was a foul copy of *The Merchant of Venice.*

When Shakespeare finally arrived, he was nearly a half hour late. Once again she noticed how fine his clothing and boots appeared — clearly, representing her, and others, was paying dividends. "Mistress," he said, nodding.

"This is not a good spot for a rendezvous," Emilia snapped.

His brows rose. "I offered to come to your residence —"

"And we both know why that is not possible."

"Yes. It is just that . . . I cannot frequent my usual haunts." Shakespeare dipped his chin. "I find myself afoul of the law."

She blinked at him. She was doing business with a criminal?

"It is nothing," he scoffed. "A writ of attachment taken out against me by William Wayte."

"Why?"

"Langley and I came to an agreement about the use of the Swan for the Lord Chamberlain's Men this summer. Wayte claims we cheated him."

Emilia narrowed her eyes, waiting for the rest.

"As a result, I cannot show my face anywhere

in the domain of the sheriff of Surrey without risking arrest." He slapped a pouch of coins into her hand. "Wayte threatened getting the Puritans involved. I assumed you'd prefer receiving payment for your faerie play to having me languish in a cell."

She fumbled in her satchel for the new play. "You will soon not be able to reach me at my current lodging. We are . . . relocating."

"As am I." Shakespeare sighed. "I find myself on the default roll for St. Helen's parish, largely thanks to you."

"It is my fault you evaded taxes?"

"It is your fault I have the wealth to do so." He took the stack of pages from her hands. "And what is the subject this time?"

"A greedy Jew and an upstart of a woman."

Shakespeare shook his head. "You really must learn the definition of comedy, my dear."

As he started off, she called after him. "If your apartments change, how will I find you?"

He smiled, feline. "It is *I* that shall find *you,* mistress. Or do you doubt my ability to do so?"

She did not doubt it in the least. It was the danger in doing business with someone who was willing to keep secrets: he had secrets of his own.

Since Alphonso's return, Emilia had managed to keep Southampton at arm's length. But the threat of being evicted made her vulnerable,

506

and when Bess slipped her a letter, Emilia hurried to the privy closet to read it.

In Southampton's bold, slanted hand was an address in Westminster.

Holywell Street.

The only other word on the paper was a date, a week hence, which gave Emilia time to figure out an excuse to leave the house. She had told Alphonso she had been hired to instruct a noblewoman's daughter on playing the lute. She would produce a coin from her own cache of funds if it meant being able to meet with Southampton. "Please them well," Alphonso had said. "Mayhap they will hire you and you will be more than just a millstone around my neck."

On the day of her meeting, Emilia dressed in one of her old brocade court dresses — tighter since her pregnancy — and picked her way through the streets of London to the address. It was a narrow building on a side street in Westminster that sat between a parish church with a small graveyard, and a butcher. The metallic smell of blood washed over Emilia as she watched the tradesman string a haunch of venison to drain in his shop.

She rapped on the door and it opened a crack. A hand snaked out, grasping her wrist, making Emilia gasp as she was tugged inside.

Southampton pushed her up against the wall, his hands framing her face as he kissed her. She melted into him. He hiked her higher, pressing her back against the plaster, as she untied his hose and dug through the foam of her skirts to bare herself. They came together like an alchemical reaction, the kind that gets mistaken for sorcery because it alters form and substance.

Afterward, they were tangled on the floor of the apartments, cool air spilling through the windows and drying the sweat on their skin. Emilia took stock of her surroundings. The rooms were small and bright and cheery. There was a scattering of furniture, covered with great white sheets billowing like the sails of ships that might carry the two of them away.

Southampton flattened one hand on Emilia's belly and traced a pattern with the other on her shoulder. "I thought you might not come," he confessed.

"You did not give a meeting time," Emilia said.

He dropped a kiss on her collarbone. "I knew it would not be easy for you to leave. And I would have waited forever."

Forever. It was such a luxury of a word.

She listened to the sound of a customer being greeted by the butcher, and the midday bells of the parish church. "Who lives here?" Emilia asked.

"You," Southampton murmured. "If you wish it."

She turned in his arms to face him. He

was asking her to be his mistress? He would keep her here, as the Baron had kept Isabella in her apartments in St. Helen's Bishopsgate. "But I am *married*," she said, her voice breaking.

"You need a home, Emilia. This could be for you, and Henry." Southampton swallowed. "And for your husband."

"You would do that for me?" she whispered.

"I already have."

"And how do I explain that I have come suddenly into a residence?" She sat up, turning away.

He sat up, too. She could feel his gaze on her back. "Tell him a relative died and left it to you."

"It would immediately become his anyway," Emilia muttered.

She felt his fingers tracing the pearls of her spine. "Then do not tell him at all," he said.

Emilia glanced over her shoulder to meet his gaze.

"What choice do we have? I have met with lawyers and solicitors," Southampton added. "There is nothing for it — if the marriage has been consummated, it cannot be dissolved. The former king had to introduce a new religion to get rid of his bride, and I do not have that sort of power."

"It is his word against mine. We could say —"

"No," Southampton softly interrupted.

"You cannot do something that puts young Henry on the wrong side of the blanket."

He was right. To annul her marriage would leave her son with the stigma of being a bastard, something he would never escape.

"You cannot remarry. Not until he is dead. But — Emilia — you can *leave* him. And I can protect you." Before she could protest he touched a finger to her lips. "No one bats an eye when married couples separate," he argued. "It is the norm more than the exception."

She knew that, of course. It was why she had been procured for Hunsdon.

"If we cannot live as man and wife," Southampton said, "let us at least be a family." He raised a brow. "And before you say you fear Lanier would retaliate against me, allow me to point out that he does not have the power to do so."

"You will need an heir."

"I have one — my dim-witted cousin. What I do *not* have is you."

She felt his hands come around her shoulders, his cheek press against hers. "I am pregnant," Emilia whispered.

She felt the tightening of his fingers, and then the silence in which he marked the weeks that had separated them. It was not his baby, it couldn't be.

Emilia had known for over a week — she hadn't bled in two months and her breasts were so tender they ached. "I have not told Alphonso yet." She had hoped — even if she had not uttered the words aloud — that nature might resolve this problem for her.

"It does not matter to me," Southampton said. "I would raise the child as if it were mine."

This man. Oh, this man. "It would be a scandal," Emilia said.

He brought her hand to his mouth and kissed her knuckles, as if she were a lady he had met at the palace, not in these sordid circumstances. "Think on it," he begged. "Do not give me your answer today."

"Sometimes I believe there are people in this world for whom happiness is not intended," Emilia admitted.

Southampton shook his head. "I would not disappoint you, love."

She could feel the words on her tongue like sharp stars: *You do not know me.*

She wished she had the conviction to reveal her secrets to him, and to know that his offer would still stand if she did.

Instead, she kissed Southampton so deeply she had no choice but to swallow those confessions. "Prove it," Emilia said, her voice husky, as she tumbled them both backward again.

They had fallen asleep. By the time she left Westminster the lamps were being lit on the streets and she found herself hurrying back

511

to Mark Lane, skirting drunkards and beggars. The key to the apartments Southampton had given her burned like a coal between her breasts.

To her surprise, when she entered her home, it was pitch-dark. There were no braces of lit candles, no dishes being cleared, no sounds at all. Emilia closed the door behind herself. "Henry?" she whispered. "Bess?"

She heard the scrape of flint and then a flame spilled from a candle, illuminating Alphonso. "Where is your lute?" he asked.

"I'm . . . sorry?"

"Your *lute*," he repeated. "You were tutoring music, were you not?"

Her eyes flicked to the surface of the table, littered with letters with broken seals. She had been a fool, but she couldn't bear to throw Southampton's letters into a fire. She had hidden them, along with the published copies of her poems, in the folds of old chemises at the bottom of her trunk of clothing.

"I am lost without you," Alphonso read. "Yours, S." He picked up another with Shakespeare's name at the bottom. "A . . . *glover*? You think me stupid enough to believe that? The only thing being gloved here is his prick, by a whore like you." He threw the letter at her, and then the printed copy of *Venus and Adonis* with Shakespeare's name upon it.

Emilia realized two things at once: Alphonso had conflated Shakespeare with the author of the letters he'd found. He did not realize S stood for Southampton; he assumed that she was carrying on an affair with someone named William Shakespeare, which was also clearly why she was in possession of his poems.

She also realized if Alphonso had found the hiding place for her letters, he had also discovered her secret stash of money.

"Alphonso," she said, breathless. "Wait —"

He toppled the chair in his haste to reach her, grabbing her by the throat and slamming her into the wall. His hands tightened. She drooled and coughed, her eyes rolling wildly. "I will fuck him out of you," her husband said, punching her head against the wall with each word. He threw her to the ground as she sucked at the sudden air, only to lose it when his booted foot caught her gut over and over.

She tried to crawl away, thinking of the child Alphonso did not know about . . . and then about the one he did. "Henry," she managed, blood running down her chin.

Alphonso jerked her still by her hair. "Cannot hear you scream," he replied, and then he punched her full in the face.

She swam to consciousness twice.

Once, when he was still beating her body.

Again, when he was done, and she felt the bloody runnel between her legs, just as she'd secretly, terribly wished.

When the sun rose the next morning, she could barely open her eyes; they were swollen into slits. Her jaw was broken, as was her arm. A patch of hair had been torn from her scalp. Her skirts were stiff with dried blood.

When she saw Alphonso staring at her, she whimpered and did her best to inch away from him.

"I cannot stop you from seeing him again," Alphonso said. "But I can stop him from seeing *you*."

She tried to wet her lips. "You would . . . kill me . . ."

"I do not think even the threat of that would give you pause," he said. "No, if ever I find that you are making a cuckold of me again, I will kill the boy."

Alphonso stood, opening the door of their home so that light bisected her like a sword. He walked outside, flexing his fist.

Not long after, Bess returned with Henry. Seeing Emilia, she tucked him behind her skirts and told him to shut his eyes tight. Then she rushed to Emilia, gingerly touching her broken body. "Mistress, oh, how you've been beat," Bess crooned.

Yes, Emilia thought dully. *I have.*

It took a week before she could sit up in bed. Another week before her hand was strong enough to hold a quill. As the weather turned colder and Emilia's body healed, she worked her mind for what she might say to Southampton.

In the end she wrote him a poem.

The world was upside down: honor misplaced, joy forsworn, maidens compromised, the innocent slandered. The good had been vanquished; and hope — which had taken the form of a key and a home that might have belonged to them both — had literally been lost in the fray.

Tir'd with all these, for restful death I cry, she began.

Art made tongue-tied by authority . . .
And folly, doctor-like, controlling skill,
And simple truth miscall'd simplicity,
And captive good attending captain ill.

She put down her quill to wipe her eyes.

Tir'd with all these, from these would I be gone,
Save that, to die, I leave my love alone.

This was her penance for loving him: because she had known joy, she would also be able to recognize its absence.

A sad tale's best for winter, she wrote. *I cannot choose between two halves of my heart. He threatens what I have borne, and that I cannot bear.*

He would read between the lines and understand that she was talking of Henry.

515

If your love be true, if you want what is best for me, then you will heed this request: Do not beg, do not rail, do not burn the world down for me. I shall not survive the loss of you twice.

"Bess," she called. Her throat was still raw, her voice an approximation.

The maid appeared, and Emilia folded the note, sealed it, and pushed it into her hand. "You must take this to Southampton House."

"I cannot leave you alone, mistress —"

"Go."

Bess skittered from the room, leaving the chamber door ajar. Emilia set aside her writing desk and collapsed backward on the bed. She closed her eyes, imagining Southampton. His smile, when he saw her handwriting.

His face, when he actually read it.

Her eyes burned, even while closed. Perhaps Emilia would hear of Southampton, mention of him threaded through the future conversations of others, and knowing that he was in the world would make it a palatable place to end out her days. Perhaps she would pray to never hear his name again, because she had never felt agony like this before. What was the point of fighting so hard to be here, when her life would only be more of the same — now without any glimmer of him.

To be, or not to be, that was the question.

It would be so much easier if she hadn't woken up after Alphonso's beating.

Emilia looked down at the knife she used

516

to trim her quills. Holding it steadily in her unbandaged hand, she pressed down on the pale skin of her wrist. She pushed down with the blade, almost fascinated by the thin line of welling blood.

A scream tore from the other room, jerking her from her dark thoughts.

She sat up, her body protesting, and dragged herself off the bed. She staggered from bedpost to wall to the doorway, holding herself upright with her good arm and cradling the broken one against her body like a wing.

Henry lay on a pallet in front of the hearth, tangled in the claws of a nightmare.

She sank to the stones beside him, brushing the damp hair from his forehead. His eyes, stormy and silver as hers, blinked open. "Mama," he said.

Her face was swollen and split and blackened. Blood smeared her wrist, an injury of her own making. She did not know herself anymore. But Henry did.

If she could not bear to lose someone she loved, how could she ever wish that fate on her son?

She stroked his back until he curled like a silkworm, breathing steadily again in sleep. Then, because she could not manage to stand on her own, she simply lay down beside him.

As it turned out, you *could* take the pound of flesh without the blood.

517

You could remove your heart, and still feel its broken pieces rattling inside.

By 1597, Emilia had lost all her angles and edges. She had sanded down whatever splinters remained, what parts of her stood out. It left her numb, which was the only way she could get through her days. If you didn't dream, if you didn't feel . . . you could not be disappointed.

She marked time by its uniformity: the baking of bread in the morning, the cleaning of the floors in the afternoon, the walks she took with Henry, the pawing of Alphonso as he pulled up her night rail. She did not write. She barely spoke.

She thought it so interesting that people lived in fear of sorcery, but no one seemed to even notice that she was a ghost that already walked among them.

She tried to soothe the ache inside her, but she could not find joy in music or poetry or any other pursuit that had once been transportive. Henry was the only bright spot in her world. He would hand her a crushed flower as a treasure, and she would feel the rusty bend of a smile; he would curl into her lap, and it was enough to make her feel substantial, instead of like a wraith. She thought perhaps the pit of loss inside her would abate if she had another child. Although she did not wish Alphonso to be the baby's father, she no longer had an option. God knew, it was bound to happen, as Alphonso used her body frequently for his own pleasure. Indeed, twice she got pregnant, and twice she miscarried, which was how she knew God would never forgive her sins — but worse, He would never *forget* her long enough for the punishment to ease.

She knew that Bess was worried. The maid had swelled to fill up the space left behind as Emilia diminished. She cooked and went to market. She breeched Henry and suggested they spend afternoons at Alma's so that he could begin to learn his letters. In truth, Emilia thought that Bess simply wanted someone else to bear witness to her mistress slipping away.

Sometimes, Henry would get close to her face and put his hands over her cheeks and stare into her eyes, like he was searching for his mother inside those smooth features.

Those were the times she started to cry.

Alphonso had secured them lodgings in Westminster, on Canon Row in Longditch. It was not far from Holywell Street, where Emilia had last met with Southampton. When she had to leave the house, she did so with her eyes downcast, just in case she might be tempted to look for a cap of copper hair, a piercing blue gaze, the love of her life.

Shakespeare, as promised, had found her with a letter at her new residence. His name had turned up once again in default of taxes in St. Helen's Bishopsgate. He was, of course, in need of funds, which meant he was in need of a new play from her. She fed the paper to the fire, not bothering to write him back at his new address in Bankside.

When the Earl of Essex was looking for gentlemen volunteers for his voyage to the Azores, Alphonso signed on. And yet, when he finally shipped out that spring, the atmosphere in the house did not feel any lighter. Emilia found herself surprisingly blank of emotion, which only reinforced the suspicion that Alphonso was right. The problem had been *her,* all along.

She found herself in Jeronimo's household one afternoon, cutting turnips for a stew with Alma while Bess mended clothing. Young Henry sat at their feet, badly playing a lute. The boy's notes were sour and jarring, but Jeronimo grinned as if he'd composed his own symphony. "We will make a player of you yet, son," he said. "Will we not, Emilia?"

Emilia had seen her cousin dozens of times since her husband had nearly beaten her to death. The first time, her face was a mincemeat, and Jeronimo had tried to meet what remained of her undamaged eye and asked after her welfare.

As if the answer had not been patently visible.

"You should introduce him to the Queen," Alma told her husband, winking at Emilia.

"It is never too early for another Bassano to become a court musician."

"Her Majesty barely wants the ones she already has," Jeronimo said, adjusting Henry's tiny hand on the bridge of the lute. "She is too melancholy for music. All her favorites are off on galleons fighting Spain with Essex. Suffolk, Raleigh, Southampton."

Southampton.

Was fighting on the same military voyage that Alphonso was on.

Emilia felt the knife she was holding slip, slicing deep into the meat of her thumb. She blinked down as her blood spilled, surrounding the turnips. It was sharp and dark, like a nightmare. She wanted to drown in it.

"Che cavalo!" Alma cried. She lurched toward Emilia, prying the paring knife from her hand and wrapping the bleeding thumb in her own apron.

Emilia stared down at her hand, caught between them. She could feel her pulse in the wound. It interested her as nothing else had for some time now. Proof that she was still among the living.

There was a bustle of communication in Italian and Jeronimo hustled little Henry outside. *"Tesora,"* Alma said softly, curving her hand around Emilia's jaw. "I knew your body was broken. I did not realize your soul was, too."

Emilia felt as if she were at the bottom of the

ocean, looking up at the sun, and wondering how she could ever muster the energy to reach it again. And then, like a miracle, Alma's words reached out and wrapped around her as surely as her arms. "What do you wish for, Emilia?"

Oh, how to answer that question.

She had wished for wings and flown too close to the sun. She would not make that mistake again. "A baby," she heard herself say.

If Henry was all the joy she had left and he was already growing up, she would need somewhere else to settle the estate of her love.

Alma's eyes caught hers, held them. "Then you shall have one," she vowed.

Doctor Simon Forman was an astrologer Alma's cousin's wife had visited when she found herself infertile. Emilia's hope was the doctor could fix whatever fault lay with her, so that by the time her husband came home from battle, she would be able to successfully carry a child to term. The baby, she hoped, would tether her back to the world from which she kept fading.

Forman was small, with strands of baby-fine hair drawn forward on his scalp to detract from the shine of his pate. His drawing room was dark, the shades pulled even though it was midday and sunny. Emilia rubbed her palms on her lap. He was a doctor, which meant that he should see her only as a patient.

And yet when he had brought her into the room, his hand had been on the small of her back and slipped lower. He had been staring at the rise of her breasts over her gown for the past ten minutes.

Emilia bit her lip. "I beg your pardon, sir. I do not know how this begins."

"It is a conversation, nothing more and nothing less. Of course, if you choose anything but honesty, I cannot be expected to help you."

"I understand."

"How old are you, Mistress Lanier?" he asked.

"Seven and twenty," she replied.

"You are married?"

She nodded.

"You wish to conceive a child?"

"Yes. I have had many . . . false conceptions."

"Your husband wishes you to be here?"

"My husband . . . has dealt harshly with me," Emilia admitted. "He has spent and consumed my goods. He does not know I am here, as he is in service with the Earl of Essex in hope of gaining preferment as a knight." She seemed to consider this. "You would know, would you not, if that will come to pass?"

Forman raised a brow. "Do you ask because you wish to become a lady?"

"I wish because it is my husband's wish," Emilia said.

"If he wishes you to become a *lady,*" the doctor mused, imbuing the word with a double meaning, "that suggests you are not one at present."

A hot flush rose to Emilia's face. "I am a faithful wife, sir."

"Are you." He took his quill and touched the tip of it to a small mark at the base of her throat. "Then why wear you the mark of the Devil?"

She clapped a hand over her neck. "I have had that mark since I was born, sir."

The doctor scrawled some notes. Emilia struggled to read them upside down. "Mistress Lanier, I should inform you of my methods. If I believe a client is keeping secrets from me . . . particularly secrets of the flesh . . . I will not hesitate to call her out as a whore." He fixed his watery eyes on her. "Your parents' names?"

She watched him sketch out two astrological figures and write down the words she spoke. *Baptista Bassano, Margaret Johnson.*

He wrote *Alphonso Lanier* in the margin.

"I was raised by the Countess of Kent," Emilia said. "After my father died and my mother went away. I was taught by the Countess herself, until she married again."

"And then?"

"When I was thirteen," Emilia said, "I became the paramour of Lord Hunsdon, the Lord Chamberlain. He kept me long, and made available to me jewels and money, and gave me forty pounds a year —"

"Yes, yes," Forman interrupted. "When did you first have sexual intercourse?"

Honesty.

"Two months after I arrived at Somerset House," Emilia replied.

"As I suspected," the doctor said. "And you took pride in this whoring."

"I took no pride in being made to be his mistress, sir."

"Were you not compensated with financial rewards for sharing a bed?"

Emilia did not understand astrology, yet she assumed that this man believed confessing her sin would unblock her womb.

"It was sex that brought you to that relationship, and I warrant it was sex that put you out of it," he said. "You were with child . . . in fornication . . . *et sodomita.*" The doctor glanced up. "Your current husband was aware of this."

"Yes," she said. "The Lord Chamberlain arranged for me to be married off to him for appearances. But rest assured my husband was compensated with financial rewards for sharing a bed."

"Were you never taught to hold your tongue?" Forman murmured, staring at her lips. "Or mayhap you were taught to use it another way entirely."

Emilia cleared her throat. "Sir, I fail to

525

understand how your accusations about my past will help me conceive in the present."

"It is not for you to understand . . . only to accept the baseness of your lust. An unweeded garden grows to seed; things rank and gross in nature possess it." Forman leaned forward, his breath sour on her face, his hand falling to her knee and squeezing. "How fortunate for you that I know all about plowing."

Emilia's second visit with Simon Forman took place in her home a month later, privately, at his request. She served the doctor ale and bread and splurged on an expensive cheese Alma had suggested; to do so Emilia herself had given up her own supper. "Have you seen my future in my charts, sir?" she asked. Forman patted the stool beside him. After a hesitation, she sat down. She watched him rip off a bit of bread and wrap it around cheese before stuffing it into his mouth. "These things take time," he said.

"These things take money I do not have," she admitted.

"You worry about funds?"

"I worry about feeding my child," Emilia corrected.

"Yet you told me how noblemen and Her Majesty favored you."

"Indeed, they did," Emilia said. "And Alphonso has spent all my money."

Forman belched. "The stars have told me

that he will return home with preferment, but that before this, he will be in peril for his life."

"Will he be knighted, then?"

The doctor shrugged. "That is a question for a different day."

"I will not be able to meet with you again on a different day," Emilia said. "I haven't the payment."

"I think you do, mistress. It is a currency with which you are familiar." He blotted his mouth with his sleeve. "I will not force a client as such to *halek,* but were it offered freely, in barter . . ." His voice trailed off.

"Halek?"

He took her hand and pressed it between his legs. She felt the skinny knob of him in her palm. "That is what I choose to call . . . intimacy," he said. He unrolled an astrological chart on the table. "I *may* be able to hold future sessions to answer your queries."

He waited.

It was a standoff.

Emilia watched the light from the lone lit candle dance over the astrologer's lines and arcs. She could not read his case notes, but that did not mean she did not understand.

She had been given to a man forty-three years her senior as a courtesan.

She had fallen in love with a noble she could never be with.

She had been forced into marriage with a

wastrel who had taken everything from her, including her pride.

But she had never, ever felt dirty until this moment.

No.

Emilia stood so quickly the stool overturned. She gripped the edges of her gown, holding them tight at her throat.

"No."

"Mistress —"

"Get out," Emilia growled, in a voice she had never heard come from her throat. "I am more than this. It does not matter what you see when you look at me, because you will never know me the way I know myself. And even if I am the only person in the world with that knowledge, it does not make it any less real."

As she paused to catch her breath she thought, *You small, stupid man.* Then she kicked the stool out from beneath Forman, leaving him cowering on the floor. She picked up the knife he'd used to carve the cheese. "By God, get out of my house," she said.

After the door slammed behind him a moment later, Emilia sat at the table, finishing the meal she had thought to give Forman. Her hand shook as she cut the wedge of cheese.

It was, as Alma had said, divine.

By the time Alphonso returned weeks later, full of self-importance despite the tragic failure of the naval mission, Emilia had conquered her melancholy. She took over the chores Bess had done when she was unable to see past her despair. She played with little Henry. To her surprise, Alphonso had sent word of his imminent arrival, so when he entered their apartments she was ready.

She had fresh flowers on the table. The house was scrubbed. Henry wore spotless clothes. A humble meal, the most she could afford, was waiting.

He stepped through the doorway, dusty and disheveled. Emilia stood with her hands clasped. The last time he had seen her, her face had been split and unrecognizable. "Husband," she said evenly.

He stilled. "Wife?"

"How lucky we are that God has seen you home," Emilia said. "You must be hungry."

He watched her over his meal the way one would watch a snake in the corner of the room — not necessarily deadly from that distance, but worth keeping in one's sights. He spoke of the Azores, the galleon, and the casualties they sustained. He made Henry laugh with stories of sand in his boots. When he finished eating, Emilia cleared the dishes. "Bess," she said, "I am sure my husband would like to wash the grime of travel from his person. Heat some water for the tub, please?"

Once the wooden tub had been hauled in front of the fire and filled, Bess took Henry to her own quarters so that Alphonso could bathe privately. Emilia scattered sage, marjoram, and chamomile across the surface of the murky water to make it smell sweet. She felt him staring at her, as if he could not quite figure out if his shrew of a wife had been replaced by faeries or if his last beating had knocked sense into her. "Allow me to help, sir," she said, dimpling prettily, and she unhooked his doublet, carefully setting it on a chair before kneeling to remove his boots and hose. He sank into the tub, sloshing water over the sides.

"May I scrub your back, Husband?" Emilia asked, standing behind him.

He glanced over his shoulder and nodded, splaying his arms along the edges of the tub. Emilia took a linen square and dipped it in the water.

"Emilia," Alphonso said, clearing his throat. "I have had time to think during our distance."

"As have I, sir."

He faced the fire, watching the flames, while her hands scrubbed his neck and curved around to his chest.

"I wish to start afresh," Alphonso continued. "I believe, with some work, you might be a fine helpmeet. A true spouse." He shifted as her hands tickled their way down his abdomen. "Indeed, it seems that you may have already come to this conclusion yourself."

"Conclusion," Emilia repeated, the steam rising around her face. "You *could* say I have come to the end, sir."

As she said the word, her hand closed around his cock, lifting it just enough for her to press the blade she'd hidden in her skirt to the edge of his testicles. Alphonso's panicked eyes locked onto hers. The linen cloth floated like an afterthought.

"You will not touch me again, not in lust and not in anger. If you do, mark my words, I will come for you. If you hurt me, I will heal from the sheer force of will. If you kill me, I shall return from the dead as a wraith. I will saw off your ballocks in your sleep, so that your quill is as good as snapped. You may live in my presence. That is all I give you leave to do."

His eyes flashed, and he moved as if to rise out of the tub. She pressed the knife into him until a ribbon of blood curled through the water. "Think you that I jest?" Emilia murmured.

Alphonso shook his head.

"You see, I, too, wish to start afresh," Emilia said.

She wrenched the blade from between his legs and slipped it back through the slit in her skirt, where she wore it now, every hour of the day, strapped to her thigh. "Good night, Alphonso," she said. "Empty the water when you're done."

531

■ ■ ■ ■

Emilia slept in Henry's chamber, curled around him like a fiddlehead fern. She did not mind giving up her own bed to Alphonso, because doing so meant she was not in it.

Five days after Alphonso's return Emilia visited the apothecary shop where Isabella had taken her years ago. The young proprietress listened carefully when she explained what she needed. A sleeping draft, a deep one, that would render her husband unfeeling.

She did not want Alphonso to touch her, but she still wanted a child. She just planned to be the one controlling the process.

So, armed with adder's-tongue fern and dwale — a concoction of lettuce, vinegar, and briony root with hemlock and henbane mixed in — Emilia served Alphonso a tea. She had been assured it would put him to sleep but leave his parts able to function.

He could barely finish his meal without his eyelids drooping. Past midnight, when she left Henry's chamber and went to Alphonso's, she found him collapsed fully clothed onto the bed. He was snoring loud enough for Emilia to feel the juddering down her spine.

She crawled onto the edge of the bed, hesitating, but Alphonso didn't budge.

She tugged at the waist of his hose until it caught at the juncture of his legs. She stared dispassionately at his penis, then began rubbing at it the way she might shuck an ear of turkey wheat. Emilia watched Alphonso's eyes flutter beneath closed lids, but he didn't wake as he hardened in her hand.

When he was stiff enough, she bunched her skirts and sank down on him. She rocked experimentally, deriving no pleasure, intent only on getting what she needed.

She shrieked when his hands suddenly gripped her hips. Emilia found herself looking directly into Alphonso's dazed gaze. "Are you . . ." he said, his voice thick, "are you an angel?"

Yes, she thought. *An avenging one.*

She leaned forward until her breasts brushed his chest. Her hand slipped between them, cupping him. She breathed over his lips. "Come," she urged.

He did, in three short jerks of his hips.

Emilia rested on Alphonso like a saddle until she was certain he was fast asleep once again. Then she left the bedchamber and returned to Henry, who stirred as she spooned him. She pressed her legs tight together and she prayed.

Alphonso awakened the next morning with the trace of a strange dream, a mouth as dry as muslin, and the smell of Emilia on his skin.

Emilia awakened pregnant.

It was late August 1598 when Emilia saw the ghost.

She was on Newgate Street in Cheapside Market, where butchers sold cuts of meat from animals slaughtered in the nearby Shambles. Today she would get a mutton joint that might serve for several meals: boiled as a soup, then carved into a stew, then pressed into a mash. She had to make it last, so that her son could have enough to eat.

And her daughter.

She rested her hand on the swell of her belly. She was sure of it; this was the girl who had haunted her dreams, giving her a second chance.

In her market basket she already had some parnsips and cooking fat and salt. She would purchase eggs and flour and then return home. "Mistress," the butcher said, handing her the wrapped mutton. She paid him his coin, turned, and *he* was there, his hair burnished like a crown, his shoulders bearing the sun.

Emilia dropped her basket, her wares tumbling into the street.

She knew she had imagined him because men like Southampton did not shop in Cheapside Market. He was so strikingly out of place here, with the silver threading in his doublet catching the light, his leather boots buffed to a high shine, jewels ringing his fingers. The crowded pulse of the market gave way for him, funneling around his presence. People gaped, some tugging their hair and bowing, others plucking at him for a handout.

He noticed none of it. He knelt on the cobblestones, unmindful of the filth, and put her items back into her market basket. "Emilia," he said softly. "Will you walk?"

She nodded, falling into step in his shadow. She rubbed her thumb over the spot between her breasts, where it felt like a wound had reopened.

Southampton led her to a narrow, arched passageway with a bee carved into its headstone. Down this little lane a bit farther were the honey merchants, but he stopped before they could reach the stalls. His eyes drank her in. "You are well?" he whispered, his gaze falling to her pregnancy.

She blurted, "Why are you here?"

"Because Thursday is when you go to market," he said simply. After a moment he sighed. "It was not difficult to find your lodgings," Southampton said. "Your husband was on my galleon, after all. I cannot tell you how many times I thought to pitch him over the gunwale and be done with it."

"Conscience does make cowards of us all," Emilia said.

"I paid a boy to watch your comings and goings," Southampton admitted. "I needed to speak with you privately."

Did he not understand that her son's life was at stake? "I asked you to never —"

"I am married," Southampton said, and Emilia felt her knees give. She pressed her shoulder blades into the building behind her.

"Heaven give you many merry days," she murmured.

"Emilia."

"I wish you and your wife good health and happiness —"

"Emilia."

He touched her then, and she vibrated like the string of a lute. He could hear it; she was certain this frequency was one common only to the two of them.

"You said we . . . could never be."

She drew in a breath, held it. Could she blame him for respecting her wishes, for finding a path to live without her?

"The only way I could let myself believe that was to behave as if it were true," Southampton said, "and pray my heart would catch up to my actions." He let his gaze slide away from hers. "Elizabeth is one of Her Majesty's maids of honor. I was in a scuffle a few months ago with Ambrose Willoughby over a game of primero when he disparaged her . . . and for a while I was out of the Queen's favor. But then I learned my Elizabeth was with child — I could not let the baby be born without the protection of my name."

My Elizabeth. Emilia heard the words over and over, in canon.

"The Queen does not know we wed without

536

her permission . . . so I leave for France tonight."

She wondered if he would return for the birth of his child. She wondered why she cared.

He stared at her swelling pregnancy. "Are you . . . happy?" Southampton asked.

Emilia regarded the beloved angles of his face, the sunlight playing with his hair as she used to. "Is anyone?" she countered.

He smiled sadly at her. "I did love you once."

"Indeed, my lord, you made me believe so."

"You should not have believed me," Southampton said. "Perhaps now you would not know such pain."

"Perhaps now you would not know such joy."

"This is not joy, Emilia," he burst out. He reached for her hand and she let him take it, only to realize that something was being pressed into her palm. Glancing down she saw her own face, the miniature that he'd had painted of her. It was a mirror of her features, and yet it wasn't. The portrait was of a woman who held a secret love. Emilia, now, was a woman who'd lost everything.

She folded his fingers around the filigree frame. "Keep it," she said softly. "If only so that I know something of us survived."

She watched Southampton slip the miniature inside his doublet, over his heart.

"If you loved me once," Emilia ventured,

taking a deep breath, "will you do one last service for me?"

"Anything," Southampton vowed.

"Close your eyes," she said.

He did, without hesitation. She stared for one beat of her heart, thinking of how easy it would be to press up on her toes and taste him. But instead, she turned on her heel and left Honey Lane. She could not bear to see him walk away from her; she had to be the one to do it. And she also knew she would never have the strength to leave if he was watching. Emilia lifted her chin, thinking of Orpheus climbing from the Underworld, listening to the music of Eurydice's footsteps behind him. She thought of how desperately he must have tried to not glance back at his love, knowing that was the surest route to Hell.

Emilia was not well made for confinement. There were only so many games of skittles one could play with Henry, with a tiny rag ball and smaller pins. Stuck in the house, she could not escape Alphonso, and often when Bess was putting Henry to bed, Emilia would find herself on one side of the hearth, bent over her writing desk, while Alphonso sat on the other side whittling or playing an instrument.

One night, she felt her husband's eyes on her while she was composing her thoughts. "What do you write?" he asked.

"Does it matter?"

He seemed to consider this, and then shrugged. "It is but pleasantry. Conversation."

She nearly laughed at that. He had broken her jaw; polite discourse was no longer part of the equation.

"They are not letters," he mused. "They are too long for that."

Emilia met his gaze. "I am writing a story for the baby, if you must know." This was not entirely untrue. It was a play, not a fairy tale, but she was superstitious about what to choose as its subject. She did not want whatever ill humors were coursing through her blood to affect the growth of the baby inside her.

"Indulge me," Alphonso said.

Emilia put down her pen. "It is about a woman who wishes to be treated well by the man she loves. She disguises herself as a boy, so he will heed her advice."

Alphonso laughed. "Think you that clothing makes a man? You have lain alone too many nights."

"I could suit myself in all points as a man," Emilia said.

"Yet you lack a man's heart."

You lack *any* heart, Emilia thought.

"Well," Alphonso said dismissively. "Your story is best served for a child, since no adult would think the premise possible."

"No? Do you not believe the differences between men and women but a whimsy,

Husband? For example, in the theater it is not the fashion to give the lady the epilogue, but it is no more unhandsome to give the lord the prologue."

"It is not the fashion because it is not done. A woman does not have the last word."

"Indeed, this would be true, since a boy plays a woman on every stage, and the audience believes it. Why would the same not hold true should a woman play a man's part?"

She could see Alphonso trying to keep up with her reasoning. She made a mental note to add a clown to this play.

"No woman could wear the disguise of a man without a man seeing through it," he said finally. "The prattle alone! You are a woman. When you think, you must speak."

"Yet a woman sits on the throne of England. When she speaks, is it because she is a woman and cannot hold her tongue in her head? Or is it because she is a ruler and her words are law?"

Alphonso scowled, backed into a corner. "What is the name of this story?"

"As You Like It," she said.

"Is it? *As you like it?*" he asked. "Do you wish that you were the man in this marriage?"

She scrutinized him in the dim light. His question was not disdainful. He was . . . curious.

"I should have been a woman by right,"

540

Emilia said. "And yet does a woman exist but as a maid, a widow, or a wife?"

He waved a hand at her writing desk. "I do not like the thought of you filling the head of my child with this foolishness."

"Then perhaps you should spend night and day with the baby when she is born. After all, I have had her to myself for nine months."

"One of us," Alphonso said, "must provide for this family."

"Of course, Husband," she said mildly. "Think you that you will still become a knight?"

He stopped whittling his block of wood. "Do you doubt it?"

Emilia shook her head. "I believe that you have never had anyone tell you that what you wish is not possible."

"But that is not true. *You* have. When I suggested that we start anew." Alphonso leaned forward, balancing his elbows on his knees. "I have not been a perfect husband. But I am the husband you have."

"More's the pity."

"That mouth on you," Alphonso said. He came out of his chair, looming over her, and threaded his hand through her hair. His thumb brushed her lip. "Would that it were put to better use."

Her eyes locked on his. She curled her tongue around his finger and sucked, then bit him so hard that she tasted blood.

Alphonso leaped backward, nearly falling into the fire.

Emilia hoisted her heavy body to her feet. "As you requested," she said, curtsying, before locking herself inside Henry's chamber for the rest of the night.

On the day Odyllia Lanier was born, in December 1598, she howled louder than the ice storm that raged outside.

On the day ten months later that she died, there was an eerie silence in the still, chill air. The birds had disappeared, virtually overnight, flying south for winter. The barges on the Thames moved sluggishly, and the church bells did not ring.

As Emilia went through the motions of preparing her infant daughter for the cemetery at St. Botolph's Bishopsgate, she thought about everything she would be burying with Odyllia. Her chance at being a mother again, for one. The birth had been difficult, like Henry's, and the midwife had told her that another might kill her. In addition to that, she had lain with Alphonso only the once, as a means to an end. She would never grant him the invitation to her body again.

She would be burying laughter, too. There had been no toy Odyllia loved more than her big brother, whose antics had led to peals of giggles that filled all the empty space in their lodgings.

And, Emilia supposed, she would be burying the false satisfaction she'd lulled herself into believing: that being a mother would satisfy all the longings in her. Sometimes, when she had itched to write, instead she would bounce Odyllia on her knee and teach her a simple song. She'd told herself that when Henry had accidentally knocked over a precious bottle of ink, the tightening of her throat was not the fear of losing her voice but rather a parent fighting the urge to scold her son.

Odyllia lay on the oak table on a clean winding-sheet. Her translucent eyelids were violet. Her chest was immobile. How many times during the past week, when Emilia had seen her daughter fight for breath, had she wished that Odyllia would stop coughing?

You would think she would have learned, by now, to be more careful with her prayers.

Emilia pulled from her pocket a small curl of paper on which she had poured out her grief. She flattened it on the table near Odyllia's foot and then took a square of muslin and dipped it into a bowl of water, one she had heated in a kettle in the hearth, even though the temperature would not make a difference.

"Shall I compare thee to a summer's day?" Emilia whispered. *"Thou art more lovely and more temperate."* She ran the muslin between the tiny toes of her daughter's right foot. *"Rough winds do shake the darling buds of May, And summer's lease hath all too short a date."*

She worked the cloth over Odyllia's leg. *"Sometime too hot the eye of heaven shines, And often is his gold complexion dimm'd. And every fair from fair sometimes declines, By chance or nature's changing course untrimm'd."*

Perhaps it was better this way, that Odyllia know nothing in her life but love. That she never reach the age where she would be hemmed in by the expectations of men.

Emilia began to wrap the cloth tight around her daughter as if she were being swaddled against the bleakest of nights. *"Thy eternal summer shall not fade,"* she vowed, *"Nor lose possession of the fair thou ow'st."* She pulled the other end of the winding cloth tight, so that only Odyllia's perfect pale face was visible. *"Nor shall death brag thou wander'st in his shade, when in eternal lines to time thou grow'st."*

Finally, she rolled the poem tight and tucked it between the wrappings of the winding-sheet for safekeeping. Like someone bringing pennies for the crossing of the river Styx, her daughter would carry these words on her journey. *"So long as men can breathe or eyes can see,"* Emilia said, kissing her daughter's cold forehead, *"so long lives this, and this gives life to thee."*

"Mama."

Emilia gasped, then turned to find Henry standing a few steps behind, watching her work.

"Where is Bess?" she asked.

"She fell asleep," Henry said, coming closer, his head just level with Emilia's hip. He reached out one finger and poked Odyllia. Then he glanced up, his eyes swimming. "What if Bess doesn't wake up, too?"

Emilia knelt and wrapped her arms around his sturdy little form. "Henry," she said, "Odyllia isn't asleep. She's dead."

"Dead means gone forever." He parroted the words Emilia had used to explain his sister's passing.

"Yes. Once Odyllia is in the churchyard, that's where she will stay."

His lower lip trembled. "Is this because I wouldn't let her hold the lute Cousin Jeronimo gave me?"

"No, darling," Emilia soothed. "It is because Odyllia was ill and her body couldn't get better."

Fat tears striped his cheeks. "I wanted her to say *Henry*. I was trying to teach her."

"I know."

"Mama," Henry said, pressing his face into her shoulder. "Will you die?"

"One day."

He shook his head. "I don't want you to be gone forever."

Emilia framed his face in her hands. "Henry," she vowed, "I will not have to leave you until many, many years from now." She tugged the fine lawn of the winding-sheet over the strawberry pucker of Odyllia's lips. Then she reached for the right side of Henry's little jerkin, rending it. *"Barukh atah Adonai Eloheinu melekh ha'olam dayan ha'emet,"* she said. "I am going to tell you a secret. This is *Kriah*. People like us, we rend our clothing so that everyone knows there is a matching tear inside our hearts."

He watched her reach for her own kirtle. Emilia barely had to tug before the fabric ripped. After so much loss, the seam gave easily, as if grief were already part of its weave.

Every moment after Odyllia's death felt like a choice: Would Emilia keep her promise to Henry, or would today be the day she did not get out of bed? Would she put one foot in front of the other, or let herself slip back into the hole she had been in after Alphonso nearly killed her? Would she remember to put food down her gullet and smile, or move through the world like a spirit untethered?

Then, after months of no contact, William Shakespeare asked her to meet at St. Mary-at-Lambeth after Evensong.

Leaving Bess with Henry, Emilia crossed the river and slipped into a pew toward the rear as the choir swung into the introit. She recalled being a child, lying on the floor in front of the hearth as her father and cousins practiced their recorder pieces for court — a minor note tugging her down, a major seventh vaulting her to the stars.

Emilia found herself paying careful attention to the words of the Magnificat, the final anthem in the service, which was a chant. In English, it celebrated Mary being told that she was going to give birth to God's son. Emilia considered that she and Christ's mother had both lost a child.

"It is beautiful, isn't it?"

She heard Shakespeare's voice before she saw him. He had slipped into the pew behind her even as other congregants were filing out of the church.

"Grief?" she qualified. "No, I think not."

"Hmm," he said. "Do not all artists start from a place of pain?"

Emilia twisted in the wooden pew so that she could glance at him. He looked thinner, older. "How did you find my new lodgings?" she asked.

"I like to keep tabs on my business acquaintances."

It sounded sinister. It was likely meant to. "Well, you're a fair-weather correspondent," Emilia said dispassionately.

"I have . . . been otherwise occupied," Shakespeare said. "The Queen's Council did a census of private grain holdings and determined that I exceeded my quantity of malted barley, as if there could be such a thing."

She narrowed her eyes. The lack of grain

crops over the past few years had led to famine, to uprisings — and to speculation by individuals who wanted to make money off other people's hunger.

"You can no longer fleece your neighbors for profit?"

He scoffed. "It is a witch hunt. I simply misjudged taxes due to the Crown."

She laughed. "Defaulted, you mean."

"Defaulted, misjudged" — he waved a hand between them — "merely words."

"Shall I tell you what I think?" Emilia said. "I think that words are the very measure of why you asked me to meet you here. I think that you find yourself in need, once again, of coin."

He leaned an elbow on the pew back between them. "And you, mistress? Do you too find yourself in need of funds?"

What did she need? She thought of Odyllia, in a churchyard across town. Sometimes, Emilia awakened to find herself standing outside, barefoot in the coldest elbow of the night, holding a blanket and a misty thought: *She must be shivering.*

Emilia turned to fully meet Shakespeare's gaze. She rubbed her hand over the polished back of the pew, releasing a scent of wax and lemon. "Your son, Hamnet," she said, swallowing. "Does the loss . . . does it ever abate?"

He stilled. She wondered how long it had been since someone spoke that name out loud to him. "It changes," he said carefully. "At times it stops pulling, like a stitch. But then I will be doing something, perhaps crossing a field where I once tossed him onto my shoulder, and I will find myself on my knees sobbing." Shakespeare cleared his throat. "They call it a loss, but that's misconstered, is it not? They remain with us." Hesitantly, he patted her hand where it rested on the pew. "Give sorrow words, mistress," he urged.

Shakespeare was a charlatan; but here he spoke truth.

She had examined love in her writing, and anger, and lust. She had canted justice on its side and shook it to better understand mercy. She had poked at religion until it snapped back. She had used comedy to tease out the tragedy of what it meant to be a woman in a world run by men.

Why not take death and grief and jealousy and turn them like the gems in a kaleidoscope? Why not see what patterns emerged?

"I have an idea for a new play," she said.

The first scene took place between soldiers, describing a bright star and its position in the sky. She remembered well Tycho Brahe's supernova, as he'd described it years ago over supper at the Danish court. She set the story at Helsingør's Kronborg Castle, peppering it with her memories of Brahe's relatives Rosenkrans and Guldensteren and the play that had been performed about Amleth, the son avenging the murder of his father, and how his inability to take swift action would be his downfall. She hid her family in the text — making the Danish prince falsely describe the play-within-a-play as the story of a widowed woman named Baptista; having him explain in detail how to play a recorder.

It was a story about what happened when the world turned inside out. When, as the supernova had shown, the heavens could change. When death broke apart a marriage. When parents outlived their children. When grief could drive you mad.

She remembered telling Tycho Brahe at dinner that the Saxo play failed its women. So when Emilia rewrote it, she made Gerutha — now Queen Gertrude — a fully realized, flawed woman. She gave the young woman sent to seduce Prince Amleth an arc of her own — finding herself pregnant and alone.

The girl, as in the original play, would die. With her lover gone and her father dead, she would turn to the queen for aid. But when Gertrude would not help, she would ingest the same herbs Emilia had taken to abort her own baby. Then Emilia gifted the girl with madness, so that she might finally speak without being silenced.

Most important, she gave the girl a name: Ophelia. In her mind, she heard *Odyllia*.

She changed the name of the tragic prince,

too, to Hamlet. In her mind, she said *Hamnet.*

When she gave Shakespeare the play, he looked twice at its title. He met her gaze, and nodded.

Silent, she nodded back.

Later, Shakespeare told her about the first performance of the play. He said when *Hamlet* was performed at the new Globe Theatre at the start of 1600, it attracted the attention of the Earl of Southampton, who by then had become the most ardent supporter of theater in London.

The Earl himself had sought out the playwright to congratulate him.

On February 5, Southampton offered Shakespeare forty shillings, asking for the players to perform *Richard II.* He wanted to lay the groundwork in the public's mind for a monarch's downfall. It was a prologue to an attempt to overthrow the Queen, which he undertook the following weekend with the Earl of Essex. The attempt failed, and he was sentenced with treason, thrown in the Tower, and condemned to death.

Court gossip was the fastest news to spread, and so Emilia knew about the plot — and Southampton's fate — almost as soon as it happened.

Emilia began going to church. Not just on Sundays but every day of the week. She would walk across the city over icy cobbles, choosing a different parish each time, sitting in a pew and offering up a prayer that Southampton's sentence would be commuted.

The world would simply not be the same without him in it.

When his sentence was changed to life in prison, Emilia stopped going to church and started walking to the Tower of London. She knew Southampton would not be able to see her, would not even know she was nearby or thinking of him, but that did not matter. As the weather became more temperate, she brought Henry, his textbooks, and a packed lunch of bread and cheese.

"Mama," Henry asked, as they scattered crumbs for birds, "why do we come where the bad men are?"

She looked up at the imposing cliffs of stone. "Even the villains are the heroes of their own stories," she said.

"I do not know what that means," Henry said, frowning.

Emilia turned to him. "It means there is nothing either good or bad," she said softly. "But thinking makes it so."

When the plague ripped through London in 1603, theaters closed again. This time, the illness was even deadlier.

The Queen's death in March — not from the plague but from melancholy after losing several close confidants — brought the end of an era. Elizabeth had ruled for forty-five years. Emilia thought of how imposing the monarch had been on her throne, sitting ramrod straight, looking down her long nose at those who came to pay tribute. She remembered how the Queen's tongue could cut like a blade. She thought she would feel more sorrow, but Emilia felt the way she did when she heard about the passing of someone whose name one recognized but did not know personally. It had been so many years since she had last curtsied to the Queen that that entire part of her life felt like a hazy dream.

Alphonso was one of fifty-nine musicians who played at her funeral. He had wormed his ways into the good graces of Lord Burghley, which had allowed him to become a court musician again. Burghley had also given him a patent — sixpence for every load of hay and three pence for straw weighed before entering London and Westminster — which became a steady source of income.

Henry was now ten years old. His head reached Emilia's shoulder and he was lean, with strawberry-blond curls and unsettling silver eyes. He was quiet and serious and attended grammar school, studying Plautus and Seneca and Latin. When the schools closed because of the plague, Emilia tutored him in all these subjects, plus literature and history and French and music. He was, even at his age, a better recorder player than Alphonso.

When Henry was working on his lessons, Emilia was writing. She knew that when King James took the throne, he had released Southampton from prison, and the Earl had again taken up his celebrated place at court. She imagined him going to the theater when it was safe again; there Emilia's language would embrace him the way she wished to.

When she wrote *Measure for Measure,* she was pondering the difference between love and lust. Isabella, about to enter a convent, found out her brother was to be put to death for having sex outside of marriage. She pleaded for her brother's life with Angelo, the duke's deputy, who told her he would grant her wish for clemency . . . if she slept with him. *To whom should I complain? Did I tell this,* Isabella asked, *Who would believe me?*

The words mirrored the ones she had said to Southampton when she told him she had married and he asked why she hadn't fought against it. She hoped he would remember.

When she wrote *Othello,* she let the character Iago stoke jealousy in his master with images from a fresco in the town square of Bassano del Grappa, where Emilia's family came from. She had described it to Southampton one lazy afternoon in Paris Garden, when he'd asked her of Italy. The frieze showed musical instruments and animals — a goat and a monkey. There were two painted windows beneath them, with a woman who represented Truth in the middle.

The last time Emilia had been there she had been a child, but she remembered the fresco was situated between two apothecary shops — one called the Moor, the other run by a man named Othello.

In the play, Othello's wife, Desdemona, was killed in the wake of her husband's jealousy. Her servant — named Emilia — was the only character wise enough to warn Desdemona that marriage could be deadly.

It was, she knew, a risk. None of the dangers that had kept her anonymous for a decade had changed. But now, when she wrote, it was not for Shakespeare. It was not for coin. It was not for art.

It was so that Southampton might hear a conversation that was meant for only the two of them.

At first, Emilia was not sure what had awakened her.

It was more than a year after the Queen's death, a cool night but not a frigid one, and the city was still boarded up under threat of the plague. She had been sleeping in Henry's room, thinking before she drifted off that he was nearly the age she had been when she left for Somerset House. Perhaps it was time to share Bess's servant's quarters. The master bedchamber, with Alphonso in it, was not and never would be an option.

She padded downstairs barefoot, drew open the door. Outside, the street was still. A rat scrabbled past; in the distance, she could hear a hacking cough.

When she glanced up, she realized that a star had burned a hole in the night sky. Glittering like a jewel, it hung almost low enough to touch. As anyone who wished fervently on the stars would know, it had never been there before this moment.

A small laugh huffed from her throat. She would not learn for years that this supernova had been spotted by Kepler, the man who was the assistant to her old dinner partner Tycho Brahe.

Suddenly she was twelve again and sitting beside the astronomer in the banquet hall at Kronborg Castle, asking him about *his* new supernova. "You know," he had confided, his gold triangle nose pointing closer to whisper, "I do not think it is actually *new.*"

"Then where did it come from?"

"It is only a theory, young mistress," Brahe had said, "but I think it is simply a star no one bothered to notice before."

"What changed?"

"Everything around it," he had explained. "If those forces compressed it to be smaller, denser, to take up less space . . . well, that could only last so long before it exploded and wasn't just visible . . . but impossible to ignore."

Emilia stepped into the street and tilted her chin up to the sky. How much pressure did one have to be under until an explosion occurred?

Emilia began to spin. She threw her arms wide, twirling, the buildings a dizzy whirl around her. She kept her gaze fixed on the supernova. Surely anyone who saw would call for her to be sent to Bethlem, with other madwomen.

She thought of Isabella, among the stars herself now: *We know what we are, but know not what we may be.*

She pictured stardust shooting from the tips of her fingers, light pouring from her mouth.

She imagined burning so bright that people could not turn away.

MELINA
SEPTEMBER 2024

Jasper made Melina a latte, because of course he had an espresso machine. He cooked her scrambled eggs with toast, and cut her some fresh strawberries. He read the paper on his phone while she ate, darting furtive glances at him and wondering how he could be so calm right now. Then again, he hadn't just destroyed his career, nearly lost his father, and broken up with his best friend all in one day.

When she thought about it like that, last night — whatever it had been — felt elusive and distant. Melina was grateful for the shoulder to cry on, the apartment to crash in, and the mindless (and mind-blowing) sex. But now it was tomorrow and her life was still the tangled snarl it had been yesterday.

She wondered if Jasper, too, could not stop replaying moments from last night — not just the ones where his hands set off little fires everywhere they touched her skin but the quieter confessions that had come in the dark. Melina had told him about Beth and how weird

558

it was to see her father with a woman who was not her mother, and how selfish she felt to say that out loud. Jasper told her about getting labeled a wiseass in elementary school when he followed literal directions. *(The teacher said, "Take a seat," so* obviously *I picked it up.)* Melina confessed that a producer once told her the problem with female playwrights is that they write about *emotions,* while men write about *ideas.* Jasper admitted that the first girl he dated in college had told him she was dying to know more about him, and he went into a spiral of depression thinking that she had only weeks or months left to live.

They shared memory after memory of how they did not fit into their work worlds or their relationships with others; and in doing so, each made space for the other.

Jasper stared at her, a little crease between his brows. Melina wiped her mouth, wondering if she had egg on it. "What?"

"You're a mess," he said.

"I know. I still don't know how I'm going to fix everything."

He frowned. "I meant that you're physically a mess. Did you want to shower?"

There was something even more intimate about being in Jasper's bathroom than about sharing his bed. To know that he used Aim and not Crest, to smell the lemon of his shampoo and realize where that scent on his hair came from, to see a bottle of Xanax sitting beside the Advil and worry about what worried him. Melina felt like she had been given a key to unlock a cave of wonders. When the little black-and-white-tiled room steamed up — either because of the hot water or because Melina was wishing Jasper was in the shower with her — she cracked the door to vent it. But then he caught her touching the handle of his razor through the opening. Their eyes met in the bathroom mirror. "Busted," he said, a grin pulling at his lips.

Melina twirled the razor between her fingertips. The handle was made of polished silver and was heavy. "I used to watch my father shave. I cannot tell you how much I wanted to do it, too."

"I cannot tell you how thrilled I am you didn't *have* to." He took the razor from her and set it on the edge of the sink. "Are you still worried about him?"

"Yeah," Melina admitted. "It meant a lot to me . . . that you drove me to the hospital."

Jasper slipped his hands into the pockets of his robe. "It was the right thing to do."

"Do you always do the right thing?"

"I try to," he admitted. "But clearly I'm not perfect, if the Bard College fiasco is any indication."

A shadow passed over Melina. "So," she said. "What happens next?"

"We wait for the column I wrote about *By Any Other Name* to be published. As soon as

560

my editor reviews it, it will go live. And then we talk to Raffe and Tyce."

We, Melina noted.

"And in the meantime?"

"I have a surprise for you," Jasper said.

While Jasper got dressed, Melina called her father. "Hi, cupcake," he said.

Just then, Jasper emerged from his bedroom, dressed for work in trousers and a crisp linen button-down. His hair was wet, darker than usual, and fell over his eyes. "Ready?" he asked and then saw she was on the phone.

"Is that Andre?" her father asked.

"No," Melina said. "I'm at someone else's apartment."

"At eight-thirty in the morning?"

She shook her head. "Just wanted to check in. I love you. Don't try to do too much too soon."

"I love you," her father said. "Use protection."

"Dad!" Melina cried, but her father had hung up.

Jasper stood in front of her, his laptop bag slung over his shoulder. "You all set?"

"I probably shouldn't be seen in public like this," she said, looking down at yesterday's sweats and T-shirt.

"You were seen in public in that very outfit yesterday," Jasper pointed out. "And besides, we aren't going to be in public, except for the subway."

That was about as public as it got, but Melina couldn't dampen Jasper's enthusiasm. She let him swipe her into the subway, emerging near Fifth Avenue. He stopped at the steps of the New York Public Library, in front of the marble lions named Patience and Fortitude — neither of whose virtues Melina had at the moment. "It's not open yet," she said.

"It is for us."

Jasper took her hand and tugged her past small clumps of tourists taking photos on the stairs, and a clot of teens vaping. At the top, he knocked on the heavy wooden door, and a security guard opened it. "How you doin', Mr. Tolle," he said, waving them in.

Melina did not think she had ever been in the library when it was this quiet. "Is this my surprise?" she asked. "I get the library to myself?"

"Not quite." Jasper led her to the Manuscripts and Archives room, where a man with an overenthusiastic mustache waited. "Ulrich!" Jasper said, shaking the man's hand. "I owe you one."

"Get me tickets for the new Audra McDonald play," Ulrich suggested.

"I'll see what I can do," Jasper promised. He put his hand on the small of Melina's back. "This is Melina Green. She's a playwright."

She could not deny the thrill of those words.

Ulrich unlocked the door to the familiar reading room, which was completely empty.

It smelled of cleaning supplies, and there was a book waiting, open, on one of the tables. Ulrich passed Jasper two sets of white cotton gloves. "Don't do anything I wouldn't do," he said, and he left them alone.

Melina's gaze fell on the yellowed paper, the fragile binding, the familiar etching by Martin Droeshout of the man from Stratford, with his absurdly high forehead and swooping fall of hair. On the left page was a poem written by Ben Jonson. On the opposite page was the title: *Mr. William Shakespeares Comedies, Histories, & Tragedies. Published according to the True Originall Copies.*

She put on the gloves, then lightly touched the delicate paper. Jasper stepped behind her, his breath on her cheek. "Have you ever seen the First Folio?"

Printed seven years after Shakespeare's death, this was a collection of thirty-six plays credited to the playwright. At the time, eighteen of them had never been published before, and several had significant changes from earlier versions. Seven hundred fifty copies had been printed, most likely, as that was a normal run for the time. Two hundred thirty-five were still in existence.

"I've seen one," Melina whispered, "but not this close, and it was behind glass."

She touched her fingertip to the name Shakespeare. "I hate that he still gets all the credit," she murmured.

"Yes, but he was saddled for eternity with that terrible portrait."

Melina twisted, so that their lips were almost touching. "There's a whole line of thought about this etching. Proof that Shakespeare wasn't the actual playwright."

"Tell me more," Jasper replied, his eyes on her mouth.

"Other poets had all these emblems surrounding them, in their portraits. Laurel wreaths, and coats of arms, stuff like that. Shakespeare's etching is weirdly blank. And given that he and his dad spent years lobbying for a family coat of arms, you'd think he would have insisted on it being in the engraving."

Jasper's eyes darkened. "Your brain," he said, "is very . . . stimulating."

She swallowed. "Then wait till you hear about his two left arms. See how the picture makes it look like his arm is attached backward? Some people believe that's a hint that this whole folio is a deception. No right arm. No *write* arm. Get it?"

Jasper pressed his mouth against her neck. "More," he growled.

"Ben Jonson," Melina gasped, "hated Shakespeare. So why would he write the introductory poem for the folio of his nemesis?"

"No idea," he murmured.

"Because he literally says, *'look not on his picture, but his book.'* He's telling you to ignore this portrait, because the real author will reveal himself in his writing."

"Or herself," Jasper added.

She groaned as his teeth closed over her earlobe. "Then, Jonson writes a eulogy for Shakespeare and spends sixteen lines telling readers not to praise the author," Melina sighed. "He warns against *ignorance, blind affection,* and *crafty malice.* That's a pretty big hint."

"Blind affection," Jasper said, spinning her around and pinning her hips with his own against the table. "Crafty malice."

He kissed her as the edges of the rooms went bright, and she had to gasp for air. Jasper ducked forward again, but Melina stopped him with a hand. "We cannot do this here!" she whispered, pointing at the Folio.

"Because he's watching?"

"Because it's a *library book.*"

"We're not whipping out a Sharpie —"

"We're not whipping out *anything,*" Melina said, moving neatly out of Jasper's arms. "You should have known better than to bring me to look at this if you wanted my undivided attention."

He smiled. "I can be patient," he said. "If you'll reward me later."

She glanced over her shoulder. "Deal," she promised.

True to his word, he watched her as she gingerly turned the pages. The thought of touching something that Emilia had touched — if not this Folio, perhaps another one — was staggering. She imagined her ancestor perusing it at a bookseller's stall, or maybe forking over the fifteen shillings it would have cost for an unbound copy. She wondered if Emilia had flipped to *Hamlet,* to *Othello,* to lines she had written. It was the closest Melina had ever come to time travel.

"Do you think Emilia wrote all of this?" Jasper asked.

Melina shook her head. "I think she was part of a group of playwrights. Oxford probably was the ringleader, and he had a stable full of writers, cranking out product that Shakespeare fronted."

"It's a hell of a secret to keep for four hundred years."

Melina nodded. "I don't know if it *was* a secret. Maybe for poets and playwrights *William Shakespeare* was a code word to the people in the theater world who were in the know. Maybe that's why Ben Jonson leaves all these little riddles in the Folio." She let her gaze fall on a soliloquy by the character Emilia in *Othello.*

Have not we affections,
Desires for sport, and frailty, as men have?

It wasn't just Ben Jonson who'd left clues behind.

"I'd heard of Oxford being mentioned as the real Shakespeare," Jasper said. "And Francis Bacon. Even Christopher Marlowe. But until you, I didn't even know Emilia Bassano existed."

"Hardly anyone does," Melina admitted. "She's pretty much flown under the radar."

He met her gaze. "Until now."

Melina wanted to nod, to repeat his words. But she couldn't, not until she knew that her own foolishness hadn't robbed Emilia, once again, of having her voice heard.

There was a quiet knock, and Ulrich poked his head in. "You've got two minutes, and then I have to take Willie S. back into hiding and let in the plebeians."

When he closed the door, Melina gently turned the pages of the Folio until it was open to the portrait, as it had been when they arrived. She rose onto her toes and softly kissed Jasper. "Thank you. I have never been seduced with a historical text before."

"Clearly," Jasper said, "you've been with the wrong guys."

He tugged on the tail of her French braid. The library hummed like an engine, fueling itself with patrons, pulling Melina out of this private bubble and back into a world where her actions had consequences.

"I have not taken a nap since I was in college," Melina said, yawning against Jasper's chest as the sun stretched greedily across the mess of sheets.

He was tracing small circles on her back. "Then you're overdue."

They had left the library with the intention of going uptown to get clothes for Melina. Jasper had insisted on going with her in case she needed emotional support while talking to Andre, although she had no idea what Jasper would have done in the moment — whipped out a sword? Stood between them like a referee? — but then the subway car had been crowded and Melina was forced up against Jasper, her back to his front. His hand had banded across her stomach to keep her steady, pulling her closer, and when she felt him getting hard she'd turned in his arms and plastered herself against him. Without saying a word, they'd gotten off at the next stop, jumped in a taxi, and wound up in Jasper's apartment again.

Melina clearly wasn't the only one who was eager to delay reality a little while longer.

"Clark Kent," she said, mostly to herself. "That's it."

"That's what?"

"Who you remind me of. The glasses. The reporter vibe."

Jasper raised a brow. "Didn't Superman have dark hair?"

"I didn't say you were Superman. Just Clark Kent."

"He *also* had dark hair," he pointed out. "And wouldn't you rather be sleeping with the superhero?"

Melina shrugged. "I don't need to be rescued. And I don't trust a guy in tights."

He stared at her, the playfulness gone. "But you trust me?"

She didn't know how to answer that. She *wanted* to trust him. Was that enough?

As if he realized that he was not going to get a response from her, Jasper cleared his throat and changed course. "You know, you can stay here, if you want."

"Thanks," Melina said softly. "But at some point, I have to stop hiding under the covers. And when I explain to the producer and director of my play why I lied to them, I'd rather not be wearing a Fall Out Boy T-shirt."

"Well, that's valid for a host of reasons. At the very least, upgrade to Paramore."

Melina lightly smacked his shoulder, and he caught her hand, singing "Uma Thurman" off-key.

"Don't quit your day job." She laughed, and he rolled over her, bracketing her with his arms.

"Are you saying I'm never going to make it on Broadway?" Jasper asked.

"You have other talents," Melina offered, and he lowered his mouth to hers at the same moment both of their phones dinged with messages.

They rolled to opposite sides of the bed to read the text. It was Elaine, the stage manager, telling them that one of the actors had tested positive for Covid. The company — and rehearsal — were on hold while they tested everyone else. "There is a God," Melina murmured.

Jasper swung himself to a sitting position. "With any luck I can get the column live before they're cleared for rehearsal. Since there's been radio silence from my editor, I'm going to stalk him in person." He pulled on a pair of boxers. "I'll text you when the piece drops."

Melina nodded. Logic told her that once Jasper's column was out, Tyce could not pull funding and Raffe couldn't pull rank without looking like misogynistic dicks. But intuition suggested that she would not be lucky enough to escape without backlash — much less a production.

She pulled on her clothes, too. "I'll go home and change," Melina said.

Jasper hesitated, buttoning his shirt. She could see him trying to figure out how to be in two places at once. "What if Andre —"

"I'm a grown woman, and it's about time I started acting like it."

Fifteen minutes later, she jogged down the subway entrance beside Jasper. At the spot where two tunnels diverged — one to go uptown, the other downtown — Melina was suddenly overcome with a dark wave of apprehension. Desperately, she grabbed the lapel of his linen jacket. "Did I say thank you? For the Folio. Breakfast. The column."

"You shouldn't be thanking me," he said, his eyes locked on hers.

In the distance was the metallic screech of a departing train, like a harpy dragging its claws. Jasper's gaze darted down the tunnel. "You should go," Melina said.

He pushed his glasses up his nose and nodded. She watched his long legs put distance between them, and then she pivoted and walked down the other tunnel. When she emerged at the northbound track, she looked across to see Jasper standing on the opposite platform. "Hey," he shouted, cupping his hands around his mouth to shout in her direction. "No matter what, don't —"

At that instant a train barreled onto the track in front of him, screaming to a stop. The doors opened with a sigh.

Don't *what*? Melina wondered.

Just before the subway doors closed, Jasper got a text from his editor, Don: *Need to discuss column.*

OK, Jasper typed. *???*

The train jerked forward. *Women have always been onstage,* his editor wrote.

Jasper rolled his eyes and started to type: *Sure, in shows by and about men.* The subway train shuddered around a corner and the lights went out. His screen glowed as his responding text got lost in the shitty cell service 180 feet underground.

A few moments later Don's reply popped onto his screen: *But there's an important story here . . .*

The subway car pulled into a station, and Jasper wrote, *Yes. Publish it ASAP.*

He watched a woman get on with a giant collection of plastic bags; she shuffled to the other end of the car. Two teenagers who should have been in school blew in like autumn leaves, dancing around each other in excitement. The doors hissed shut.

He stared at the three hovering dots, his editor's next comments caught somewhere in the ether between them.

No changes?

Seizing the little window of cell service, Jasper immediately texted a thumbs-up emoji. He waited for the resulting whoosh that told him it had been sent and slipped the phone back into his pocket.

It wasn't until Jasper reached his destination and emerged aboveground that all the unsent messages from Don and to Don scrolled into his app, fleshing out the abortive conversation.

Need to discuss column.

OK. ???

This is not an exposé.
Women have always been onstage.

Sure, in shows by and about men.

But there's an important story here . . .
One you totally missed:
White woman takes center stage away from
Black man.
I sent an email with my suggested edits, do
you approve?

Yes. Publish it ASAP.

No changes?

Jasper, however, did not check his phone
until he reached the offices of *The New York
Times* and made a pit stop at the staff room to
get coffee before heading to his cubicle. Clarence Field was there, a Black editor for the
opinions page. "Jasper," he said, wary. "That
column was . . . unexpected."

Ah, Jasper thought. It's out. "How so?" he
asked mildly.

"I've just never really seen you address insti-
tutional oppression in your pieces."

Jasper made a noise of agreement as he
poured his coffee.

"It's about time someone *white* called out

racism in theater." The editor clapped him on the back. "Well done."

As Clarence left, his words sank in. Hurrying to his desk, Jasper pulled up the column online. He started to read, words he had never written. Panicking, he scrolled through his messages app, reading the entirety of the conversation he had not known he'd been having with his editor.

For God's sake, the miscommunication was Shakespearean in scope — like Friar John quarantined with the plague so Romeo doesn't get the missive saying Juliet's only *playing* dead. Like Antony, given false news that Cleopatra has died, then trying to kill himself. "Fuck," Jasper breathed, opening his work email and scanning all the unwarranted changes that had been made to his piece, completely altering the focus and the message.

Heart pounding, Jasper stormed into his editor's office without knocking. "What the hell, Don? That is *not* what I wrote."

"Yeah, it's better," his editor said, leaning back in his chair.

"I didn't *mean* to give permission for your changes — I was on the subway and . . . Look, forget it. Just take it down."

Don shook his head. "It's only been fifteen minutes and it's already getting more comments than your last three reviews. Positive comments, I might add. Theater's having a

574

racial reckoning; it's good for the *Times* to double down on that."

"Yes but —"

"You're welcome, Tolle. I realize it's an adjustment for your readers to not think you're a jerk, but you'll survive."

He looked down at a stack of papers on his desk, dismissing Jasper wordlessly. Jasper went back to his cubicle, rubbing his temples, sweating to figure out a way to fix this. Don was dead wrong. Jasper didn't care about his readers, there was only one whose opinion he valued. Melina would read this and think he was the biggest asshole who ever lived.

Because Jasper had publicly destroyed her . . . again.

The notification from *The New York Times* popped up as Melina was exiting the subway. Her heart was pounding before Jasper's column even loaded. She started reading as she was propelled by other passengers up the staircase and into the sunlight.

She stood still as the world whirled around her.

Melina Green submitted her work to the festival pretending to be a male playwright . . .

. . . convinced Andre Washington, a Black playwright with no produced work of his own, to front the play without giving him any credit.

. . . evidence of the egregious disparity

in theater that still exists for those who are marginalized . . .

"Hey!" A kid with Beats headphones on slammed into her. "Move, lady."

So she did. On numb legs, with fingers in a rictus grip around the story that cast her as a liar, a racist, a fraud.

At 181st Street, she drifted to the brick wall outside a bodega, leaning against it as she shook with rage, with shock.

She had *trusted* Jasper.

She'd *believed* him when he said he understood.

She'd *slept* with him, and in return, he'd fucked her over.

Her mind snagged on the penultimate words he'd said that morning, as they stood in the bowels of a subway station: *You shouldn't be thanking me.*

Her phone began to buzz, and Jasper's name flashed on the screen. Melina declined the call. Almost immediately, it started ringing again, so she turned her phone off.

He'd said before he didn't lie, but that had to have been false, given what he'd told her he was writing. Was he so slavishly devoted to keeping his reputation intact that he couldn't risk going down with a sinking ship? Was an exposé the way he'd hoped to save his own hide as the production he'd catalyzed fell like a house of cards?

Or — worse — had Jasper known *all along*

576

that Melina was the same playwright he'd excoriated at Bard? Had he assumed something was not quite right when she gave a fake name? Had he gone along with her ruse, feigning memory loss, so that he could strike the killing blow before she had struck hers?

Had he been playing her the whole time?

Melina felt young and stupid and betrayed. No matter how many conversations she and Jasper had had about gender and theater, they had been only empty, hot air.

Melina wandered toward the Hudson. She passed joggers sweating to silent music, nannies pushing strollers, dog walkers holding earthbound balloon sprays of yappy, leashed dogs. No one looked at her twice.

She sat down on a grassy bank, the metal dragon of the George Washington Bridge stretched behind her, huffing clouds. She knew that she needed to speak to Tyce and to Raffe, and, well, everyone at rehearsal. But she also knew that if she turned on her phone, Jasper would relentlessly call or text until she responded.

She threw herself a little pity party, crying a bit before she used the hem of her T-shirt to wipe her eyes. Then she turned on her phone.

There were seventeen voicemails from Jasper.

Melina, please, pick up, the first one said.

Melina? Are you there? Let me explain.

She deleted the rest without listening.

There was a text from Raffe saying that the actor playing Alphonso had Covid and did she know why Mel wasn't answering his calls?

There was an email from Tyce asking her, tersely, to call his cell to discuss recent developments.

She could almost hear Andre's voice in her head: *Well, shit, Mel. What did you* think *was gonna happen?*

Taking a deep breath, Melina pulled Jasper's column up on her phone again, reading about the clueless, privileged white woman who had tried to pull one over on the theater industry at the expense of someone with even less agency than she had.

Access as a playwright should never have devolved into levels of marginalization. If you were a woman of color, you were at the bottom of the totem pole, and Melina winced a little as she conceded that for all her complaining, it would have been exponentially harder to get a toehold in this business if she wasn't Caucasian.

Melina read Jasper's beautifully crafted takedown of her character — beneath his pen, she became a white woman so single-mindedly focused on obtaining recognition that she erased the accomplishments of the Black gay man she'd roped into the scam.

For the first time, she saw herself from that perspective, too. Not as the wronged female playwright but as a person so blind she didn't realize the impossible position into which she'd put Andre. Either he refused to help his best friend, or he had to feign excitement over this accomplishment while knowing that his *own* plays — about being BIPOC and queer in America — were equally (if not more) unlikely to be produced.

She thought of how she and Andre had once spent five hours learning all the choreography from the WAP video. How they could make and receive references to the Real Housewives that bordered on ESP. How they had once rated everyone they knew by the order in which they'd die in a zombie apocalypse.

She also thought of how Andre sometimes brought her black-and-white cookies when she was writing like there was a demon on her back, because he knew they were the only food she could not turn down. How, when Andre's last boyfriend cheated on him, she had paid the barista at the dickhead's local Starbucks to put half a box of salt in his Americano. How she'd thought that their relationship had transcended race and gender because none of that mattered when you found your best friend.

She wasn't the racist, egocentric monster Jasper had made her out to be.

But, Melina realized, she wasn't *not* one, either.

The first time Melina had written a play, she was seven years old. The play was about a duck and a fish that met on a pond and became best friends. She wrote lines for both characters, carefully cutting up her script and gluing them into prompt books — one for her mother and one for her father.

"You're the duck," she told her father. "You're the fish," she said to her mom. She sat on the floor and waited for them to read their parts.

Hello, read her father.

Hello, said her mother.

I see you're a fish.

And you, her mother replied, *are a duck.*

Let's swim.

Melina read the stage directions. "So they swam for hours, and then the duck said . . ."

Hey, Fish, why don't you come to dinner?

I'd love to, her mother answered. *I will see you later.* But as the duck swam off to get ready, the fish wondered, *What if I am dinner?*

Melina's mother and father had looked at each other. "Well," her mother said, smiling, "that's some big dramatic tension right there."

"That's not one of your lines," Melina complained.

Hello, Duck, her mother read. *I'm here for dinner but I'm afraid you might eat me.*

Okay, her father replied. *I will become a vegetarian.*

Melina beamed. "And that's how," she finished, "they stayed best friends, forever."

Even though she still had keys to the apartment, she knocked. Melina saw a shadow cross the peephole and a moment later Andre opened the door. He was wearing her silk bathrobe over his tank top and shorts.

She knew, from his face, that he'd read Jasper's column. Who hadn't? On the walk to their building, she had scrolled through seventeen hundred comments. About a third of them insisted there was no racism in America post-Obama. The majority said Jasper's column was proof that people in power could change and that it was about damn time.

There was a flicker, a faltering, over Andre's features that gave Melina the courage to speak. "I'm sorry," she burst out, just as Andre said the exact same words.

He shook his head. "I was pissed at you, Mel, but I didn't mean for *this* to happen." She realized he was holding his phone. "Jasper's called me four times."

"What did he say?"

"He wanted to find you. I said I had no clue where you were," Andre replied.

Melina walked into their apartment and sank onto the ratty couch. The television was on — *RuPaul's Drag Race*. "You watched without me?" she said.

Andre sat down beside her. "For all I knew you were never speaking to me again. I wasn't going to waste a whole season because you were being a bitch."

"I know," Melina sighed. "I'm sorry about that. Really, really, sorry, Andre. I didn't realize how much I was asking of you, to go along with this whole stupid plan. I was so wrapped up in how hostile this business is to me that I didn't think about how hostile it is to *you*. And asking you to pretend that my play was your play was just plain . . ." She trailed off, unable to find the right words.

"Soul crushing?" Andre suggested. "Demeaning?"

"Either works," Melina agreed. "You're a writer, too, and yesterday I acted like you didn't deserve to even *edit* my play." She glanced up at him again. "For the record, I still want you to write my eulogy when I die."

"Do I get credit, or do I have to pretend I'm just reading what you wrote?"

Melina flinched. "I deserve that."

Andre reached for the remote and paused a queen doing a death drop as she sang for her life. "Well, at least we have something in common. I submitted your play because I wanted to help you. You convinced me to lie . . . because *you* wanted to help you."

Melina winced. "You have every right to hate me. My big break should never have been at your expense. I know I've got access and privileges you don't have because I'm white.

582

But somehow this stupid theater business pitted us against each other." She drew in a breath. "I want you to be famous as hell," Melina said. "I want your stories out there, about people I'm not, and lives I'll never live. But I want my work out there, too. *Yes* to Black theater and brown theater and playwrights with disabilities and queer musicals. *Yes* to all of it. But . . . I'm still here. I feel like I keep getting told: *Step aside, it's not your time yet.*" Melina twisted her hands in her lap. "I was thinking so much about me, I forgot to think about *you* . . . or anyone else who's still trying to make a place for themselves in this industry. I don't know how to be ambitious *and* be an ally, Andre," she said. "I don't know how to advocate for myself as a woman without sounding petty or entitled. I just know that theater is about as postfeminist as it is postracial."

Andre met her gaze. "Envy is part of being human, Mel. You can be jealous of someone without taking that win away from them. It doesn't have to be an *or.* It can be an *and.* Besides," he said, with a rueful smile, "I'm the one who submitted the play, not you."

"You were drunk."

"Fine, then, let's just blame the prosecco." He shrugged. "I know you weren't trying to make me feel like shit. You were only trying to get even with Jasper Tolle."

He missed Melina's blush because he started scrolling through his phone. "I guess I can change your contact info back."

"You deleted me?"

"No," Andre replied. "I changed your name from Mel to *Karen*." He tossed the phone into the cushions between them. "I really am sorry that you're being dragged like this, Mel."

"Well, I'm the one who dragged *you* into this," Melina admitted. "And I'm sorrier."

Andre rolled his eyes. "Always so competitive . . ."

She threw herself at him, hugging him tight. "I hated you being mad at me."

"I hated being mad at you more," Andre admitted.

"I have to tell you something," Melina blurted out. "I slept with Jasper."

"What!" He drew back, genuinely shocked. "I do not know how or why you wound up in Jasper Tolle's bed, but I do want to know if his apartment is wallpapered with *Playbill*s of the shows he trashed."

"No," Melina said. "But he moisturizes nightly with the tears of ingenues whose careers he ruined."

Andre sobered. "Did you know he was going to —"

"No," Melina interrupted, before he could ask the question.

"What about your show?" he asked. "What happens now?"

"I don't know," she said.

He squeezed her hand. "For what it's worth, I know how much you wanted this."

"I *needed* this," Melina corrected.

She needed people to know who Emilia was, and what she'd crafted.

She needed to write plays that would be judged on their own merit, which was doubly impossible after today's column.

She *wanted* to be back in Jasper's apartment, feeling precious, not rotten.

She *wanted* to go back in time and withdraw from the fringe festival.

There was a world of difference between the two.

Melina looked at Andre. "There's a lot I want that I can't have. But what I want right now is my robe back."

He reached for the remote and clicked. The drag queen hit the floor in a split. "We'll discuss," Andre demurred, starting the show over from its beginning.

During Jasper's first week at the *Times,* the senior theater critic had swung into his cubicle. "Can I pick your brain?" he'd asked.

"Absolutely not," Jasper had said, picturing a primitive lobotomy. "Get the fuck out of here."

Needless to say, his relationship with his superior had been a rocky one. He'd worked remotely long before the pandemic, because he sometimes felt it was easier being alone than trying to communicate.

He had gradually found friends in the city who understood his quirks. He became proficient at his job, enough that he gained respect instead of scorn. But on an island with 1.6 million people, Jasper often felt isolated.

And then he'd run into Melina Green, a.k.a. Andrea Washington, at the New York Public Library. He could only remember a few times in his life when conversation had been so effortless. He loved how she (like Jasper) got passionate about a subject — in her case, Emilia Bassano; in his, theater in general. They were two oddballs, but somehow, they fit.

He had fought his physical attraction to her because it seemed inappropriate. But it had been like holding a torch to kindling and telling it not to catch fire.

In Shakespearean plays, comedies ended with a marriage; tragedies ended with nearly everyone dead. Jasper had been sure he'd been living the former, but he'd been thrust into the latter.

And why? Because the subway didn't have Wi-Fi? It seemed like a truly mercurial reason for his life to come crashing down.

His editor, Don, had been right. Jasper was being canonized for talking about the lack of diversity among Broadway creatives, when in his opinion, it was ridiculous to applaud a white man for belatedly recognizing his privilege.

Melina had been right, too: no one was talking about gender discrimination in theater.

He wanted to explain to her. He wanted to apologize. He wanted to kiss her again.

He had reviewed what he would say, if he could, a hundred times in his mind: as he walked miles on city streets, as he showered, as he waited for sleep to claim him. He had the words; he just didn't have the opportunity. Every time he tried to contact Melina, her phone was off. His texts went unread. As days passed, she had not returned to the theater — but then again, neither had anyone else, as half the cast was quarantined with Covid now. Tyce had also gone MIA after the news about the true author dropped. Jasper had never been to the apartment she shared with Andre, so he didn't know where it was. Andre had taken his first call but now let them roll to voicemail.

He couldn't find her, a silver needle in the vast haystack of Manhattan. So Jasper decided to draw her out instead.

He met Tyce D'Onofrio at Bar Centrale, the unmarked quiet space above Joe Allen, a popular restaurant. Tyce was already waiting in a booth when Jasper arrived. He called over a waiter so that Jasper could order a martini.

"Where have you been hiding?" Jasper asked.

"Oklahoma," Tyce said. "Moving my mom

into a memory care unit. But I've been telling people I went to Positano. Sounds way more mysterious, right?"

"I guess."

"Or it did, anyway, until your little column hit the internet." Tyce scowled. "Now it looks like I was running from something. What the actual fuck happened?"

Jasper rubbed his hand over his face. "That was not my column," he said.

"Could have fooled me."

"You can't blame Melina for this," Jasper insisted. "She had good reason to lie to you." The reason, of course, was Jasper himself, but he didn't share that.

"It's weird," Tyce said. "Why didn't she just say who she was? Women write plays all the time."

"Name five," Jasper challenged.

"Five what?"

"Five female playwrights."

Tyce rolled his eyes. "Suzan-Lori Parks, Theresa Rebeck. Lynn Nottage." He hesitated. "That other one, the one who did *Topdog/Underdog*."

"That's Suzan-Lori Parks, too."

"Paula Vogel!" Tyce crowed, triumphant.

Jasper waited for a fifth name. And waited.

"Okay, whatever," Tyce said. "What's your point?"

"Do you think Melina Green is a good playwright?"

"Sure."

"Wrong," Jasper barked. "She is a *great* playwright, but no one is willing to take a chance on producing her work."

"Well, it's not going to be me," Tyce said. "Come on, Jasper. You know if I don't pull this show, I'm going to look like an idiot. She's a punch line right now. Did you see *Colbert* last night?"

"She is not a punch line," Jasper gritted out. "Rewrite the narrative, Tyce. Grow a pair and produce the damn play."

They stopped talking as the waiter brought Jasper his drink. He took a long, strong sip.

"I can't. The optics are bad. If I did, I'd have the Black Theatre Coalition breathing down my neck." Tyce flattened his hands on the table. "However, I am not averse to making lemonade out of lemons. What if I produce one of *Andre's* plays? I checked out some of his work from when he was a student at Bard — it's unpolished, but he was younger then — and the dude can *write,* man. Frankly, I don't know why he's wasting his talent at a casting agency."

Because, Jasper thought, *if not for this clusterfuck, you might never have bothered to read one of his plays.*

Tyce shrugged. "Plus, it's great PR. The guy who was slighted gets recognition and acclaim. Who doesn't like a Cinderella story?"

Jasper ran a finger around the lip of his

martini glass. He was desperate. Maybe if he found a way to elevate Andre and his writing, Melina would see it as a peace offering?

Jasper nodded. "Keep talking," he said.

Summer dried up like a corn husk, blowing away with chilly winds and the onset of autumn. In Central Park, the trees were alight, a bonfire of nature against a crystalline blue sky. The Broadway Briefing ran a notice about the cancellation of Tyce D'Onofrio's Off-Broadway play. The contract Andre had signed with Tyce's production company was void — it was so blatantly obvious that entertainment lawyers hadn't even gotten involved.

Melina got a job babysitting twins in Brooklyn. Jasper stopped trying to contact her with any frequency.

She read his columns like she was starving and they were a feast. She tried to hear the sentences in the cadence of his voice, admired his clear-eyed observations, made without artifice. She still didn't understand how a man who couldn't lie had deceived her.

Andre was her shadow, glued to her side — determined to dispel any notion that they'd fallen out over what she'd done. She was headed to Connecticut for the long weekend and Andre had agreed to join her, but only in return for a favor. Melina had expected him to want to borrow her Swarovski hoops again to wear out clubbing, but he'd demanded something far more costly.

He wanted her to get back into the saddle after being thrown from the horse.

Today, she had set up two meetings with producers. The first had been with a woman who hadn't had a lead production yet but had invested in several Broadway shows. She was in her seventies and had invited Melina to her exclusive club on Central Park West for brunch. Everyone addressed her as Mrs. Westenham, and as Melina took a seat across from her at the table, she noted that one of the giant South Sea pearls on the woman's necklace would pay the rent on her apartment for two months.

"It means so much that you were willing to meet with me," Melina said, offering her brightest smile. "I have several finished plays ready to go!"

"Oh," Mrs. Westenham said, "I'm not actively producing right now. I was just anxious to meet you, after that column!" She leaned closer, conspiratorial. "One of the girls in my book group sat next to Martha Stewart on a plane, but that was pre-felony, so it hardly counts."

The second producer — Davey Gunn — was, to Melina's surprise, her own age. "Wow," she said, unable to keep the surprise out of her voice. "You're not what I expected."

The young man — debonair, with dark hair

591

and dark skin and dark jeans — looked at her, assessing. "Same," he said. He jotted notes in a small Moleskine book, and then picked up his phone. "Is it okay if I take a pic for Davey?"

"You're not Davey?"

"As if," the man said. "I'm just his PA. He's on set."

"On set," Melina repeated. "So, he's a film producer?"

"Yeah. I'm kinda surprised that the admin assistant didn't tell you this when she booked the meeting,'" he said. "We're doing a series on reverse racism, and how you can't even bring it up without being canceled, which is kind of proof that it exists, right? We've got Rachel Dolezal confirmed, and an Asian-American girl who's suing Harvard —"

"No," Melina said, holding up her hand. "Not interested." She scraped back her chair and walked away so fast that she left her umbrella behind.

She'd known it would be a shitty day, but she hadn't expected the universe to overdeliver.

By Any Other Name would have opened tonight, in approximately three hours. On another time line she'd be getting dressed in an outfit Andre chose for her. She'd be photographed with Jasper holding her hand in front of a step-and-repeat. She'd be watching her show with tears in her eyes and would shoot to her feet for a standing ovation at the end. She would have stayed out past the after-party, and she'd be eating late-night diner burgers with Jasper and Andre, waiting for one of Jasper's colleagues to drop their review.

A rave, he would have said proudly. *I told you so.*

He would have kissed her. *Now, everyone will know your name.*

Get a room, Andre would have joked.

Instead, Melina was meeting Andre at Grand Central and taking the train to her father's house. If that dream scenario was not to be, at least she'd be with people she loved. Andre stood beneath the constellation of Taurus on the domed ceiling of the station, their usual meeting spot. He'd brought her overnight bag so she didn't have to take it to the meetings with the producers. "How did it go?" he asked, pushing a venti Starbucks cup into her hand.

"Don't want to talk about it." Melina took a sip and her eyes widened. "Andre, this is a chai latte."

"I know."

"They're like six bucks!" she exclaimed. They were both cheap when it came to Star-bucks and usually ordered drip coffee if they went there at all. She narrowed her eyes. "Why are you buttering me up?"

"I'm not," Andre said, but he already looked guilty. "Okay, I am."

She raised her brows.

"I had a meeting with Tyce D'Onofrio. He wants to read my play." Andre covered his face with one hand and peeked out through split fingers. "Would you hate me?"

"No," Melina said immediately. "Not if it makes you finally finish it." She slipped her arm through his. "At least one of us will get produced. For what it's worth, Andre, I could never hate you."

"You may want to reserve judgment," Andre murmured, and he nodded at something over Melina's shoulder.

She turned to find Jasper standing there.

"Jasper was at the meeting, too," Andre explained. "He begged me to tell him where to find you, Mel, because you won't take his calls —"

"For a reason!" Melina hissed.

Her face was hot, her hands shaking. Chai spilled over her wrist, and Andre took the cup from her. "Five minutes," he said quietly. "Five minutes, and then never again."

She jerked her chin once.

Andre took a step toward Jasper. "If you make things worse," he said, "I will cut out your liver and bedazzle it into a change purse."

"Noted," Jasper murmured, but his eyes never left Melina's face.

He looked exactly the way she had fixed him in her memory: those owlish glasses, that pale sheaf of hair falling over his forehead; the long legs and nervous fingers, always in motion. "I miss you," he said simply.

She had expected *How are you?* or *I'm sorry.*

Melina didn't speak. She didn't trust herself to speak. She was afraid that if she opened her mouth, all the pain and frustration would pour forth like a swarm of bees.

"This isn't how I wanted things to go," Jasper began. "It was a comedy —"

"Real funny," she interjected, two fired bullets.

"— of errors." He dipped his head like a penitent.

Melina chewed on her response. "You hurt me," she said finally.

His gaze flew to hers. "I know," Jasper said. "But it wasn't my fault."

"Really? Your name was in the byline," Melina said. "No matter *why* you wrote it, you could have printed a retraction."

"I could have," he admitted. "I *wanted* to. But it wouldn't have changed anything. Once the piece goes viral the way that one did, it's out there. Forever."

"Is that supposed to make me feel better?" she snapped.

"Give me a chance to explain —"

She closed her eyes. "Not a good idea."

"Please, look at me," he begged. "When you don't, it's hard for me to read your expressions."

Melina stared right into his eyes. "I don't

want to talk to you," she articulated. "Is that clear enough?"

She turned away to search out Andre, but Jasper caught her. The pressure of his fingers on her skin was a live wire. "You said you wanted a producer to give you the benefit of the doubt. To see potential and take the risk. Why aren't you willing to do the same with me?"

"I *did*. Ten years ago, I had stars in my eyes because the great Jasper Tolle was actually going to give me — a complete novice — feedback on my work. Giving someone the benefit of the doubt after they have publicly shamed you is one thing, Jasper. Doing it twice is pathetic."

"I didn't know you the first time."

"You didn't know me the second time, either," Melina said. "You just thought you did."

"I want to make this better," Jasper said. His eyes were overly bright, the lines of his face haggard. "I want to fix this."

Suddenly, Melina was so tired she didn't think she could stand. "You can't fix the problem, Jasper, when you *are* the problem."

"Mel," Jasper said, the first time he'd called her that — the name of the writer who had swept him away, the wordsmith he'd loved before he knew it was her. "I only want to help."

She realized that her cheeks were wet. "If

you really want to help," Melina said, "leave me alone."

This time when she turned, he reached for her again.

This time, she found enough strength to wrench herself free.

She sobbed blindly, until Andre closed his arms around her, letting her cry against his chest. He stroked her back and her hair and let her wring herself out.

When the boarding announcement was made, Melina followed Andre silently down to the track and onto the train, letting him settle her next to the window. She used the hem of her shirt to wipe her runny nose while Andre plucked her phone from her purse, entered her passcode, and found Jasper's name. He blocked the number, and then deleted the entire contact. "There," he said gently. "All done."

BY ANY OTHER NAME
Rehearsal Script

EMILIA
(shoves all the papers off
the table)

I need air.

(she exits)

THE WOMAN
(gathering the papers)

For months she had been
fussing with poems, hoping for
perfection. No woman had ever
published a book of poetry.
She was determined to prove to
Shakespeare that it wasn't his
name selling his plays — it was
her writing.

TRANSITION to a busy
market.

BOOKSELLER

Shake-Speare's Sonnets. Written by
the famous playwright hisself!

EMILIA

How much?

BOOKSELLER

A shilling.

THE WOMAN

There were 154 poems, including
the sonnet she had written for
Odyllia.

EMILIA

That rat bastard.

THE WOMAN

It took a year to find a
publisher willing to meet with a
woman who had no man at her side.

    RICHARD BONIAN enters,
    a titan behind his desk,
    master of his domain.

BONIAN
(reading the manuscript)

Salve Deus Rex Judaeorum. That's the
title?

EMILIA

Yes. Hail God, King of the Jews.

BONIAN

It is a psalter, then.

> EMILIA

Not a book of psalms, sir. A book of poetry.

> BONIAN

Women do not write poetry.

> EMILIA

What you hold in your hands proves otherwise.

EMILIA
1604–1611

Emilia is 35–42

Emilia knew she was not the only person who wrote for Shakespeare. Kit had mentioned it years ago, hinting at the Earl of Oxford and others. There were certainly plays being produced with the name *William Shakespeare* on them that Emilia had not written.

She had asked Shakespeare, from time to time, who else he . . . well, *represented,* for want of a better term. He was coy. He said that he was bound to silence, much as he'd promised Emilia herself. Once, he asked her why it mattered. "When you go to the butcher for a haunch of meat," he'd said, "does it make a difference which housewife preceded you or came after you, so long as you were able to walk away with your roast?"

It was possibly the sole proof she had of Shakespeare's code of morality, murky as it was.

Yet Emilia had wondered at the *housewife*

reference. Was she not the only woman he represented? She could not decide if the thought made her feel more competitive, or gleeful.

It was possible, Emilia supposed, that the additional plays allegedly penned by Shakespeare were indeed written by him. But he was a full-time actor with the King's Men, as well as a shareholder. Even if he never slept, Emilia had ample opportunity to read his writing every time he sent her a letter. Nowhere in those missives was evidence of the literary skill in "his" plays. She imagined Shakespeare's work had never improved much past the point of his *Titus Andronicus,* which she'd gussied up for him. If he was still writing at all, he had an editor, one who could take the straw Shakespeare put on the page and spin it into gold. More likely, he slapped his own brand on the works of others.

And what a brand it had become.

When Emilia had begun writing plays a decade earlier for Shakespeare, she had only wanted her words to be heard on a public stage, and to secure a modest income. She had required anonymity, and so, she'd borrowed the name of a man who was a nobody.

And unwittingly, she made him a *somebody.*

With the exception of Kit, and Ben Jonson, very few playwrights were name brands.

Playwrights and players were both seen as the very dregs of society — until the quality of plays was genuinely elevated. A Shakespeare play was now in this category. Crowds thronged to the Globe to see them performed; sometimes they even cost a bit more. Legends had begun to spring up around him: *he only brings fair copies to the King's Men, never foul, because his work needs no revision. He dreams up new words in his sleep.*

Shakespeare preened under the attention, which was as necessary as air for him. The coat of arms he and his father had finally been granted was emblazoned anywhere he could put it; he bragged to Emilia that he could not enter a tavern without a young playwright offering to buy him a pint.

When Kit proposed using Shakespeare's allonym, Emilia had worried it might not work.

Now she worried that it might have worked too well.

Emilia had asked Shakespeare for a meeting, but he'd said he was busy preparing with the King's Men to perform *Othello* for the first time. The actors would be doing their read-through of the play at the Falcon Inn, in preparation for the performance at Whitehall for King James.

She had practiced her speech to him, but when she reached the inn's courtyard, she could not bring herself to enter. There were too many ghosts inside this building — of Kit, of her youth, and now, of her very own words read by the boisterous players inside.

After she'd spent about an hour of shivering in the cold breath of October, the actors began to bleed from the inn, clutching their parts. Some elbowed each other, deep in conversation as they passed her. Some stumbled, dizzy on ale. Shakespeare walked out with Richard Burbage, the actor who was starring in the tragedy. When he saw Emilia, he raised a brow and then clapped Burbage on the back. "I shall meet up with you anon," Shakespeare said.

Burbage's eyes alit on Emilia. Although she was no young woman anymore, she still attracted leers. "So you shall, Will," the actor said, laughing as he walked in the direction of the Globe.

"I should have thought you'd come inside," Shakespeare said. "Did you not wish to hear the play read?"

She folded her arms. "Burbage is playing the Moor?"

"He is the finest the King's Men has," Shakespeare replied.

"He is the wrong color," Emilia pointed out.

Shakespeare rolled his eyes. "There is paint for that," he said. "Now. What is the reason for your visit? Have you a new play for me?"

Emilia swallowed. "No, and I shall not, until we come to terms."

"We have come to terms, mistress."

"A decade ago. As a businessman you must recognize that when the market alters, so does the negotiation."

"Speak plainly," Shakespeare said.

"I would like to be compensated in proportion to the measure of your success." She swallowed. "Thirty shillings, instead of fifteen, for each play sold."

He smirked. "Why on earth would I give up a piece of my share?"

"Because without me you would be getting nothing at all."

Shakespeare folded his arms. "I could copy the Book of Common Prayer, slap my name at the top, and sell out a week of performances. People aren't flocking to the theaters because of your words. They come because they trust the name William Shakespeare."

"What do you think earned that trust?"

"Mayhap at first," he conceded. "But now?" Shakespeare shrugged. "They will consume anything I serve them. And there are other capable cooks."

"Are you so certain your audience will not notice a change in the work?" Emilia said.

"Are you so certain they *shall*?"

Emilia swallowed. She could hear the words she had written into *As You Like It: My pride fell with my fortunes.*

"I wish you well, then, sir," she said, lifting her chin.

To her surprise, Shakespeare laughed. "So

that is that," he said. "I did not expect such righteousness from a practical woman."

"That was your first mistake." She picked up her skirts, intending to walk away.

"Jonson is jabbering about his plays," Shakespeare said. "Calling them his *works* and hinting that he means to publish them as a collection." He waited for Emilia to turn and meet his gaze. "I may do the same."

"They are not yours," she said, her voice low.

"You were paid. The transaction is complete. They are owned by the shareholders of the Globe now. Of which I am one." He smiled at her. "It has been a pleasure doing business with you, mistress."

She hurried toward the Falcon Stairs to the ferry landing. It was not until she reached the dock that she stopped to catch her breath, gulping in air thick with the stench of rotting fish.

Emilia squeezed her eyes shut. "Dear God," she whispered. "What have I done?"

She quickly realized she would need new work. Alphonso's income rarely made it to their table in the form of food; he gambled or swilled it away. Capitalizing on the education she had received with the Countess, she reinvented herself as a tutor.

Life with Margaret Clifford, Countess of Cumberland, was not what she had been expecting. Her first inkling came when she arrived at the country estate to teach Lady Clifford's fourteen-year-old daughter, Anne. It was two days after the death of the Earl of Cumberland, and out of respect, Emilia wore black. She was ushered upon arrival into a room in the far wing of the manor house, one that reminded her of the one Mary Sidney had used. Similar glass phials and tubing were suspended over candles, held at the throat with metal clamps. Lady Clifford, a tall woman with a blade of a nose and overplucked brows, was scrawling notes on a piece of paper beside a bubbling brew that smelled strongly of vinegar and thyme.

"Hand me that, will you," the lady said, snapping her fingers and pointing at what looked like a finely woven fisherman's net.

Emilia passed it to Lady Clifford, who proceeded to turn the arm holding the glass phial and spill the contents through the sieve. Tiny spores of herbs caught in the weave, and the rest of the fluid gushed into another waiting silver bowl. The countess peered into it, then touched her pinkie finger to the fluid and licked it. "Still silver. That's disappointing." She sat back, wiping her hands on her apron. "You must be the music tutor."

"Yes, milady," Emilia said, curtsying.

"Do you know about alchemical matters?"

She blinked. "I knew a lady, once, who studied."

"I am more interested in physic and chirurgery and the distillation of medicines," the countess said. "But alchemy has its place."

Emilia assumed she was trying to change the silver bowl to gold. She looked up to find the woman staring at her. "My humble apologies, mistress," Lady Clifford said. "I have not offered you condolences on your loss."

Emilia blinked at her. "My . . . loss?"

Lady Clifford jerked her chin in the direction of Emilia's dark clothing. "How dedicated to your craft you must be, to make this journey in your grief."

"I did not — I have not —" Emilia cleared her throat. "I beg your pardon, my lady. I sought only to show respect for *your* loss."

Lady Clifford looked at her for a moment. "*My* loss?" she said, and then she threw back her head and laughed so deeply it filled the bright laboratory. "My dear," she said, "the only regret I have for George's death is that I wasn't the one to kill him."

Margaret Clifford had removed to her country house years ago when her husband, George, began swiving every female at court and spreading the lie that it was her incompetence as a wife that had driven him to seek comfort in the arms of others. Instead of trying to clear her reputation, she plucked her daughter, Anne, out of London and decided to educate her with the same devotion she would have given to her two sons, had they survived childhood. If her daughter was destined, as Lady Clifford had been, to find herself at war with a man, then she wanted her armed to the teeth.

Londesborough Hall was in Yorkshire, which meant that Emilia had to leave Henry behind. She had entrusted him to Bess's care, and Alma's, knowing that they would keep him away from Alphonso while she was absent. When Emilia wasn't instructing Anne she was treated as an esteemed guest and not a hired tutor. She and Lady Clifford and Anne traipsed through the moors at dawn, mist nipping at their walking boots. After the evening meal, Emilia would play an instrument to accompany Anne as she sang, or to provide entertainment while Lady Clifford worked on her embroidery.

It took Emilia several days to figure out what was so different about this household. Yes, it was run by a pious, educated woman who believed her daughter had every right to an education as well. But that ethos seemed baked into the food they consumed and plastered into the walls surrounding them. There were both male and female servants in the house, but only the maids were part of the inner sanctum. It was a sort of paradise of women, a Themiscyra where Amazons might lay down their weapons and simply enjoy the company of their sisters.

"Is it not interesting," Lady Clifford said one afternoon, when they had finished a round of lawn bowling, "that there is not a male word for *slut*."

Emilia's jaw dropped.

"There are so many terms to describe a woman who undertook the same behavior as my late husband, after all," Lady Clifford mused. "Whore, dollcommon, harlot. Moll. Prostitute."

Emilia glanced at Anne, who was still an innocent, but the girl was avidly nodding. "Wench," Anne added. "Bawd. Crushabell."

"Men are never the fornicators," Lady Clifford said. "Merely the ones who are cuckolded."

Emilia cleared her throat. "It does make one wonder who the women are bedding."

"Precisely!" Lady Clifford clapped her hands. "And why the English language has so very many ways to shame a woman into submission."

"I believe it comes down to obedience," Emilia said. "A woman who speaks when she is not asked to or who gives away the prize of her chastity has violated the natural order of things by asserting power."

"Indeed. I have often thought that the reason young ladies are denied a classical education is because, all things being equal, men would be left behind in the dust." Lady Clifford shrugged. "It is all of a kind, you know.

The name-calling, the limits to learning, the reminder that a weakness of body must mean a weakness of spirit . . . why, it puts me in mind of a time the late earl refused to race a horse against one of Leicester's unless the man weighed his gelding down with stones."

"And a woman who flouts convention must needs be a witch," Emilia added. Both women turned sharply.

Margaret Clifford might be unusual, but she was a devout Puritan, and Emilia suddenly realized she may have crossed a line.

"Do you believe God favors man over woman, Mistress Lanier?" Lady Clifford asked.

Emilia's heart pounded; this felt like a test. "I believe that we are all God's children," she said carefully. "If we were made in His image, should we not be equal in His regard?"

Lady Clifford nodded, satisfied. "The Clifford estates are entailed in a way that would suggest the same," she said. "They descend to the eldest heir, male or female, and have done so since the time of Edward II."

It took Emilia a moment to process what Lady Clifford was saying. She turned to Anne, who was the presumptive heir, then, to the Cumberland properties — which included castles in Skipton and Brougham and Appleby. "'Tis true," Anne said. "I am a baron. Perhaps the only one in skirts." She jumped up to set the pins for lawn bowling again.

"You are likely the prettiest baron in the realm, darling," Lady Clifford said, watching Anne roll the ball. "But I'd wager you are also the smartest and most just — and far better suited to running the estates than your uncle Francis."

"Your turn, Mistress Lanier," the girl said, setting the pins again.

Emilia took the ball as Lady Clifford continued. "My late husband, determined to humiliate me posthumously, did not leave Anne her due. He bequeathed the earldom to his brother. Anne inherited the title Baron de Clifford only because it was created by writ. Oh, and a paltry sum of fifteen thousand pounds."

Emilia's swing flew wide. *Paltry.*

"But I shall fight the King if I must, to give my daughter her rightful inheritance."

"Mama is no stranger to battles like this," Anne said. "Mistress Lanier, do you know of Beamsley? It is an almshouse near Skipton for widows. My mother began the construction in 1593, and ever since, it has been a refuge for women of little means."

"Your charity is a credit to you, Lady Clifford," Emilia said.

Margaret Clifford stood, tossing the ball from hand to hand, squinting at the pins. "I wished only for my goodwill to outlive me," she said. "Yet there will come a time when I am no longer here to give voice to my wishes.

I needed to be able to direct my legacy from beyond the grave."

"Hundreds of years from now, those buildings will still be earmarked as a haven for widows," Anne said. "It's part of the deed."

"Yes," Lady Clifford said, drawing back her arm. "They can never be sold or taken over. A man can't decide one day that he wants them. If you want to create something that men cannot dismantle," she said, letting the ball fly, "you must beat them at their own game."

Anne squealed. "Mama! You knocked them all down!"

Lady Clifford smiled. "Didn't I just," she said.

My darling boy,

I think you would like the place where I am staying. There is a moor that sucks at your feet when you walk upon it, and a home that feels crowded with ghosts. The young woman who is my pupil is learning quickly and, Henry, she is a lady *and* a baron! I know you think it impossible for those two words to sit side by side — and yet such impossibilities exist all around us: open secrets, sweet sorrow, civil war.

I have had word from Cousin Alma that you are applying yourself to your studies and so you must; so too should you heed Cousin Jeronimo in your musical education.

He says you have composed a piece on re-corder; pray, practice it so that I might hear it the moment I return.

I am sorry to tell you, my love, that I will not be with you for Christmastide. The Countess of Cumberland has asked me to attend her when she visits Cooke-ham, her brother's estate in Berkshire. There is sure to be a feast in the likes of which I have never par-taken.

And yet, I shall be starving, because you are all that sustains me.

Your loving mother

"I will never fall in love," Anne announced one day when she and Emilia were walking the forest grounds at Cooke-ham. Frost sil-vered the trees and their footsteps crunched on the snow.

"I do not know that it is a choice," Emilia replied.

The girl stopped walking. "You speak from experience, then? You are wholly devoted to your husband?"

Emilia picked up her skirts and began to move again. "I do not think your mother is the sort who would force you to marry if you do not wish it."

"Oh, I will likely marry," Anne said, shrug-ging. "I do not see how we will be able to litigate without the patronage of a man. But I would much rather get what is due me as heir than produce a successor for someone else's line." She glanced at Emilia. "I bore witness to my parents' marriage, mistress. I know very few marry for love."

"You are too young to be cynical."

"Were you not at my age?" Anne asked.

At Anne's age, she was two years in Hunsdon's bed. "No," she said softly. "I was too practical to be cynical."

"What does it feel like?" Anne asked. "Love?"

Emilia moved aside a low-hanging branch and considered the question. "Like drowning, I think."

Anne smirked. "And you call *me* cynical."

"I have heard it said that the hardest part is just allowing it to happen. That once you stop fighting it is quite . . . peaceful."

"Do all the dead wash up on the shore to tell you so?"

Emilia laughed and tugged at Anne's braid. "Minx," she said. "This is wholly anecdotal."

"If you mean to champion love, using the language of death to describe it is perhaps not the soundest argument."

"And if you mean to elude it you may find yourself still blindsided."

"That's exactly it," Anne said. "It's like fighting with your sword arm up the castle stairs, and leaving your heart exposed. Why make yourself vulnerable?"

"Well, for the same reason your lady mother distills metals and spirits. There are certain alchemical reactions where two distinct elements can come together and form something greater than the individual parts."

Anne smirked. "Half the time she blows things up by accident."

A twig cracked, and they looked up to find a doe staring at them from a clearing. Her ears twitched before she bounded deeper into the woods.

"Deer do not mate for life," Anne mused. "They travel separately, by sex, and come together in the woods only when the doe chooses to mate." It was an oversimplification, but Emilia knew she was not wrong. "The mamas raise their fawns without the stags anywhere nearby. The males serve their purpose . . . and then move on."

"True," Emilia said, "but you are not a doe."

"More's the pity." Anne turned. "How do you *know*? That a man is . . . the one?"

Emilia thought of Southampton. It had been years since she had seen him, but she could not smell the first grass of spring without thinking of what it was like to lie with him on the banks of the marsh in Paris Garden. There were times she still was certain she saw him in a crowd, then blinked only to find the sun in her eyes. She could replay every encounter they had ever had like beads on a strand of pearls, polishing each moment in her memory. "When he is with you," Emilia said carefully, "you cannot be in the moment, because you are thinking of what it will feel like when he is gone. And when he is gone, you are missing the piece of yourself you care for most."

"That sounds miserable," Anne said.

"There are boons as well" — Emilia laughed — "but those are not for maidens to know."

"So a person who overwhelms you like a tide, who makes you forget yourself — *willingly,* and whose lovemaking causes your heart to beat faster, or whatnot — that is one's true love?"

"In brief, yes." Emilia slid a glance at her. "Have I convinced you, then, to open your mind to it?"

Anne shook her head vehemently. "No," she said, "but now I know what to avoid."

Lady Clifford decided to remain at her brother's estate past the holiday, and within a few months, spring exploded across Berkshire. Cooke-ham sparkled like a tiara jeweled with sapphire ponds and emerald lawns and amethyst blossoms bursting from the lilac trees. Emilia scribbled ideas for the beginning of a poem while Anne studied Euclidian theorems. Lady Clifford had spent the morning attempting to smelt iron with coal, but frustration brought her outside to join them. It was an Eden, Emilia realized. A garden of knowledge that, this time, was unrestricted to women.

Sweet Cooke-ham, where I first obtained / Grace from that grace where perfect grace remained, Emilia wrote.

If Emilia was Eve in this paradise, then it was the Countess of Cumberland from whom she was receiving favor. If only she could guarantee an income forever here, and not have to worry about the fact that when Anne married, she would once again be penniless. If only she did not need Shakespeare to share her writing.

She had never imagined there was a noblewoman like Margaret Clifford, who would champion equality not just in her own daughter's education but in a public court of law that would award Anne the inheritance she deserved.

What if there were others?

What if Emilia could *find* them?

It was common practice for poets to dedicate their work to noble benefactors who they hoped might support them. If Emilia could garner the patronage of strong, educated women — well, perhaps she would never again have to rely upon men.

Beat them at their own game, Lady Clifford had said.

Emilia could not write plays under her own name. But there was no reason she could not use *poetry* to write about faith and godliness

618

and all the other qualities men wished women to have. She personally did not give a fig about Jesus — for Emilia the Bible ended with the first volume — but who would dare criticize her if she wrote about Christ on the cross?

Emilia looked up from her writing desk and smiled.

Lady Clifford caught her eye. "You look as if you've discovered the philosopher's stone."

"Mayhap," Emilia said, "there is more than one way to achieve eternal life."

Another outbreak of the plague in 1606 sent Emilia back home, as Lady Clifford and Anne traveled abroad to escape the pestilence. She was overjoyed to reunite with Henry but was once again forced into proximity with Alphonso.

She spent hours sitting at the oak table writing, as her husband stomped around their home. His hay patent provided minimal income, but disease kept people from coming and going in the city, so their budget for rent and food was once again reduced. Bess found ways to stretch a meal, but there was no coin from Emilia's plays to purchase herbs that could be fashioned into remedies or preventatives for disease that she might sell as she had done during previous epidemics. Instead, Alphonso watched her with hooded eyes. "Can you not find another paid position?" he demanded.

"Hmm," she said, hardly giving him attention. "Indeed, that is what I attempt to do."

Scattered across the table were ten different poems dedicated to women of great standing and piety — from Lady Clifford and her daughter to Queen Anne and her daughter Princess Elizabeth and Lucy Russell, Countess of Bedford. She wanted these ladies to be her patrons. If she could use her poems to celebrate their devotion and piety, then she hoped they would offer her charity. Surely *not* doing so would make them look considerably less devoted and pious.

It was harder to write as herself than it had been to write as Shakespeare. Stylistically, she did not want to invite comparison — there was still too much risk. The cadence of the prose must be different from what she usually wrote. She found herself forcing her natural lyrical style into the base expectations of what a female poet might be, and making it formulaic and strained instead.

Bess appeared with a trencher. "Mistress? Shall I serve?"

"Of course," Emilia said. "I am nearly finished with this . . . letter." She looked at Alphonso. "You know, you, too, could tutor music."

He scoffed. "I am so proficient I could not lower myself to work with a beginner."

God save her from stupid men.

Bess placed a knife beside her, and a loaf of

bread wrapped in linen. Henry clattered down the stairs, drawn by the smell of the meal.

"Darling," Emilia said, smiling at him. "How is the Cicero?"

"Tedious," he said. He sank down into his usual seat on the far bench. He was thirteen now, more man than boy, with a fine fuzz on his upper lip and a voice that broke in the middle of sentences. He was growing up too fast, and she knew he would leave her house soon.

All the more reason for her to focus on her book of poetry. It truly was her last hope.

She was working today on the longest poem in the collection, a defense of Eve. The Christians believed that the pain of childbirth was recompense for Eve's original sin, but dear God, all the woman had done was offer a piece of fruit to her partner.

Surely Adam cannot be excus'd.
Her fault, though great, yet he was most to
*   blame;*
What Weakness offered, Strength might have
*   refus'd,*
Being Lord of all, the greater was his shame.

If man was so very superior, might he not just have said he wasn't hungry?

"Wife," Alphonso ordered. "Stop your scribbling."

Emilia looked up at him, set down her quill, and gathered her papers. "Yes, of course."

621

She handed the pile to Bess, taking a trencher in return.

"Wife. You are sitting in my seat."

She blinked up at him innocently. It was true that in all the years they had lived in this house, Alphonso had taken his meals at the head of the table, where Emilia now settled. Henry sat opposite, and Emilia and Bess shared the long bench on the side. "Why is this your seat?" she asked.

"Because . . ." He frowned. "Because it is where I always sit."

"So your position is accorded simply by habit?"

"My position is accorded by me being the head of this household," Alphonso said. "By me being the man of the family."

Henry watched this exchange, chewing his food.

"Why *that* seat?" Emilia pressed.

"It is the best," Alphonso said, although there was nothing unique about his chair. If anything, it was rickety.

"Ah." She nodded, then moved to the long bench. "It is odd, Husband, that you'd not choose the longest seat, then. Biggest is best, no?"

He narrowed his eyes. Then he grabbed his trencher and shoved it to the side of the table. "Move," Alphonso ordered, sitting down nearly on top of her before Emilia could return to the head of the table.

"To be clear," she said, "is *that* now your

seat? I wouldn't want to mistake it again and cause distress."

Alphonso grunted, and Henry smothered a laugh with a cough.

"So it turns out that a man's position is not accorded by habit," Emilia mused.

Alphonso pushed back his trencher. "You sour my stomach, woman," he groused, and he stalked out the front door.

Emilia took a sip of ale and tore a hunk of bread from the loaf. She looked at Henry. "Another serving, darling?" she asked, and she winked.

Over the next few years, Emilia balanced her household chores with her writing, perfecting her poetry. One day, while at a market buying cooking grease, she passed a bookseller displaying his newest wares. "Fancy a read, missus?" he asked. Before she could say no, she noticed the title page.

Shake-Speares Sonnets. Never before Imprinted.

"How much?" she heard herself say.

"A shilling."

She counted the poems: 154 of them, followed by a long piece called "A Lover's Complaint." She walked until she found a spot to sit and read.

Several poems that she had sold him over the years — including the sonnet she had written for Odyllia — were included.

623

The rest, she could only assume, he had purchased from some other poets. It was outrageous to claim that the pittance paid to them at the time of sale encompassed the right to publish them again, even more widely, without compensation.

That rat bastard.

Forgetting the rest of her shopping list, Emilia hurried back to her lodgings, where she pulled out the stack of papers that would become her book of religious poetry. For too long, she had been refining it. She really had only one chance to acquire the financial support of the ten patronesses in her dedications.

But this?

This was war.

It took Emilia over a year to find a publisher who was willing to meet with a woman.

Bess helped Emilia air out the one court gown that she had not sold during the past decade to put food on the table. It was hopelessly out of fashion but still made of the finest velvet, with pearls sewn into the fabric and a lace collar and cuffs that they bleached in the sun to restore to snowy white. Bess would accompany her to the meeting — a lady would always be attended by her maid.

Richard Bonian's publishing offices were not far from her lodgings, but it was a warm day and she had walked there in her heavy dress. She was flushed and sweating, partly because of the weather and partly because of nerves. Bess sat in a chair in the corner of the room, her eyes wide as saucers, while Master Bonian took Emilia's manuscript into his ham-size hands.

"*Salve Deus Rex Judæorum,*" he read aloud.

"Yes, that is the title," Emilia said. "Hail God, King of the Jews."

"It is a psalter then?"

Emilia shook her head. "Not a book of psalms, sir, but a book of poetry."

"Women do not write poetry," Bonian said.

She smoothed her hands over her skirt. "What you hold in your hands proves otherwise."

He assessed her elaborately pinned hair, her dated dress. "You are married, Mistress Lanier? And your husband supports this strange endeavor?"

"He is indeed the very reason I am called to write," Emilia said. Bess coughed.

Bonian shuffled through the pages, skimming her work. "*You came not in the world without our pain . . . Make that a bar against your cruelty. Your fault being greater, why should you disdain / Our being your equals, free from tyranny?*" He raised a brow. "A Defense of *Eve*? From the point of view of a woman?"

"Indeed," Emilia replied. "How else should I see the world?"

"This is heretical," Bonian said. "No male wishes to be called out as cruel or flawed."

"No female wishes that, either."

"Yes, but they are not buying the books I publish."

Emilia leaned forward. *"Yet,"* she said. "You are a businessman, sir. Most noblewomen can read."

"And so they do — the Bible or the Sidney Psalter."

"Because there is little else published that celebrates their virtue and their faith," Emilia argued. "If the material does not exist, then naturally they cannot purchase it."

Bonian drummed his fingers on his desk.

She lowered her gaze. "I could never claim to understand the tides of business," Emilia said. "I speak only as a woman myself, called on by God to reflect on the piety of those who are my betters."

Bonian pursed his lips. "It will be too expensive to print. Cut it down to five dedicatory poems."

"You ask me to choose between my right hand and my left. It would be impossible to leave out any of these patronesses."

The publisher shook his head. "I cannot accommodate you, then. The cost would be prohibitive."

Emilia hesitated. If she cut five of the dedications, that was five fewer women she was appealing to for money. "I see," she said, rising to her feet. "Thank you for your time, Master Bonian. Bess, come. Master Thorpe will not wish to wait."

Emilia tried to silently communicate to Bess to follow her lead, though they did not have another meeting set up. She was bluffing.

"Thorpe?" Bonian said. "Thomas Thorpe?"

Emilia nodded. "You are acquainted?"

She did not know Thomas Thorpe. She only knew that his name was listed as publisher on Shakespeare's book of sonnets.

"I believe he has recently published a book of poetry," Emilia said. "And is looking for more."

She watched Bonian's face flush and thought how wonderfully predictable men could be. "Fine," he said. "I will publish your book. It must be a limited print run if you insist on keeping all the prefatory material. Otherwise it is too risky an endeavor, and Thorpe would tell you the same. You are no Shakespeare."

Emilia smiled, sinking back into the chair. "Of course not," she said.

She never would truly know why her book was not successful. Was it because she hinted at dangerous ideas in these poems? Was it that she hadn't dared to create literary fireworks while writing in her own name?

Was it because the husbands of the women she had hoped to entice would not allow their wives to read a female author? Did they fear the blank canvases of women's minds could be filled with thoughts of something other than them?

Of the ten ladies Emilia had hoped to attract as patrons for her writing, not one stepped forward. Not even Margaret Clifford and Lady Anne, who — to be fair — were embroiled in the court battle to wrangle Anne's inheritance back from her uncle. It stung. She had written a passionate elegy championing women, only to have women turn their backs on her.

By the time winter snarled into London in 1611, there was no money left. Henry was working with Alphonso, occasionally playing at court to fill in for one of the recorder players or flutists, and they were still collecting the hay patent money — but Alphonso drank away the coin almost as soon as it was made. For the first time in her life, Emilia had no secret stash of income to fall back upon. There were nights they skipped meals. Alma would visit with a basket of table leavings, saying that they had more than they could consume, and although Emilia's cheeks burned to accept such charity, her belly ached too much to turn her cousin away.

One night, Emilia found herself unable to sleep. Ever since Henry had grown, she had bedded down with Bess, the maid willingly giving up half her tiny room for her mistress. Careful not to wake Bess, Emilia carried a candle downstairs, listening to the wind hiss through the cracks in the door.

At forty-two, she would have to re-create herself, once again. But she was so, so tired.

She found her writing desk where Bess had stored it near the dark hearth. Pulling her wrap tighter around her shoulders, she slipped free a piece of paper and removed the bottle of ink she now watered down to make it last longer. She cut a fresh point to her quill.

She gripped the quill in her hands, and for the first time ever had no idea what to write.

Words had transported her when she was a child trapped by circumstance. Words had helped her escape her prison as a woman and had knit back the bones she broke as a wife. Words had bricked the wall she had started to build sixteen years ago, after aborting the child of the only man she would ever love.

"A sad tale," she whispered softly, "is best for winter."

She had convinced herself that suffering was bearable if it meant justice in the end. But what if her struggles did not change the perception of those whose lives her work had brushed against? What if she was less than a footnote, bound to be forgotten?

Since what I am to say must be that
Which contradicts my accusation, and
The testimony on my part no other
But what comes from myself, it shall scarce boot me
To say "Not guilty": mine integrity
Being counted falsehood, shall, as I express it,

Be so received. But thus: if powers divine
Behold our human actions, as they do,
I doubt not then but innocence shall make
False accusation blush and tyranny
Tremble at patience.

She wrote in a stream of consciousness, the plea of one who had already been found at fault, one who had nothing left in her arsenal with which to fight.

This would be a story about a woman who had done nothing wrong.

She'd be exiled, pregnant, because of her husband's jealousy.

Sixteen years would pass, and he would believe his wife was dead . . . until he saw her again. Would the husband realize his mistake and learn to trust those he loves, or would any change in his behavior simply be due to amazement at seeing her alive again? Emilia wasn't certain. But one thing was clear: neither husband nor wife would ever wipe away the losses they'd suffered.

At dawn, Bess found Emilia asleep at the table. As soon as Bess gently shook her awake, Emilia knew what she had to do.

The crowd at the Mermaid Tavern was well in their cups. Not much had changed since Emilia had last visited the Bread Street establishment, with Kit. It was the first Friday of the month, and the Sireniacal Fraternity

630

— a drinking club — was loud and boisterous, each member trying to best the others with a raunchy joke.

She had sold a posy ring for funds so that she could pay a beggar boy outside the Globe to tell her where Shakespeare went for company and drink. Now, she sat with her back to the wall in a corner, her cloak hiding her face, so that she could remain as anonymous as possible. She recognized Ben Jonson from her meeting at Mary Sidney's poetry salon years ago, but his eyes skated over her, as if he found her features familiar but was unable to place them.

A tavern maid brought Emilia another ale, along with a bowl of stew. She handed over the last of her coin — she would be walking home, then, no hack for her. "Mind they don't spill on ye," the woman said, jerking her chin in the direction of one of the drunk men, who was now inexplicably wearing a pair of smallclothes on his head, tied beneath the chin like a baby's bonnet. "Last meeting, they tried to see if one of the half-wits could swim by dumping a pitcher of ale on his head."

As she walked off, the rowdy lot began banging on the table, and Shakespeare was ferried forward, spilling the contents of his mug on his doublet. "Give us a jest, Will!" one of the men yelled.

He brushed his hair off his face with his free

631

hand and began. "'Twas a girl from the forest of Arden . . ."

Arden. It was the name of the forest in *As You Like It* — a fingerprint she had intentionally left behind, a nod to the title of the first play she had ever written.

"Who was blowing a lad in the garden!" Shakespeare continued, and the crowd roared in delight. "He said, *I don't follow, it seems you are hollow* . . . and she belched and said, *Do beg yer pardon!*"

He took a stumbling bow as the others toasted him. Emilia stood, clapping, and when the rest of the crowd had sunk to their benches again to drain their drink, she remained on her feet until Shakespeare noticed her.

He walked over and sat down at her table. "Mistress. I did not know you frequented the Mermaid."

"I do not," she admitted. "I was hoping to find you." Emilia took a deep breath. "I have come to apologize."

"Ah." Shakespeare smirked. "I thought that was the only word in the English language you did not know."

"I have written a play," Emilia said, drawing out the manuscript she had completed, tied with string. "It is a comedy of sorts."

"I have not been producing comedies," he said.

This was true; *King Lear* and *Macbeth* and

Antony and Cleopatra and *Timon of Athens* — all written in the years during which they had not spoken, presumably crafted by other playwrights whose work he brokered — were the very opposite.

"All the more reason it is time for one."

He pursed his lips. "I do not know how much longer I shall keep up the charade. I find myself wishing to retire to Stratford. The business is wearying."

Emilia did not have the luxury of rest. "*The Winter's Tale* is not *just* a comedy," she clarified. "It is one born of tragedy at the start."

He tilted his head. "How so?"

She leaned forward. "A jealous king, Leontes, accuses his wife, Hermione, of infidelity with his best friend — though she's innocent. The king imprisons her, she gives birth, and the baby girl is hidden away and raised by shepherds. When she is brought to trial, her son dies of distress, and hearing that, so does she."

"This sounds miserable," Shakespeare said.

"No, because sixteen years have passed. King Leontes realizes his judgment was harsh. Meanwhile, his baby daughter grows up unaware of any of this. Perdita falls in love with the son of a prince, whose father does not approve of them because of the difference in their station. But this prince is the very son of King Leontes's best friend — and when it is discovered that Perdita is the king's long-lost daughter, the marriage is allowed. Everyone is reunited, Leontes and his best friend are reconciled, Perdita can get married."

"Well," Shakespeare said. "This is happier."

"But wait! A statue is presented — a rendering of Hermione, the wronged queen. Leontes is stunned by how realistic and beautiful it is . . . and then it comes to life." Emilia met his gaze. "You see? Time heals all wounds."

They were no longer speaking of the play. "And yet," he said, his voice chilled, "scars remain."

"I beg of you, Master Shakespeare. I need this. I need . . . *you*."

For a long moment, he regarded her. She felt like a mouse in a field with a hawk circling. "I read your book," he said finally.

She blinked; she had not anticipated this. "You," she said wryly, "and six others in the whole of England."

"It did not sound like you. By which I mean: it did not sound like *me*."

"That was my hope," Emilia replied.

Shakespeare scratched at his beard. "Our partnership is but a riddle. What grows bigger the more one takes away?"

"A hole," Emilia answered.

"Or a man," he said quietly, "who takes credit due another."

It was, she thought, the closest thing to contrition she would ever hear from Shakespeare. She supposed there was a different sort of emptiness in knowing that you were praised for work that was not your own. How strange that there had been two of them sharing this name, and neither one felt complete.

"You always had such *hubris,* mistress," Shakespeare said. "It is interesting to see you groveling."

Emilia's eyes flashed. "I am not —"

"Ah" — he grinned — "so it *is* you, after all." He plucked the play from her grasp. "One last play . . . for old times' sake." He stood up. "However, terms cannot be as they were. Ten shillings."

Before, he had paid her fifteen.

"Yes," Emilia said, swallowing. "Of course."

She did not see Shakespeare again, nor did she see *The Winter's Tale* performed. She had ten shillings that had to last her, and she could no longer afford to go to the theater.

She taught music for a few pence a week to local children; she sewed herbs into muslin bags to create teas that could cure a headache, get rid of moles and rashes, prevent conception. Her business spread by word of mouth, and she operated from her home whenever Alphonso was not around to grow angry. Local women who patronized her knew that when she hung a lavender wreath on her door, she was open for business.

It was on a blustery September day in 1613 when Alphonso was at court that Emilia was preparing a tisane for a midwife who was going through the change of life. "Cold one minute, and boiling the next," the woman was saying. "I scarce know whether to wear all me skirts at once or take them off and run stark naked down the street —"

At a knock on the door, Bess left her post at the hearth, where she was shelling walnuts. "Master Jeronimo," she said loudly, warning Emilia.

"Mistress Sitwell," Emilia murmured, pushing the loose herbs into a pouch and handing them to her, "perhaps we can finish our conversation later."

The midwife nodded, glancing to Jeronimo, who stood in the doorway, holding his hat in his hands. He turned to allow the woman to pass, and then looked at Bess.

"Bess," Emilia said. "Give us a moment."

"*Piccolina,*" Jeronimo said, taking Emilia's hand and leading her to the chair by the fire.

She did not have to hear the words to know. "Alphonso is dead?"

Her cousin nodded. "Yes. I wanted you to hear it from me."

"How?"

His throat bobbed. "He went to bed and he did not wake up."

Emilia narrowed her eyes. "*Whose* bed, Jeronimo?"

"A singer who accompanied the recorder troupe for King James."

A laugh startled out of Emilia, and she clapped her hand over her mouth. She dissolved into giggles, clutching her sides. "Well," she said, finally. "At least he went doing what he loved."

Jeronimo backed away. "Should I get Alma for you?"

"That will not be necessary," Emilia said. "I thank you for coming to tell me."

He walked toward the door, hesitating at the threshold. "I know, Cousin, that it was not always easy for you."

Emilia smiled faintly. "We must not speak of it. It's over."

She waited until the door closed behind him. There would be much to do — receiving the body, purchasing a winding-sheet, contacting Saint James in Clerkenwell so that Alphonso might be buried in the churchyard. She would have to speak to Henry, who — at court — would have heard the news. She would have to talk to Alphonso's brother about the hay patent to make sure she continued to receive some of the income due — she was quite certain Alphonso had not written a will. Those who think they are invincible rarely do.

Her hands went to the neck of her kirtle to make the customary tear. But instead of ripping the rough fabric, she patted the space over her heart.

Emilia walked to the back of the apartments, where the master bedchamber was. She pulled the coverlet from the bed and stripped the blankets and linens from the wool-stuffed mattress. She balled these up and threw them across the room. She went to Bess's room and carefully opened the stitches at the top of the feather bed, slipping her fingers inside to retrieve the miniature of Southampton she had moved into the chamber when she began sleeping there. She took it back to the master bedchamber, fisting it in her palm. Then she lay facedown on the bare mattress, her hand clasped around the image of the man who'd held her heart, and she slept better than she had for years.

The quality of mercy is not strained, Emilia thought. It was impossible not to think of the indefatigable character of Portia as Emilia now sat in a court of law, facing her brother-in-law, Innocent. She was the only woman in a sea of men, and she was attempting to get what was rightfully hers.

As Alphonso's widow, she should have continued to receive a portion of the hay patent her husband had secured years earlier, but Innocent had kept the money himself. When she could not bully him into paying her share, she brought the petition before the assizes, where it was heard by a judge who moved the case to the King's Bench.

She had thought often about Lady Clifford and Lady Anne, whose inheritance battles had only grown more complicated. When a court had decided that Lady Anne was entitled to half the old earl's estate, she refused, saying she deserved all of it.

Emilia wondered if those two noble ladies felt more confident amid the clerks and barristers that moved through Westminster Hall in their dark robes. She thought about Christine de Pizan's assertion that women and men were both capable of learning the law. She thought of how in her play, Portia had played at being a man in court.

"Mistress Lanier," the chief justice before her said. "I shall ask you one more time. Are you certain you wish to represent yourself?"

She could not afford a lawyer. "Who else could better tell my story, sir?"

The chief justice shook his head. "Proceed."

"I base my argument on the precedent set by Slade's case," Emilia said, rising, "through the action of assumpsit. By failing to pay me money due from the patent left to me as my husband's widow, Innocent Lanier has committed deceit, and is liable." She sat back down in a rustle of skirts, listening to the hushed whispers flying around the room. From the corner of her eye, she saw Innocent's barrister, a serjeant-at-law, lean toward him and murmur in his ear.

The chief justice blinked at her. "Have you legal training, mistress?"

"I . . . read, sir. Widely."

Innocent's barrister stood. "The defense

wishes for a stay," he said. "We did not expect the plaintiff to have such a comprehensive understanding of English contract law."

There was a clamor behind Emilia. "Are you truly claiming," a voice said, "that the defense wishes it had prepared a defense? You should not have assumed your plaintiff was not a worthy adversary."

The speaker approached the chief justice. "My lord," the justice said. "You honor us with your interest in these proceedings."

Southampton turned, his gaze skating over Emilia, then settling pointedly on Innocent's lawyer. "Well," he said, "*someone* has to." He turned to Emilia, his face impassive. "Mistress, am I correct in understanding that the patent of which you speak is the very same that my former guardian, Lord Burghley, arranged for your husband?"

"Yes, my lord," Emilia managed. She stared at his long hair, still red, if threaded now with gray. His bright eyes. The smile that tipped higher on one side than the other.

"What debt is owed?"

A lifetime, she thought.

"Eighteen pounds," she said.

His gaze was locked on hers. He took a step closer, and then stopped. Slowly, he turned to Innocent. "And you, Master Lanier, what claim do you hold on the patent?"

"My brother said it was mine to do with as I wish."

640

"You have written proof of this claim?" Southampton said.

She had forgotten so much about him. That he commanded attention without even trying. That he had a small scar through his right eyebrow, from swordplay with sticks when he was a child. That he had been trained in the law at Gray's Inn and could likely argue circles around everyone in this chamber.

"I have it . . . somewhere," Innocent replied.

"Unless you can produce it, I should think it is in the best interests of the court to follow the letter of the patent law as decreed by Lord Burghley originally." He smiled at the chief justice. "But of course, this is not my bench."

The chief justice could not be seen contradicting the Earl of Southampton; as a legal strategy, what the Earl said was effective. "Indeed, this was to be my judgment," he said. "The plaintiff in this action upon assumpsit shall recover not only damages but also the whole debt. The defendant will be required to pay Mistress Lanier twenty pounds."

The observers in the chamber erupted in discussion as the justice called for the chamber to be vacated. Innocent started toward Emilia, but Southampton stepped between them. "Mistress," he said quietly. "A moment of your time?"

The room emptied until she was left standing in a shaft of sunlight with Southampton. She smelled the tallow of the candles sputtering in sconces and the faint thread of tobacco. She smoothed her hair and ducked her face, suddenly aware she was thirteen years older than when they were last together.

He caught her hand. "Don't," he murmured. He looked down at her fingers, resting in his, and dropped them suddenly as if they were glowing coals.

"Thank you," Emilia said simply.

Southampton smiled faintly. "I could not let him continue to torment you beyond the grave, could I?"

"How did you know?"

"Your brother-in-law crossed my path at an inn," he said. "Foolish men brag when they drink."

She let herself study him — the fine sprays of lines at the corners of his eyes, the parentheses carved around his smile. "You are well?"

He nodded. "And you?"

"I am better now," she confessed.

He tilted his head. "How is he?"

She knew immediately what he was asking, and she felt that familiar rush of pride swell through her, blooming on her face. "Henry is lovely," Emilia said. "He is kind, and thoughtful, and smart as a blade. He is the best musician in my family."

"I have heard him play once or twice at court," Southampton said. "I wished to talk to him. But I did not know . . ." His words dried like dust. "I did not."

Emilia wondered if her son would remember Southampton. He had been so little when they spent time together in Paris Garden, pretending to be a family.

"I have two daughters and two sons," he blurted out, and she froze.

"I know."

His breath huffed between them, falling like a stone. "I do not know why I said that."

"To remind me," she whispered, "that you still can never be mine."

He met her gaze. "So much has changed, Emilia," he said, "and so much has not."

She felt her throat tighten and her eyes filling with tears, so she turned away. "I must go."

Immediately, he stepped away, clasping his hands behind his back. "If your brother-in-law does not pay you expediently, have you another income?"

For one brief, terrifying moment, she thought he might suggest employing her again. Perhaps this time for his daughters and sons, as a tutor. She thought if he spoke the words, she would leave this building and walk straight into the Thames.

"I shall survive," Emilia said. "I always do." She swallowed, stuck in the tar of memory. "Do you regret it?" she asked, grateful that she could not see his face.

The weight of their history pressed down on them. She thought he might not answer, to spare her from hearing the truth.

Then Southampton said, "I don't think there is right, or wrong. There are only choices, and consequences." He hesitated. *"What we changed was innocence for innocence."*

Her heart began to pound as he quoted *The Winter's Tale* to her. She turned and took a step toward him, finishing the line. *"We knew not the doctrine of ill-doing, nor dreamed that any did."*

"You are a fan of theater, too," Southampton said. "That play, it is my favorite. It stayed with me."

She could barely form her lips around words. "Did it?"

"Exit, pursued by a bear," he said, quoting one of the stage directions — words she had written after remembering the story he'd told young Henry at Paris Garden. "Time appeared on the stage as a character itself, to mark the passage of sixteen years in the play. And strangely, that performance was sixteen years after the happiest summer of my life." Southampton took her hand, rubbing his thumb over her palm. "I read your last letter so often it fell apart, Emilia. But it did not matter, because I knew the words by heart. *A sad tale's best for winter,*" he quoted.

For years Emilia had felt like the sole occupant of a lighthouse, sending a beam toward

644

him over the dark ocean. For years there had been no response. And now? To know that her words had not only reached him but guided him to her shore?

A small cry climbed the ladder of her throat, and then she was in his arms and pressed against him and his mouth was crushed to hers. His hands speared into her hair, scattering the pins like raindrops around them. She melted like wax, shaped against him, remade.

Emilia was twenty-three, looking up at him with the sun a halo on his hair, as he traced a message over the flat of her belly: *Mine.* She was twenty-four, swallowing the herbs that would flush the proof of that from her body. She was twenty-nine, attempting to stay upright as he told her he was married. And now this. Their time together had never been linear; it was a loop, and they were destined to keep returning to the start, and getting nowhere.

When they finally drew apart, she put her hands against Southampton's chest.

"Did you think of me, when you were writing it?" he asked, his lips against her temple.

"Yes," she confessed. "And also when I wasn't."

Then she realized what she had just admitted. "My lord," she said, panicking. "You . . . you cannot —"

"I would never," he said quickly. "It has been so many years since I alone knew your secrets. I would not be so unwise as to give up that honor again."

She lay her palm against his cheek. "Oh, Henry," Emilia said.

He caught her hand in his again and brushed his lips against her knuckles, a goodbye.

Emilia closed her eyes. She squeezed his fingers, as if she might be able to hold on to him this time. *Do not leave me,* she prayed, silently. *Just one more breath, one more moment, with you.*

But she was an expert in being disappointed.

MELINA
JUNE 2027

In the three years since Melina's father's bypass surgery, he'd healed, and so had she. She'd moved back home and watched his relationship with Beth blossom. He seemed perpetually in awe to have found himself in a situation where he was the one being cared for, instead of doing the caring — and Melina could not begrudge him that. Beth wasn't her mother, but she never tried to be, either. There were times she caught Beth with the little shoebox she kept in her closet, spinning her late husband's wedding ring around her thumb. There was a beauty, Melina realized, to knowing that there would always be a door closed off to your new significant other, where you stashed the pieces of your heart that had broken before you met.

At their wedding, Melina had walked her father down the aisle. Beth and her father were going to Mexico for their honeymoon — some all-inclusive senior resort — and Melina was alone in the house with her dog,

Typo — a six-year-old Jack Russell terrier she had rescued. Every morning she got up and dressed, fed Typo, and then took him for a two-mile walk into the center of town. As she went, she'd pick up the newspapers that the cranky preteen delivery girl tossed heedlessly into the street, moving them onto driveways. She'd pull the trash can over the curb for Mr. Chandrashakar, who was eighty-eight and living alone.

It wasn't strange to be back in the Connecticut town where she had grown up. If anything, it was familiar as hell. Melina knew, to the minute, how long it would take to reach the general store at the center green. She knew the brand of coffee they brewed. She knew there would be two stacks of newspapers for sale — *The New York Times* and *The Boston Globe,* papers from the big-sister cities between which her hometown sat squarely — and she knew she would pick up a copy of the *Globe* and read it on the porch while birds serenaded each other and Typo chased squirrels.

Melina had not read *The New York Times* in three years, and she had no intention of doing so again.

Since leaving Manhattan, Melina had taken on freelance writing jobs. It turned out that wrestling with language was a tool as much as an art, and could be applied broadly. She wrote mostly for technical journals, but every now and then a company would ask her to do an instruction booklet. Melina relished those tasks. There was something about making things simpler that appealed to her. In her own small way she believed helping other people find clarity would balance the fact that she hadn't been able to find it herself.

How to assemble this nightstand.

How to take a pregnancy test.

How to install an electric fence.

Sometimes, Melina would wake from a dream in which she'd written her own instruction book: How to be happy.

But every time she peeked inside the pamphlet, it was blank.

Andre's newest play was a retelling of *A Doll's House,* in which the main character (Neveah, instead of Nora) was a Black woman who marries into a Southern white family. The play put race — especially the sexualization of Black women — under a microscope, and when Melina first read a draft, she knew *this* was the one for which he'd win a national drama award. He was developing it at Goodspeed Opera House and was either on his way to a set visit in East Haddam or headed home from there — Melina couldn't remember which. But he was coming for lunch, so she had thrown together a salad and a flatbread with caramelized onions and Gruyère. He sat across from her in clothes he couldn't have afforded three years ago, hot cheese strung like a clothesline between the crust and his lips. "I am having an orgasm," he murmured, his mouth full.

"Things Melina does not need to know," she replied.

"Seriously, where did you get this? I want to eat it every day for the rest of my life. I want to buy the restaurant and make the chef my love slave."

"Hard pass," Melina said, "since this is the restaurant and I'm the chef."

Andre reared back, surprised. "You couldn't pour milk into cereal three years ago."

"And now I am someone who makes home-made pizza dough." She shrugged.

There had been a plan. Melina was going to leave New York City for a few weeks until the scandal died down. Soon enough, there would be a fresh scandal in the Broadway community and hers would fade. She would stay in Connecticut and help her dad with rehab. But when weeks turned into months and Melina still had not returned, Andre found a new roommate. Then his play transferred to Broadway, and he got a bigger place near Lincoln Center, where he lived alone. There *were* fresh scandals — Andre told her about them when they FaceTimed — but eventually, he stopped asking Melina when she was coming back.

"I have news," Andre announced.

"What?"

He folded his hands on the table. "I told my parents I'm gay."

Melina felt her lips twitch. "And did the house catch fire? Did locusts descend?"

"Do not say *I told you so*," Andre warned. "It's gauche. Anyway, they did not care, provided I'm still planning on giving them grandkids."

"I would hazard a guess that your sexual orientation didn't rank as news for your parents, either," Melina said.

"That's because I buried the lede. I think I may have found a baby daddy."

Melina grabbed his wrist. "What? Who!"

"His name is Josiah. He built the set for the Goodspeed show. Wears a carpenter belt without any irony and serves Village People vibes."

"How long have you been together?"

"Six months," Andre said.

"You kept this from me for half a year?"

"I had to make sure it was going to last!" he argued. "But enough about me. Who's keeping you warm these nights?"

Melina shook her head. "I told you, there is no one within a sixty-mile radius I want to go out with. I went on one date with a mortician who asked if I wanted to see his collection of death photos. Another guy stole my credit card and cash from my wallet."

Andre frowned. "What about the one with the dimples?"

The last time Andre had been here, he wouldn't leave until they'd gone through Bumble and matched Melina with someone. "Nice guy. Narcoleptic. Fell asleep twice during our dinner, which sort of undermined my confidence," Melina said.

"And then?"

She reached down and pulled Typo onto her lap. "Then I got a dog."

"Don't you miss it?"

"Sex?"

Andre shook his head. "Making theater."

Melina had five finished plays hiding in a drawer in her childhood bedroom. As it turned out, you did not have to have readers to be a writer. "No," she lied. "Not one bit, Andre."

"I don't believe you."

"I'm still *writing*," Melina pointed out.

He scoffed. "Yeah, manuals on how to unclog your toilet. What's the endgame here, Mel? When your dad comes back and you're living with the newlyweds —"

"Technically, I've been living with them both since I moved out of our apartment."

"So you're just going to become like those trees in California?"

Melina frowned. "Redwoods?"

"No! The ones turned to stone."

"The Petrified Forest," Melina corrected. "It's in Arizona."

"I don't care where it is," Andre said. "You

are going to waste away here in Mayberry, USA, sleeping in the same bed you slept in as a kid."

Melina looked down at herself. "I am hardly wasting away," she said. "I'm busy. I'm fine."

She remembered nights when she was little that storms rolled in. Jagged lines of light would split the sky and thunder shook the entire house. When she called out in terror, her father couldn't always come. He was with her mother — giving her meds, sponge-bathing her, whatever. So Melina would pull the covers up to her chin and tell herself, *I'm fine.*

It didn't make the lightning any less intimidating or the thunder softer. But if she said it often enough, surely it would come true.

"I'm *fine*," she repeated now.

Andre took the last slice of the flatbread. "Hair is fine. Sharpies are fine. Idris Elba is fine. You," he said, "are delusional."

When Andre left, Melina sat on the porch with her laptop, working on edits for a scientific journal article, while Typo leaped in the yard, trying to eat fireflies.

A soft ding alerted her that an email had landed in her work inbox. She had a very rudimentary website so that clients could see samples of her work and, she hoped, hire her.

Melina opened the message.

Melina quickly closed the email. She shut her laptop, went into the house, and got a large glass of wine. She drank it all, then called Typo in and went to bed.

The next day, she didn't look at any email at all.

The third day, she could feel the message in her inbox festering like a sore.

With a groan torn from deep inside, Melina opened her computer, hit Reply, and started to type.

She was picking wild strawberries in the field behind the house when she got the call.

"Is this Melina Green?" said a woman's voice.

Melina stood, squinting into the sun. Typo circled between her feet. "Yes?"

"This is Katherine Marsh. I'm the associate —"

"I know who you are," Melina interrupted, and her face instantly flamed. Had she been a recluse so long she had forgotten how to have a polite conversation?

"I'm so glad you responded. I'd like to arrange a meeting in person to discuss this further."

In the space that the woman left for her reply, Melina thought: *Of course you would. You want to make sure you won't get canceled, like I was.*

"I can work around your schedule. And I'd be happy to cover the cost of your travel," Katherine said into the silence. "If that's an issue."

"I have a car." Melina wanted to be able to beat a hasty retreat if she did not gather enough courage to cross the threshold of a theater again.

"If I may say so . . . I've never read anything like your play," the woman gushed.

Melina looked at Typo, who cocked his head. Her father would not be home for a week. Tomorrow was Trash Day. "How's Wednesday?" she asked.

Explosives.
Opioids.
Nuclear weapons.
None of them could hold a candle to

hope, the most dangerous commodity in the world.

Melina had awakened before dawn, packed an overnight bag just in case, threw in a Ziploc bag of dog food and some bottled water. She and Typo crossed the Connecticut border before the sun rose.

Because she had reached Maine hours before her scheduled meeting time, she pulled off at a public beach. She let Typo loose, removed her sneakers and socks, and rolled up the legs of her jeans to walk down to the spot where the ocean lapped at the rocky shore. Although it was June, the water felt like ice, and she jumped back.

Typo barked at a crab that scuttled beneath a jut of rock. He looked curious and comfortable away from home, while Melina could barely take a deep breath because of her anxiety.

She forced herself to put her toes in the surf again, gasping at the frigid rush.

Do not get your expectations too high, she lectured herself. *The theater probably has seven seats. Or it's run by a phantom in a mask. Or they want to perform the play with puppets.*

She looked at the horizon. The ocean bled blue into the sky.

Somewhere across this sea was the country where Emilia Bassano had struggled and loved and lost and survived.

Melina realized her ankles had gone numb,

or maybe she had just become accustomed to the temperature.

It was amazing, really, how quickly one could adapt.

The theater was tiny but charming. One hundred seventy-eight seats, arranged three-quarters of the way around a thrust stage that was bordered in pickled white shiplap. A peaked, vaulted ceiling swathed in white satin for noise reduction. The satin gave it the feeling of a circus tent, and Melina thought this was fitting for whatever spectacle was about to occur.

It was cool enough to leave Typo in the car, windows cracked, while she approached the box office. Melina had told the summer intern working there that she had an appointment with Katherine Marsh. "Oh, right," the kid said. "I'm supposed to bring you into the theater."

But the theater had been empty — lights dimmed, the ghost light lonely on the stage. The intern told Melina to make herself comfortable while she found the artistic director.

Melina stood in front of the stage, her hand resting on the scarred flooring. She could hear echoes of soliloquies and sword fights and tap dancing, like aftershocks of the stories that had been told here.

"Don't leave."

Melina whirled around to see a figure

silhouetted in the back of one aisle. Before he stepped into a shaft of light that illuminated his cornsilk hair and before she saw the glasses perched on his nose, she knew. She could tell from the way he moved, from how the air in the room bristled like a thunderstorm.

"You are not Katherine Marsh," Melina said to Jasper.

"No," he admitted. "Sorry to disappoint."

"It's not the first time," she retorted. It had been three years, surely whatever anger she'd had toward him had dissipated a little. Surely she could act like an adult for five minutes. "Why are you even here?"

He came to stand in front of her, studying her face. "I work here," Jasper said. "I'm the artistic director. Katherine works with me."

He could not have shocked Melina more. "*You* run a theater?"

His mouth curved. "Someone once told me that a critic shouldn't be allowed to criticize without getting his hands dirty and writing or directing a play himself."

"What about your column?"

"I quit the *Times* three years ago. Not long after we . . ." His voice trailed off.

She hadn't known, because she studiously avoided that publication. And Andre hadn't told her, because they had a long-standing pact to never utter Jasper Tolle's name.

"I started Athena because I made a promise to you, and I intended to keep it. We only perform works written by women or non-binary writers," Jasper said.

Melina's jaw dropped.

"I know you don't believe me," Jasper hurried to add, "and that you may *never* believe me. But I wrote the piece I told you I'd write. My editor made those changes. He didn't think a story on gender discrimination was going to get as many hits as one about racial discrimination. And it turned out, he was right. It forced a lot of white theater makers to stop making excuses for their choices."

Melina knew this was true; Andre was one of the writers of color who had benefited.

"But all that good came at a really significant cost." Jasper rubbed his hand over the back of his neck, grimacing. "I truly did want everyone to know your name. Just not . . . that way."

Melina's head spun. As apologies went, this was the grandest of gestures. Jasper had been a household name, the most famous theater critic. He was telling her he'd walked away from all of it out of a sense of . . . what? Guilt? Responsibility?

Love?

Her lips felt wooden, her tongue stiff. "Was the email just a trick to get me here in person?"

Jasper shook his head. "No. I really do want to direct your play. I want the whole world — fuck, at least all of southeastern Maine — to know what Emilia wrote. And I want everyone to know what *you* wrote." Very slowly, he reached for her hand. "I made a bigger table," Jasper said quietly, "but I've been saving a seat for you."

Melina glanced down at their palms pressed together.

The initial discussion between a writer and a director typically explored their joint vision for the production. Melina's eyes met Jasper's. She asked a question that had a dozen others nested within it.

"So," she said. "How does it start?"

He exits, leaving EMILIA alone.

She crosses to sit on a carved bench beneath the embrace of a lush emerald willow. At her feet is a faerie house.

THE WOMAN

A theater.

EMILIA

An audience.

THE WOMAN

A comedy.

EMILIA

A tragedy.

THE WOMAN

There once was a girl who became invisible so that her words might not be.

EMILIA

There once was a girl. A beginning and an end.

THE WOMAN

There was a story, whether or not
others ever chose to listen.

Blackout

THE END

EMILIA
1618–1645

Emilia is 49–76

Emilia didn't find out about Shakespeare's death until a month or so after it happened, in the spring of 1616. The public wondered if there might be one last play — perhaps even an unfinished one — in his estate. She found herself thinking about that. She wondered what people would make of it — how a playwright who, she'd heard, had meticulously divvied up his belongings might not have any of the tools of the trade in his possession. When Kit had died, the detritus of his life as playwright was all that remained; his landlady had even let Emilia sort through the stacks of books he used for research and take a few. When Nashe and Watson and Greene and other poets had passed, their unfinished works went to their patrons or to other writers to finish.

She considered the mythology that had sprung up around Shakespeare — his

663

reputation for never having to revise his plays; his ability to write one commercial success after another despite also being a full-time actor; his unorthodox method of working alone instead of collaborating like other playwrights — and she shrugged. There were just some people who were meant to go through the world with a patina of invincibility glimmering on them, and he was one of them.

And then, Emilia reasoned, there were people like her.

Emilia snaked between the tables where six young girls sat, bent over a poem in the original French. "Now," she said, "what is the message of *Bisclavret*?"

Little Olivia, the youngest of her pupils and the most precocious, raised her hand. "That we should have a school dog," she announced. "It would be ever so handy for cleaning up after supper."

Her older sister, Caterina, hushed her. "It's a werewolf, not a dog, stupid. And we can't have a school werewolf because it would eat us."

"I'm not stupid!"

"Girls," Emilia interrupted, before this could spiral even further. "I would like you each to write down your interpretation of the piece, and we shall read them aloud." She turned as the girls picked up their quills. *"En français,"* she added, and they groaned.

It was 1619 and she had reinvented herself again. Henry was gone more often than he was home, following the King from palace to palace as a royal musician. She supported herself and Bess by starting a school, instructing young women who were excluded from the local grammar school by their gender, and from private tutoring by their families' limited income. The parents she had convinced to pay her small tuition were mostly immigrants who lived near Alma and Jeronimo. Some were musicians, some were mercers, some were glassblowers.

In forming her curricula she used the same works that Henry had been taught when he was a young boy in grammar school, supplemented by the texts that the Countess had given Emilia when she was little. She leased a house in St. Giles-in-the-Fields that accommodated herself and the girls. It was the cheapest property in a good location, and as a result, there was plenty wrong with it — from rot in the threshold of the doorway to a wobbly handrail on the staircase. Her landlord, Edward Smith, had promised to fix these things two years ago, when she first leased the building, and still had not. She had withheld her rent; he had sued her for defaulting on her lease. She had countersued, asserting that she had a right to deduct the cost of repairs he had not made.

"Mistress?" One of her students tugged on her skirts. "Is there somewhere else I can sit?"

Emilia looked at the spot where the girl had been and saw a steady stream of water pouring from the ceiling, as it was apt to do when it rained. "Come work over here," she sighed, bringing the girl to another bench and asking the others seated there to squeeze together to make room.

Her oldest student suddenly threw down her quill, splattering ink across the page of the girl beside her. "Maria," Emilia said sharply. "I can only assume that means you are finished."

The girl stood, her face mottled. "This is *stupid,*" she muttered. "This is all so bloody stupid." Shoving past Emilia, Maria ran outside into the driving rain.

Maria was sixteen and a role model for her other students; Emilia had never seen the child with a cross word for anyone. "Girls," she instructed. "Continue."

She found Maria sitting on a small bench beside the school entrance, protected from the rain by the overhang of the roof. The girl scrubbed her hands across her face and looked away, but not before Emilia saw that she had been crying. Without saying a word, she settled beside Maria and waited.

"What is the point of learning this?" Maria finally exploded.

"Bisclavret?"

"All of it," she gusted. "Why learn when I'm never going to use it? It doesn't matter if I can speak French fluently or conjugate Latin verbs when all I'm meant for is to keep house and squeeze out babes."

Emilia rocked back, resting against the wall of the building. "Perhaps you will do more than those things."

"You're wrong, mistress," Maria argued. "And it makes it worse when you have a taste of learning you'll never use."

"Stop it," Emilia snapped, grabbing the girl's shoulders and shaking her. "If you say that, they've already won. They've convinced you that your life is so small, you shouldn't even hope for better." At Maria's frightened gaze, she relaxed her hold, her fingers flexing. "When I was a child, a bird — a kite — flew inside the Queen's palace and got trapped. It could see outside through the windowpane, so it kept flying into the glass. Over and over."

Maria's eyes widened. "Did it break through?"

"No, it broke its neck."

"That's a terrible story." The girl scowled.

"Perhaps," Emilia said softly. "Some time afterward, the glass in that windowpane shattered. There must have been a hairline crack no one had seen. A glazier was called in to replace it, but the new glass broke, too. Every time it was fixed, a few weeks later, it would fracture. The damage must have created a structural flaw in the frame. That windowpane was very high up, mind you, and eventually it was just left open to the elements." She turned to Maria. "Escape may not be possible in my lifetime. Mayhap I am like that bird, beating against the window for naught. But you — or your daughter, or your daughter's daughter — may be the one to fly through the hole."

Maria threw herself into Emilia's arms. "I'm to be married by the end of the month," she sobbed. "To a silk merchant who's old enough to be my father. He only cares if my hips are wide enough to survive childbirth . . . not whether I've read Ovid."

Emilia wasn't surprised. These girls would be wed in alliances that would further their families' status or their wealth or their connections — she only hoped that before then, they would be fully armed with an education. She stroked Maria's hair. "He likely can't conjugate Latin, either," Emilia murmured.

That, at least, got a faint smile from the girl. Emilia drew back, wiping Maria's tears with her thumb. "Are you not tired?" Maria asked. "Of struggling?"

"All the time," Emilia admitted. "I think that is what it is to be a woman."

The rain fell in sheets, cutting them off from the rest of the world. "*I* think," Maria mused, "you are a very good tutor."

Emilia looked at her. "I wasn't always one. Once," she murmured, "I published . . ."

. . . plays that the whole world loved.

But she could not tell this to Maria, because it only proved the girl's point.

"I published a book of poetry. That very few people read," she added wryly.

Maria considered this information, something she had not known about her schoolmistress. "Mayhap that matters less than the fact that you wrote it."

Emilia was an old woman now. She knew the difference between idealism and practicality; she knew that clinging to your principles did not put food on your table. And yet, she was a survivor. That was both the blessing and the curse of hope: it turned a weary *why* into a seductive *why not.* Even when you were wise enough to understand the odds of failure, all you saw was that sliver of possible success.

Emilia could see Maria's mind working out this puzzle of how to exist in a world that would rather erase her. Of all the curricula she had devised, this might be the only lesson that mattered.

She squeezed Maria's hand. "Shall we go back to *Bisclavret*?"

Sometime later, when the girls had moved on to Latin conjugations, there was a violent pounding on the door. Emilia peered through the window slats to find her landlord standing in the pouring rain beside a constable and a watchman.

"Girls," she said, "upstairs. Now."

The men pushed their way inside. "That's

her," Smith said, jabbing a finger toward Emilia. "She's the one who owes me."

Emilia set her hands on her hips. "I can only assume you've come in the middle of a torrential downpour so that you can witness firsthand the repairs you haven't made to the roof."

The constable grabbed her elbow, hard. "Let's go. Yer under arrest, mistress."

There was a gasp from the staircase, and Emilia's gaze flew to find her students, huddled at the top of the landing.

"I cannot leave these young women unaccompanied," she said. "I am a schoolmistress."

"Not if you don't pay for the schoolroom," Smith said.

She turned to the watchman, who was pulling her arms behind her back as if she were a common criminal. "Please. They cannot remain here alone."

"They're welcome to join you at Fleet Prison," the constable said.

Emilia caught Maria's gaze, projecting more calm than she felt. "Go to Mistress Wormheld, the seamstress on the corner. Ask her to deliver a message to your parents, explaining that I am indisposed and that the school had to shut its doors temporarily. Please tell them I shall write to let them know when we are back in session."

The girl swallowed. "Yes, mistress."

When she was released from debtor's prison,

the parents of her students were not bound to look favorably upon a schoolmistress who had been jailed. She wondered if she would see Maria again before the girl was married.

"Go," Emilia said softly, and Maria scuttled down the staircase, knocking into the handrail in her haste; it listed and then collapsed like kittle pins.

The Knight's Side of Fleet Prison was for those who were awaiting punishment but had no coin to bribe the wardens into settling them into the Master's Side, where there was decent food, cleaner bedding, relative privacy, and the hope of a visit from family. Emilia did not have money; she did not even have a way of letting Henry or Alma or Jeronimo know she'd been arrested. Although she was not in the worst of the accommodations at Fleet — those were the fetid basement cells called Bartholomew Fair — she was jammed into a cell with six others: two women barely covered by their dresses, two who looked like ordinary working-class women, another who had not stopped praying, and a beggar who was missing a foot.

"'ello, luv," said one of the ladies, whose breasts were spilling over the neck of her dress. "What they nab ye fer?"

"A misunderstanding," Emilia said. "I do not belong here."

The light-skirt laughed, revealing a mouth

of missing teeth. "Wouldn't ye know it, ain't a one of us who *does*."

There was no day and no night in the cell, just candles that burned and sputtered outside and the occasional scrape of a key in a lock or a chain on the ground. In addition to the two prostitutes, the common women had been charged with adultery. The praying woman was a cutpurse, and the beggar was mute.

Once a day a pail of water was set in the cell, with a skin of mold floating on the top. A guard would toss a hunk of cheese in, too, and then laugh when the women attacked one another to get to it first. Emilia did not join the fray. She pressed her back against the wall and closed her eyes, reciting sonnets in her head.

Some days, she lay in the faerie bower where Titania and Oberon had fought over the little Indian boy.

Others, she walked the parapet with the soldiers of Elsinore Castle, seeing the ghost of the old king.

She ran through the forest of Arden with Rosalind, trading her skirts for the freedom of a man's hose.

She watched Desdemona stare at her husband with nothing but devotion, even as Othello choked her life from her.

She inserted herself in a half dozen different settings, anywhere but here.

Several days into her incarceration, the

candles outside the cell hissed into blackness, and the rats came out. They crawled around her ankles and scratched at the soles of her boots. She dozed and woke to the splash of the beggar urinating on her hand.

Scrabbling backward, inadvertently kicking one of the other women as she went, Emilia found the spot where the wall of the cell met the iron bars.

"Ssh, love," she heard, a whisper in her ear. "Don't fight so."

Emilia turned and found Southampton beside her. "You are not here," she whispered.

"I am if you need it to be so," he said.

She knew she was dreaming, and willed herself to stay asleep.

"Do you remember the day we were at Paris Garden?" he asked. "And a red kite swooped down and stole your drawers?"

Emilia nodded. "I felt indecent, the whole ferry ride home."

"And I thought the kite was the smartest bird, to have secured such a treasure."

She smiled. "I spent days looking up in the sky, expecting my underclothes to fall."

He leaned closer. "So did I."

"Does it seem so long ago to you?"

"It feels like only moments have passed," he said softly. "Don't blink."

She stared into his eyes. "Don't blink," she repeated.

Truly, it took only a beat of the heart before

the baby in your arms was a young man on the brink of starting a family of his own. A moment ago, she had been learning the power of her own body at Isabella's. Just yesterday she had broken her fast with Hunsdon, kissed Southampton, argued with Kit. How did time move so very slowly and so dizzyingly quickly all at once?

"You," a voice said, and the rusty hinges of the cell groaned. Emilia startled; she had blinked after all. The vision of Southampton was gone. She tumbled backward, catching herself with her elbow and sending a shooting pain up to her shoulder. The guard yanked her upright, pulling her down the hall.

"Put in a good word for me, luv," said one of the prostitutes.

Emilia was dragged up a set of stairs with puddles in their sagging stone bellies and into a room so bright that she was blinded. It took her a few seconds to realize that her son was standing beside the warden, horror written across his face.

Henry put an arm around her. It never failed to amaze her how her child was now a head taller than she was, broad enough to support her when she stumbled. His mouth was tight as he led her out of Fleet, past the gates, into the bustle of the London streets. Only then did he stop and hold her shoulders, assessing her for damage. "Are you all right, Mama? Shall I find a doctor?"

Her face softened. "I am fine, darling. Or I will be once I'm rid of the stench of the cell."

"I did not know," he said, his eyes welling. "I came as soon as I heard."

He had been at Nonsuch, playing flute for the King. She had no idea where he had come up with the money to pay her debt and whatever else it would have cost to have her released.

"I am sorry you were in there for so long."

She wanted to ask Henry how long it had been. As she hadn't eaten for days, she'd begun to lose track of time. But she thought that might frighten him. Even if he was bigger and stronger than she was, he would always be her child, and she would do what she could to protect him.

"I had company," Emilia said.

The last person Emilia expected to find at the door when she opened it was Ben Jonson.

"Mistress Lanier," the writer said, sweeping his hat from his head. "Well met."

Five years ago, Jonson had bundled all his plays together into a folio. Prior to this, no playwright considered mere scripts to be great literature; theater was a snack for consumption rather than a meal of state for dignitaries. Jonson had the hubris to refer to his plays and masques as if they were part of an oeuvre. Even more shocking — his folio had sold well.

Now, it was 1621, and Jonson's work was

famous. On the other hand, Emilia herself had not written a play for years, not since Shakespeare's death. She had lost her conduit into the business; she was trapped inland with no access to a port. What could Jonson possibly want with her?

She, who was rarely tongue-tied, did not know what to say. Should she feign ignorance of their association? What were the odds that he even remembered Hunsdon's shy wisp of a courtesan from so long ago, reading Mary Sidney's closet drama after hours? Or the time they crossed paths in a tavern, when he was drunk, and she was crawling her way back into Shakespeare's good graces?

"I beg your pardon, sir," Emilia said, deciding to assume that he did not recall any of that. "Are we acquainted?"

She felt Bess come into the room, curious about the stranger at the door.

"Apologies," Jonson replied. "I am Ben Jonson. I often forget that a poet's words are more recognizable than his face."

Emilia felt a trickle of sweat run down her spine. "Bess," she said, turning. "Would you bring some ale for Master Jonson?"

The servant disappeared into the back of their lodgings. Emilia led Jonson into the main room and invited him to take a seat before the fire. "I hope it is not too presumptuous to think you are familiar with my writing," he said.

"Sir, I doubt there is a soul in England who is unfamiliar with your writing," she replied.

"You are a poet as well."

Bess settled a tray between them. Emilia squeezed her hands to steady them before pouring a cup of ale for Jonson and passing it to him.

"I do recall thinking, when I saw your book, *Where did she come from?*" Jonson said, chuckling. "And then I remembered you, in the poetry salon run by the Countess of Pembroke. At which point I wondered, *Where did she* go?" He leaned forward, the mug balanced on his knee. "How odd, it seemed to me, that a writer with such youthful promise might simply vanish for so many years before arriving in printed form."

Emilia folded her hands in her lap. "I have been a wife and mother."

"Neither of which excludes picking up a quill."

She met his gaze, steely. "I am unsure of why you are here, Master Jonson. Why do you play at solving a mystery where there is none?"

He sank back in his seat, regarding her. "Do you know the plays of Shakespeare?"

"Who does not?" she replied.

"And by chance, have you seen my play *Every Man out of His Humour*?"

Emilia shook her head. It had come out around 1600, when she did not have coin to attend the theater. "There is a clown, Sogliardo," Jonson explained. "He pretends to be a poet, but he in fact steals poems or hires others to write them. He has money, but there is no explanation for how he received that wealth. In my play, Sogliardo wants a coat of arms more than anything else in the world."

Just like Shakespeare. When the shield was finally granted, the motto read *Non Sanz Droict,* Not Without Right.

"It is suggested to Sogliardo that his coat of arms bear the motto Not Without Mustard."

Emilia laughed.

Jonson leveled his gaze at her. "Most playwrights start as actors, or vice versa, did you know that, mistress? It becomes clear enough to which role one is suited. As an actor, I, for example, am not worth the price of admission to the theater . . . but I can write. Shakespeare began in this business as a playwright — a middling to awful one, if I may be so base — and instead went on to tread the boards. I have always wondered how he overcame his literary ineptitude to become such a celebrated poet. It simply did not add up. And such has been the root of my rivalry, as it were, with the man."

"So you seek to bury him further in the ground?" Emilia asked.

"No. I come here to relay a conversation from several years ago."

Emilia pressed her lips together.

"I was in Stratford during the spring of 1616," Jonson said. "My friend Michael Drayton — he was writing for the Lord Admiral's Men at the time — took me out to raise a glass in celebration of my folio being published. Shakespeare was at the pub and sat down with us." He flicked his glance toward Emilia. "Well, the man could not hold his beer. Ale made Shakespeare's tongue loose, and the conversation flowed in ways I did not expect. He went off about how he would have had his own folio published before mine had the source of his writing not dried up."

Emilia swallowed. "He was not visited by his muse, then?"

"'Twas not the muse he missed, as it turned out. It was the Earl of Oxford, and others, who'd been providing the wheat for him to mill into grain. Many were part of Oxford's merry band of writers at some point — Kyd, Nashe, Middleton, Bacon — for various reasons. For Oxford and Bacon it was anonymity. But others, it was simply to have enough money to put food in their bellies, and a play with Shakespeare's name on it was a guaranteed, quick sale. When Oxford died, there were some extant plays and a few playwrights from his little cabal that continued to provide material. But then Shakespeare mentioned someone who had not been one of Oxford's men. A side deal, I imagine. He said Emilia had been — and these were his exact words — his golden goose."

Emilia turned to stare at the fire, her heart pounding.

"Of course I wished to know what he meant. Emilia is such a unique name. I had first heard it when introduced to you at Mary Sidney's literary salon, and then numerous times in the Shakespearean plays. When I said as much, Shakespeare told me that when Fletcher gave him *Two Noble Kinsmen* to sell, he'd renamed the object of the men's affections *Emilia,* a coded message that he hoped would summon the woman who had written for him some years before. So I said, plainly, *You collaborate with a woman?* And Shakespeare said, *Collaborated.*" Jonson met her gaze. "Days later, he was dead of a fever."

"Why are you here?" Emilia said sharply.

He set down his cup. "Did you know I am editing a folio of the plays credited to Shakespeare? It is a herculean task. I cannot even say why exactly I am undertaking it, given my dislike of the fellow. But as it turns out, my rivalry had never been a fair fight — I was one man, against multitudes. And I think, mayhap, that is why I have undertaken this project." He hesitated. "Thomas Middleton modified *Macbeth,* adding in witches from some of his earlier work. He is writing for the King's Men now and tailoring *Measure for Measure* to best fit the troupe. It made me wonder if I might approach the original writers of the so-called Shakespeare plays and let them — for want of a better term — speak for themselves."

He took a roll of papers from his satchel, handing them to Emilia. She tugged at the ribbon binding them to find several plays. Resting on top was the foul copy of *Othello,* likely the one last used in performance.

"In case you would like to make changes," Jonson said.

Emilia felt herself nearly vibrating with tension; she was surprised a single note of worry didn't echo around them. "Whose name will be on this folio?"

"The one you — and others — made famous," Jonson said. "But your texts deserve to outlive the man who brokered them." He rose, slinging his satchel over one shoulder. "I thank you for your hospitality, mistress. And your stories. I have always wondered how Shakespeare seemed to know so much about what it meant to be a woman."

"We are human first," Emilia replied. "That's all I wanted to share."

Jonson grinned. "Think on that," he said, "when you revise."

What do you say, when you know the words will be your last?

Revisiting *Othello* was like summoning Alphonso back to life: there was so much in that story of a jealous husband, of the wife he killed. Emilia had placed herself into the text as well — choosing to literally name a character Emilia — Iago's wife, the woman strong enough to stand up to Othello after he murdered Desdemona. She threatened to expose her own husband's role in the tragedy. And then, like Desdemona, Emilia was killed by her husband — another man who did not want to hear the truth.

When Emilia had first written the play, she had not been able to imagine a happy ending for these women.

She still could not.

She turned the pages until she found a spot where her namesake character, Emilia, was describing men to her mistress, Desdemona:

They are all but stomachs, and we all but food;
They eat us hungerly, and when they are full
They belch us.

And then they blame us for their indigestion, Emilia thought.

It did not matter that Desdemona had not been unfaithful to Othello — if he believed it, it must be so.

But it also did not matter that Emilia herself had been untrue to Alphonso — because betrayal, in some cases, is indistinguishable from survival.

A woman who was unfaithful might have a

hundred hidden reasons to be so.

She turned the pages until she found a later scene between Desdemona and Emilia, discussing infidelity. As she'd written it years ago, Desdemona was shocked by Emilia's admission that there were circumstances under which she would have been unfaithful.

Would thou do such a deed for all the world? Desdemona had asked.

The world's a huge thing, her maid replied. *It is a great price, for a small vice.*

Now, Emilia dipped her quill in the ink.

She would not be able to argue with God about the choices she had made. She would not be able to convince society that she was not a sinner.

But her namesake could.

She added a hundred and sixty more lines in her revision, giving many of them to the outspoken servant Emilia.

*I do think it is their husbands' faults
If wives do fall. Say that they slack their
    duties,
And pour our treasures into foreign laps;
Or else break out in peevish jealousies,
Throwing restraint upon us. Or say they strike
    us,
Or scant our former having in despite.
Why, we have galls, and though we have
    some grace,
Yet have we some revenge.*

She hesitated, and then a wide smile un-spooled across Emilia's face. Suddenly, she knew exactly what to write.

Let husbands know

Their wives have sense like them. They see, and smell,
And have their palates both for sweet and sour,
As husbands have. What is it that they do
When they change us for others? Is it sport?
I think it is. And doth affection breed it?
I think it doth. Is 't frailty that thus errs?
It is so too. And have not we affections,
Desires for sport, and frailty, as men have?
Then let them use us well. Else let them know,
The ills we do, their ills instruct us so.

What was the most frightening thing one could possibly say to a man? That a woman's dreams, hopes, desires, flaws, and foibles were no different from his.

That men and women were *equals.*

She sat back at her desk — Henry's old school desk — and gave both Desdemona and Emilia a proper literary burial, adding lines for Desdemona. When she'd first written the play, she had barely mentioned the song sung by Desdemona's mother's maid, Barbary, as she died:

684

My mother had a maid called Barbary.
She was in love, and he she loved proved mad
And did forsake her. She had a song of willow,
An old thing 'twas, but it expressed her fortune,
And she died singing it. That song tonight
Will not go from my mind . . .

Now, though, Emilia created the very tune and lyrics for Desdemona. As her quill scratched over the margins, she thought of her father, playing his recorder, and how her mother's bearing would change as if he were the charmer and she the snake. She thought of Jeronimo and her cousins in the musicians' gallery in the Queen's Court, and the way the jagged edges of a tense political standoff could be sanded smooth with a flourish of a madrigal or a lively pavane. She thought of audiences that grieved with minor chords and soared with arpeggios.

Emilia closed her eyes and hummed the tune that circled the edges of her mind, drawing it closer until the melody tumbled and rose and took form:

The poor soul sat sighing by a sycamore tree,
Sing all a green willow.
Her hand on her bosom, her head on her knee,

Sing willow, willow, willow.
The fresh streams ran by her and murmured
*   her moans,*
Sing willow, willow, willow.
The salt tears fell from her, and softened the
*   stones —*

She stopped herself, interrupting the scene and the ballad. It would stay unfinished until the end of the play, when Emilia was killed by Iago, and she called back the refrain.

What did thy song bode, lady?
Hark, canst thou hear me? I will play the swan
And die in music.

"I will die in music," she said aloud now, her voice filling all the space in the empty room.

Just like the character Emilia, this would be her swan song.

What do you say when you know your words will be your last?

I was here.
I mattered.

Emilia looked down at the printed pages that sat on the oblong table, still smelling of ink and damp to the touch. Two years had passed since Jonson approached her about the folio of Shakespeare plays, and now it was coming to fruition. She did not know if he'd invited any of the other authors to see the work in progress, but she was honored to be asked.

The publishers were Edward Blount and Isaac Jaggard. Isaac's father, William, was to have been the printer, but he'd died during the time it took to compile the massive book, and so Isaac was now directing the actual production of the material. Jonson had introduced Emilia to him when she first arrived, before they'd gone to examine the copies of the front matter.

He handed her a page with an illustration of Shakespeare drawn by Martin Droeshout, an engraver.

"What do you think?" Jonson asked.

Emilia hesitated. She did not want to demean the artist, but she had known William Shakespeare, and this image of him was ridiculous. His forehead was so high as to seem deformed, his hair uneven. His doublet appeared to be worn backward, and he had two left arms. "If I were to be remembered thusly after my death," Emilia said, "I should come back to haunt you."

He threw back his head and laughed. "That is exactly what I am going for," Jonson said, his forefinger hovering over the sketch. "Mark this double line on the neck, as if he is wearing a mask."

Her lips twitched. "Clever."

"I cannot imagine anyone who knew the

man being able to look at this and not read between the lines. But, just in case . . ."

He offered her the page that would sit opposite this bizarre engraving — a poem by Jonson, introducing the reader to the work:

This Figure, that thou here seest put,
It was for gentle Shakespeare cut,
Wherein the Graver had a strike
With Nature, to out-do the life;
O, could he but have drawn his wit
As well in brass, as he hath hit
His face, the Print would then surpass
All that was ever writ in brass.
But since he cannot, Reader, look
Not on his Picture, but his book.

"You could not have said more bluntly that the real writer isn't in this picture but rather is found in the text," Emilia said, impressed.

Jonson smirked. "Yes, well, you're a playwright. You know that sometimes the audience is clay-brained." He clapped his hands together. "Right. So this next bit is going to be a letter from Heminges and Condell."

"The actors from the King's Men?"

"The very same."

"But they have not written it yet?" Emilia asked.

"They were never asked," Jonson said. "The entirety of this folio is deception. Plus, when have you ever known actors to be able to write anything coherent themselves? They are but heralds crying out what the castle wishes known. I am still working on their false compliments, but I shall make them sufficiently superfluous, so that it is impossible to believe this is the work of a man rather than a God." He extemporized. " 'His mind and hand went together' . . . 'we have scarce received from him a blot in his papers' . . . all that rot."

"Is that not too much, sir?" Emilia asked. "You hope to stoke doubt, not cause a riot."

He raised a brow. "Does your Hamlet not substitute a forged copy of the letter Claudius uses to have him executed?"

She rolled her eyes and touched another loose page, this one titled *To the memory of my beloved, the Author Mr. William Shakespeare: And what he hath left us.* "That's quite inclusive," Emilia said.

"One tries."

Jonson began to read his poem:

To draw no envy (Shakespeare) on thy name
Am I thus ample to thy Book, and Fame;
While I confess thy writings to be such,
As neither Man, nor Muse, can praise too
*   much;*

Emilia covered her mouth with her hand, stifling laughter. "Is it not so?" Jonson challenged. "You cannot praise work that a man never wrote." He skated his finger down the page. "This next bit is for you."

These are, as some infamous Bawd, or
*   Whore*
Should praise a Matron. What could hurt her
*   more?*

False praise, he was suggesting, was as distasteful as a harlot comparing herself to a godly wife. It was an odd metaphor for a poet of Jonson's caliber to choose, since the playwrights who would be erroneously comparing themselves to the great Shakespeare were all men.

Unless, of course, they weren't.

"Oh, this is the best part," Jonson said gleefully.

My Shakespeare, rise; I will not lodge thee by
Chaucer or Spenser or bid Beaumont lie
A little further, to make thee a room.
Thou are a monument, without a tomb,
And art alive still, while thy Book doth live
And we have wits to read, and praise to give.

All of it was true. Shakespeare was not buried in Poets' Corner of Westminster Abbey with Chaucer or Spenser or Beaumont, the great literati. And compliments were due not to him but to the texts within.

It was subversive and smart, for those in the

know. But if you bought the Folio and you were not reading carefully, you would simply think Jonson, like everyone else, believed Shakespeare was worthy of temples erected in his name, flowers strewn in the wake of his coffin, mourners tearing out their hair.

Jonson smoothed the edges of the paper, settling it carefully back onto the long table. "What think you?"

"It is not a set of plays you've created, but a series of puzzles," Emilia said.

He clasped a hand over his heart. "Guilty, mistress. I cannot bear the thought of that gull being anointed with laurels others carried."

"It was our choice," Emilia said softly. The alternative would have been to remain unheard. She may have used someone else's name, but the words had been her own.

She looked at Jonson, who had inked his own demons and regret and jealousy into these poems of his. "Think you one day someone will crack this cipher? Long after we both are gone?"

He met her gaze. "With time and thought, and all these clues," Jonson said, "how could they not?"

It was not long after the Folio was printed that Emilia noticed something different about her son. Henry would be in the middle of a conversation and suddenly start to laugh, as if he'd heard a joke that no one else could.

He missed suppers, and more than once she found him sneaking into the house in the wee hours of the morning. His laundry bore grass stains and mud patches, hardly normal for a flutist, and she found herself remembering her own hems, stained from rolling in the marshy grass with Southampton.

When, one day, he shyly brought sweet, candy-cheeked Joyce Mansfield to meet her, she already knew that this was the woman he would marry.

On the day of her son's wedding, Emilia dressed in the finest clothing she had: a red silk gown that made her skin look like rich honey and her hair as blue-black as the wing of a crow. Joyce was at her family's home; they would meet at the church.

The ceremony was at midday, and as the sun crawled higher through a streaky web of clouds, Emilia finished arranging the bread and meats that would be part of the wedding meal for her relatives and Henry's new family. Bess fluttered beside her, having borrowed pitchers and mugs from neighbors to hold ale. Bess had been included, of course, as a guest at Henry's wedding — she had raised that boy as much as Emilia herself had.

"Henry!" Emilia called again, her voice carrying up the narrow stairs.

Bess smiled. "Nervous bridegroom. Mayhap he don't wish to be the center of attention."

"I doubt it. He's played instruments before

kings and queens. What is standing up before a priest?"

"Everything, when it's the rest of yer life, mistress. As a child, he did not have such a fine model of a marriage."

Emilia looked at her maid, surprised that this thought had not occurred to her before. "Bess," she suggested, "why don't you run up to the church, and let them know we're on our way?"

She climbed the stairs to Henry's room and knocked softly on the closed door. When he didn't answer, she opened it and peered inside. "Henry?"

He lay on his bed, facedown, still in his shirtsleeves and hose.

"Are you well?" Emilia asked, sitting down on the mattress beside him, her skirts rustling. She placed her hand on the small of his back, the way she had when he was little and woke from a nightmare.

He rolled to his side, and to her surprise, his eyes were rimmed red. "Henry," she said, "have you changed your mind? We can . . ." She grasped at thoughts. "Pack a satchel. Hire a horse, if we must. We can spirit you out of London before anyone even knows you've broken a promise —"

"Mama," Henry quietly interrupted. "What if I'm like him?"

She could feel the ghost of Alphonso. He was *just* there, in the cold breath at the back of her neck, in the flash of light in the looking glass. "There is not a bone in your body that is like his," Emilia replied.

Henry sat up, legs crossed on the mattress. "So it's true."

They had never spoken of his paternity. What mother would tell her child he was illegitimate; that she had been a courtesan; that he was the reason she had lived as another man's shame for so many years?

"Children can be cruel," Henry said, by way of explanation.

He watched the chase of emotions on her face: fear, embarrassment, pain, resolve. Emilia picked through words as if she were choosing cherries, trying to find only the sweetest fruit to offer him. "Your . . . real father . . . was a good man," she said.

"I wish I'd met him," Henry sighed.

Emilia realized two things in that moment: that he assumed Hunsdon was his father — Hunsdon, who had died when he was a baby. Or perhaps Henry was so young when she was being courted by Southampton that he did not remember the time they had spent together.

Then again, Emilia could not definitively say which of the two men was Henry's father.

"Here is what I think," she said. "Whether your father was a good man does not signify. The girl who is waiting for you at the church is marrying *you.* She loves you, Henry, I can see it every time you come into a room and she turns like a flower to the sun. She loves you because *you* are a good man."

He puzzled over her words as if they were a song he was writing, and if he just concentrated hard enough, the melody would manifest. "I may not know how to be a husband," he said thoughtfully, "but I know how to love."

Emilia shook her head and laughed. "Pity your poor mother's ears, Henry! I am not certain I need to hear the details —"

He grinned. "I meant that I know to put someone first, no matter what." Henry took her hand and squeezed. "You taught me that."

A year later, Emilia shared lodging with Henry and Joyce. She'd begun a new trade — brewing ale, and selling her wares to a tavern at the end of the street. One morning she was at market, haggling over the price of a large canvas sack of malt, when she heard the word *Southampton* uttered by two matrons who were trading the currency of court gossip.

Did you hear?

Southampton had been in the Netherlands, commanding volunteers to fight against the Spanish.

Did you know?

He had only just arrived at Roosendaal when his son, Lord Wriothesley, had contracted a fever.

What a pity.

When the young man died, his father had brought his body to Bergen op Zoom and had been laid low by the same fever.

Such devotion.

Their bodies had returned to England with a heroes' welcome.

Imagine losing both a husband and a son.

They'd be buried in Titchfield.

That poor wife.

The next moment Emilia was walking — heart pumping, hands shaking in the cold. She continued until she stood on the bank of the Thames and stared toward Southwark, where she and Southampton used to meet.

She'd had no contact from him after he intervened in the lawsuit about Alphonso's hay patent — and that had turned out to be a pyrrhic victory. In spite of the judge ruling in her favor, she received no payment from Innocent. Emilia had spent more years apart from Southampton now than she'd had with him. His distance was a blessing, because she truly believed that seeing him again would only make the pain more acute.

But she also believed that there was an invisible thread that snaked from her heart to his. She was certain that when he crossed her mind in the middle of something mundane — baking bread, sweeping the hearth — it was because he had thought of her at that exact moment in the soft center of his own day. Emilia had also believed that the reason she was still alive and so many she loved were not was that she and Southampton were meant to inhabit the same time and place, even if they were not together.

She'd thought: *If I die, he will know. He will be on horseback and suddenly go cold as ice. He will be in a conversation and lose all his thoughts. He will look out the window at the sky and know that even if it seems as it did a moment ago, everything has altered.*

She'd thought the same would hold true for herself, were he the one to die first.

But Southampton was gone, and had she not been buying malt at that moment the gossips had passed, she might not have even known.

She doubled over as if she had been struck hard in the belly. Circling through her head was a single thought: she hadn't gotten to say goodbye.

Emilia stood at the edge of the river until her tears froze on her eyelashes. A constable ambled past. "Mistress?" he asked. "Are ye well?"

She was broken and hollow.

She was alone.

Emilia looked at the watchman. "I will be," she said.

She sold the ale she had stockpiled at home, and then negotiated with the tavern owner to sell him all her brew-making supplies. She scrawled a note for Henry, who would return from playing for the King sometime before Twelfth Night. Emilia did not know how long this would take, and she did not want her son to worry.

She, who had never ridden well, bought a horse. She wore three layers of kirtles and two cloaks, as buttoned up against the biting wind and snow as she could be. The first day, she managed only five miles before she had to stop at an inn and rest her sore muscles. No one questioned an old woman traveling alone; she had nothing worth stealing — not belongings or beauty or chastity.

On the third day, she sold the horse to an innkeeper and paid a farmer and his wife hauling a cart south to let her ride in the back with the timber they were transporting.

The farmer was a taciturn, burly man who likely had grown more and more silent in the incessant tide of his wife's chatter. Emilia engaged politely at first: Yes, she was a widow. No, she and her late husband had not been blessed with children. Yes, she was headed to Titchfield for Christmastide, to visit her sister. No, she had never been this far south before. Then she began to feign sleep just for a moment's peace.

Despite the cold, they passed others traveling. There were drovers herding sheep, men selling grain, crates of poultry and pigs. Twice the cart hit a trough and they had to empty it entirely so that a wheel could be repaired, leaving Emilia with broken fingernails and splinters she had to pull with her teeth. Once, a tree had fallen and needed to be chopped before they could pass. Snow made the travel a crawl.

On the sixth day, the farmer and his wife left her at the road that would take them to Poole. Emilia thanked them, paid for her passage, and set off on foot for the last sixteen miles to Titchfield.

By the time she reached the town where Southampton's barony sat, she was, quite literally, numb. Her hair was white with falling snow; her hands curled inside her gloves. Inside her thin boots, she could not feel her feet.

She had arrived on January 7, after Twelfth Night, when Christmastide celebrations had ended and the village was back to business as usual. In this, she was lucky; surely the entirety of the town would have been at church just a day earlier. St. Peter's sat in the center, bordered by a graveyard as white as a virgin's robe.

It was there Emilia began her search. But there was no disturbed ground, no maw of earth that had been recently dug to accommodate a coffin. She realized her mistake almost immediately: the Southampton family would of course have a vault *inside* the church.

The wooden doors, thank God, were unlocked. Inside it was only nominally warmer.

Emilia waited for her fingers to burn and tingle, proof of life, before she went farther.

The tomb was easy to find, draped with lilies and white roses. It sat separated from the pews and the nave and the altar by a black iron gate. Four obelisks formed the corners of the marble monument, with the carved form of the second earl's wife lying on a stone bier. She was flanked by stone effigies of the first and second earls of Southampton.

It was her love's mother, Mary, who had commissioned the tomb. She had been the daughter of Viscount Montagu. It was why Emilia had used that family name in *Romeo and Juliet,* the first play she wrote while thinking about Southampton.

Emilia found herself picturing Romeo fighting his way into the crypt until he could hold with his own arms what he thought to be the body of Juliet.

Henry would not be in these stone coffins; his body would be in a crypt somewhere below.

She did not have access to the actual vault. In fact, the gate surrounding the tomb was locked. Emilia looked around, but the church was empty. She shed her cloak and set her satchel on the tile floor, then hiked her skirts up in a knot between her legs. With a wince for her stiff limbs, she climbed the iron gate and dropped inside, stepping toward the marble tomb.

Emilia circled the stone monument, looking for an entry to the crypt. When she could not locate one, she fell to her knees in front of a panel that depicted two children praying. She touched her fingers to the smooth cheek of the marble boy and thought about her own son, and the daughter that she and Southampton had conceived.

She borrowed Romeo's words. "Here's to my love," she murmured.

She flattened herself on the cold floor, as close to the tomb as she could get. She had heard that in the tombs of nobility, corpses were preserved in honey, and she hoped this was true, so that his afterlife would be sweet.

She peeled back the years, imagining the feel of Southampton's stubble scratching her cheek, the pliant heat of his arms around her. She remembered how his gemstone eyes would darken when he caught sight of her coming toward him. She thought of the time that he'd tried to teach her to whistle, and they had laughed so hard at her abject failure that they could not catch their breath.

Then she closed her eyes and drifted off to sleep beside Southampton one final time.

Winter softened into spring, then ripened into summer. Henry's wife fell pregnant and lost the babe, remaining so ill that she sometimes could not even stand up from bed. She was weak and wan, and so Emilia sourced chamomile and gingerroot and peppermint from the apothecary, hoping to create a tea that would allow Joyce to keep food down and regain her strength.

She was humming to herself as she turned onto her street, but the notes fell away as she noticed a nobleman standing in front of her door.

Not a nobleman, exactly. More like a young buck. He couldn't have been more than sixteen, but he was dressed as finely as a courtier. Perhaps a boy hoping for Henry to play at a fete. "If you've come to see my son," Emilia said, "I'm afraid he is not at home."

"Mistress Lanier?" the boy said, his face lighting with recognition.

He was staring at her so intently that she felt a shudder race down her spine. "Sir?" she asked. "Have we met?"

"In a manner," he said. He glanced down the street at a woman who was beating a feather bed and watching them nosily. "Have you a place we might speak privately?"

Emilia nodded, inviting him into her home. Joyce was sleeping, and Bess was still at market. She offered him ale, which he declined. He shifted uncomfortably, as if he could not find the words to explain what he wished.

She waited, and then she sighed. "You have me at a disadvantage, sir," Emilia said. "As you know me, yet I do not know you."

"I am Southampton," the boy said, and she fell back as if she'd been struck.

The fourth Earl of Southampton did not look like his father. He had black hair and dark eyes and narrow features. He could likely feel her gaze roaming over his face, and he offered a small smile. "It is said I take after my mother," he offered.

"I am sorry for your loss, my lord," Emilia said.

"I am sorry for yours," he replied. He pulled a small velvet pouch from the inside of his doublet. Reaching for her hand, he spilled the contents into her palm. Emilia's own face, in miniature, looked up at her.

"This was among his personal effects, when he . . . when his body was returned to us," the young earl said. "He kept it with him, always. When I was just a boy, I found it once on his dressing table and he thrashed me for even touching it. It was the only time he paid attention to me, in truth." He took a step backward, as if he knew he'd said too much. "I think you should keep it, mistress. I would not wish for my mother to have to stumble upon this and suffer the loss of him twice."

She nodded, closing her hands around the small brooch. The filigree of the frame bit into her skin. She wondered to whom the young man had shown the tiny painting to identify her by name. If the courtier who had seen it

said, *Oh yes, that's Hunsdon's former piece.*
"Thank you, my lord," Emilia managed.

"Call me Thomas. Please." He looked at her for a long moment. "You made him happy?"

How to answer? She did not know his history and did not deserve to. Had Thomas been the product of a marriage that was merely a business transaction? Had he never seen love modeled for him? Had he wondered what made his father distant, what piece of the man he would never have?

"I believe I did, for a while," Emilia said softly.

He jerked his chin, as if coming to a decision. "I am glad of it." He turned, preparing to leave.

"Wait," Emilia called. "He, too, was young, when he became earl." She wanted to give him a gift, as he had given her. "He didn't like it."

Thomas smiled ruefully. "Perhaps we have something in common after all."

"Very few of us get the lives we wish for," Emilia said.

The boy let the words settle between them. "All the more reason," he said gently, "to find those few minutes that we are happy." He started for the door. "God be with you, mistress."

When he left, Emilia stood in the silence, looking at the woman she used to be. She turned on her heel and went into her bedroom. She no longer kept the miniature of Southampton hidden in her feather bed; she had no reason to. Instead, it was in a small wooden chest with the most precious things she owned: her first publication, a ribbon Kit had used as a bookmark, a wooden heart that her son had whittled for her.

She slipped the miniature inside, nestling it beside the ivory oval with Southampton's portrait. "There," Emilia said, softly touching her fingertips to both paintings.

They were tangible proof that, once, she had been beloved. That she had loved.

She liked to think that Southampton, wherever he was now, was watching. That he knew, too, they were finally together.

When Emilia had been younger, she had drawn attention at times she did not wish to, due to her dark skin and light eyes and plush lips. It had been her beauty that engaged Hunsdon, that ensorcelled Southampton, that enraged Alphonso. But as she aged, her features faded.

The older women grew, the more invisible they became. As the currency of her face and form diminished — the only valuable parts of a woman, to society — so did she. Perhaps as a woman got older, her body and mind made the unconscious decision to live more in the past than the here and now — and that was why she hardly seemed present. Even in her own home, now occupied by Henry and Joyce and three-year-old Mary and baby Harry, Emilia often felt lonely. Today, the family was chattering about when Henry was going to court again and whether Harry had a tooth coming in. Emilia realized it had been hours since she had uttered a word . . . and no one missed her contributions.

"Well," Henry said, pushing back from the table where he had broken his fast. "If I am to ride with the others, I cannot be late." He was now an official flutist for the King, which provided security and income, and he traveled the circuit as the royal family decamped from palace to palace. Emilia had lost track of where they were headed today.

He wrapped his arms around Joyce's middle from behind. She squealed, dimpling at him over her shoulder. If Emilia was proud of anything, it was that Henry had found himself a love match. Little Harry was banging a spoon on the table while he sat on Bess's lap as she tried to feed him some sort of mash that popped out of his mouth as quickly as she popped it in. Mary lifted her arms to be picked up by Henry. "Papa," she cried, "I don't want you to go."

He stepped away from his wife and whirled his daughter into the air. "But," he reminded her, "I always come back, do I not?"

In her silence, from the sidelines, Emilia watched the play before her like the spectator she had become. *A comedy,* she thought. Henry has created his own happy ending.

Suddenly there was a scream as Mary fell hard to the stone floor. She started sobbing, and Joyce rushed to her side to soothe her. Harry burst into fearful tears at the clatter, too, distracting Bess — which meant that only Emilia saw what had happened.

One moment her son had been tossing his little girl into the air with a wide smile on his face, and the next, he had crumpled like a rag, his entire body buckling as he clutched his hand over his chest.

"Henry!" she cried, vaulting from the table to kneel at his side. He had collapsed on his belly and she rolled him over, seeing the blood gush from where he'd hit his nose, and his hand still spasming over his chest. His eyes were wide and frightened, the silver sparking like lightning. "Mama . . ." The tendons of his throat stretched, his face a rictus of agony.

She grabbed his hand. "Henry, I'm right here."

By now, Joyce realized he had fallen. She threw herself across his body, crying, until Emilia grabbed her hard by her shoulders. "Take the children away," she said, her voice low and fierce. "We must find a doctor."

"Daddy?" Mary said, her face a pinched white oval.

"Joyce," Emilia ordered, and her daughter-in-law snapped into action, sweeping the little

girl into her arms and plucking the baby from Bess's lap.

"I'll go for the doctor," Bess said, and she ran out the door.

Emilia heard Joyce bustling the children up the stairs, but she did not take her eyes off Henry's face. He was staring at her the way he had as a child, when thunderstorms shook the beams of the ceiling, when nightmares clawed at him from beneath the bed: as if her proximity was the only thing keeping danger at bay. "I am here," Emilia whispered again, squeezing his hand.

"Mama." He swallowed, struggling, gasping. His body was tighter than the strings of a lute. His fingers curled into a fist over his ribs, and she knew — even though she was no physician — that was what had seized up inside him.

An apoplexy.

Henry's heart, the one constant in her life. It had beat for her, it had bled for her, it had been large enough to hold her mistakes. How could she not have anticipated that it would break underneath the load it had borne for so many years?

Joyce returned, falling to her knees on Henry's other side. "You will be well, my sweet," she said, a smile pasted on a face streaked with tears.

Henry looked at her, and then turned back to Emilia. "Mama, promise."

She could not speak. Her throat was dammed.

"Love them," Henry ground out, and the light banked in his eyes.

A year after Henry died, so did Joyce.

At sixty-six, Emilia was raising Mary and Harry. She, who had always wanted more children, now had two of the sweetest in her care. She read to them, she fed them, she coddled them, she sang to them. The lullaby they liked the most was the tune she had written for Desdemona in the revision to *Othello*: "Willow, willow, willow." It had become the story of her life. Even as the tree's branches were dragged low by wind or rain or ice, it never broke. It gave, just enough, to survive.

As the money she had received for her share of the Folio dried up, Emilia found herself struggling to provide for her grandchildren. Her cousin Jeronimo had died earlier that year, so she did not have him to turn to. When Emilia was desperate for income to cover expenses for her household and Alma's, she sued Alphonso's other brother, Clement, who had taken over the hay patent after Innocent's death.

She sat in the King's Bench courtroom at Westminster Hall, once again facing down a relative of Alphonso's: she had played this scene before. The older she grew, the more her life felt like that. She would be at the table with her hands in a heap of flour and little Mary beside her, fashioning a small mouse out of dough that would be baked in the ashes of the hearth, just like her father had done for Emilia at her age. She would hold Harry in her arms as they crossed the Thames in a wherry, pointing at the splash of the oars and telling him stories of sea monsters who lived in the waves and the mermaids they loved, and she would be whisked back to a similar voyage with Henry in her arms.

Sometimes Emilia felt so old. Other times she was twenty-three, her face flushed with sunlight and lovemaking, the whole of her life spread out before her like a vibrant bolt of silk. She was a strange chimera — an old woman's form wrapped like loose batting around a young woman's dreams. Back then she had believed that every action, every step, would bring her closer to God. Now she knew it was so, but in a much more literal way. When you knew you would be gone soon, what scores did you settle before you left?

She knew she had said these same phrases before to a chief justice about assumpsit and debts owed.

She glanced over her shoulder, hoping for a ghost.

"I have two grandchildren to provide for," she told the chief justice.

That last spoken sentence, at least, was new.

The chief justice pushed his spectacles up

his nose. "You are saying, Mistress Lanier, that although you were owed twenty pounds over these years, you have received only eight pounds?"

"That is correct, sir."

He turned to Clement. "What say you?"

Like all of Alphonso's brothers, he had a face like a fox — black eyes, twitchy nose. "This is the first I've heard of it."

"He lies," Emilia snapped.

The serjeant representing Clement shuffled through some papers. "A man cannot be blamed for that which he does not know."

"Why not?" Emilia said. "Women are, all the time."

There was a collective huff in the courtroom, and for a moment, Emilia wondered if she had overstepped. She knew matrons who'd said less provocative words yet had been thrown into prison on the presumption of witchery.

But the chief justice laughed. "Mistress, I hope your grandchildren pay heed to you, lest they face the sharp edge of your tongue. Master Lanier, you will be obliged to pay Mistress Lanier the remaining twelve pounds owed."

Emilia sat for a moment, staring down at her hands as if they belonged to a stranger: the brown age spots, the fine wrinkles. These were not the graceful fingers of a courtesan and had not been so for a long time. They were the hands of a woman who had worked hard to survive. They had clawed her to safety, grabbed at wishes, mixed and baked and bleached and swept, shaken and soothed, held her son and her son's son, bled ink. They told her story.

Emilia glanced over her shoulder again, wishing for Southampton, but this time he wasn't there.

This time, Emilia had rescued herself.

The bride was missing. Henry Young stood at the altar with the priest, shifting uncomfortably from side to side. The groom's mother and uncle kept darting glances across the church to the pew where Emilia sat beside her grandson. "Gram," Harry whispered, "where is Badger?"

His voice cracked on the endearment he used for his sister — the endearment that he'd used to taunt her when they were small. Back then, it had been the way little Harry could get a surefire rise out of Mary, nearly four years older and apt to ignore him. Now the word held all the affection he felt for his sister, and his worry. At fourteen Harry was only trying on the shape of manhood, with his narrow shoulders broadening and fuzz on his upper lip — but his protective instincts were already firm. "Do you think she's well?"

Emilia didn't know how to answer that. She and Harry had left Mary, in her finest dress with a crown of flowers in her hair, in the vestibule at the rear of the church. The girl had seemed hopeful, happy.

She stood, smiling, and put her hand on Harry's arm. "Leave it with me," she said. The Young family began whispering to each other; she knew that they felt Henry was marrying below their station already; this was yet another strike against Mary. Emilia leaned toward Harry, murmuring, "Do keep them from bloodshed."

When she reached the vestibule she knocked softly. The door swung open beneath her hand, but the room was empty.

Emilia glanced toward the waiting groom and the clergyman, and then slipped quietly into the churchyard and down the street, deep in thought. Where would Mary have gone?

She found herself gravitating not toward their lodging but to the part of town where they had lived when her son and his wife were still alive. Emilia had moved several times since then with her grandchildren and Bess. But that first set of rooms — where she had become a widow, where Henry had brought his new wife, where Mary had been born — held the happiest ghosts. When she thought back to those apartments, she heard the music of Henry's flute and a crackling hearth and the giggles of babes. It was the symphony of *family*.

Perhaps Mary felt the same.

New renters lived in the rooms now, but there was a small patch of woods not far away, a garden that had once belonged to a grand lord and had been lured back to wildness. Emilia picked through a thicket that tore at her stockings until she found the elm tree she herself had taught her grandchildren how to climb. On the overgrown grass at its base sat a flower crown. Emilia glanced up to see two booted feet dangling from an upper limb. Mary's face was obscured by leaves and branches.

"Well," Emilia said. "I certainly can't climb up there anymore, so you'd best get down."

Mary's face peered through the greenery. "You found me," she said.

"Always," Emilia promised. She waited for the girl to make her way to the ground, landing light as a cat at her side.

"Does everyone hate me?" Mary asked, her eyes damp.

Emilia threaded her arm through her granddaughter's. "Nobody hates you," she said. "Do you wish to talk about it?"

"What if I don't?"

"Then we shall sit here," Emilia said, "until the sun goes down, and rises again."

A small laugh hiccuped out of Mary. "We'll grow hungry."

"Well," Emilia agreed, "there is that." She smoothed the girl's hair. "What is it, sweetling?"

"I cannot bear to marry him," Mary burst out.

Emilia had been expecting this. "You are young yet." Mary was only seventeen. "You do not have to be in a rush."

"But I love him!"

"If he loves you," Emilia replied, "he will wait until you're ready."

Mary leaned against the wide trunk of the tree, her brow pinched. "When you married, Gram," she asked, "were you scared?"

How to respond? Emilia had been furious, humiliated, broken. She had not wanted Alphonso; she would have run to the ends of England to get away from him, if it were possible. "What you're feeling is what every bride feels," she said finally.

Mary seemed relieved. "You understand then how terrifying it is to care so much." Another tear streaked down her cheek. "What if I lose Henry, too?"

This was not what Emilia had expected after all. Mary wasn't having second thoughts. Instead she suffered from a surfeit of good sense: once you had everything you'd ever wished for, you could not help but fear the moment you wouldn't.

She folded her granddaughter into her arms. Mary's father and mother had died in quick succession. Emilia could not speak to loving a spouse so wholly, but she knew what it was to give yourself completely to someone, only

715

to be left behind. They took the best parts of you with them. "Oh, chicken," she sighed. "That's the cost of finding your soulmate."

"If I do not marry," Mary said stubbornly, "then I'll never have to worry about living without him."

"Do you truly think your feelings for Henry will fade simply because you do not put your name beside his in the church register? If he's the one for you, and you choose not to spend your days with him out of fear of loving too much, you're only punishing yourself." Emilia smiled gently. "He adores you, Mary."

"I know."

"There is so much in the world to diminish us. If you find someone or something that makes you feel larger than life, my darling, grab tight with both hands. You may be thrown to the ground at some point. You may break into pieces." Emilia touched her granddaughter's cheek. "But, oh, Mary . . . what a ride."

Mary reached for her flower crown and turned it in her hands like a wheel. "Even though it hurts?" she asked, her voice small.

Emilia looked into the girl's eyes. They were silver; her eyes, her son's eyes. Mary would go on to marry Henry Young, and they would have a daughter one day with the same unusual eyes. That daughter would have a daughter, and so on, and so on — passing along the gaze that gleamed like a polished blade, that could cut as cleanly. But Emilia's features were not all that would be handed down through generations. She imagined Mary telling her own granddaughter one day that a life well loved was a life well lived. "Even though it hurts," Emilia repeated, nodding.

"I wish my parents could be here at the wedding," Mary confessed.

"They will be," Emilia promised. So would Southampton and Hunsdon, Jeronimo and Alma, Odyllia — all the people whose threads were woven into the history of this sensitive, beautiful young woman. Maybe that was the lesson Emilia had been struggling to learn all this time — that being remembered by many was far less important than being remembered by a few who mattered.

Suddenly Mary turned a panicked gaze toward her. "What excuse shall I give?"

"That you forgot to bank the fire."

"But it is June. There is no fire in the hearth."

"A wise husband," Emilia said, smiling, "knows better than to contradict his wife." She took the flower crown and set it on her granddaughter's red hair. "There," she pronounced. "You are perfect."

As if the coronet had transformed her, Mary dashed forward, any lingering doubt evaporating like mist. She leaped into the brambles that carpeted the forest floor. "Come, Gram," she teased. "We are already late!"

Emilia laughed. "Yes, yes," she said. She ran a few steps until a cough rattled her, and she fought to catch her breath.

"Gram?" Mary asked, turning back. "Are you well?"

Emilia held one hand to her chest, the other resting on her hip. She took small sips of air. "My granddaughter is getting married," she said brightly. "I have never been better."

It had begun with the cough, and had evolved into an ailment that even children suffered, that Emilia herself had contracted and recovered from a dozen or more times over the course of her seventy-six years. She felt her skin sear, too sensitive even to be covered by the light blanket Bess tried to throw over her. She marveled that she had survived multiple outbreaks of the plague in England, yet would be felled by a common cold.

But it hadn't been common. The cough had only gotten worse, dry and hacking. The scratch in the back of her throat had turned pustulant and swollen. Then the fever had come, bringing a strange haze that blurred the line between waking and sleep.

She did not think it would be long now.

Bess tried to spoon cool ale into her mouth, but Emilia knocked the liquid away. "Bring me . . ." she rasped. She lifted a shaking hand, pointing to the latched wooden box that sat beside her hairbrush.

"Yes, mistress," Bess said, letting go of her hand only to do her bidding. Bess, who'd been so long at Emilia's side.

She starting coughing again, and Bess hauled her slight frame more upright, so that she could breathe easier. The wooden box sat in her lap, the blanket pooled around it. Emilia tried to undo the clasp, and when she couldn't, Bess reached over to flip it free.

The wooden heart that her son had carved her from wood years ago was gone; she'd given it to Harry when he came to visit earlier today — or had that been yesterday? She had given Mary the ribbon that once had belonged to Kit. There was relief in knowing they were settled. Mary and her husband would take care of Harry until he struck out on his own.

She knew they would remember her as the grandmother who had raised them, who had held them when they were ill. The one who taught them how to split open the seedlings of a maple with your thumb and drop them from a height so that they plummeted from the sky. She'd told them how a falcon's broken wing could be fixed with the feather of another bird, knit together like new. She'd described how a pineapple burst on your tongue, sweet and sour all at once. And she'd spun them so many stories, of doomed lovers and jealous faeries and clever girls, playing all the parts at once.

Emilia pushed the box toward Bess. "Keep these for me, when I am gone."

The maid peered inside. Two miniatures stared up at her, faces Bess would easily recognize. "Mistress, I cannot —"

"There will come a time when you may need to trade them for coin," Emilia interrupted. "When you do, all I ask is that you sell them together."

Bess nodded, her fingertips glancing over the ivory oval of Southampton's portrait, and the spikier edge of Emilia's. Beneath them, yellowed and folded into quarters, was the first play Emilia had ever written. *Arden of Faversham* curled at the edges, cushioning the bottom of the box as newsprint lined a birdcage. Bess, who had never learned to read, would think it nothing more than padding to keep the miniatures safe and dry.

Perhaps that was the only thing it was good for, after all.

She could hear Bess crying softly, and she reached for the maid's hand. "You have been my constant," Emilia whispered. "I am glad it was you with me, at the end."

She wished she could say more. She wished there were enough words to thank Bess. She wished she could apologize for taking the maid, all those years ago, from the relative comfort of Somerset House and consigning her to a service where she had once shared a bed with her mistress to ensure Emilia wasn't killed by her husband.

Emilia closed her eyes. *All right, God,* she thought. *I am ready.*

One moment, Emilia was clutching the edge of the blanket so tight, and the next, she was not.

She was standing, shivering in her shift, but she was not the woman she had been that morning. The gray tangle of her hair was again a black braid twining halfway down her back. Her arms were smooth, her face unlined. Her eyes were so clear that the edges of the door-way in front of her were sharper than a knife.

She knew this door. It was the one that had led from the Baron's study to the gardens behind Willoughby House. Back then Emilia had struggled to unlatch the heavy door, to escape to the hedges, where she could create make-believe worlds.

Now, when Emilia reached for the handle, it opened easily.

It did not lead outside, however. She found herself in a white space with no walls or ceiling or floor. It was just light, as if she'd blinked and found herself on the glowing surface of the moon.

"Hello."

When she heard a man's voice behind her, she spun so fast she nearly tripped. Her heart slugged against her ribs. *Please let it be him who has come for me.*

But when her eyes adjusted, it was not Southampton at all. It was Kit, arms folded, impatient, as if he'd been there for a while.

"Oh," Emilia cried. "I've missed you."

His eyes gleamed. "Death, it turns out, is an excellent professional move," Kit said. "But, Mouse, we've all been waiting for you."

She took a step forward and realized that there was nothing tethering her. "You . . . have?"

"You did not think we would start without you, did you?"

There was so much she wanted to ask. She heard herself say, "Will they know me?"

Kit softened. "You've done so much more than most women could," he said.

Her eyes filled with tears. "I do not think it made a difference."

"Did it not? Even if you do not feel the shade of the tree you planted, others will."

She looked up at him. "But what of the person who planted the seed?"

"Is that more important than what she produced?"

"Why must it be one or the other?" Emilia challenged. "Why not both?"

He held out his hand. "Mouse?"

She took it, and they began walking. Since everything was painfully white, she could not see any progress they made. "You know, it takes a hundred years for a river to change course, from silt or stone deposits under the surface," Kit said. "No one sees what's causing it, but a century later, the water flows in a different direction. No one can dispute the change."

Emilia considered this. Facts, seen from different angles, could be dismissed as fictions, and vice versa. There was a reason you could not create history without writing the word *story*.

She looked at the dear, familiar face of her friend. "How far do we have to go?"

"Ages," Kit replied.

Emilia glanced down to see something beneath her feet, a black curl of smoke that pressed against each sole whenever she took a step. No, not smoke. Words. One for each tread. She began to string them together, speaking haltingly out loud. *"From . . . hence . . . your memory . . . death cannot take,"* she read. *"Although in me each part will be forgotten . . . Your name from hence immortal life shall have . . ."*

Kit had stopped walking. *"Though I, once gone, to all the world must die."* He smiled at Emilia. "I rather liked that one."

It had been a sonnet, one she'd traded to Shakespeare like a magic bean from a fairy tale in hopes that the greater reward would be hers.

The poetry would last. The poet would not.

Emilia swallowed, because she knew that Kit was using her poem to say it was time, it was the end. Her eyes darted over his shoulder, hoping to see what came next. But what she spied was unfamiliar: buildings that pierced clouds, girls dressed like boys, carriages pulled by sorcery.

She thought, for just a moment, there was something she recognized.

A theater. An audience. A woman with silver eyes. A comedy, a tragedy.

There once was a girl who became invisible so that her words might not be.

She turned to ask Kit about this vision, but he was gone, and she was no longer in the white space. She was sitting on a carved bench beneath the embrace of a lush emerald willow, a tale on her tongue.

There once was a girl, Emilia thought: *A beginning and an end.*

There was poetry that, once spoken, could not be unheard.

There was a story, whether or not others ever chose to listen.

MELINA
DECEMBER 2027

"There once was a girl," said the narrator, standing in a narrow shaft of light, "who became invisible so that her words might not be."

The actress playing Emilia stepped forward. "There once was a girl. A beginning and an end."

They linked hands. "There was a story," the narrator finished, "whether or not others ever chose to listen."

Blackout.

The most extraordinary moment of any show was the hiccup of time between the last line and the applause. It took only a heartbeat for the audience to leave the world of the play to regain footing in this one — but, oh, those seconds were precious. It was the proof that they'd taken a journey; and that they'd come home changed.

Melina sat in the front row at the Athena Playhouse, listening to the final sentence of the play she had written.

Opening night of *By Any Other Name* was a

sellout, as would be the rest of its run. Melina felt Andre jump to his feet to the left of her, and wolf whistle at the line of actors.

She had kept his revised ending, because Andre was right. Being named *was* important. It gave you credit for the work you put into the world, but it also held you responsible for your words and deeds when you hurt the people you loved, even inadvertently. In the *Playbill,* Andre was acknowledged for contributing additional material.

To her right, her father let go of Beth's hand to clap furiously. When he'd seen that in her *Playbill* bio Melina had dedicated this show to her mother, he'd teared up. Now, he threw his arms around Melina and hugged her so tight she couldn't breathe.

It didn't matter. If she died now, she would die happy.

The actors took another bow as Jasper emerged from stage right to another enthusiastic round of appreciation. He was carrying a huge bouquet of roses in one hand. "Tonight we have the honor of having the playwright in the house," he said, looking down at Melina.

She shook her head, paralyzed. Last night, Jasper had pleaded with her to take a bow. He'd been relentless, really, creatively finding ways to make her agree. She had been half out of her mind at the feeling of his hands on her body; had she actually promised him she would take the stage?

Andre took the decision from her, spinning Melina and giving her a push toward the steps that led to stage left. She surfed the wave of a standing ovation as she climbed the stairs and ducked behind the curtain. She could see Jasper grinning, and the beaming, exhausted smiles of the actors.

To Melina's great shock, there was an actress in the wings blocking her way.

The woman was in period costume, likely a member of the ensemble. Melina hated the thought that one of the performers had not made it onstage quickly enough to take a bow. "You should be out there," she said, over the roar of clapping, and the actress turned.

Melina found herself staring into a shrewd pair of silver eyes.

As silver as a metal that would never be as precious as gold.

As silver as the hopeful lining of a cloud.

As silver as her own.

Melina felt a hard shove between her shoulder blades and stumbled onto the stage. She glanced over her shoulder, but the spot where the woman had been a moment before was utterly empty.

Jasper was waiting. So was the company that had brought her words to life; and all the future ideas she had yet to voice.

There once was a girl, Melina thought, as she stepped front and center, *who was seen.*

AUTHOR'S NOTE

As an English major in the 1980s, I'd been introduced to the question of Shakespeare's authorship only in passing, since most professors who make their living teaching Shakespeare have little inclination to bite the hand that feeds them. I decided to do a bit of digging on the actual historical records we have for the man from Stratford — and what I found completely rocked my beliefs.

What do we know about William Shakespeare? He was the son of a glover. He had three children — a daughter, Susanna, and then twins — one of which, Hamnet, died of the plague. He was not formally educated. He acted in various theatrical troupes, and there are pay stubs to prove it. He was a shareholder in the Lord Chamberlain's Men, which became the King's Men. He and his father were obsessed with obtaining a family crest, which they finally did.

He also was kind of a jerk.

He married Anne Hathaway after getting

her pregnant. He evaded taxes, twice, and had a restraining order taken out on him by colleagues. He was fined for hoarding grain during a famine and hiking up the price to gouge his neighbors.

Here's what there is *no record* of in Shakespeare's life: that he was an author.

True, documentation from four hundred years ago is not abundant. But other playwrights and poets of the time referenced each other. Their names and authorship were written in the ledgers of theater company owners. They were lauded publicly at the time of their death or buried in Poets' Corner at Westminster Abbey. They left behind books and manuscripts in their wills.

Moreover, although every other playwright of the time collaborated — there were no copyrights back then, and plays were adjusted by whoever was available to fit the growth and ebb of theater companies — Shakespeare apparently did *not.* In fact, a mythology has sprung up that Shakespeare managed to write thirty-seven plays alone while simultaneously being a full-time actor and producer.

Yet other writers of the time questioned Shakespeare's authorship. In 1595, poet Thomas Edwards, in " 'Narcissus,' L'Envoy" *(Cephalus and Procris),* referred to the writer of *Venus and Adonis* as "deafly masking thro / Stately troupes rich conceited." In other words, whoever the author was, they were hiding behind a literary mask. Joseph Hall, in 1597, described an unnamed author as a cuttlefish, someone hidden in "the Black cloud" of ink who shifted their fame "onto another's name." Even if it wasn't Shakespeare he was discussing, it suggests that using an allonym was common practice at the time. In 1611, poet John Davies praised "Our English Terence Mr. Will: Shakespeare." On the surface this is a compliment, comparing Shakespeare to the Roman playwright known for his comedies. But it was also widely believed that some of Terence's work was written by other authors, like Scipio and Laelius, who relinquished the credit to him.

There is nothing suggesting Shakespeare ever played a musical instrument, although there are a couple thousand musical references in his plays. He humanized Jews, at a time when anti-Semitism was the norm. He never spent time at court or in the military, although these feature in his writing. He was not a lawyer but wrote extensively about the law. He never went to Denmark, but described the actual layout of Kronborg Castle in *Hamlet,* and used the unique names Rosencrantz and Guildenstern — visitors to the court whom he had not met. He never went to Italy but decided to write multiple Italian wedding comedies — peppering them not just with formal Italian but colloquialisms

731

transliterated into English. Although other famous men of his time documented their travels religiously, there's no evidence Shakespeare ever left England — however, his plays mention things that were not written about in the guidebooks of the time: interior canal systems in Italy that are mentioned in *Two Gentlemen of Verona* and that were known only to locals; a fresco in the town of Bassano, Italy, that features heavily in *Othello;* a sycamore grove mentioned by Benvolio in *Romeo and Juliet* that is geographically very specific and accurate.

But what really irked me (and stuck like a splinter in my mind) was that Shakespeare had created some of the most clever, fierce, protofeminist characters in all of literature — Portia, Beatrice, Rosalind, Viola, Lady Macbeth, Juliet, Katherine, Cleopatra — but he never taught his own daughters to read or write. They both signed with a mark.

I. Do. Not. Buy. It.

As Melina muses, just because there is an absence of evidence doesn't mean there is evidence of absence. It seemed logical to me that there might have been other explanations and other writers who were contributors or authors of the plays attributed to Shakespeare who, for one reason or another, had been elided from history. But it was Elizabeth Winkler's essay in *The Atlantic,* "Was Shakespeare a Woman?" that caught my attention.

732

She wrote about Emilia Bassano — someone I'd never heard of — a converso Jew who was the first woman to publish a book of poetry in England.

There is very little known of Emilia's actual life, but the spare facts we do have come from the diary of Simon Forman, the astrologer/doctor she visited when she hoped to conceive another child. In "Astrologicalle Judgmentes of Physick," Forman says that if a female client had secrets about her past, especially sexual ones, he would focus his consultation on sex (MS Ashmole 363, ff. 138v–140v, paragraph 1930). Emilia's initial visit on May 17, 1597, illustrates this technique (MS Ashmole, 226, f. 95v). He insults her and she responds by describing herself as a sophisticated, tasteful woman. He adds she "had a child in fornication . . . et sodomita" (the child was illegitimate and she was sexually progressive) and "She was paramour to my old L. of Hunsdean that was L Chamberline and was maintained in great pride and yt seams that being with child she was for collour married to a minstrel." We also learn that Emilia was brought up by the Countess of Kent, and that Hunsdon "kept her longe." Forman concludes Emilia needs money and will have sex with him in return for it (he uses the term *halek* for intercourse). According to his notes, she never consented.

Other salient moments from the casebooks:

May 13, 1597: Forman incorrectly calls her Millia and mistakes her age for twenty-four (she was twenty-seven). Her address is mentioned: Longditch at Westminster.

May 17, 1597: Labels her as the daughter of "Baptista Bassane and Margarete Jhonson [*sic*]." Alphonso Lanier, her husband's name, is written in the margins.

June 3, 1597: Emilia asks Forman whether her husband will be made a knight, and whether she will get pregnant again. Forman says "he shall . . . but shalbe first in despaire of it" and he says she will miscarry. Emilia also discusses her financial situation with Hunsdon, who kept her in "great pomp" and gave her "40 pounds a yere." Forman says she is "hie minded" and boastful of her beauty. He also notes "she hath a son his name is henri."

June 16, 1597: Emilia asks again whether Alphonso will have military success; Forman says yes, but he'll be "in perill of his life" first.

September 2, 1597: Emilia admits that her husband has spent all her money. The entry concludes with a physical observation of "a wart or a moulle in the pit of [her] throte."

September 10, 1597: Forman asks Emilia if she will "halek" with him.

September 11, 1597: Forman says he was invited to Emilia's home, but "could not hallek."

September 17, 1597: Forman does not respond to Emilia's request for a visit since she turned down his advances: "She seemed a freind [*sic*] and is not so."
There are also diary entries on September 29 and November 25, 1597, and January 7, 1600. In the last, he asks "wher she intende any more villani or noe." In addition to being a predator, he apparently did not take rejection well.
These facts and others about Emilia in my novel were scrupulously curated through research in books and interviews with academics. I have tried to be as accurate as possible, but because this is a novel, there were a few places I chose to depart from fact:

1. Fletcher and Beaumont *were* arrested for treason for discussing how to kill a fictional king in a co-written play — but in 1620, years after I placed the conversation in Marlowe's mouth.

2. We don't know where Shakespeare was in 1586. It's part of the "lost years," but it has been hypothesized he could have been part of the troupe the Queen's Men after they swung through Stratford and may have gone from there

into Lord Strange's Men with the actor John Heminges. Also, we know that the Queen's Men performed histories that might have led to the Henry plays and King John. It is widely believed that by 1592, when I theorize Emilia met Shakespeare, he was acting with Pembroke's Men — and that is indeed the troupe that first performed *The Taming of the Shrew.*

3. The Earl of Southampton has never been linked romantically to Emilia Bassano. They would have met and traveled in the same circles for the ten years she was with Lord Hunsdon. He was considered very handsome, and was much closer to her age. The fawning dedications to him in the long poems *Venus and Adonis* and *Rape of Lucrece* started a whole scholarly tangent on whether Shakespeare was bisexual. This is of course possible . . . or perhaps the poems were written by a straight woman and dedicated to her male lover — particularly *Venus and Adonis,* which is about an older woman seducing a younger, innocent man. (It is worth noting, too, that although academics are quick to say that Southampton was a great patron of the arts and that's why Shakespeare dedicated the long poems to him, Southampton was

a teenager at the time and likely not the mover and shaker in the theater world that he became in later life.) We also know historically that Southampton is descended from Viscount Montagu — Romeo's surname. Additionally, *Romeo and Juliet* is the only Shakespearean play where a female character's age is mentioned multiple times (Juliet is thirteen, the same age Emilia was when she became Hunsdon's mistress, and much is made of whether she is ready for marriage). Finally, Southampton *did* legally intercede for Emilia, in her later years, to get money she was due for her dead husband's hay patent. It seemed to me that if he was involved with her later in life, she likely had a connection with him earlier. I saw enough historical threads to weave them into a relationship — plus I wanted Emilia, fictionally, to have a little happiness. (More on this later.)

4. We do not know for certain if Emilia wrote *Hamlet,* but she was either in Denmark or in very close proximity to the Danish ambassador, Peregrine Bertie — the Baron in my novel who was the brother of the Countess of Kent, Emilia's guardian. It felt more realistic for me to ascribe that text to her than to

Shakespeare, who never went to Denmark and would have had no reason to know the namesakes for Rosencrantz and Guildenstern, or the Amleth mythology, or the very specific references to recorder playing given to the players by Hamlet. Also, Ophelia's name is so close to Odyllia, Emilia's deceased daughter — to me it felt like an immortalization of her in text, and I felt that as a grieving parent, Emilia might also immortalize Shakespeare's deceased son by renaming the tortured hero from the Saxo myth (Amleth) to Hamlet (which is stylistically equivalent to the name of Shakespeare's boy, Hamnet, back in the 1600s when spelling wasn't standardized).

5. There's no proof that Alphonso beat Emilia, but we do know that their marriage was never a happy one, and that he did squander away all the money Hunsdon settled on her when they parted ways.

6. Emilia's letter to the unborn Henry is fictional, but we know it was very common for pregnant women during that time period to write "mother's legacies," which basically recognized the danger of childbirth. In these legacies, women would tell their unborn child, "I may

not live to see you, so I want to shape your personality with these words I leave behind for you." These letters are some of the only documented writing we have left from women in Elizabethan times.

7. We do not know for certain if Emilia wrote any of the sonnets, but we do know that other poets wrote child loss elegies — like Ben Jonson's "On My First Son." The sonnet I attributed to Emilia after Odyllia's death reads quite differently when you frame it as a mother lost in grief.

Over the years, people who are skeptical of Shakespeare's authorship have latched on to various potential authors. Christopher Marlowe has been proposed as a candidate, but he died before all the plays were written. The Earl of Oxford is a frontrunner because of his travels, his love of theater and music, his personal knowledge of Italy, his bisexuality, his extensive education, his access to court and military life and the law. As part of the aristocracy, he could patronize theater troupes but it would have been scandalous to be credited as a playwright. However, Oxford, too, died before all the plays were completed. Francis Bacon is a contender but had no connection to theater and his work for the Queen left him little time to write thirty-seven plays.

Mary Sidney Herbert is one candidate who didn't die before Shakespeare, and whose love life mirrored the relationships in the sonnets: after her husband died, she had an affair with Matthew Lister, a young doctor she couldn't marry because he was not nobility. Mary Sidney Herbert also was a known writer, editing her brother's books after his death, and creating closet dramas she presented at her country home.

And then there's Emilia Bassano. There are elements of Emilia's life — her hidden Judaism, her placement as a courtesan for a much older man, her legendary beauty, her Italian heritage, her musically gifted family, her wild swings from a courtier's life to a woman who outlived her children and was buried in an unmarked grave — that spoke to me of what it was like to be a woman with something to say, who was never given a voice. For that reason, I've chosen to make her the star of this novel.

In reality, Alexander Waugh is probably right — he's proposed the theory that Edward de Vere, the Earl of Oxford, organized a writer's room of sorts, and that Shakespeare was an allonym used by them all; that the plays and poems we credit to a single man were penned by multiple writers. I believe that among these collaborators were Mary Sidney Herbert and Emilia Bassano.

How could Emilia have gotten connected to the Earl of Oxford? Well, Oxford's sister, Mary de Vere, married the Baron — Peregrine Bertie. And, of course, Oxford and Lord Hunsdon would have moved in the same circles at court.

I get a lot of hate mail — it's part of the job when one's novels cover gun control, abortion rights, Covid, and more — but I'm expecting the antagonism to be off the charts for this novel. When Elizabeth Winkler wrote the *Atlantic* piece about other authorship, she received more hate mail than she ever had in her life. Shakespeare is not just a playwright; he's practically a religion. Despite the gaps in his history, many highly intelligent people are still not willing to entertain any other explanation except that the man from Stratford wrote those plays solo. In her new book, *Shakespeare Was a Woman and Other Heresies* (which I cannot recommend highly enough), Winkler wades through the transformation of Shakespeare from man to myth. His birthplace is a tourist attraction — *Come see where he took his meals! Here's where he is buried! Buy this tea towel with his face on it!* — and as a result of this bardolatry, Shakespeare has become a cottage industry. There are many reasons for this elevation of Shakespeare to a god — from the fall of organized religion in England post–Queen Victoria, to the creation of English literature as a subject meant to keep women occupied, to Germany's love of Shakespeare during WWI that made England claim him as a national product. Questioning his authorship is unwelcome; saying that the actual playwright was a woman is a whole other thing.

Why do people get even *more* upset at the thought that the real Shakespeare was a woman? Because there's no precedent for it, and it requires us to reevaluate everything we've been taught. For years we have been given a version of Shakespeare's work through a patriarchal lens, and it's hard to unlearn that. But it's vitally important to try to recover the writing women may have done in Elizabethan times — writing that was erased because it was not considered important. In addition to the "mother's legacies" — most of which have not survived the passage of time — we know that women were doing science in their kitchens: crafting medicines, testing methods of preservation, discovering pH balance. Women were grafting roots in their gardens, making cheese, growing rare plants — and as men learned about these endeavors and published the knowledge, the women's names fell away as the historical scientists of origin. Similarly, Shakespeare acolytes say there was no proof of women collaborating on plays at commercial playhouses. This is true. But just because we don't have written evidence doesn't mean it didn't happen. We know women were writing closet dramas for home performance. We know women were shareholders in theaters, costumers, ticket sellers. Not long after Emilia's death, in the 1660s, Aphra Behn became the first female professional playwright. Who's to say an Elizabethan woman didn't figure out how to anonymously get her words in front of audiences before that?

I'd like to leave you with Sonnet 81 — a sonnet that scholars have struggled to interpret, because it was written when the name Shakespeare was widely known and celebrated . . . yet reveals an author who knew he or she would be forgotten.

Or I shall live your epitaph to make,
Or you survive when I in earth am rotten,
From hence your memory death cannot
    take,
Although in me each part will be forgotten.
Your name from hence immortal life shall
    have,
Though I, once gone, to all the world must
    die:
The earth can yield me but a common
    grave,
When you entombed in men's eyes shall
    lie.
Your monument shall be my gentle verse,
Which eyes not yet created shall o'er-read;
And tongues to be your being shall
    rehearse,
When all the breathers of this world are
    dead;

You still shall live, such virtue hath my
  pen,
Where breath most breathes, even in the
  mouths of men.

But now imagine those words were written
by a brilliant woman who had been silenced
by societal restrictions. A woman who had
swung from a life on the arm of one of the
most important men in Queen Elizabeth's
court to one of virtual poverty. A woman
who outlived her lovers and her children. A
woman who grew up watching how her family's musical performances could move men
to tears and inspire them with courage. A
woman who immortalized herself and those
she loved in plays, at the great cost of losing
credit for those very words.

To paraphrase the final couplet of the sonnet: *Once I'm gone, I'm gone forever . . . but not
you. I will build you a monument of words. The
only power I have is in my pen — so you will live
on where life has no limit: in the mouths of men.*

Life has no limit, in the mouths of men.

That sonnet hits differently . . . when you
imagine Emilia writing it.

Although I cannot prove to you that Emilia
Bassano wrote any parts of the plays attributed to Shakespeare, neither can anyone prove
to me that she *didn't.* Certainly, she deserves
to be more than a footnote in history on her
own merit, because of the great achievement

of publishing a book of poetry at a time when women simply didn't *do* that.

No matter what, if you had not heard of Emilia before reading my novel, I hope that now you will never forget her.

I think she'd be pleased.

— *Jodi Picoult, June 2023*

Addendum, October 2023

After writing this manuscript, I went to London for work, and contacted the archivists at the Victoria and Albert Museum, where the famous miniature of Emilia Bassano is kept hidden away. Two very smart women, Dr. Adriana Concin and Dr. Rosalind McKever, showed me Emilia's portrait. Believed to be painted by Isaac Oliver, the student of Nicholas Hilliard, the miniature was set in a glass case with a handful of others accredited to Hilliard's studio. As remarkable as it was to see and hold Emilia's four-hundred-year-old portrait in my hands, my eye was drawn repeatedly to the miniature beside it — a young man with long, curly red hair, his hand slipped between the fastenings of his lacy shirt to cover his heart. Unlike the rest of the Hilliard/Oliver miniatures, the background was not a bright blue field, but a black one. "Who's that?" I asked the archivists, and I was told the portrait was of an "unknown man."

I took out my phone and pulled up a painting of the Earl of Southampton, Henry Wriothesley, aged twenty-one. The "unknown man" miniature looked like a younger version of the Earl.

The archivists were just as excited as I was. They checked the provenance of the miniature and confirmed that this "unknown man" and the Emilia miniature were painted at approximately the same time — around 1590. They told me that the miniature of the man was unusual because of the black background — which definitely would have been the choice of the person sitting for the portrait. On the back of the vellum on which the painting was made was the print of a playing card: the six of hearts.

The six of hearts, in cartomancy (the equivalent of tarot in Elizabethan times), represented romantic love — but the kind that couldn't last. It was a doomed love, a soulmate you would not have forever, an affair that was ephemeral. It's a card of romance, of transition, of loss. It would have been the choice of the person commissioning the portrait to have the painter include this as well.

You cannot imagine how stunned I was. There is no way of knowing, of course, that Southampton and Emilia sat for the portraits at the same time, or that when the "unknown man" asked the painter to put a black background of despair behind his image and to paint the six of hearts on the back of the miniature, he was sending a message about the impossibility of their relationship. But the archivists were as intrigued as I was and promised to do further research.

During the editing of *By Any Other Name,* I discovered a painting by John de Critz showing Southampton in his teens. The image had a remarkable similarity to the miniature of the "unknown man" at the Victoria and Albert museum. This inspired me to find the provenance of the first portrait of Southampton that I had pulled up on my phone to show the archivists. It is, as it turns out, a miniature of Southampton, painted when he was twenty-one, by Nicholas Hilliard — the very same artist who created the miniature of the "unknown man" about four years earlier. On the back of this later miniature, however, is the playing card of the *three* of hearts — which, in cartomancy, is a warning. It signifies that someone else has entered the bounds of your relationship with a loved one — someone who could ruin it.

That later miniature was painted in 1594 — the year that I posit, in my fictional account, that Emilia is beaten so badly by her husband, she winds up crawling to Southampton's house for help.

The archivists at the Victoria and Albert Museum are still doing research for confirmation, but agree that their miniature of the "unknown man" may indeed be a portrait of the teenage Southampton.

In a very weird, small, and beautiful way I feel like I might have given Emilia back the man she loved. Maybe fiction is fact; maybe the embellished history I created for her truly happened. But no matter what, in the archives of the Victoria and Albert Museum, Emilia Bassano gets to spend eternity nestled beside the Earl of Southampton — and something about that just feels *right*.

Portrait of Emilia Bassano (left), attributed to Isaac Oliver, c. 1590, in the archives of the Victoria and Albert Museum; portrait of an "unknown man" (right), attributed to Nicholas Hilliard, c. 1590, with the six of hearts printed on its back, in the archives of the V&A.

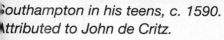

Southampton in his teens, c. 1590.
Attributed to John de Critz.

Miniature of Henry Wriothesley, third
Earl of Southampton, c. 1594.
Attributed to Nicholas Hilliard.
Vellum, with the three of hearts on
its back.

ACKNOWLEDGMENTS

Unlike those who have elevated Shakespeare to a one-man wonder who penned every word by himself, I am aware that no writing happens without collaboration. I was incredibly lucky, on this journey, to have so many people along for the ride to offer help, knowledge, and support.

I would like to thank the following:

For entertaining my theories about Emilia and/or inspiring me with their mastery of Shakespeare: Alicia Andrzejewski, Deborah Harkness, Elizabeth Winkler, Emma Whipday, John Hudson, Wendy Wall, Will Tosh, Lotte Wakeham, Morgan Lloyd Malcolm, and Sir Mark Rylance.

For sharing what it means to be a woman in theater: Theresa Rebeck, Natalie Margolin, and Kristen Anderson-Lopez.

For discussing the nuances of race and theater: Jiana Odland, Christine Pride, Jo Piazza, and Nikki Payne.

Thanks to Saskia Nesja, whom I taught

eighth-grade English and who — decades later — let me examine a First Folio at Eton.

Thank you to Dr. Adriana Concin and Dr. Rosalind McKever of the Victoria and Albert Museum, for being as swept away by Emilia as I am.

I greatly appreciate Clarence A. Haynes and Amber Salik for their nuanced sensitivity reads of the manuscript, and for their suggestions, which allowed me to make this a smarter, more empathetic book.

For being early readers, support systems, or for answering random texts, like "Where can someone disappear inside the NYPL?": Reba Gordon, Elyssa Samsel, Kate Anderson, Caroline White, Ashlee Latimer, Katie Desmond, Melody Wukitch, Michael Wagoner, Brigid Kemmerer, and S. J. Arnegger.

Thanks, Samantha van Leer, for letting me co-opt your story about the fish and the duck that meet on a pond. (She didn't write that as a play, but as a twenty-two-page short story, at age seven.)

A shout-out to Katherine Marsh, the president and librarian of the East Blue Hill Library in Maine, whose trustees bid in a character-naming auction and won her a mention in this novel.

Timothy Allen McDonald is my co-librettist for all my theater projects, including the script pages between these chapters. It doesn't escape me that this time around, a male

752

playwright is the silent partner of a woman playwright.

For keeping the Jodiverse alive: Laura Gross, Sanyu Dillon, Kara Welsh, Kim Hovey, Deb Aroff, Rachel Kind, Denise Cronin, Scott Shannon, Matthew Schwartz, Theresa Zoro, Paolo Pepe, Wendy Wong, Kathleen Quinlan, Corina Diez, Angie Campusano, Hope Hathcock, Kelly Chian, Susan Turner, Maggie Hart. Emily Isayeff and Susan Corcoran are proof that girls really do run the world; they've been cheering me on for years as I put this book together. Jennifer Hershey is the best editor in the business and the biggest champion of my writing — if Jennifer had been around in Elizabethan times, she would have made Emilia a household name and we'd be saying, "Shakespeare *who?*"

Finally, to Tim van Leer, the collaborator with whom I created my favorite three masterpieces — thanks for welcoming Emilia into our home while I obsessed about her, and for loving her as thoroughly as I did. Southampton's got *nothing* on you.

SHAKESPEAREAN
REFERENCES

Throughout the novel, Easter eggs have been left for those who wish to see how the events of Emilia's life, in my imagination, might have inspired writing that was attributed to Shakespeare:

Pp. 34, 44: Titania and Oberon: In *A Midsummer Night's Dream,* the fairy king, Oberon, becomes jealous when his queen, Titania, dotes on a little Indian boy. Oberon has his servant Puck find a magic plant that, when brushed over the eyes of someone asleep, makes them fall in love with whatever they first see. Titania thus falls in love with a traveling player, whose head Oberon turns into that of a donkey.

Pp. 61–62: *Hamlet:* The ghost of the King of Denmark, seeking revenge, asks his son, Hamlet, to kill the new king — Hamlet's uncle. To do so, Hamlet pretends to be insane. He sleeps with his girlfriend, Ophelia, who kills herself. Hamlet's uncle sends him to England with his friends Rosencrantz and Guildenstern, along with a note that Hamlet should be killed on arrival, but Hamlet foils the plan — swapping notes so that Rosencrantz and Guildenstern are killed instead. Hamlet returns to the castle and kills his uncle. Everyone dies at the end.

Hamlet is set in the castle at Helsingør (Elsinore). The name "Hamlet" is a variation of "Amleth," protagonist of the Saxo tale described here. Rosencrantz and Guildenstern were truly relatives of Tycho Brahe the astronomer — whose theories are mentioned in many of the Shakespearean plays, although there is no indication Shakespeare ever met any of these men.

P. 74: We know what we are, but we know not what we may be.
> — Ophelia, *Hamlet* (IV.v.47)

P. 76:
> What's in a name? That which we call a rose
> By any other name would smell as sweet.
>> — Juliet, *Romeo and Juliet* (II.ii.46–47)

P. 109:
> Petruchio: Come, come, you wasp, i'faith you are too angry.
> Katherine: If I be waspish, best beware my sting.

Petruchio: My remedy is then to pluck it
out.
— *The Taming of the Shrew* (II.i.207–09)

P. 109:
If love be rough with you, be rough with
love.
Prick love for pricking and you beat love
down.
— Mercutio, *Romeo and Juliet* (I.iv.25–26)

P. 110: The course of true love never did run
smooth.
— Lysander, *A Midsummer Night's Dream*
(I.i.137)

P. 111:
I am one, sir, that comes to tell you your
daughter
and the Moor are now making the beast
with two backs.
— Iago, *Othello* (I.i.106–07)

P. 113: *Hamlet:* Ophelia, having gone truly
mad, hands out a variety of flowers with different hidden meanings. Rue, she keeps for
herself. Many female scholars believe it is
because it is an abortifacient, and if you read
Ophelia's madness as springing from an un-
wanted pregnancy due to premarital sex with
Hamlet, her despair feels very real.
Ophelia: There's rosemary, that's for

remembrance; pray you, love, remember. And there is pansies, that's for thoughts.

Laertes: A document in madness, thoughts and remembrance fitted.

Ophelia: There's fennel for you, and columbines. There's rue for you, and here's some for me; we may call it herb of grace o' Sundays. O you must wear your rue with a difference.

— *Hamlet* (IV.v.170–77)

P. 122:

The very instant that I saw you, did
My heart fly to your service.

— Ferdinand, *The Tempest* (III.i.71)

P. 123:

A good leg will fall, a straight back will
  stoop, a black
beard will turn white, a curled pate will
  grow bald,
a fair face will wither, a full eye will wax
  hollow: but
a good heart, Kate, is the sun and the
  moon . . .

— Henry, *Henry V* (V.ii.159–64)

P. 130:

My falcon now is sharp and passing empty,
And till she stoop, she must not be
  full-gorged,
For then she never looks upon her lure.

Another way I have to man my haggard,
To make her come and know her keeper's
  call.
That is to watch her, as we watch these
  kites
That bate and beat, and will not be
  obedient.
> — Petruchio, *The Taming of the Shrew*
> (IV.i.171–77)

P. 134: I will wear my heart upon my sleeve.
> — Iago, *Othello* (I.i.66)

P. 135:
How low am I, thou painted maypole?
  Speak,
How low am I? I am not yet so low
But that my nails can reach unto thine eyes.
> — Hermia, *A Midsummer Night's Dream*
> (III.ii.296–99)

P. 135: And though she be but little, she is
fierce.
> — Helena, *A Midsummer Night's Dream*
> (III.ii.342)

P. 139: You kiss by th' book.
> — Juliet, *Romeo and Juliet* (I.v.122)

P. 140: All the world's a stage, and all the men
and women merely Players.
> — Jaques, *As You Like It* (II.vii.146)

P. 140:

There's something tells me (but it is not love)
I would not lose you.
— Portia, *The Merchant of Venice* (III.ii.4–5)

P. 147: I will play the swan, and die in music.
— Emilia, *Othello* (V.ii.296–97)

Pp. 147–48:

There is written her fair neck round about:
Noli me tangere, for Caesar's I am,
And wild for to hold, though I seem tame.
— Sir Thomas Wyatt, "Whoso List to Hunt" (lines 12–14)

P. 170:

How all occasions do inform against me,
And spur my dull revenge!
— *Hamlet* (IV.iv.34–35)

P. 179:

Love comforteth like sunshine after rain,
But Lust's effect is tempest after sun.
Love's gentle spring doth always fresh remain;
Lust's winter comes ere summer half be done.
Love surfeit's not, Lust like a glutton dies.
Love is all truth, Lust full of forged lies.
— *Venus and Adonis* (lines 799–804)

P. 183: Let your wisdom let that they not fall into this tyrant's hands.

— Mary Sidney Herbert's *The Tragedy of Antony,* translated from Robert Garnier's original

P. 194:

Romeo: O, wilt thou leave me so unsatisfied?
Juliet: What satisfaction canst thou have tonight?

— *Romeo and Juliet* (II.ii.125–26)

P. 195: Who can control his fate?

— Othello, *Othello* (V.ii.316)

P. 195:

Juliet: I have forgot why I did call thee back
Romeo: Let me stand here till thou re-member it.

— *Romeo and Juliet* (II.ii.172–73)

P. 200: If you prick us, do we not bleed?

— Shylock, *The Merchant of Venice* (III.i.59)

P. 204:

This bud of love, by summer's ripening breath,
May prove a beauteous flower when next we meet.

— Juliet, *Romeo and Juliet* (II.ii.128–29)

P. 213:

Even as the sun with purple-colour'd face
Had ta'en his last leave of the weeping morn,
Rose-cheek'd Adonis hied him to the chase;
Hunting he lov'd, but love he laugh'd to
scorn;
Sick-thoughted Venus makes amain unto
him
And like a bold-faced suitor 'gins to woo
him.

"Thrice-fairer than myself," thus she
began,
"The field's chief flower, sweet above
compare,
Stain to all nymphs, more lovely than a
man,
More white and red than doves or roses
are;
Nature that made thee, with herself at
strife,
Saith that the world hath ending with thy
life."
— *Venus and Adonis* (lines 24–35)

P. 216: You heedless joltheads and unmanner'd
slaves!
— Petruchio, *The Taming of the Shrew*
(IV.i.166)

P. 233: Emilia's poem, based on a tale from
Ovid's *Fasti,* is the plot of *The Rape of*

Lucrece, a second long-form poem dedicated to Southampton.

P. 234: The *Groatsworth* pamphlet, published by Robert Greene in 1592, included the terms "upstart crow" and "Shake-scene." Recent scholars think this was a reference not to Shakespeare, but to actor Edward Alleyn. At the time, there was no record of Shakespeare being an actor, much less a writer.

Pp. 237–38: The "Complaint and Lamentation of Mistress Arden of Feversham in Kent" is a seventeenth-century English ballad about the murder of Thomas Arden by his wife, Alice; her lover, Mosby; and several others in 1551 in the town of Faversham. The story was well-known and also described in *Holinshed's Chronicles: The Historie of England.* The play *Arden of Faversham* was published anonymously in 1592. It has been attributed to Marlowe, Kyd, Watson, and/or Shakespeare because of the strength of the writing, the emotional content, and the anti-hero character of Alice but several female Elizabethan scholars have suggested that it was actually penned by a woman.

P. 239: Love is a god, and marriage is but words.
— Alice, *Arden of Faversham* (I.101)

P. 278:

'Tis fearful sleeping in a serpent's bed
And I will cleanly rid my hands of her.
— Mosby, *Arden of Faversham*
(VIII.42–43)

Pp. 278–79:

Mosby: It is not love that loves to anger
love.
Alice: It is not love that loves to murder love.
Mosby: How mean you that?
Alice: Thou knowest how dearly Arden
loved me.
Mosby: And then?
Alice: And then — conceal the rest, for 'tis
too bad,
Lest that my words be carried with the
wind
And published in the world to both our
shames.
— *Arden of Faversham* (VIII.58–65)

P. 280:

A fount once troubled is not thickened still.
Be clear again, I'll ne'er more trouble thee.
— Alice, *Arden of Faversham* (VIII.147–48)
(This is repeated, almost verbatim, in *The
Taming of the Shrew.*)
A woman mov'd is like a fountain troubled,
Muddy, ill-seeming, thick, bereft of beauty.
— Katherine, *The Taming of the Shrew*
(V.ii.158–59)

P. 282:
    If thou cry war, there is no peace for me;
    I will do penance for offending thee,
    And burn this prayer-book, where I here use
    The holy word that had converted me.

    See, Mosbie, I will tear away the leaves,
    And all the leaves, and in this golden cover
    Shall thy sweet phrases and thy letters dwell;
    And thereon will I chiefly meditate
    And hold no other sect but such devotion.
                    — Alice, *Arden of Faversham*
                                    (III.v.114–22)

P. 287:
    Give me my Romeo, and when I shall die,
    Take him and cut him out in little stars,
    And he will make the face of heaven so fine
    That all the world will be in love with night
    And pay no worship to the garish sun.
        — Juliet, *Romeo and Juliet* (III.ii.21–25)

Pp. 287–88:
    Frown not on me when we meet in heaven;
    in heaven I'll love thee, though on earth I
    did not.
        — Alice, *Arden of Faversham* (V.iii.10–11)

Pp. 300, 301: I have seen Sackerson loose
twenty times . . .
                    — Slender, referring to the bear in
            The Merry Wives of Windsor (I.i.293)

765

P. 348:
I fear,
All the expected good we're like to hear
For this play at this time, is only in
The merciful construction of good women;
For such a one we show'd 'em: if they smile,
And say 'twill do, I know, within a while
    All the best men are ours; for 'tis ill hap,
If they hold when their ladies bid 'em clap.
            — Chorus, *Henry VIII* (V.v.3464–77)

Pp. 358–59:
. . . the searchers of the town,
Suspecting that we both were in a house
Where the infectious pestilence did reign,
Sealed up the doors, and would not let us
    forth,
So that my speed to Mantua there was
    stayed.
        — Friar John, explaining why he did not
    deliver the information that Juliet was not
    truly dead, *Romeo and Juliet* (V.ii.8–12)

P. 380:
In sooth, I know not why I am so sad.
It wearies me, you say it wearies you.
            — Antonio, *The Merchant of Venice*
                                        (I.i.1–2)

P. 386:
When, in disgrace with fortune and men's
    eyes,

I all alone beweep my outcast state,
And trouble deaf heaven with my bootless
  cries,
And look upon myself and curse my fate,
Wishing me like to one more rich in hope,
Featured like him, like him with friends
  possessed,
Desiring this man's art and that man's
  scope,
With what I most enjoy contented least;
Yet in these thoughts myself almost
  despising,
Haply I think on thee, and then my state,
(Like to the lark at break of day arising
From sullen earth) sings hymns at heaven's
  gate;
  For thy sweet love remembered such
    wealth brings
  That then I scorn to change my state
    with kings.
                    — Sonnet 29

P. 390: To whom should I complain, did I tell
this?
    — Isabella, *Measure for Measure* (II.iv.185)

P. 392:
  Emilia: I have laid those sheets you bade
    me on the bed.
  Desdemona: All's one. Good faith, how
    foolish are our minds!
    If I do die before thee, prithee shroud me

In one of those same sheets.
— *Othello* (IV.iii.23–26)

P. 413: Love comforteth, like sunshine after rain.
— *Venus and Adonis* (line 799)

P. 420: The character Æmelius is a Roman noble in *Titus Andronicus,* and Bassanius is in love with Titus's daughter Lavinia.

Bawdy jokes:
Demetrius: Villain, what hast thou done?
Aaron: That which thou canst not undo.
Chiron: Thou hast undone our mother.
Aaron: Villain, I have done thy mother.
— *Titus Andronicus* (IV.ii.77–80)

P. 420:
Grumio: How say you to a fat tripe finely broiled?
Katherine: I like it well. Good Grumio, fetch it me.
Grumio: I cannot tell. I fear 'tis choleric. What say you to a piece of beef and mustard?
Katherine: A dish that I do love to feed upon.
Grumio: Ay, but the mustard is too hot a little.
Katherine: Why then, the beef, and let the mustard rest.

Grumio: Nay then, I will not. You shall
have the mustard
Or else you get no beef of Grumio.
Katherine: Then both, or one, or any thing
thou wilt.
Grumio: Why then, the mustard without
the beef.
Katherine: Go, get thee gone, thou false
deluding slave,
That feed'st me with the very name of
meat.
— *The Taming of the Shrew* (IV.iii.20–32)

P. 423:
I am ashamed that women are so simple
To offer war where they should kneel for
peace,
Or seek for rule, supremacy, and sway
When they are bound to serve, love, and
obey.
Why are our bodies soft and weak and
smooth,
Unapt to toil and trouble in the world,
But that our soft conditions and our hearts
Should well agree with our external parts?
Come, come, you froward and unable
worms!
My mind hath been as big as one of yours,
My heart as great, my reason haply more,
To bandy word for word and frown for
frown;
But now I see our lances are but straws,

769

Our strength as weak, our weakness past
   compare,
That seeming to be most which we indeed
   least are.
Then vail your stomachs, for it is no boot,
And place your hands below your hus-
   band's foot;
In token of which duty, if he please,
My hand is ready, may it do him ease.
        — Katherine, *The Taming of the Shrew*
                        (V.ii.177–95)

P. 429: Think'st thou I'd make a life of
jealousy . . .
        — Othello, *Othello* (III.iii.208)

P. 433:
  O beware my lord, of jealousy!
  It is the green-ey'd monster which doth
    mock
  The meat it feeds on.
        — Iago, *Othello* (III.iii.195–97)

P. 436:
  Paris: Younger than she are happy mothers
    made.
  Capulet: And too soon marred are those so
    early made.
        — *Romeo and Juliet* (I.ii.12–13)

P. 487: Exit, pursued by bear.
    — stage direction, *The Winter's Tale* (III.iii)

P. 500:
   But now I was the lord
Of this fair mansion, master of my
   servants,
Queen o'er myself; and even now,
   but now,
This house, these servants, and this same
   myself
Are yours, my lord's. I give them with this
   ring.
Which, when you part from, lose, or give
   away,
Let it presage the ruin of your love,
And be my vantage to exclaim on you.
             — Portia, *The Merchant of Venice*
                          (III.ii.171–78)

P. 501:
   I am a Jew. Hath not
a Jew eyes? Hath not a Jew hands, organs,
   dimensions,
senses, affections, passions? Fed with the
same food, hurt with the same weapons,
   subject to
the same diseases, healed by the same
   means,
warmed and cooled by the same winter
   and summer,
as a Christian is? If you prick us,
   do we not
bleed? If you tickle us, do we not laugh? If
   you

771

poison us, do we not die? And if you wrong us, shall
we not revenge?
— Shylock, *The Merchant of Venice*
(III.i.57–66)

P. 502: The villainy you teach me I will execute.
— Shylock, *The Merchant of Venice*
(III.i.70–71)

P. 502:
By Heaven, I will ne'er come in your bed
Until I see the ring.
— Portia, *The Merchant of Venice*
(V.i.204–05)

P. 515:
Tir'd with all these, for restful death I cry,
As, to behold desert a beggar born,
And needy nothing trimm'd in jollity,
And purest faith unhappily forsworn,
And gilded honour shamefully misplac'd,
And maiden virtue rudely strumpeted,
And right perfection wrongfully disgrac'd,
And strength by limping sway disabled,
And art made tongue-tied by authority,
And folly, doctor-like, controlling skill,
And simple truth miscall'd simplicity,
And captive good attending captain ill.
Tir'd with all these, from these would I be gone,

Save that, to die, I leave my love alone.
— Sonnet 66

P. 515: A sad tale's best for winter.
— Maximillius, *The Winter's Tale* (II.i.33)

P. 516: To be, or not to be, that is the question.
— Hamlet, *Hamlet* (III.i.57)

P. 526:
. . . 'tis an unweeded garden
That grows to seed; things rank and gross
  in nature
Possess it merely.
— Hamlet, *Hamlet* (I.ii.139–41)

P. 535: Thus conscience does make cowards
of us all.
— Hamlet, *Hamlet* (III.i.91)

P. 536: Heaven give you many, many merry
days.
— Mistress Page, *The Merry Wives
of Windsor* (V.v.248)

P 537:
  Hamlet: I did love you once.
  Ophelia: Indeed, my lord, you made me
    believe so.
  Hamlet: You should not have believed
    me . . .
— *Hamlet* (III.i.125–27)

P. 539:
Were it not better,
Because that I am more than common tall,
That I did suit me all points like a man?
— Rosalind, *As You Like It* (I.iii.121–23)

Pp. 539–40: You a man? You lack a man's heart.
— Oliver, *As You Like It* (IV.iii.174)

It is not the fashion to see the lady the
epilogue, but it is no more unhandsome
   than to see
the lord the prologue.
— Rosalind, *As You Like It*
(V.Epilogue.1–3)

Pp. 540–41:
Do you not know I am a woman? When I
think, I must speak.
— Rosalind, *As You Like It*
(III.ii. 253–54)

I should have been a woman by right.
— Rosalind, *As You Like It*
(IV.iii.185–86)
Duke Vincentio: What, are you married?
Mariana: No, my lord.
Duke Vincentio: Are you a maid?
Mariana: No, my lord.
Duke Vincentio: A widow, then?
Mariana: Neither, my lord.

Duke Vincentio: Why you are nothing,
then, neither maid, widow, nor wife?
— *Measure for Measure* (V.i.197–206)

Pp. 543–44:
Shall I compare thee to a summer's day?
Thou art more lovely and more temperate:
Rough winds do shake the darling buds of
May,
And summer's lease hath all too short a
date;
Sometime too hot the eye of heaven shines,
And often is his gold complexion dimm'd;
And every fair from fair sometime declines,
By chance or nature's changing course
untrimm'd;
But thy eternal summer shall not fade,
Nor lose possession of that fair thou ow'st;
Nor shall death brag thou wander'st in his
shade,
When in eternal lines to time thou grow'st:
So long as men can breathe or eyes can see,
So long lives this, and this gives life to
thee.
— Sonnet 18

P. 549:
Give sorrow words: the grief that does not
speak
Whispers the o'er-fraught heart and bids it
break.
— Malcolm, *Macbeth* (IV.iii.246–47)

P. 552: There is nothing either good or bad, but thinking makes it so.
> — Hamlet, *Hamlet* (II.ii.268–70)

Pp. 554–55:
It is impossible you should see this,
Were they as prime as goats, as hot as
  monkeys,
As salt as wolves in pride, and fools as
  gross
As ignorance made drunk. But yet I say,
If imputation and strong circumstances
Which lead directly to the door of truth
Will give you satisfaction, you might have
  't.
> — Iago, *Othello* (III.iii.459–65)

P. 605: My pride fell with my fortunes.
> — Rosalind, *As You Like It* (I.ii.252)

P. 618:
Farewell (sweet Cooke-ham) where I first
  obtain'd
Grace from that Grace where perfit Grace
  remain'd;
And where the Muses gaue their full
  consent . . .
> — Emilia Lanier, "Description of Cooke-
> ham," *Salve Deus Rex Judæorum*

P. 621:
But surely Adam cannot be excus'd.

Her fault, though great, yet he was most
    too blame;
What Weakness offred Strength might
    haue refus'd,
Being Lord of all the greater was his
    shame.
> — Emilia Lanier, "A Defense of Eve,"
> *Salve Deus Rex Judæorum*

P. 625:
You came not in the world without our
    paine,
Make that a barre against your crueltie;
Your fault beeing greater, why should you
    disdaine
Our beeing your equals, free from tyranny?
> — Emilia Lanier, "A Defense of Eve,"
> *Salve Deus Rex Judæorum*

Pp. 629–30:
Since what I am to say must be but that
Which contradicts my accusation, and
The testimony on my part no other
But what comes from myself, it shall scarce
    boot me
To say "Not guilty." Mine integrity
Being counted falsehood, shall, as I express
    it,
Be so received. But thus: if powers divine
Behold our human actions, as they do,
I doubt not then but innocence shall make
False accusation blush and tyranny

Tremble at patience.
> — Hermione, *The Winter's Tale*
> (III.ii.23–33)

P. 638: The quality of mercy is not strained.
— Portia, *The Merchant of Venice* (IV.i.190)

P. 644:
What we changed
Was innocence for innocence. We knew not
The doctrine of ill-doing, nor dreamed
That any did.
> — Polixenes, *The Winter's Tale*
> (I.ii.86–89)

P. 682:
They are all but stomachs, and we all but
food;
They eat us hungerly, and when they are
full
They belch us.
> — Emilia, *Othello* (III.iv.121–23)

Pp. 683–84:
[But I do think it is their husbands' faults
If wives do fall. Say that they slack their
duties,
And pour our treasures into foreign laps;
Or else break out in peevish jealousies,
Throwing restraint upon us. Or say they
strike us,
Or scant our former having in despite.

Why, we have galls, and though we have
  some grace,
Yet have we some revenge. Let husbands
  know
Their wives have sense like them. They
  see, and smell,
And have their palates both for sweet and
  sour,
As husbands have. What is it that they do
When they change us for others? Is it
  sport?
I think it is. And doth affection breed it?
I think it doth. Is 't frailty that thus errs?
It is so too. And have not we affections,
Desires for sport, and frailty, as men have?
Then let them use us well. Else let them
  know,
The ills we do, their ills instruct us so.]
                    — Emilia, *Othello* (IV.iii.97–115)

Pp. 685–86:
My mother had a maid called Barbary.
She was in love, and he she loved proved
  mad
And did forsake her. She had a song of
  willow,
An old thing 'twas, but it expressed her
  fortune,
And she died singing it. That song tonight
Will not go from my mind . . .
The poor soul sat sighing by a sycamore
  tree,

Sing all a green willow.
Her hand on her bosom, her head on her
  knee,
Sing willow, willow, willow.
> — Desdemona, *Othello*
> (IV.iii.28–33, 43–46)

P. 686:
What did thy song bode, lady?
Hark, canst thou hear me? I will play the
  swan
And die in music.
> — Emilia, *Othello* (V.ii.295–97)

P. 688:
This Figure that thou here seest put,
It was for gentle Shakespeare cut,
Wherein the Graver had a strife
With Nature, to out-do the life.
O, could he but have drawn his wit
As well in brass, as he hath hit
His face; the Print would then surpass
All that was ever writ in brass.
But since he cannot, Reader, look
Not on his Picture, but his Book.
> — Ben Jonson, Introduction to First Folio

Pp. 689–90:
To draw no envy, SHAKSPEARE, on thy
  name
Am I thus ample to thy Book, and Fame;
While I confess thy writings to be such,

As neither Man, nor Muse, can praise too
much;
'Tis true, and all men's suffrage. But these
ways
Were not the paths I meant unto thy
praise;
For seeliest ignorance on these may light,
Which, when it sounds at best, but echoes
right;
Or blind affection, which doth ne'er
advance
The truth, but gropes, and urgeth all by
chance;
Or crafty malice might pretend this praise,
And think to ruin, where it seem'd to raise.
These are, as some infamous Bawd, or
Whore
Should praise a Matron. What could hurt
her more?
. . .
My SHAKSPEARE, rise! I will not lodge
thee by
Chaucer or Spenser or bid Beaumont lie
A little further, to make thee a room.
Thou are a monument, without a tomb,
And art alive still, while thy Book doth live
And we have wits to read, and praise to
give.

— Ben Jonson, "To the Memory of
My Beloved, the Author Mr. William
Shakespeare: And What He Hath
Left Us" from First Folio

P. 701: Here's to my love.
   — Romeo, *Romeo and Juliet* (V.iii.119)

P. 723:
From hence your memory death cannot
   take,
Although in me each part will be forgotten.
Your name from hence immortal life shall
   have,
Though I, once gone, to all the world must
   die.
   — Sonnet 81

SOURCES AND RESOURCES

The Agas Map. https://mapoflondon.uvic.ca /agas.htm

Andrzejewski, Alicia. "Shakespeare Already Wrote About What Happens When Women Don't Have Bodily Autonomy." *Electric Literature,* August 2022. https://electricliterature. com/shakespeare-abortion-bodily-autonomy -alicia-andrzejewski/

Andrzejewski, Alicia. "What Black Playwrights Taught Me About Shakespeare." *Huffington Post,* 2022.

Anonymous. *Arden of Feversham.* https://www. gutenberg.org/files/43440/43440-h/43440 -h.htm

Beaumont, Francis. *The Knight of the Burning Pestle* (1613). London: Bloomsbury Methuen Drama, 1969.

Bensusan, S. L. William Shakespeare: His Homes and Haunts. London: T. C. and E. C. Jack. https://www.gutenberg.org/cache/epub/29611/pg29611-images.html

Blanding, Michael. *North by Shakespeare: A Rogue Scholar's Quest for the Truth Behind the Bard's Work.* New York: Hachette, 2021.

Bradbeer, Mark. *Aemilia Lanyer as Shakespeare's Co-Author.* Oxon: Routledge, 2022.

Bryson, Bill. *Shakesepeare: The World as Stage.* New York: HarperCollins, 2007.

De France, Marie; Shoaf, Judith P. (translator). "Bisclavret." *The Lais of Marie De France.* https://people.clas.ufl.edu/jshoaf/marie_lais/

Delahoyd, Michael. "The Taming of a Shrew." Washington State University. https://public.wsu.edu/~delahoyd/shakespeare/taming.html

Edmondson, Paul. "John Heminges and Henry Condell." *The Shakespeare Circle: An Alternative Biography* (ed. Paul Edmondson and Stanley Wells). Cambridge, 2015.

Gilvary, Kevin. "A Storm Called Emilia." www.deveresociety.co.uk, January 2020.

Herrick, Linda. "Outing the Dark Lady." *New Zealand Listener,* Issue 10, 2020.

Hodgson, Elizabeth M. A. "Prophecy and Gendered Mourning in Lanyer's *Salve Deus Rex Judaeorum.*" SEL 43:1, Winter 2002, 101–16.

Hudson, John. "A Midsummer Night's Dream: A Religious Allegory." *University of Birmingham Journal of Literature and Language.*

Hudson, John. *Shakespeare's Dark Lady: Amelia Bassano Lanier, The Woman Behind Shakespeare's Plays?* Stroud: Amberley Publishing, 2016.

Korda, Natasha. *Labors Lost: Women's Work and the Early Modern English Stage.* Philadelphia: University of Pennsylvania Press, 2011.

Lanier, Emilia; Rowse, A. L. (introduction). *The Poems of Shakespeare's Dark Lady.* New York: Potter, 1969.

Lanyer, Aemilia; Woods, Susanna (editor). *The Poems of Aemilia Lanyer: Salve Deus Rex Judaeorum.* Oxford: Oxford University Press, 1993.

Lasocki, David. "The Bassano Family, The Recorder, and the Writer Known as

Shakespeare." www.americanrecorder.org, Winter 2015.

Lasocki, David; Prior, Roger. *The Bassanos.* Oxon: Routledge, 2016.

Orlin, Lena Cowen. *The Private Life of William Shakespeare.* Oxford: Oxford University Press, 2021.

Oxford Dictionary of National Biography. "Lanier [née Bassano], Emilia." September 2004. https://doi.org/10.1093/ref:odnb /37653

Posner, Michael. "Unmasking Shakespeare." *Reform Judaism,* Summer 2010, pp. 36–39, 46.

Price, Diana. *Shakespeare's Unorthodox Biography: New Evidence of an Authorship Problem.* Westport: Greenwood Press, 2001.

Rackin, Phyllis. "The Hidden Women Writers of the Elizabethan Theater." *The Atlantic,* June 2019. https://www.theatlantic.com /entertainment/archive/2019/06/shakespeares -female-contemporaries/590392/

Rebeck, Theresa. "A Racial Reckoning Is Underway in Theater. Where Is the Gender Reckoning?" *New York Times,* October 2021.

Russ, Joanna. *How to Suppress Women's Writing.* Austin: University of Texas Press, 2018.

Schafer, Liz, Royal Holloway University of London. "A Shrew and the Shrew." https://www.bl.uk/treasures/shakespeare/shrew.html

Shahan, John M.; Waugh, Alexander. *Shakespeare Beyond Doubt? Exposing an Industry in Denial.* Claremont: Shakespeare Authorship Coalition, 2016.

Shapiro, James. *Contested Will: Who Wrote Shakespeare?* New York: Simon & Schuster, 2010.

Shapiro, James. *A Year in the Life of William Shakespeare: 1599.* New York: Harper, 2005.

Simon, Ed. "Amelia Lanyer, the First Female Jewish English Poet and Shakespeare's Dark Lady?" *Tablet Magazine,* April 2016. https://www.tabletmag.com/sections/arts-letters/articles/amelia-lanyer-english-poet

Whipday, Emma. "What If Shakespeare Had Been a Woman?" *Voices Magazine,* British Council, June 2016. https://www.britishcouncil.org/voices-magazine/what-if-shakespeare-had-been-woman

787

Winkler, Elizabeth. *Shakespeare Was a Woman and Other Heresies.* New York: Simon & Schuster, 2023.

Woods, Susanne. *Lanyer: A Renaissance Woman Poet.* New York: Oxford University Press, 1999.

https://www.british-history.ac.uk/survey-london/vol22/pp94-100

https://elizabethan.org/compendium/home.html

https://folgerpedia.folger.edu/The_Elizabethan_Court_Day_by_Day

https://mapoflondon.uvic.ca/FALC1.htm

Othello, Folio 1, 1623: https://internetshakespeare.uvic.ca/doc/Oth_F1/index.html

Othello, Quarto 1, 1622: https://internetshakespeare.uvic.ca/doc/Oth_Q1/index.html

https://shakespearedocumented.folger.edu/resource/document/taming-shrew-first-edition

ABOUT THE AUTHOR

Jodi Picoult is the #1 *New York Times* best-selling author of twenty-nine novels, including *Mad Honey* (with Jennifer Finney Boylan), *Wish You Were Here*, *The Book of Two Ways*, *A Spark of Light*, *Small Great Things*, *Leaving Time*, and *My Sister's Keeper*, and, with daughter Samantha van Leer, two young adult novels, *Between the Lines* and *Off the Page*. She lives in New Hampshire with her husband.

jodipicoult.com
Facebook.com/jodipicoult
X: @jodipicoult
Instagram: @jodipicoult
TikTok: @jodipicoult